DAISY CHAIN

Also by Maggie Ritchie

Paris Kiss
Looking for Evelyn

DAISY CHAIN

Maggie Ritchie

First published in Great Britain in 2021 by Two Roads
An Imprint of John Murray Press
An Hachette UK company

1

A CIP catalogue record for this title is available from the British Library

Hardback ISBN 9781529366389
eBook ISBN 9781529366402
Audio Digital Download ISBN 9781529366426

Typeset in Plantin Light by
Palimpsest Book Production Ltd, Falkirk, Stirlingshire

Printed and bound in Great Britain by Clays Ltd, Elcograf S.p.A.

John Murray policy is to use papers that are natural, renewable and
recyclable products and made from wood grown in sustainable forests.
The logging and manufacturing processes are expected to conform
to the environmental regulations of the country of origin.

Two Roads
Carmelite House
50 Victoria Embankment
London EC4Y 0DZ

www.tworoadsbooks.com

For Michael and Adam

Prologue

~ Lily and Jeanie ~

~ Kirkcudbright, Scotland, 1901 ~

Two young girls sit in the green-golden shade of a weeping willow. The buttery late-afternoon sun dapples their arms and lights up their heads, one dark and one copper, bent together over a daisy chain. Their fingers are stained with the juice from the stems and they are whispering, their voices dipping and diving like swallows. They are safe in their secret green chamber where they are weaving their hopes for a life that stretches before them and will take them over the Galloway Hills and beyond. The peculiar, magical light dances on their skin, shimmering and changing colour, iridescent as a trout in a gravel stream. Lily and Jeanie. Lily as pale as the creamy milk that comes from the herd in the pasture below, Jeanie as brown as the hazel-nuts gathered by her friends, the tinkers encamped on the sandy beach known as the Doon.

Lily crowns her friend with a daisy garland and sits back on her heels to admire the way the tiny white petals edged with pink sit on Jeanie's untidy dark curls. 'When I'm a famous artist, I will paint you every day,' she says. 'You're the queen of the forest.'

Jeanie's teeth flash in a face smudged with dirt. 'No, you're the one that's more like a queen.' She edges closer. 'Tell me again where we'll live when we are grown women?'

Lily lets her hands rest in her lap and closes her eyes. 'In my studio in Glasgow.'

1

'The city! That would be fine, just fine. We can eat cream cakes off fancy plates with silver forks. And I'll be a famous dancer. The tinkers have been learning me to tumble and the high-wire lady shows me fancy tricks like pirouettes and the splits. She used to be a dancer and told me there's a theatre in Glasgow with its own sea for the mermaids, and a waterfall for the horses that come galloping through the water with real-live injuns riding them. I'll wear a sparkly costume and feathers in my hair and kick higher than all the other dancers. But don't worry, I'll be sure to give you a wee wave in the audience.'

'I'll have to be quick with my pencil if I'm to sketch all that,' Lily says.

'Draw me now, doing this, look!' Jeanie springs up, lithe as a cat, and cartwheels through a gap in the willow branches and out onto the open hilltop, her ragged skirt riding up to show bare flanks as she lands in the splits.

Lily runs out after her, laughing. 'You'd better wear drawers when you're a dancer.'

Jeanie's thin arms held high in fifth position make a graceful arc, the way she has been taught by the former prima ballerina now reduced to dancing for coppers at country fairs.

A faint call rings out from a stone house in the valley below. 'That will be Mama.' Lily shades her eyes to make out the distant figure waving at the garden gate. A flicker of movement makes her turn. A man is watching them, half hidden by a copse of beech trees. He sits hunched on a camping stool under a large white umbrella and works on a canvas. Lily nudges Jeanie so she collapses in a heap of skinny brown legs and arms.

'What did you do that for, you daftie?' Jeanie says, pulling her fingers through her tangled hair to remove burrs and twigs.

2

Lily shades her eyes to get a better look. 'It's the artist from the pink house in the High Street. I think he saw your bare bottom.'

Jeanie jumps up and sticks her tongue out at him, hands on hips, skinny legs astride. 'He shouldn't have been keeking at my arse, the dirty midden. He still hasn't paid me the penny he promised for painting me and my wee sisters down by the burn. We sat so long we got pins and needles.' She tugs at Lily's sleeve. 'Never mind him. Race you down the hill. Last one's a scabby dug!'

Golden light pools over the hills and a ragged black cloud of starlings rises and falls against the summer sky. The two girls run down the steep slope, white specks against the green while the shadows lengthen behind them, purple as a bruise.

PART 1

~ *A Country Childhood* ~

1901–1911

∼ Lily and Jeanie ∼

Lily was gazing out of the schoolroom window, chin on hand, watching a pair of wood pigeons duck their heads and kiss their beaks in a courtship dance. Her other hand drew the birds, covering the pages of her jotter in thumbnail sketches. Jeanie nudged her, jolting her back to the clatter and hum of the classroom, but it was too late – the teacher was standing before her.

'Lily Crawford, how many times do I have to tell you to pay attention? You're an awful lass for having your head in the clouds.'

Lily bent her head. 'Yes, Miss Clarkson.'

The teacher started to walk away only to turn around and catch Jeanie screwing up her face and crossing her eyes, making Lily snort with laughter behind her hand.

'Right, that's it! I've had enough of your cheek, Jean Taylor. Hold out your hand.' Jeanie bit her lips to stop herself crying as the leather tawse stung her palm.

Lily stood up, colour mounting in her cheeks. 'That's not fair, miss. Jeanie was only trying to cheer me up, and it was me who was distracted and being told off, not her.'

'Don't you dare talk back to me, young lady. You may be the doctor's daughter, but I'll have none of your airs and graces in this schoolroom. Hold out your hand.' Lily glared at her, stony-faced, while the tawse bit into her palm. 'Now go on outside, both of you, and sit on the steps for the rest of the class and have a good think to yourselves.'

When the bell rang at the end of the school day, the two

girls found themselves surrounded by a circle of jeering boys.

A farmer's son, his shoulders already broad, his fists like mallets, sneered at Lily where she sat with Jeanie on the steps. 'Got what was coming to you, eh, Miss Hoity-Toity, fancy-pants? You think you're better than us because you speak as if you've a mouth full of boules?'

A skinny lad with a face like a rat squealed and pointed at Jeanie's tear-streaked cheeks. 'Wee cry baby! At least your face is getting a wash for a change, ya dirty cow.' He kicked at the ragged skirt of her dress. 'When's your mammy going to make you a new dress – or is she too busy hoorin'?'

With a snarl, Jeanie leapt up and on her tormentor like a wildcat clinging to a tree trunk. Startled, the boy fell into the dirt of the playground and screamed as Jeanie pummelled him with her fists. The farm boy went to help his friend, but Lily was too quick for him and stuck out a leg and he fell face first, banging his nose in a starburst of blood. Before he could recover, she pulled Jeanie off the rat-faced boy and they ran out of the playground. They didn't stop until they'd passed the harbour where the queenie boats were tied up after the day's fishing and they'd reached the beach.

The two girls hunkered down at the edge of the water and dipped their throbbing hands into the coolness. Jeanie's back heaved with sobs and Lily put her arms around her, feeling how her spine and shoulder blades stuck out.

'Don't mind them, Jeanie. They're ignorant boys and you're the queen of Kirkcudbright.'

Jeanie sniffed and wiped her red eyes. 'They can go to hell. I hate them all. I hate this place. I don't want to be the queen of Kirkcudbright, I want to get out of here.'

Lily looked across the estuary at the hills beyond and felt the wind ruffle through her hair and the spring sun

8

warm her face. Above them, seagulls wheeled and mewled like newborn babies. School was a trial, but she bore it by retreating into a daydream. Her jotters were full of sketches and doodles. Jeanie, she knew, was different; she couldn't sit still in the stuffy classroom and itched to be outdoors, leaping and running and dancing, climbing trees and stretching her brown limbs. Lily knew how to cheer Jeanie up.

She stood up and pulled off her dress. 'Come on, last one in's a hairy egg!' Lily waded into the estuary and plunged in head first.

Jeanie splashed after her, not bothering to take off her dress. She sank down and let the waves lap over her shoulders and floated on her back. Squinting up at the sky with its scudding clouds, she grinned as the icy water crept through her hair and over her face, washing away the dirt of poverty and the taunts of the school day.

∼ Lily ∼

Lily was shaken awake by a gentle hand. She rubbed her eyes and opened them to see her mother.

'What time is it, Mama?'

'I don't know, darling, but it's early.' Lily's mother drew back the curtains to reveal a dawn sky suffused with pink. She opened the window wide and birdsong filled the room. 'If we go to the woods now, we'll have all morning.'

Lily threw back the covers and dressed quickly. They stole out of the sleeping house and into the dew-damp morning. The town was quiet, their footsteps the only sound on the cobbled streets as they made their way past the pastel-coloured houses and through narrow wynds to Barrhill Wood. They climbed the stile and entered the woods, their canvas bags slung across their chests. Bluebells carpeted the ground between the trees. As they walked deeper into the woods, Lily's mother pointed out the way the quality of the light and shade deepened or brightened the colours. They stopped at a pond and sat with their sketchbooks open to wait and watch. After a while a red squirrel crept down a tree trunk, pausing to sniff the air, before dashing along an overhanging branch to the water's edge, dipping its acorn-shaped head to drink. Lily's charcoal flew across the page to capture the movements of its feathery tail, the way the tiny claws curved and gripped the bark. Her mother glanced at her drawing and nodded before returning to her own work.

They spent the morning walking and sketching, making careful studies of the minute hanging bells on the wild hyacinths, and of the yellow siskins and scarlet crossbills flitting through the trees to feast on the green budding pine cones.

By the time they returned home with twigs and pine needles in their hair and the hems of their skirts stained with mud and grass, Lily was ravenous and followed her nose and the smell of bacon and coffee to the dining room. She stopped at the door at the sight of her father, glowering behind his newspaper at the head of the table. He folded his newspaper and stood; his expression was thunderous. Lily felt her mother's hand on her shoulder.

'I work hard all week tending to the ailments of the good people of this town and I expect to rest on Sunday. How foolish of me! Instead, my morning is interrupted by having to read this note from Lily's teacher, which you, my dear, seem to have forgotten to bring to me.' He moved a scrap of paper on his desk and Lily bit her lip. It must have fallen out of her pocket and been picked up by Bridie, the daily. Her father narrowed his eyes. 'It's a long and dreary litany of complaints about your behaviour. I nearly nodded off while reading it, but am I to understand that you and that little ragamuffin of a friend were given the belt?'

Lily lifted her chin. 'Miss Clarkson was picking on Jeanie again, it wasn't fair.'

Her father removed his spectacles and rubbed the space between his eyebrows. 'God grant me patience! Instead of coming with us to visit your aunts, you'll go to your room and stay there.' He picked up his newspaper again and shook it. Lily took the hint and raced up the stairs. She was delighted with her punishment, which meant she'd have the rest of the day to work up her

11

sketches. Her fingers already itched for the delicious box of pastels her mother had bought her for her last birthday. There was just the right shade of ochre for the red squirrel.

∼ Jeanie ∼

Jeanie stirred the porridge pot and tried not to breathe in the fumes from the handkerchiefs boiling away on the range. The kitchen stank of the dirty laundry her mother took in for a pittance and the pulley was festooned with undershirts waiting to be starched and ironed. Her little brothers and sisters sat around the kitchen table with their empty bowls. Jeanie thinned the porridge with water from the kettle to make it go further and served it up with a jug of milk.

'What about you, Jeanie?' one of her brothers asked, as he scraped up the last spoonful.

'I'm no hungry,' she said. But the familiar hollow feeling in her stomach started to burn. After she'd shooed them outside, she went to help her mother, who was pounding clothes into a lather of grey suds in the wash house. Together, they hauled the wet clothes out of the rinsing water and twisted them, one at each end, before Jeanie fed them through the ringer. Her mother stopped and clutched her lower back and Jeanie brought her a cup of water.

She drank and wiped her mouth. 'You're a good lass,' she said, turning to pick up a petticoat from the heap of dirty laundry. Jeanie knew by the size of the pile that her mother had been up since dawn. The wash house darkened and Jeanie turned around to see her mother's latest bidie-in standing in the doorway.

'Look at the pair of you, hard at work, you're making me feel tired!' Calum Mackay laughed and beckoned to

Jeanie's mother. 'Come and have a rest, it's Sunday after all.' Jeanie's lips tightened as her mother flew to his arms and rested her head on his chest. She was besotted and seemed to lose her senses when Calum was around. He grabbed her around the waist and swung her around and whispered into her ear. She giggled and they headed back to the cottage: no doubt the big brass bed she now shared with him would soon be rattling and squeaking. Jeanie grimaced and turned back to the sink to rinse the petticoat and put it through the ringer. Her mother had been so happy since Calum had stopped at their gate one day, offering to mend the fence and chop firewood. Ma had asked him to stay for supper and her eyes had lit up when he'd pulled out a half-pint bottle of whisky from his waistcoat. The fire was soon roaring with the logs he'd cut, the room transformed with warmth and laughter as Calum told stories of his travels and the sights he'd seen as a salesman, a small child on each knee. When he rose and put on his hat, Ma had said he could stay and sleep in front of the fire. When Jeanie had come down the next morning his shoes were by the grate but there was no sign of him.

It only took Calum a few days to become the man of the house, shovelling down huge helpings of stovies or mutton stew while the little ones made do with bread and dripping. But at least Ma was singing again and planting wee kisses on the top of his head. He'd pull at her apron strings to tease her, and she'd blush and bat him away. The little children soon took to clambering on his lap and pulling at his sideburns, but Jeanie was wary of this charming stranger; as the eldest, she'd seen a few men come and go from the cottage. Some of them had been rough with her brothers and sisters and had given Ma the odd black eye, but this Calum had a gentle voice and spoke proper, like Lily and her family. It was obvious from his silk handkerchiefs and patched but quality clothes that he was a cut above the sprawling Taylors, who were at the bottom of the pile in Kirkcudbright, and Jeanie wondered why such a fine gentleman was holed up in their damp cottage. Jeanie had asked him one night, when he was picking his teeth, feet up on the hearth, and his answer was smooth and too swift, as if he'd thought it out before.

'I had a top job as a clerk for one of the big law firms in Glasgow, but it was too stuffy for me. I wanted the freedom of the open road, an adventure, and look what I found, the pot of gold at the end of the rainbow.' He'd grabbed Ma by the waist and kissed her until she wriggled and squealed with delight. Jeanie hadn't believed a word of it.

Now she heaved the basket of wet clothes out to the green and pegged the contents on the line. The sun had burned off the early morning mist and a soft wind carried the briny scent of the sea towards her, and she lifted her face and closed her eyes to breath it in. She'd go down to the Doon on the north side of the estuary, to the tinkers' camp, and see Tatiana, who always made time for her. She had once danced with the finest Russian ballet companies but left her career behind to marry one of the show people. Jeanie's stomach rumbled at the thought of Tatiana's thick meat stews and the bread she baked every morning.

~

Tatiana watched Jeanie as she mopped her plate with the last piece of bread. 'Do you want another dance lesson today?' Jeanie nodded, her mouth too full to talk, and Tatiana shook her head. 'You'll get a cramp dancing on a full stomach.' She picked up a basket. 'We'll walk down to the water's edge and I'll show you how to find better food than you can buy in any shop.'

15

On the beach, she taught Jeanie how to dig cockles and spoots out of the sand and prise mussels off the rocks. They gathered dulse, the red, meaty seaweed Tatiana added to her stews, and moved inland to the salt marshes to gather sea aster for its tangy leaves, and further out for wild garlic, nettles and dandelion leaves.

Back at the camp, Jeanie sat on the steps of Tatiana's wagon and waited for her lesson. She watched a group of children pull a dog around in a cart. Like Jeanie, their faces were streaked with dirt, their knees filthy and their hair tangled. One of the older girls shouted for her to come and play, and Jeanie jumped off the steps and took up one of the ropes as they raced around the camp past broken chairs and sagging sofas with the dog barking encouragement. Jeanie, laughing at the dog with its one blue and one green eye and running with children who didn't care that she had holes in her dress and no shoes, forgot all about the dark, damp cottage full of other people's dirty clothes and Calum's sidelong looks. When the game was over, she ran over to Tatiana, who had come out to watch them play. The dancer smiled and waited for Jeanie to settle.

'Stand straight, pulling up, up, up from the belly. Feet in first position and arms in *bras bas*. Good, let's begin.'

～ *Lily* ～

Lily's mother had found her an art tutor, the man she and Jeanie often saw painting outdoors. On her first day, she stood outside the pink house on the High Street and pulled on the bell, wondering what it looked like inside. Lily and Jeanie had often crept up to a window to peek inside, but it had always been too gloomy to see much. Now the housekeeper opened the door and led Lily into a dark and musty library. She waited for what seemed like an age, but just when Lily was beginning to wish she'd never come, the housekeeper returned and led her through the house, hurrying her through a long gallery hung with paintings, and into the artist's studio. Here, in the vast double-height room, canvases at different stages of completion were propped on easels or against the walls. Lily was intoxicated by the jumble of brushes in jam jars and by the smell of oil paint. The artist stood in front of one of the huge canvases, a palette loaded with paint in one hand and brush in the other, lost in concentration. She stood and watched him work for a while before he turned and noticed her.

Without preamble, he said: 'I need you to look at this.' Lily walked over to the canvas and saw two girls seated among bluebells and poppies. He frowned and pointed with his brush. 'Is this the right blue?' Lily thought back to her walks with her mother and of how the sunlight filtering through the trees changed the colour of the wild hyacinths.

'I think it needs a bit more red, they're more purple in some lights than blue.'

He nodded and handed her the palette. 'Mix up the colour for me, and then fetch a palette for yourself and a small canvas and go into the garden. I want you to paint whatever you see there, using as many colours as you can.'

Lily sat on a bench underneath a blossoming cherry tree and looked at the garden, seeing a riot of lush greens with bright splashes of blue, pink, orange and red. She began to dab at her canvas, at first tentatively and then more and more exuberantly, filling the white space with colour. She was so absorbed she didn't realise the artist was standing behind her until he put a hand on her shoulder. He picked up her canvas and studied it.

'When your mother asked me to take you on, I wasn't keen, but she assured me you had talent.' He narrowed his eyes at the canvas and Lily shifted on the bench. 'She's right, but you need to learn to look like an artist does and see what is there and not what you think should be there.' He pointed out shapes and tones and colours so that Lily began to see the flowers and plants and stones as unfamiliar objects.

Lily spent as much time as she could in the artist's studio and in his garden. Summer days were best, when she would bring Jeanie, who leapt and danced while Lily and the artist painted her. Over cream teas, he'd tell the two girls about his trip to Japan, about the women in their silk costumes, faces painted chalk white with scarlet lips and coal black eyebrows, and about the samurai with their swords and shaven heads, while they sat wide-eyed.

'Remember,' he said to them. 'Go after what you want and don't listen to anyone who says you can't have it. Let nothing and no one stop you.'

~ *Jeanie* ~

Jeanie was fourteen when the trouble at home started.

She'd known for some time now what Calum wanted, ever since he'd come into the kitchen and seen her standing in the tin tub, seen her body with its budding breasts and the down starting between her legs. Calum had stopped in his tracks and stared at her until Ma called from outside for him to split some wood. He'd muttered an apology and slunk out with a sheepish grin, as if it had been an accident, but he'd lingered too long. Until then he'd won the family over with his ready laugh and the patience he'd taken with the little children, playing with them endlessly and not seeming to mind them pulling at his mop of blonde curls. Even Jeanie was beginning to get used to him. She had settled down at school under a new teacher, who had noticed how bright she was and lent her books. Calum had noticed her new studiousness and was careful to ask Jeanie about her schoolwork and admire her copperplate as she did her homework at the kitchen table. Jeanie had lowered her guard.

That night at supper, after he'd seen her naked, she couldn't meet his eyes, but he only smiled at her as if nothing were amiss. Just as Jeanie was beginning to think she must have imagined the greedy expression on his face when he'd caught her bathing, Calum grinned at her mother.

'Our wee Jeanie's growing up, she's going to be a beauty, like her mammy.'

Ma smiled and laid her hand on Jeanie's head. 'Aye, she'll be winching soon and getting a home of her own, although the lads around here aren't up to much.' Mary Taylor was from Glasgow and thought herself a cut above the country folk she lived among, despite having arrived in Kircudbright with a string of children, a baby in her belly and a brass curtain ring on her finger that had fooled nobody.

Jeanie had become increasingly aware of Calum watching her, and over the next few days began to feel uneasy around him, making sure she was never alone with him. One night as she slept in the big brass bed with some of the little ones, she was woken by the creak of a heavy tread. Before she could gather her wits, a hand was clamped over her mouth and Calum's whisky breath was in her nostrils. His eyes shone blackly in the darkness and his mouth was twisted into a leer, so he looked like a devil of the night, not the easy-going man who had tricked them all with his laughing ways.

'Hold still and I won't hurt you,' he whispered.

Jeanie's eyes widened in the dark and she bit him, hard.

Calum snatched his hand away and cursed and sucked at the bleeding wound. 'You wee besom. I'll teach you some manners!'

He smacked her across the face and dragged her out of the bed. The young ones she shared the bed with didn't waken. They were deep in the untroubled sleep of little children and Jeanie thought if she could fight him off without screaming, they wouldn't waken up and see their big friendly Uncle Calum attacking their sister. She braced her heels against the bare floorboards, ignoring the splinters that pierced her skin, but he was too strong for her. He dragged her by the hair over the floor to a pile of clothes and threw her down as if she were a rag doll. Jeanie, who had seen the beasts in the fields coupling and had grown up hearing noises from her mother's bedroom, knew fine well what he meant to do to her. Now he was on top of her, pinning her shoulders down and panting in her face. He tried to shove her legs apart with his knee, but she summoned all her strength and fury and managed to bring hers up and catch him a good one in the balls. Calum rolled off her, doubled up in pain and winded, and Jeanie made a tear for the door. She wrenched it open and was down the stairs and outside before he could recover.

Jeanie didn't stop running until she reached the tinkers' encampment. The fairground people came to Kirkcudbright every summer with their painted mechanical wonders, and over the years she'd grown close to Tatiana, who, with no children of her own, doted on Jeanie, giving her the kind of mothering she'd never had.

Now Jeanie's bare feet sank into cold sand as she scrabbled along the Doon towards the dull glow of a campfire. It was late and the moon was a bright penny pressed among scudding clouds, but there were still dark figures hunched around the flames. Their heads turned as she ran past them, but she didn't stop until she reached Tatiana's wagon. She climbed the steps but hesitated at the closed door until she heard movements. A tentative knock brought Tatiana out. She was in a nightgown and her dark hair was plaited for sleep, but she was alert and after a swift look at the blood on Jeanie's face, she ushered her inside.

A small lamp cast enough light to show they were alone in the wagon. Tatiana must have guessed what Jeanie was thinking. 'My husband is with the other men and he won't be back for a while. Show me where you're hurt.'

Jeanie lifted her dress to show the scratches on her inner thighs. The bruises would start to show soon but for now they were red marks.

21

'Did he hurt you, inside?'

Jeanie shook her head. 'I got away, before— I . . .'

Tatiana stroked her hair. 'You don't have to tell me if you don't want to, but I think I know who did this to you. Your stepfather?'

Jeanie glanced at the floor, too ashamed to meet her eyes, and nodded mutely.

Tatiana grimaced. 'Calum Mackay is well known around here – he comes sniffing around the young girls, sweet-talking them. The men have had to chase him away a few times. Do you want me to come home with you so you can tell your mother?'

Jeanie looked up, terrified. 'No! She won't believe me. He's got her wrapped around his finger. I can't go back there! Please don't make me go back, he'll be at me again! Can't I stay with you?' She threw her arms around Tatiana and at last the tears came.

'All right, don't fret, little darling, you can come with us. We're moving out in a few days. You can send a note to your mother, tell her you've gone to find work, and meanwhile lay low. From what I know about Mary Taylor, she won't care as long as you send her money. And I can't imagine Calum telling her what really happened.'

Jeanie tightened her grip and nodded into Tatiana's neck. The older woman patted her back and rocked her, crooning a lullaby in a language Jeanie didn't understand, and soon she was asleep.

For the next few days she stayed close to Tatiana's wagon, only ducking out to relieve herself. When she woke one morning, the wagon was on the move. She drew back the curtain and watched as they left Kirkcudbright behind.

6

~ Lily ~

After a week of neither sight nor sound of Jeanie, Lily could bear it no longer, and went down to her cottage. Her mother, a worn-out woman with a toddler on her hip, answered the door.

'She's run away from home with them tinkers, and good riddance!' Mary Taylor said, and shut the door in her face.

Lily couldn't understand why Jeanie had left without saying goodbye to her. They were from different worlds – Lily was the doctor's daughter, an only child who lived in a big stone house, while Jeanie lived in a damp cottage with thirteen noisy brothers and sisters who never seemed to get enough to eat – but it had never mattered, they had always been inseparable, from their first day at school. Now, without warning, Jeanie had disappeared. One day they had been whispering about their changing bodies and beginning to notice boys they liked, the next she was gone.

~

Lily threw herself into painting but never stopped wondering what had happened to her friend. The years passed and she left school, spending more time than ever at her tutor's house. As she approached her twentieth birthday, he began to talk to her about art school.

'Do you really think I could go? Do they let women in? I know some of the universities are beginning to let women study medicine and law, but I'm not sure about art schools.'

'Glasgow School of Art is one of the few, along with the Slade, that has women students. The director insists half the students are female. Fra Newbery's a good friend of mine, and I can write to him about you, if you like.'

Lily took a deep breath. She had never thought of turning what had always been considered a hobby for girls like her into a profession, and, besides, she knew no women artists. Now the prospect tantalised her until she could think of nothing else. The image of her father, his expression stern and immutable as a statue, rose up before her and she closed her eyes in despair.

'Papa will never allow it.'

The artist frowned. 'So, you're going to give up, just like that, because your father doesn't approve? If you want this, you must fight for it. I can talk to him if you like, but you must do your bit.'

Lily looked around the studio and imagined what it would be like to be able to paint every day, be surrounded by other artists, and to leave behind the daily chores and at-homes she was forced to endure as a member of a prominent Kirkcudbright family. For some time now, the townswomen had been sending their sons round to ask her out for walks, hoping that marrying into the Crawford family would give them a leg up the social ladder. Lily thought of her mother, and knew she would help her. While her father had always been a distant figure, closeted in his study when he wasn't tending patients in the surgery, Victoria Crawford was a gentle, loving creature who had always been ready to scoop Lily into her lap when she was little and seemed to get as much fun out of her games and imaginary worlds as she did. She had illustrated Lily's bedtime stories with clever little sketches and had spotted her daughter's talent at an early age, encouraging her to draw and showing her what she called 'tricks of the trade'.

As Lily grew, she had let her spend hours drawing rather than forcing her to learn more practical skills such as sewing or running a household.

When Lily asked to go to art school, her mother clapped her hands.

'Of course, you must go! You can't waste this gift you have. You're more of an artist than I could ever have been.' She lowered her eyes to hide her regret, but it was too late.

'Nonsense, Ma, you taught me everything, you're far more talented than me.'

Her mother looked up and smiled. 'I never had any formal training. If your tutor thinks it's time for you to go further, then so be it.'

Lily felt as if a tight bandage had loosened from around her ribcage. The dreams of becoming an artist that had sustained her through the tedium of social visits and small-town mores were about to become a reality. Then a thought occurred to her like a splash of cold water: in her excitement she'd forgotten about her father.

'What about Papa?' She already knew the answer. Her father was an old-fashioned Victorian who believed his daughter's place was in the home – her own if she were to marry and if not then with her parents to look after them in their old age. He had taken to rattling the newspaper furiously every morning as he read about the campaign to give women the vote, and only tolerated Lily's devotion to art because he believed it to be a harmless distraction.

Her mother frowned. 'You leave your father to me. Let me talk to him tonight after dinner. I'll get Cook to make his favourite roast.'

That evening, after the door to the study had closed behind her parents, Lily stood in the corridor listening. At first she heard her mother's gentle murmur, followed by a silence, and then her father's raised voice. He yanked the door open and glared at her.

'I want a word with you, Lily.'

Her heart sank. She should have known it wouldn't be easy. 'Yes, Father.'

He paced up and down in front of the fireplace, ranting, for a full half hour – Lily kept an eye on the clock on the mantel to keep the tears at bay – before she could speak.

'If you do this,' he shouted, 'you'll never make a decent marriage. No respectable man will look at you. You'll end up an old maid.' He stopped pacing and pointed at her. 'And the type of people you'll be mixing with! If you fall, you'll ruin our family's good name.' Lily stood up. She found, to her surprise, that she was calm and unafraid.

'Am I to be an old maid and a fallen woman? Can one be both?' She waited for the explosion but instead saw the corners of his mouth twitch. Donald Crawford was a logical man, a scientist, and she knew she had to appeal to his reason. 'Father, you know me, I've never given you the slightest cause for concern when it comes to young men – unlike the lawyer's daughter, who had a saintly reputation until she ran off with the grocer's boy and got herself in the family way.'

He flinched. The affair had scandalised the polite layer of Kirkcudbright society and delighted the tradespeople, who barely took the trouble to hide their sniggers when the girl's mother finally dared to show her face in their shops.

'You and Mama have brought me up well, and I have you to thank for the sensible head on my shoulders.' She crossed her arms. 'Papa, you know if you don't let me go I shall be miserable. I'm like you, I need an occupation. I can't stay at home tatting rugs and waiting for some local boy to come courting. Surely you can see that?' Lily could tell he was about to give way. Despite all his bluster, he admired spirit. She laid a conciliatory hand on his. 'I promise to make you proud. This isn't a whim.'

Her mother joined them and looked up at her husband. 'Donald, please. You know I would never suggest anything that would put Lily in harm's way.'

He sighed. 'I have my reservations, but if your heart is truly set on it, you may go to art school.'

Lily whooped and flung her arms around his neck, ignoring her father's discomfort as he tried to disentangle himself. She picked up her skirts and ran from the room before he could change his mind.

She had won the first skirmish, but her father continued to raise objections. At night she heard her parents arguing, her mother raising her voice uncharacteristically, and during the next day they were coolly polite with each other when their paths crossed. Lily's father clearly blamed his wife for spoiling her.

She'd often wondered how two such different people as her parents had ended up together, and if her mother was happy. Her suspicions about her parents' marriage were borne out the night before she left for Glasgow. While the two women were packing her trunk, her mother stopped and held her hands.

'Darling girl, you're about to have an opportunity that I could only dream about – don't waste it. Promise me that you'll put your work as an artist above everything. Children are a blessing, but marriage and motherhood are not easy. They crushed any hopes I had of becoming an artist, and there's not a day goes by that I don't struggle with the urge to walk out the door and never come back. I don't want you to end up like me, living a half-life. Whatever you do, fight to be your own person.'

PART 2

～ *Oil Paint and Footlights* ～

1911–1914

7

~ *Lily* ~

~ *Glasgow, September 1911* ~

Lily climbed the stone stairs and stopped in front of the black double doors, her portfolio under her arm. It was her first day at Glasgow School of Art and she had never been so unsure of herself. The building loomed over her, unlike anything she'd seen before, its sandstone facade trussed by ironwork like bindweed. She looked up at the mullioned windows that blindly reflected the sky and used a hand to steady herself against the brass plaque that was engraved with the word IN. From below the steep hill where the school perched, the wind carried the sounds of the River Clyde: the clatter of the shipyards and the whistles of vessels of every size, from tiny puffers and tugs to merchants' ships loaded with bounty from all over the Empire.

Lily's throat, more used to the country air, ached from the soot that belched from the factories to choke the city. Sweat trickled down her back, her scalp itched under her cartwheel hat and her breath came in shallow gasps from the tight corset. It had been a mistake born of vanity to wear her new dress with its fashionably cinched-in waist on her first day. A swell of voices and footsteps rose from inside the building; she tried to move aside just as the door swung open and a stream of students pushed past, turning Lily into a helpless spinning top. The portfolio slipped from under her arm and slid down the steps, spilling paper from between the broken ties. She shrank into the corner and closed her eyes, wishing herself back in Kirkcudbright where the skies were high and wide and blue, and a body could stand alone rather than be shoved out of the way by an unseeing crowd. When she opened her eyes, a young man was sitting at the foot of the steps looking through her sketches.

Lily ran down the steps and held out her hand. 'What do you think you're doing? Give those back at once!'

The stranger handed her the drawings and smiled so broadly her anger drained away. 'Sorry, couldn't resist. I wanted to see what the competition was like this year. I was hoping they'd be rubbish but unfortunately you seem to be a fine draughtswoman.'

He stood up and brushed the seat of his tweed trousers, giving Lily the chance to study him. He was a full head taller than her, which made her warm to him even more. In Glasgow, where the city-bred folk seemed to grow poorly in the dull light and dank air, she stood out like the milk-and-butter-fed country girl she was.

They walked up the stairs together and this time the door swung open without mishap. The man stretched his arm above her to hold the door open.

'I'm John Petrie, but everyone calls me Jack. What do they call you?'

'Lily Crawford.'

'Like the tall flower with its pale petals; it suits you. Your parents chose well. Just imagine how awkward it would be if you'd grown up short and dark with a less pleasing countenance.'

Lily knew she ought to think him impertinent but couldn't help smiling at the compliment.

Jack followed her through the door. 'Well, Miss Crawford, I hope you'll be happy here.' He tipped his hat and she realised he was about to leave her.

The empty hall still seemed to echo with footsteps and chatter. Lily had only been here once before, when the director, Fra Newbery, had interviewed her. He'd been sitting at a simple wooden desk tucked into an arched window, benign but with an unmistakable air of authority. The director had steepled his hands and told her of his policy of women making up half the students.

'I've worked hard to banish the stereotype of the amateur lady artist – the dilettante young lady who decorates milking stools with impossible sunflowers has been entirely weeded out from the School, I'm glad to say. So, you're not to dismiss your talents through false modesty – you're a professional artist now.'

Lily had felt herself grow in stature as Newbery talked on, outlining the courses she would take. 'You're a painter, I believe, and should flourish under our exacting tutors. But you'll also learn crafts – embroidery, metalwork or repoussé, bookbinding and illustrating.' He caught Lily's frown; she'd stubbornly refused to learn needlework at home and much preferred to wield a sable brush than sit hunched over an embroidery frame. Newbery stood to pace the Turkish rug and continue his lecture. 'There's no need to be sniffy. Here we value the crafts and the principles of design that have made this city's industries stand head and shoulders above those of the rest of the country.'

Lily had followed Newbery out to the exhibition hall where he had shown her some of the works made by these craftswomen. She had been impressed by the intricacy of the designs and the richness of imagination: there was a pewter box decorated with amethysts and garnets; a pair of Christening mittens covered with tiny silk stitches; a fairy book tooled in gold leaf that was open at exquisitely detailed pen-and ink illustrations.

She had had to tear herself away from these treasures

to catch her train, and hadn't been able to take up Newbery's offer to show her around the rest of the Mackintosh Building. Now, here at last, Lily stood frozen in the hall with corridors stretching to either side of her and stairs in front of her, unsure of which way to turn. Jack must have seen her panic because he turned back and offered her his elbow.

'I don't have anywhere pressing to be just now, so shall I give you the grand tour? It's a bit of a warren, but you'll soon get used to it.'

She took his arm gratefully and he began to question her about artistic influences as they walked.

'Are you a fan of the Belgians? I find their *art nouveau* rather too flamboyant, but then I prefer our more austere Glasgow style.

Lily hesitated, aware of her ignorance, and wary of being laughed at. She straightened her shoulders; she wouldn't be intimidated. Jack would have to take her as he found her, as her mother said. Besides, something told her that he would not be cruel enough to mock her, despite his air of urbanity.

She kept her voice casual. 'I'm afraid I don't know much about modern art.'

Jack spread his hands as if to show he meant no offence. 'But that's splendid! You're in for a real treat. I'll explain as we go along, but seeing is the best way for us artists to understand, don't you find, Miss Crawford?' He stopped and disarmed her once again with a smile. 'What say we throw caution to the wind and call each other by our Christian names?' He lowered his head to hers. 'So much less stuffy, and I could tell the minute I laid eyes on you that we were destined to be friends.'

Lily smiled back, relieved he hadn't sneered at her ignorance and gratified to be treated as an equal, not like a child to be petted and patronised as so many other men did back home: her father, the minister, even the spotty butcher's boy wasn't above the odd condescending smirk. Kirkcudbright with its twitching curtains and small-town gossip, where you couldn't chap a male friend's door without attracting curious glances and whispers, was a world away from big, sprawling Glasgow, its streets crowded with people too busy with their own business to mind yours. What would the good townsfolk make of her now, walking unchaperoned with a strange man? Lily suppressed a bubble of laughter, thrilled at the newness of everything, and at the realisation she was free to do much as she pleased. But she was also eager to make new friends with people who shared her love of art and thirst for new ideas. Jack, friendly and engaging, was a start. Her fingers curled more tightly around his arm.

As they walked through the wide corridors, Jack talked about the emerging style of art centred around the school. 'There are a lot of naysayers; of course, there always are when artists try to shake things up. You should have seen what the critics have been saying about this building, that it looks more like a house of correction or a poorhouse than a place of learning. But we love it, so much so that some of us have given it a nickname, as you would a friend.'

'What's that?'

'The Mack.'

Lily smiled. 'The Mack, I like it.' She was already enchanted with the school and knew that she would come to know and love every inch of it. 'The critics are idiots – how could anyone not see how impressive, how utterly extraordinary and different it is? It makes me feel more of an artist, that this is a place where art is taken seriously.'

Jack was delighted. 'Exactly so! I knew we were going to hit it off.'

They climbed the stairs and reached a glassed-in corridor. The September sun had turned the space as warm as a greenhouse and the city rooftops stretched out below.

'Impressive, isn't it?' Jack said. 'The men students have already come up with a name for it: the Hen Run.'

'Why do they call it that?'

Jack cleared his throat. 'Well, the women's studios are at one end and the – er – conveniences are at the other. There's not much time between classes, so there's a bit of a dash sometimes.'

Lily laughed. 'Why, Jack, I do believe you are blushing. Most becoming!' She looked down the length of the corridor and couldn't resist an impulse to run as she had done as a child down her favourite hill back home. 'Shall I see if the Hen Run lives up to its nickname?' Without waiting for a reply, she lifted her skirts and raced along the corridor, skidding towards the end and nearly running into the wall, before turning on her heels and dashing back. Her lungs ached with the effort of running in a corset and she had a stitch, but she didn't care.

Jack grinned. 'I do believe you are going to fit right in here.' He held out his elbow again. 'Come on, we'd better get you matriculated and into your first class.'

A little while later, duly enrolled at the front office, Jack led her back up the stairs. 'You haven't seen the lecture theatre or the library yet. You're in for a treat with the library – it's like a magical forest – but you haven't time now, your first class has already started, and Nellie Grayson is a stickler for timekeeping. All the tutors are, and I'd try to be early if I were you.' When he saw the worried look on Lily's face he said, 'Don't worry, I'll introduce you; Nellie can be rather aloof and cool, but she has a bit of a soft spot for me, if I say so myself.'

Lily was amused by this tiny display of vanity. Jack was

clearly aware of his good looks, but rather than making him insufferable, somehow it only added to his charm. They pushed through another set of double doors into a cavernous studio with enormous windows that flooded the room with light. Breathing in the scents of her new world – of charcoal, turpentine and oil paint – Lily was daunted. She'd been used to her private classes with the artist and had never shown her work. Now she was in a room full of students, many of them no doubt more experienced and talented. She looked around to assess the competition: serious-faced men and women in smocks stood in front of easels, too absorbed in their work to look up. Only the model, dressed as Britannia, turned her head to stare at Lily, but resumed the pose when a murmur of protest arose from the students.

'Why are there so many women and so few men?' Lily whispered to Jack.

'Most of the men come to the evening classes from their day jobs so the women mostly have the place to themselves during the day, apart from a few lucky chaps like me who don't need to be shackled to a place of work.'

Lily looked more closely at Jack, taking in the subtle signs of wealth: the faded but well-cut tweed suit, the gold cufflinks and watch and fob. But most telling of all had been the way he had shown her around the Mack as if he owned the place. His easy charm betrayed his class: Jack had been born at the top of the heap and had no reason to feel threatened by others.

He bowed his head and murmured. 'Look lively, here comes your painting tutor.' The tutor walked slowly between the easels, pausing here and there to make a remark. She wore a cream coat, its wide lapels cut away to show off a coral dress, and an embroidered band held back her hair to show off a handsome face. The effect was bohemian but elegant.

Noticing Lily, the tutor walked over and frowned at the ledger she was carrying. 'I take it you're Miss Crawford?'

Lily took a breath to steady her nerves. 'Yes, that's right.'

'Nice of you to join us.' Her tone was arch. 'I abhor tardiness, so unprofessional.'

Lily's face burned. In an instant she was transported back to the schoolroom, being barked at by a teacher. Well, she was no longer a schoolgirl. She drew back her shoulders but before she could deliver a sharp reply, Jack stepped forward.

'My deepest apologies, entirely my fault: I've been showing Miss Crawford around and simply lost track of time.' He turned to Lily. 'Allow me to present the best tutor and finest portrait painter in Scotland: Nellie Grayson.'

The tutor's expression softened. 'I can see Jack has already been using his charms on you, but you mustn't allow yourself to be distracted from your work, Miss Crawford. The work always comes first, understood?' Lily nodded. 'Good. In future, I will expect you to arrive a quarter of an hour early for class to give you time to set up.' Nellie Grayson looked over at an easel leaning against the far wall. Lily took the hint and hurried off, turning to wave to Jack. When he had left, it was as if some of the air had gone out of the room with him. Lily's shoulders drooped, but her spirits lifted when she saw the door pushed open a crack and Jack's head reappear. The tutor's back was turned so she went over to him.

'What is it? You're going to get me into trouble again,' she whispered.

'I don't suppose I could see you again, after your last class? Embroidery, I believe. I took the liberty of having a squint at your timetable while you were enrolling.'

Lily tried not to show her delight. 'Thank you, that would be agreeable.'

Jack's face broke into a broad smile. 'Agreeable! Marvellous! You are a cool one. Cheerio, then. I'll meet you on the front steps.'

Still grinning, Lily strode across the room to pry her easel from the stack against the wall. She had some trouble with the butterfly screw and another student came to her aid.

'They're terribly stiff these easels, but there's a knack to it. Here, let me. Father's an engineer, wanted a boy and got me instead, so I was brought up to be handy.' Her helper pushed a springy curl of hair behind her ear and straightened up. 'There!' She had grey eyes fringed with dark lashes that slanted like a cat's, high cheekbones and a wide mouth made for smiling. Lily's shoulders relaxed and her courage returned. This girl was so friendly and open, not at all intimidating. 'I'm Katharine Mackenzie, but everyone calls me Kit. It's your first day, isn't it? I remember being so nervous when I started last year.' She squeezed Lily's arm. 'Don't worry, we're a friendly bunch and you'll soon feel at home.' She kept her voice low and glanced at the tutor, who was looking their way. Kit picked up her easel. 'Come on, let's find you a good spot; Purple Patch isn't so bad, but she likes a quiet studio.'

Nellie Grayson was now frowning at them, so Lily didn't dare answer, but once her easel was set up and unjammed by Kit's nimble fingers, she whispered: 'Purple Patch?'

'That's what we call her because she's always telling us to look for the colour in shadows. Right, that's you sorted. See you at needlework and we can have a proper chat: the embroidery tutor is more easy-oasy and lets us talk while we work.'

Alone and in front of her easel, Lily picked up a piece of charcoal. Her fingers felt stiff and she was seized with a sudden uncertainty faced with the blank sheet of paper.

39

Back home, drawing had come naturally, her pencil seemed to have a mind of its own. Now she was frozen. She closed her eyes and recalled a comforting memory of home: a green bower, a flash of brown legs, two heads pressed together over a daisy chain. Jeanie. As the sun cast squares of light on the studio floor, Lily began to sketch the model, her hand moving quickly across the paper, and wondered, as she had done so many times over the years, where her old friend was now.

8

~ *Jeanie* ~

While Lily was putting the finishing touches to her drawing, only a mile away Jeanie swung her empty basket as she walked over Kelvinbridge in the West End. The autumn sunshine was warm on her face, lifting the tiredness that dogged her. Old Ma Graham's messages could wait: the sun was out and it had chased the grey clouds away; the sky was a rare, clear, high blue. She stopped and leaned against the bridge's iron parapet to watch the people walking past and the horses pulling the carts and omnibuses, their hooves ringing out on the cobblestones.

Jeanie still loved the bustle and hum of the city streets; it was only her work as a maid in one of the big houses along Great Western Road that had turned her life into a purgatory she dragged her weary feet through day after day. She looked down at her shoes: they were trodden down at the back. But at least she had shoes, and food in her belly. What she had fled from in Kirkcudbright was far worse than rising at four in the morning to empty the chamber pots, clean ashes out of the grates and scrub the kitchen floor for crabbit Pamela Graham and her whiskery husband with his port-brandy nose. The couple didn't have children, and Jeanie had thought that would mean less work, but now she wished she'd been taken on by a family. Ma Graham wanted every mahogany surface buffed and her fancy Turkish rugs beaten near to death every day. Children would have brought some cheer to that dreary household, as well as a few smudges from sticky fingers. She missed the tumbling joyfulness of her little brothers and sisters. It was for them that she'd had to leave home and disappear into the anonymity of the city, and she'd do it again if she had to. She leaned over the parapet to watch the river swirling below and thought back to how she had got here.

~

After leaving Kirkcudbright, Jeanie had travelled around the country with the show people for the next four years, spending the winter months at Vinegar Hill in the East End of Glasgow. Tatiana had kept up their dance classes when Jeanie wasn't helping at the geggies on Glasgow Green, doing tumbles and cartwheels for pennies. Jeanie worked hard to entertain the punters and tried to give whatever she didn't send back to her mother to Tatiana for her bed and board, but Tatiana would take nothing.

'You'll need this some day. It's important for a woman to have running-away money.' She lowered her voice. 'I have too, but don't tell Sean, he'd spend it on drink for his friends, acting the big man.'

Jeanie knew Tatiana's husband only tolerated her and had tried to keep out of his way and out of the couple's wagon as much as possible. But at night she could hear them arguing – about his drinking, about her failure to give him a son, about having another mouth to feed. In Jeanie's fourth year, when spring arrived and the show people had begun to tie up the big and little machines to go back on the road, Jeanie knew she'd have to move on, no matter that Tatiana insisted she stay. Early one morning, Jeanie had crept out of the wagon with her dance shoes in a small bundle of possessions. But Tatiana must have heard the creak of the stairs and had appeared at the door, rubbing the sleep from her eyes.

'There's no need to leave. Stay.'

'I'll be fine, don't worry about me; I'll get work as a maid. I hear the big new houses in the West End are aye looking for servants. Besides, I have to earn more money to send back home now that Ma's on her own.' Word had got back from Kirkcudbright that Calum had disappeared one night, taking the laundry money Ma kept in a tea caddy. 'She'll be struggling to look after all the bairns and take in washing without me there to help her.' Jeanie had reached up to take Tatiana's hand and pressed it to her cheek. 'You've been like a mother to me, and I'll always be thankful to you, but it's time I stood on my own two feet.'

Tatiana had pulled her into her arms. 'And you have been like a daughter to me.'

~

Now Jeanie sighed as she stood on Great Western Bridge, wishing herself back on the road with the warm, raucous show people who had treated her like one of their own. Come Christmas, it would be a whole year since she'd said goodbye to Tatiana and been grafting for Ma Graham, the miserable old besom. A breeze lifted her bonnet's ribbons and she rubbed her face, weary at the thought of the back-breaking work that waited for her. Her wages didn't amount to much, but she sent back what she could to her mother. No, she'd just have to thole it at Ma Graham's. At nearly twenty, life was bleak and cheerless. Jeanie's head drooped. The swirling waters looked tempting. What else did she have to look forward to but a drab and exhausting future?

She shook off the black thought and was about to pick up her heavy basket but couldn't bear the thought of going back to that gloomy old house, not when the sun was still shining. Instead, she kicked off her shoes and shinned up the balustrade. Jeanie was small – the hunger in her belly as a child meant she'd never grown tall or fattened up around the hips and bosom like other girls her age – but she was strong and wiry. Tatiana had been teaching her the tightrope before she left and now she easily balanced on the narrow parapet, the tough soles of her feet gripping the raised iron edge. She stretched out her arms and walked, toes pointed, lithe and controlled as a dancer, just like the pictures of Blondin she'd seen pinned to the wall of Tatiana's wagon. She listened to the river rushing below and imagined she was inching along a tightrope over Niagara Falls. Jeanie pointed her right leg behind her and stretched out her arms gracefully in an arabesque.

'The trick is never to look down,' Tatiana had told her. A crowd gathered and began to clap as she steadied herself and took a bow. A young man called out: 'Haw, hen, you should be on the stage, you're bonny enough!'

A bear of a man in a top hat and astrakhan coat stepped up to the balustrade and reached a leather-clad hand up to her. 'Let me help you down, young lady.' He had a strange, guttural accent, his tongue curling around the Ls. When she was standing in front of him, he looked her up and down, as she'd seen farmers sizing up the beasts at the mart.

She glared at him. 'What are you looking at, mister?'

He rubbed his chin. 'My new dancer, I hope. Where did you learn to do that?'

Jeanie couldn't help grinning. 'From my friend, Tatiana, she used to be with some famous Russian ballet company before she fell in love with a showman and ran off with him.'

'How like a Russian to follow her heart! She taught you well, this romantic Tatiana, and you have natural grace, the correct build, like a little bird.' He pulled a card from his

44

pocket and handed it to her with a small bow. 'If you're interested in a position with my dance company, come and see me at the Theatre Royal.' He tipped his hat and walked off.

Jeanie looked at the embossed lettering on the card: VIKTOR IVANOV, IMPRESARIO. She tucked it into her pocket, picked up her basket and began walking slowly up Great Western Road, where a dirty kitchen floor waited to be scrubbed. As she toiled past the Botanic Gardens with her heavy basket, she had to push past a gaggle of students, talking excitedly. What would it be like to have such freedom? Jeanie reached for the card in her skirt pocket and curled her fingers round it. She would be mad to give up her steady job – her brothers and sisters needed her wages.

A flock of pigeons rose in a clatter of wings from a rooftop and Jeanie stopped to watch them fly away.

9

~ *Lily* ~

Lily strolled along Kelvinbridge in the last of the sunlight. She stopped to watch a duck glide through the air to land on the water. In Kirkcudbright the hills would be pooling with gold as the sun sank behind them and the scallop fishermen would be tying up their boats for the night. In the little town it would be country-dark soon as households drew the curtains and went to bed, but here the city still hummed with activity. Soon people would be spilling out of their homes and heading to theatres or to visit friends, the streets ablaze with light and the air full of the rumble of carriage wheels and the sharp retorts of horses' hooves. A flock of pigeons rushed overhead in a clatter of wings. Back home, the sky would be thick with swallows readying themselves for the winter exodus. After having fought so hard to leave home, Lily hadn't imagined she'd miss it so much. Now, she almost wished herself back in Kirkcudbright, even though the last few months there had been fraught.

As she watched the River Kelvin flow under the bridge, the doubts that had been gnawing at Lily during her first day at the Mack rose once more. She'd found art school to be not all she'd dreamed of, and that rather than finding herself at home, her talent shining among other gifted peers, she was surrounded by more technically skilled and knowledgeable artists. She'd made a horrible mess in needlework, too resentful of being forced to take up the ladylike pursuit she'd always detested to listen to the tutor's gentle instructions and explanations that these so-called womanly crafts were as valuable as the fine arts. And her painting and drawing tutor, Nellie Grayson, whom she had so wanted to impress, had only paused at Lily's easel to point out how she'd got the proportions wrong.

'These are basic skills that I expect my students to have acquired already. You'll find books on the Golden Rule in the library,' she'd said before turning her attention to another easel. Lily had gritted her teeth as she heard the other student's work being praised.

Lily looked down at her hands gripping the bridge's iron balustrade and touched the amethyst and mother-of-pearl bracelet her mother had given her. Mama believed in her talent, had nurtured it as if it were her own. Lily remembered her interview with Fra Newbery, and she knew she wouldn't have got in if she hadn't shown real talent. Lily would show Nellie bloody Grayson what she was capable of, and she would make her mother proud.

10

∼ *Lily* ∼

As Lily settled at Glasgow School of Art, she gradually shed the remnants of her old life. First to go were the tight corsets that had stifled her breath, replaced by billowing, gloriously loose dresses in the aesthetic style that she made herself and decorated with embroidery, felt flowers, beads and winking circles of mirrored glass. Her stitches were still uneven but the patient needlework tutor had encouraged her to use wool on calico so the rustic effect was pleasing, and had reassured her that while others, such as Kit, were skilled at recreating scenes from fairy tales and Arthurian legends, it was enough to make honest, workaday clothes that honoured the arts and crafts principles laid down by William Morris.

Lily now wore her coppery hair softly gathered at the nape, ignoring the scandalised looks from conventionally dressed women in the streets and the sneers of men rushing to their office jobs in their monochrome work suits. It had taken some courage at first to step out without a hat, her unpinned hair flowing down her back in waves like the pre-Raphaelite beauties so admired by her new friends, but she found that she could weather the disdain – what did it matter to her what anyone thought? She was an artist now and would dress as she damned well pleased. Her landlady had got to her, though, glaring at her when she returned, and talking loudly on the stairs outside her room about the loose morals of young women today and the trash she was forced to take in to earn a crust, despite Lily following the rules pinned to her door that included no men callers.

When Kit told her she'd found a studio flat in a Garnethill tenement, only a few minutes' walk from the Mack and cheaper than both their lodgings if they shared, Lily readily agreed to move in with her.

'You'll come to a bad end, that's for sure,' the landlady sniffed.

'So I've been told,' Lily said as she handed her a week's rent in lieu of notice. However, she wasn't brave enough to weather the storm that would no doubt break at home if her father found out she was living independently, able to come and go as she pleased and have whoever she liked visit her unchaperoned. She wrote to her parents with her new address but left out the change in circumstances. They didn't need to know everything about her new life in Glasgow; it would only worry them and confirm her father's worst fears.

Having their own space to work gave Lily and Kit the chance to work on late into the night without a nosy landlady banging on the ceiling with a broom. They decorated the flat to their own tastes, covering the walls with paintings, drawings and tapestries they had made at the Mack, and the worn-out sofa and armchairs with embroidered panels and Paisley-patterned shawls. The two women hauled down the velvet curtains, heavy with dust and soot, and hung yards of muslin that let in the light through the newly cleaned windows. Friends from the art school gave them a mirror made from pewter and studded with semi-precious stones, as well as pottery vases and bowls finished with iridescent glazes. When the tiny flat was arranged to their satisfaction, Kit threw herself down on an armchair and propped her boots on the ottoman.

She stretched and put her hands behind her head and

grinned up at Lily, who stood in front of the banked-up coal fire. 'Our place, Lil, ours!'

The two friends were busy at the Mack but at the end of each day they locked the storm doors and settled in for the evening, talking and talking over tea sipped from hand-painted cups, and taking turns to listen intently as the other discussed ideas or technical problems. When Kit landed her first commission to illustrate a series of fairy tale books, Lily was just as excited, her friend's success encouraging her to redouble her efforts now that there was proof people would actually pay for their work. Lily advised on colour and composition, looking on admiringly as Kit sketched curlicues and tendrils for the half-hidden details that would delight the reader when they looked closer: a frog peering from under a leaf in a corner or an imp perched high on the branches of a tree, all so different from her own bold paints and broad brushstrokes.

Lily was still struggling at art school under Nellie Grayson's cool appraisals, as she tried one style after the other. She worked her way through the art books and copies of *Studio* magazine in the library, seeking inspiration and in a vain attempt to please the only tutor whose opinion really mattered to her.

'I see you have been looking at Mr Beardsley's illustrations,' Nellie said during one class when she stopped at Lily's pen and ink drawing. 'It's all very well mimicking another artist, but any decent draughtsman can make a copy. You need to go deeper into your own emotions, really look at the world and at your subject, and develop your own style. Until you do that, you may have a good eye, but you won't be an artist.'

The blood sang in Lily's head; she grabbed the sheet of paper off the easel and tore it in two. 'It's rubbish, so I'll treat it like rubbish.' She expected a reprimand, but Nellie merely nodded.

'Never be afraid of throwing away your work, no matter how long you've spent on it. I want to see you waste paper, lots of it, and use charcoal, it'll let your hand flow – you're a painter, not an illustrator. Make a mess, fail. It doesn't matter. Find your own style.'

Baffled at first by her advice, Lily stopped trying to imitate other artists and began to trust her own instincts, going through sheet after expensive sheet of paper until she started using brown butcher's paper and old newspapers to sketch her own ideas. On Nellie's advice, she took to spending the first half-hour of a life class just looking at the model, discovering the kaleidoscope of greens, yellows, violets, blues and reds that make up a person's skin, the hollows and bumps, the dark and light that brought the sitter to life.

The hours she spent standing at her easel, concentrating so hard the rest of the world fell away, were exhausting. Lily's back and feet ached like a shop girl's, and her eyes were dry and her mind wrung out. But it was the same for the other students, and she revelled in the camaraderie during the breaks. At the end of class, Jack would be waiting on the steps outside the Mack, his hat tipped to the back of his head, his hands in his pockets. In their free time they would take in the latest exhibition or sketch in the Botanic Gardens. He was always respectful of her person and reputation, but Lily could tell he had warm feelings for her, and she had to quell her nerves and steady her breathing when she caught sight of him.

In the beginning they talked shop: Lily about the techniques she was learning and the styles she was experimenting with, and Jack about his enthusiasm for the avant-garde art he'd seen in Vienna, Brussels and Paris. Lily was jealous

51

of his freedom and vowed she too would travel the world one day. As the weeks passed and they grew closer, Lily tried to put her mother's warnings out of her mind; Jack was an enlightened, modern man, nothing like her father. Besides, they were friends, nothing more. That's what she told herself until one afternoon when they were sketching orchids in one of the Botanic Gardens' glasshouses.

Lily wiped her brow. 'It's so hot in here; I feel sorry for those women in their tight dresses. They've been giving me strange looks, but who is the cooler and more comfortable?' She paused and put down her pencil. 'Although they do look terrific in the latest fashion.'

Jack glanced at the two women with their cartwheel hats and wasplike waists before returning to his sketch. 'They couldn't hold a candle to you.' He looked at her softly. 'You're the most beautiful woman I've ever met; you'd make a sack cloth look good.'

He was looking at her with such intensity that Lily caught her breath. She laughed nervously. 'Thanks a lot – I know my dressmaking skills aren't up to much.'

The moment was gone. Jack smiled and went back to his sketch. Lily felt a pang as she picked up her pencil and tried to concentrate on her drawing.

11

~ *Jeanie* ~

Jeanie sat on the floor of the empty rehearsal room, dripping with sweat. She stretched her aching calf and pointed her toes to the ceiling to try to get rid of a cramp. Every muscle in her body ached; she had never been so tired, not even as a maid. She wiped away the sweat that was stinging her eyes and leaned her head against the mirrored wall. Months after joining Viktor's dance company, she still lagged behind the other dancers in ballet class. She picked up steps and routines easily enough in rehearsals, and was as fit, flexible and strong as the next person, but the exacting ballet lessons left her feeling like a clumsy fool, ignorant of the French instructions the ballet mistress rapped out and which the others knew like clockwork, having been schooled in them from early childhood. The other dancers called her 'tweenie', after she'd let slip she'd been a house servant, and mocked her thick country accent. The male dancers weren't so bad; they appreciated how light she was to lift and the way she picked up steps instinctively and seamlessly followed their lead. Jeanie knew she was getting better every day, that she wanted this more than any of those stuck-up bitches. One day she'd get out of the chorus line and into the spotlight; she'd show them. She would never go back to skivvying and she'd never be poor again.

The company was rehearsing for the Christmas show at the Theatre Royal, and Jeanie was determined to stay on later to perfect the dance routines. Before they left the studio, one of the dancers had broken off from the gaggle heading off to eat to ask her to come with them, but Jeanie had only shaken her head and mumbled an apology. Instead she'd stayed by herself, working on the steps over and over again until the pain had made her sink down to the floor.

Jeanie heard a heavy tread and looked up to see Viktor leaning on his cane. Without his hat, she could see the silver in his hair and how the lines around his eyes creased, as if he were amused at a private joke. Her stomach dipped. She'd begun to find his dark Russian looks attractive; more than attractive. For a while now Jeanie had found herself watching him as he directed rehearsals, and now and then she caught him watching her with a dark intensity.

'Rehearsing again?' he said. 'You'll dance yourself into the ground if you're not careful.'

Jeanie leapt to her feet. 'I'm not tired, not even a wee bit.' But she couldn't help wincing as her calf went into spasm again. Viktor got down on his haunches, pulled her leg towards him and began massaging her muscle and pushing her foot flat. She nearly cried out, but it soon eased.

Viktor smiled up at her. 'Better?'

She nodded. His hands were warm. No man had ever touched her with such gentleness.

'I've been watching you over the past few months; you've come on. I knew you were a natural, little bird, from the moment I set eyes on you. My instincts are always right.' He smiled. 'So, I'd like to give you a little solo spot in the show. It'll mean more work, but I think you can handle it.'

Jeanie forgot her aches and pains. She grinned down at him. 'Thank you! I won't let you down, cross my heart and swear to die.'

'Oh, I wouldn't like that, not at all.' With his hands still on her, he looked at her searchingly. His eyes were so dark she couldn't see the pupils. 'You know, I'm married,' he said. 'But Anna hates this world now that she can't dance any more. When she left, she said she'd had enough of living out of a suitcase, enough of draughty theatres, and enough of me. That was years ago. Now she lives in St Petersburg with her dogs and her dresser and is quite happy.'

Jeanie gently withdrew her leg from his grasp. He rose and waited in front of her.

'So?' he said. 'Are we to be together? I would like that very much.'

Jeanie looked at him, losing herself in the kindness of his dark eyes. Slowly, she reached up to kiss him on the mouth. After a while, Viktor took her by the hand, and she followed him out of the studio.

12

~ *Jeanie* ~

A few weeks before they were due to open, Madame Lebret clapped her hands to get the dancers' attention as they stretched.

'I have an announcement to make – one of our newest recruits will be taking on her first solo role in the Christmas show.' She turned to Jeanie, who had been dipping her shoes in powder and now stared at her, wide-eyed. The other lassies would be spitting feathers; they'd hate her even more. And what if they found out about Viktor? They'd been discreet, leaving the theatre separately to meet at his hotel, but it was hard to keep secrets in this closed world. Everyone would think she'd got the part because she was sleeping with the impresario.

With a graceful wave of her arm, the choreographer beckoned to Jeanie to stand by her side. 'Our little Jeanie only came to us recently, somewhat rough around the edges, I admit, but she has blossomed and is now ready to take centre stage.'

Jeanie closed her eyes; she couldn't bear to see the hatred in the other dancers' faces. Instead of the silent resentment she'd been expecting, a wave of applause went around the studio. When she dared to look, the company was clapping, their expressions open and delighted.

'Brava! Brava!' they cried and, one after the other, they came up to kiss her on the cheeks and embrace her.

'After all your hard work, you deserve this,' a French dancer, who Jeanie had thought the haughtiest, said with a wide smile. 'Congratulations, *chèrie*.' She kissed her three times on the cheek, in the Parisian way that Jeanie still found embarrassing.

The dancers crowded around her and one of the male dancers, an Italian, placed his hands around Jeanie's waist and lifted her high. She grinned at their upturned faces, the cheers and their wildly clapping hands, before covering her face. He placed her gently back on her feet. 'Now you must come out with us, to celebrate, yes?'

Madame Lebret put her arm around Jeanie's shoulders. 'Go with your companions. Viktor will pay for the champagne – he always does when the star is cast.' The company cheered again, and she laughed.

Jeanie cleared her throat and hoped the tears in her eyes wouldn't betray her. 'I just want a word with Madame, and then I'd love to join you all; thank you.' She hugged herself. 'I can't wait; I've never tasted champagne.' A small lie in the middle of her joy – Viktor always had a bottle chilling in his suite. Once they had all left the rehearsal studio in a chorus of good wishes, Jeanie turned to Madame Lebret. 'I don't know how to begin to thank you for trusting me with this role.'

The dance tutor put her arm around her shoulders. 'It's time, my dear, that you took a bigger role. As you can see from the reaction of the others, I'm not the only one who recognises your talent.'

'I thought they'd hate me for taking the best part.'

'A dance company is not like that; we're a family. I've noticed that you keep yourself to yourself, but you must let the other dancers get close. It's the only way you'll survive in this game; they'll support you in your moments of triumph, and, more importantly, in darker times.'

'They were so kind just now, so generous. I thought they

57

looked down on me, calling me "tweenie" because I was a maid.'

Madame Lebret laughed. 'So sensitive! You have the artistic temperament, my dear, but you must grow a thicker skin. They call you Teeny because you are so petite.' She led her towards the door. 'You must learn to trust people more; it was hard for me too – I came from a poor background, a small village, and when I arrived in Paris I thought everyone was laughing at my country accent and my simple ways. The first time I tasted foie gras I spat it out, and I thought burgundy tasted like vinegar. But in our world, all you need is talent and hard work; it doesn't matter where you come from. Now, go and join the company, and let them show you how happy they are for you. Who more than they know what you have gone through to earn this part?'

Jeanie reached up and kissed the dance instructor on the cheek three times. 'Thank you, Madame.'

Madame Lebret chucked her under the chin. 'You see, you are learning already.'

13

∼ *Lily* ∼

Lily could no longer fool herself: she was beginning to fall for Jack, although she was careful not to betray her feelings again. In turn, he kept a careful distance, teasing her as if she were no more than a sister. Lily sometimes caught Jack staring at her rather than at his sketchbook, but instead of looking flustered, he would only smile and bend his head to his work again. He was patient with her and she suspected he was playing the long game: if he'd pressed himself on her, she would have drawn back, but, contrarily, the more he behaved as if nothing had changed between them, the more Lily was drawn to him. And it was Jack she desperately wanted to see after her breakthrough at the Mack, when she at last won her tutor's respect.

∼

Nellie Grayson stood silently contemplating Lily's latest painting. Lily had put aside any attempt to follow trends, returning instead to the landscape of her childhood, to the luminous, shifting colours of Galloway. For this painting, she was exploring colour and light: a young woman leaning against a tree, the sunlight dappling through its leaves to pool in greens and golds on her pale skin. But this was no shy and innocent rustic lass – she looked boldly out of the canvas, her head at an unorthodox tilt as if daring the viewer to see her as more than a decorative object.

Lily clasped her hands behind her back and waited for

Nellie's verdict. When it came, she listened as she never had before.

'You have talent, real talent,' Nellie said finally. 'I wasn't sure you were mature enough to find your own way and avoid the clichés, but Fra was right about you. This is exceptional; we should put it forward for the Royal Academy awards.'

These were treasured words Lily knew she would recall and exult in again and again when she was alone, but right now she wanted to repeat them back to Jack. As soon as class was over, she hurried to find him. He looked up from his easel, surprised to see her in his studio; usually they met on the outside steps. He stood and wiped his hands with a rag.

'Lily! Is there anything wrong?'

Forgetting her usual restraint around him, Lily rushed up to him and held onto his arms, repeating everything Nellie had said. Jack's grin was broad and bright.

'The Royal Academy, no less! Oh, Lily, you deserve this; it's your breakthrough.' He grabbed his jacket and pulled it on. 'Come on, we're going to celebrate! Champagne and dinner at the Central Hotel are in order, I believe. And then I'm taking you to a party.'

Lily glanced down at her handmade dress in dismay and put a hand to her hair, which hung in tangles after a day in the studio. 'A party? But I must go home and change first.'

'No time! You look absolutely splendid the way you are – a natural beauty! And it's an artists' party, so the dress code will hardly be conventional. I was told to bring a rising star from the Mack, and I think you fit the bill, don't you?'

Lily clapped her hands together to stop herself hugging him. 'What are you waiting for? Let's go!'

'Hold your horses, Miss Crawford,' he said as he caught up with her.

'Whose party is it?' she said as they hurried out the Mack and into the street.

'Some artist friends of mine who live in the West End, a lovely couple, both very talented in their own right, both successful and deliriously happy with each other, despite the bonds of matrimony.' Lily shot him a look, but he didn't return it. 'There'll be quite a crowd, a real mixed bag, not just artists but people who can actually afford to buy art – a canny move by the hostess, who, I warn you now, is rather formidable.'

~

Jack was right: the lady of the house was utterly terrifying. She sat on a throne-like chair in the middle of a strange, stark white room like a queen holding court. The room was filled with people who all seemed to know each other, talking at the top of their voices. To quell her nerves, Lily concentrated on the clean lines and simple textures, so different from the prevailing fashion for dark furniture, ferns in brass pots and stuffed birds suffocating under domes of glass. In contrast, this home was modern and austere, but there was also a softness and elegance to the pieces of pink, purple and green glass decorating the white furniture, like so many jewels. Everything else was white or cream, down to the carpets, and Lily caught herself wondering how the maid could possibly keep such a room clean of soot. The heat from the coal fire and the press of bodies was oppressive; she slipped away from Jack, who seemed perfectly at ease mingling with the throng, and sat in a window seat.

'I, too, find these soirées rather overwhelming. May I join you?'

Lily looked up to see a smoothly handsome face

frowning down at her. His features were delicate but his mouth full, his dark hair slicked back like lacquered ebony, giving him the air of a sleek oriental cat. He was quite the most beautiful man she'd ever seen, and her fingers itched for a sketchbook. Lily smiled at him and he sat down next to her.

'Ned Raeside,' he said with a slight bow of the head. Beside them three young men were talking loudly about commissions and the cost of framing. Ned raised his eyebrows and lowered his voice. 'Shop talk! So tedious, whether it's artists or lawyers. And I should know, I'm one of the latter.' Lily opened her mouth to introduce herself, but he raised a slim hand. 'You are Miss Crawford, of course, how could you not be?' He studied Lily. He wore impeccable evening dress and she became acutely aware of her unbrushed hair, her clumsily embroidered dress, and the paint spatters on her hands. He seemed to sense her discomfort and smiled to himself as he took a cigarette case out of his pocket. 'My dear friend, Jack, has told me *all* about you.' His tone was arch, making Lily wonder exactly what Jack had said. Ned studied her a moment before tapping his cigarette on the silver case. 'Hmm, I can see the obvious attraction. Jack's always had an eye for a pretty girl, but you must be quite exceptional to have held his attention this long.'

Lily was too startled to realise she'd been insulted. 'Oh, but you're mistaken, we aren't . . .'

Ned went on as if she hadn't spoken. 'You see, the poor dear bores so easily, always has done.' He spoke quietly so she had to lean in close enough to smell his verbena cologne. 'Even as a boy he'd tire of a new toy after he'd played with it once. Spoiled, you see, the golden child. But you, my dear, seem to have captured his interest.' Lily watched as if hypnotised, while he took his time inserting a cigarette into an ivory holder and lighting it. 'In fact, in all the years I've known him, I've never seen him so smitten.' His lips curved to reveal even, white teeth. 'Clever girl to have kept him hanging on.' His dark eyes gleamed with malice as he watched the effect of his words.

Lily recoiled and the corners of Ned's mouth twitched as he saw he'd hit his mark. She knew she shouldn't rise to this baiting, that she should walk away to preserve her dignity, but when she turned her head to look for Jack and saw him leaning against a bookcase in the corner, he was standing too close to an elegant woman, her blonde hair caught in the latest style and her evening dress cut low to show off a creamy bosom. Lily had never thought of Jack as frivolous in his affections and had always assumed he was sincere in his devotion to her. Now she thought back to how patiently he'd waited for her, playing the long game, and wondered if this obnoxious Ned was right, and that the real Jack was a callow adventurer only interested in the chase. She straightened her back and made herself turn back to her mocking tormentor, reminding herself that she knew Jack well enough by now to judge his character. This man, who purported to be his friend, was out to make trouble, for whatever reason.

Lily's temper flared. She resented above all Ned's implication that she'd been trying to hook Jack with a tawdry cat-and-mouse game, feigning reluctance like the heroine in a Victorian melodrama. She despised women who primped and fluttered their eyelashes to get what they wanted. This so-called friend of Jack's needed putting in his place.

'Ned Raeside, you say?' She frowned as if trying to search her memory, and then shook her head. 'You may have heard about me, but I've never heard of you. Do you know? Jack has never spoken about you, not once. Odd, since you say you're so tight with him.' It was all she could think of at the time and not exactly a stinging counterattack, but Ned's mouth turned down at the corners, giving him the air of a sulky child. Lily suppressed the urge to laugh; she had clearly hit a nerve. After a moment, he regained his composure.

'Well, perhaps he doesn't confide in you fully yet, Miss Crawford,' he drawled. 'But I can assure you, we are the best of friends, as he will tell you himself. Look, there he is over there, talking to that bouncy little blonde. What do you say? Shall we break them up?'

Ned walked off without waiting for Lily's reply. She watched Jack turn from the irritatingly attractive woman and greet Ned warmly. Lily could tell by the way they patted each other down like police officers arresting a suspect just how fond the two men were of each other. Jack beckoned her over and she joined them just as the other woman slipped away, blowing a kiss.

'Lily!' Jack said. 'I'm delighted you've already met Ned, my dearest and oldest friend – and quite the cleverest chap I know. He's training to be an advocate, and I wager he'll become Scotland's youngest judge before too long.' Ned looked abashed; Lily could see he'd lost some of his wasp-ishness in Jack's company. He took out another cigarette and tapped it on the case, like a cat grooming itself to recover its equanimity.

'Don't be an idiot, Jack,' he drawled. 'We both know you keep in with me because I'm your only normal friend among a host of moonstruck bohemians.'

'Not true! Why, there's Florence over there, and she is as far from a moonstruck bohemian as you could wish.' Jack beckoned to a serious-looking young woman in a grey skirt and a striped, mannish shirt, its cuffs turned back as if she were about to embark on a practical task. When she came over, he said: 'Lily, I'd like you to meet Florence Anderson, one of the few women medical students at Glasgow University – a rose among thorns, eh Flo? All those drunken medical students playing pranks with bits of dead bodies,' he said with a shudder. 'Don't know how they turn into doctors: I wouldn't let any of them loose on a patient.'

'They're not so bad, as long as you don't take their jokes to heart,' Florence said, a smile transforming her plain face. 'Fortunately, I have a thick skin. Besides, now we're in our final year, we all work so hard there's no time for pranks.' She shook Lily's hand firmly. 'Jack speaks fondly of you; he's been promising to bring you to tea for an age but keeps forgetting.'

'He's hopeless,' Lily said, warming to this straightforward woman. 'I should love to come to tea.'

'It's settled, then. Jack is in awe of your talent and can talk of little else.' They both glanced at Jack, who looked at his feet.

'Guilty as charged, I'm afraid.'

Florence took Lily's arm. 'So refreshing to meet another independent woman.'

Ned rolled his eyes and sighed dramatically. 'Please! Stop, I beg you! You'll be chaining yourselves to the railings and blowing up postboxes next, like those ghastly suffragettes.'

Lily was about to retaliate when Florence waved her hand, as if batting away an indulged child. 'Don't listen to him, Lily; he's a terrible tease. In fact, Ned defended one of those ghastly suffragettes. She would have ended up in jail if it weren't for him.' Lily looked at Ned with renewed interest. He looked back at her coolly but was the first to break the staring contest with a soft chuckle.

The rest of the evening passed in a blur of talk and

laughter. Ned stopped aiming barbs at Lily and entertained them all with colourful anecdotes from the courts that made them gasp with scandalised laughter.

'You might like this salty little tale, with my apologies in advance to the ladies,' Ned said. 'The judge, a rather lenient fellow in my opinion, told the ne'er-do-well he was sentencing: "Although I find you a fecund liar, I will not send you to prison." To which the grateful defendant replied: "Thank you, your Honour, and you're a fecund good judge."'

Lily, emboldened by several glasses of champagne, laughed until tears sprang from her eyes. She was enjoying herself immensely and could see why Jack was so fond of Ned, who grew warmer and funnier the more relaxed he became and the more he sipped at the glass of whisky in his hand. She put his earlier sharpness down to shyness and an odd prickly defensiveness in his nature, as if he were forever on the lookout for potential enemies. At any rate, he'd clearly decided that Lily had passed some kind of test and was now using his considerable charm and wit to win her over.

As midnight grew nearer and the room grew smokier, Lily's head began to ache from the champagne, and she excused herself and stepped outside for some fresh air. The night air was mild and the sky clear of its customary blanket of clouds so she could see the stars above and the lights of Glasgow spread out below. The dark outline of the hills in the distance made her think of home. Soon it would be Christmas, and she would be with Ma and Pa in Kirkcudbright. In the darkness, a cough made her jump: there was someone out here with her.

'Who's there?'

'I'm sorry, my dear, I startled you.' A man stepped forward into the yellow glow of the street lamp. He had greying hair and a moustache; the loosely tied bow at his neck marked him out as an artist rather than a potential danger.

'Not at all,' Lily said. 'Lovely night – I needed some air.'

'I hope you're enjoying the party; we like our little get-togethers – a chance to keep in touch with the younger set coming out of the Mack.' He put his hands in his trouser pockets, revealing an embroidered waistcoat, and studied her. 'Forgive me, my dear, but I'm assuming you're an art student?' When Lily nodded, he said: 'Are you one of my wife's protégées?'

'No, Nellie Grayson is my tutor.'

'Ah, a painter then.'

'I hope so.' She smiled at him. 'Yes, a painter.'

'That's the spirit! No need to minimise your talent – plenty of other people will be only too eager to do that for you.' Lily detected a note of bitterness despite his smile.

'Are you doing well?'

'Beginning to. Nellie wants to put one of my paintings up for a Royal Academy medal.'

'Good to see a youngster on the way up. Enjoy your success while it lasts, my dear, but brace yourself for a bumpy ride. At some point we all fail while others succeed. It can eat you up.'

Lily thought back to her delight at Kit's commission. 'Oh no, I'm sure I'll always be happy when my friends succeed, aren't you?'

The older man laughed. 'I would have to be a saint not to resent the plaudits given to my peers, each a dagger in my heart. It's particularly excruciating if you feel your own talents remain undiscovered and unappreciated.

'My wife, for instance, is also my artistic partner, but she's overlooked all the time, her beautiful gessoes sneered at by the so-called cognoscenti as overly feminine.' He shrugged. 'It's unfair, but that's how it is in our world.' He turned to her and she could see him frown in the half-light. 'Tell me, what do you hope for now?'

Lily decided against false modesty. 'To win a medal and have a solo exhibition.'

He put his head to one side as if considering her. 'Difficult for a woman, but not impossible, as long as you have a good dealer. You must learn to be a businesswoman as well as an artist.' He smiled. 'Don't listen to me; I'm an old cynic who has long ago put aside his dreams of fame and fortune. You're right to aim high, but early success can be a curse for an artist.' He spread his arms over the city. 'The view is sublime from up here, but it's a long way down.'

The front door opened, flooding them with the warm indoor light and breaking the intimacy they had shared in the darkness.

The man bowed slightly and took her hand. 'Goodnight, good luck, and *bon courage*.' As he turned to go, the light from inside caught him and she recognised him from a photograph she'd seen in the *Studio*.

Lily was still thinking over the conversation she'd just had when Jack stepped out into the garden beside her.

'Why are you hiding out here all alone?' he said.

'But I haven't been alone. Jack, you'll never guess who I've been talking to.'

14

~ *Jeanie* ~

The swell of orchestra music faded, and the stage darkened. When the spotlight came up, it revealed Jeanie, resplendent in a costume encrusted with diamanté, shining like a star in the night sky. As the musicians began the next movement, she began to dance, first-night nerves forgotten as she lost herself in the music, pirouetting and leaping, light and agile as a cat. As she danced, she caught glimpses of the rest of the company crowded in the wings to watch and encourage her. She danced as she'd never danced before, ignoring her trembling muscles and jarred ankles, alone at first and then with a partner in an intense and passionate routine. All too soon, her moment of glory was over, and the rest of the dancers joined them, merging in lines and overlapping circles to form moving patterns on the stage. Before she knew it, the show was over and the whole company was on stage, holding hands and bowing while thunderous applause filled the vast gilt and red velvet glory of the theatre. Jeanie's partner held out his arm and brought her to the front of the stage, where she curtseyed low as the clapping grew louder and cries of 'Bravo!' broke out. Jeanie's bones seemed to vibrate in sympathy with the ruckus and her heart swelled as the noise wrapped itself around her small body. The applause rose even higher as Viktor came out of the wings to present her with a bouquet of roses. She cradled them in her arms before stepping back into line. The roses were dark red, their petals like velvet, and their scent so heady she could smell them over the grease paint. Wrung out, drenched with sweat, excruciating pain cramping her legs and feet, Jeanie had never been happier.

~

A bath with salts had helped ease her aching limbs and now Jeanie sat in her dressing room in a silk peignoir. Her own dressing room! It was a gift for tonight only from Viktor, for her solo debut. Used to bumping up against half-clothed women taking off their make-up and chatting at full volume, she relished the quiet. She wiped the cold cream off her fingers and studied her reflection. Her eyes were still lined with the remnants of kohl, so they appeared huge. She clipped on the emerald earrings Viktor had bought her and touched the French scent to her pulse points. Her stomach rumbled and she was acutely aware of her empty belly. Any minute now, Viktor would come and take her to his hotel where they'd eat steak, bloody and rare as he'd taught her, and drink champagne and expensive claret. He always laughed at her appetite.

'I love to watch you eat – where do you put it all? You never put on an ounce.' Jeanie would only shrug and help herself to another buttered potato.

She in turn loved the luxuries that came with Viktor: the starched linen sheets changed daily in his suite, the baskets of fruit, the champagne chilling in its silver basin, the fresh flowers on every polished table, the jewellery and, above all, the clothes. Jeanie glanced at the red velvet dress hanging behind her door and gave a sigh of contentment. Her new life had brought her all this, but the memories of poverty hovered in the back of her mind like a spectre. Viktor knew where she'd come from and took pleasure in her delight as he plied her with gifts and took her out for meals with his theatre friends, now that they no longer hid their affair.

Sometimes she missed the excitement of their early days together when a well-tipped doorman would smuggle her into Viktor's hotel. Their lovemaking had been a revelation. She'd been expecting pain the first time and had been shy of undressing in front of him, but Viktor had been kind and gentle, his knowing hands making her lose herself in a pleasure so intense it left her trembling and spent, and eager for more. Jeanie let her fingers drift over her chest and shivered with anticipation. There was a knock at the door and her insides twisted. She turned from the mirror, letting her silk dressing gown fall open slightly. The door opened to reveal a familiar face.

'Tatiana!' Jeanie leapt up to embrace her old friend and ushered her into the room. 'You're back in the city! Of course, it's winter, I should have come to see you at the wintering grounds.'

'Don't worry about me, I can see you've been busy.' Tatiana stroked her face and kissed her cheek. 'When I heard you'd become a professional dancer, I couldn't wait to come and see you. I assumed you'd be in the chorus line but imagine my joy when I saw you dance solo.'

'I can hardly believe it myself,' Jeanie said. 'It's you I have to thank, you taught me how to dance.'

'Ah, but those were only tricks and tumbles for the geggies; you're now a real dancer. I'm so proud, I could weep!'

Jeanie hugged her again, more tightly, and felt rather than heard Tatiana's shuddering sob.

'What's the matter?'

Tatiana sniffed. 'It's nothing, it's just so good to see you again.'

Jeanie studied her friend, taking in the powder that failed to cover up the dark circles and eyes reddened with crying. 'How are things with Sean?'

71

Tatiana sat down heavily on Jeanie's dressing stool. Her voice was hollow. 'He's been seeing another woman, younger than me. Everyone in the camp knew about it except me. When he found out she was expecting his child, he started a fight over nothing and threw me out.' She put her head in her hands. 'I've nowhere to live, my running-away money will tide me over for a few days but I've no way of earning money. I don't know what to do.'

Jeanie stroked her hair. 'Don't be silly, you have me. I'll help you, just as you helped me when I had nobody to turn to. Things look dark now, but really he's done you a favour.'

Tatiana lifted her head. 'What do you mean?'

'You were always too good for that act – the high wire for a former prima ballerina – *pah!*' Her fingertips touched the bruise on Tatiana's face. 'And as for the toerag who did this, you were too good for him too.' She poured a glass of water for Tatiana. 'I can ask if there's work for you here if you like?'

'Would you?'

'Of course! They're always looking for dressers and ward-robe mistresses, if you didn't mind doing work like that?'

Tatiana looked around the small dressing room. She smiled at Jeanie. 'I would love to be back in the theatre and working with dancers – and to be close to you again. I've told you before: you're like a daughter to me.'

Jeanie put her arms around the older woman. 'I know, Tatiana, and you're like a mother to me, the best I could hope for.'

15

∼ *Lily* ∼

Lily's conviction that she would never succumb to professional jealousy was put to the test soon after her encounter
at the West End party. It was the opening night, or
varnishing as she'd learned to call it, of the Glasgow Society
of Lady Artists' Christmas exhibition, where her work was
being shown for the first time. Lily had been working hard
in the intervening weeks and two of her paintings were on
show: the portrait so admired by Nellie Grayson, and a
rustic scene of two little girls making daisy chains in the
shade of a willow tree. It had caused her the most trouble,
trying to recreate the Galloway light, but she was now
quietly pleased with it. Both paintings had been hung in
prime positions and were attracting a lot of attention when
she came into the exhibition hall.

Kit spotted her and broke from the crowd surrounding
Lily's paintings. 'Here's the artist!' she announced. Admirers
gathered around murmuring praise: *breaking new ground
. . . such talent . . . a fresh perspective . . .* She soaked it
up like parched soil drinking in the rain. Kit nudged her
and she looked around to see a small portly man approaching
her. She recognised him as a prominent art dealer who
supplied the city's wealthy tobacco and sugar merchants
with paintings to decorate the blank walls of their grand
new homes. He stopped at her work and examined it in
minute detail, like a jeweller scrutinising gemstones.

He turned to Lily, who was standing next to her work
like a mother bear guarding her cub. 'These are yours?'

She nodded, not trusting her voice. 'They show a great deal of potential, Miss . . .?' He leaned in to see the handwritten note on the wall. 'Crawford.' He reached into his waistcoat pocket and handed her a card. 'Sandy Munro's the name. May I suggest you make an appointment with my secretary? I have a wealthy gentleman in mind who is fond of these bucolic scenes.' He gestured at the painting of the two young girls, then bent to peer at the portrait and straightened up. 'And this could work for a line of commissions. This wealthy gent's wife, for instance, is quite striking, what the French call *une jolie-laide*, or in the pithier Glaswegian argot of the streets, she has a face a like a torn scone.' Lily's nerves dissolved into laughter and Munro grinned. 'I believe you'd do this fine lady justice, you'd be able to bring out her, um, singular personality.' He patted her arm and strode away to look at other paintings.

Kit's eyes were shining. 'You lucky thing! To be picked up by none other than Sandy Munro at your first exhibition.' She put her arms around Lily and squeezed the breath out of her. 'I knew you'd be a star the moment I met you.'

Lily smiled, embarrassed but delighted. 'Don't be silly! I'm sure his sales pitch is well rehearsed.' Nevertheless, she couldn't wait to tell Jack, who had promised to look in on the way to the Glasgow Art Club varnishing. When he came in late with Ned, she rushed up to him and told him her news. But she knew she'd lost his attention when he looked over her shoulder and waved. She turned to see Sandy Munro bearing down on them and stepped forward to meet him with a smile that died on her face when the art dealer brushed past her to clap Jack on the back.

'Petrie, dear boy! I've sold that landscape – the one with the wee shepherd laddie who looks like he could do with a good wash behind the ears – to one of my best clients, and now he's clamouring for more from "the most promising young artist to come out of Scotland". Or at least, that's what I've told him.' Munro guffawed and Jack grinned: unlike Lily, he didn't appear the least embarrassed by the compliment. Lily realised Ned had been right: Jack was used to being praised and even expected it as his due.

Munro drew Jack closer, turning his back on Lily. 'Have you any more quaint country scenes hidden away in your studio? I can't sell enough of them, in Glasgow at least. London won't touch them until we get you into one of the big galleries. They haven't caught up with the new French trends yet.' Munro lowered his voice and moved further into the crowd with Jack, forcing Lily to step nearer to hear what he said next. 'Talking of which, I may have a lead that could get you exhibited at the Royal Academy, no less. What do you say we leave this amateur ladies' sale of works and head across the road to the Art Club to talk business over a wee dram, away from the fussing hens and their wee daubs, eh?'

The fizz of triumph Lily had felt earlier went as flat as the tepid glass of champagne in her hand. She'd been foolish to think the dealer's interest was genuine when he was clearly of the art establishment's view that women couldn't and shouldn't make art. Her fingers tightened around the stem of the coupe glass. The two men would now retire to the Glasgow Art Club where the real business deals were struck by men and women were only tolerated as visitors or, if they were there, hired to sweep the hearths and scrub the stairs. The Society of Lady Artists had been set up in protest, to give women like her the chance to exhibit, but the real power remained firmly in the hands of the male art elite.

Lily turned back to her *Girl with a Rose* and saw its flaws: the clumsy brushwork, the subject matter too cosy and safe, the tilt of the head she'd once thought proud and independent that now just looked silly. As if to echo her feelings, she could hear Sandy Munro chortling with Jack as they walked away. She frowned at Jack's retreating back. He could have easily included her in the conversation had he not been too busy looking after his own interests. He probably didn't even realise he'd stolen her limelight. He was so arrogant and self-assured! The two men turned, as if in afterthought, and tipped their hats to Lily before resuming their conversation. The coupe glass broke in her hand and champagne spilled over her fingers. She didn't notice Jack's lawyer friend, Ned, until he spoke.

'Funny thing about our Jackie-boy,' Ned drawled as they watched the two men leave. 'He always lands on his feet. Used to infuriate me when we were at school. I'd be grafting away, and he'd sail off with the Dux medal at the end of the year without having done a stroke of work. I blame his parents – they worship Jack and have always given him anything he wants. It was the same at school; everyone adored him, even the dominies. The Great Jack Petrie: star on and off the rugby pitch. Didn't have to try at all, not like us lesser mortals. I suppose some people are just born lucky. Sickening, isn't it?'

Lily kept her voice even. 'Jack is a talented artist and a fine man, why shouldn't he be so well loved?' But Ned was not fooled and only smirked at her before she turned on her heel.

~

Ned had hit the mark again, homing in on her nascent jealousy. Lily was still fuming about Jack at the varnishing dinner at the Society later that evening. He hadn't returned after his meeting with Munro and must have stayed on at the Art Club, where the men were holding their own varnishing dinner. She tried to enjoy the company of the other women, but the speeches were long and many. Lily soon fell into a worse gloom.

They moved through to the gallery where some of the women were gathered around the piano, choosing music for a singsong. Lily longed for the evening to be over and was thinking about going home when Kit rushed up to her, breathless, her cheeks pink and her hair escaping from an embroidered hair ornament. Lily struggled to muster a smile for her friend.

'There's a spey wife here, a fortune teller, who has read my cards,' Kit said. 'She sees a romantic liaison for me with a tall, dark man. She says we have a deep spiritual connection as we met in another life. Oh, Lily, you don't suppose she could mean Henry, do you?'

Lily suppressed a groan. Henry Geddes was a new painting teacher who Fra had enticed over from Edinburgh. She found his adherence to symbolism and the Celtic Revival rather old hat, but romantic Kit was spellbound by his talk of fairy queens and Druids and was clearly smitten with him.

Lily, preoccupied with Jack's selfishness and what she perceived to be his betrayal, was in no mood to indulge Kit, who was mesmerised by Geddes's ideas about the artist occupying a higher plane. When Lily had heard that he claimed to be guided by a spirit from the other side, she had decided he was either delusional or trying to make himself seem important. But Kit was so enraptured by Geddes that Lily hadn't the heart to say what she really thought, until now. Tonight, though, her nerves were on edge and the humiliating episode with Munro and Jack made her cruel.

'Geddes is a pompous windbag who likes to have you hanging on his every word as an adoring and unquestioning acolyte. I can't imagine what you see in him.' Kit's eyes brimmed and Lily regretted her intemperance. 'I'm sorry, that was unkind. I don't know what got into me.' She took her friend's hands in hers. 'But I do worry about you. I just don't want you to get hurt.'

Kit sighed. 'I know I'm being foolish, but all my life, since I was old enough to read all those fairy tales about knights and princesses, I've longed and longed to fall in love. You have Jack, but I have no one, and sometimes I think I never will.'

Lily had been feeling sorry for her friend but was irritated by the mention of Jack.

'There's nothing between Jack and me – we're friends, that's all.' His casual lack of consideration towards her on the very night when he should have been cheering her on had left its mark. Lily was more determined than ever not to be distracted from her work. Ned was right: Jack was used to getting his own way; if she let him, he would only hurt her. Who was she to warn Kit when she'd come so close to making the same mistake? She spotted Geddes across the room, his head bent too near to a young female student. She loathed men like him, with their sidelong looks and caressing smiles. At least Jack was straightforward, even if he was infuriatingly self-absorbed.

An urchin in ragged trousers with bare, dirty feet pulled at Lily's skirts, interrupting her thoughts. 'Are you Miss Crawford, missus?' She nodded and he placed a note in her hand. 'Mr Petrie said I was to run through the lane from the Glasgow Art Club and give you this.'

Lily unfolded the note and what she read there weakened her resolution to keep Jack at arm's length. The self-control with which she had kept her feelings in check vanished and she felt herself relax. Why shouldn't she allow herself to love him? He was a modern-thinking man who she now knew would not stand in the way of her ambitions, a man who had written:

It's not right that I am here at the Art Club and you are not. I've just proposed a toast to the Lady Artists saying that I hope next year this ridiculous ban will be lifted and a lane will no longer divide us.

Forgive me for rushing off earlier – Sandy Munro is a hard man to say no to and I've been having some trouble selling my paintings to him recently. Regardless, I should have stayed with you on your big night. I've felt awful all evening. Can you forgive this empty-headed fool? I'm outside, please come and meet me.

Jack was waiting for her at the railings of Blythswood Square's garden, a dark figure silvered by the full moon that rode high and shone hard and bright as a new sixpence. As Lily stepped into his shadow, she stumbled and fell against him. Jack put his arms around her and, without stopping to think, she tilted her face to his just as the wind dropped and all was still. His mouth was warm, and heat spread through her despite her bare shoulders and throat. After a while she leaned into him and felt his chest rise and fall in a sigh.

'At last,' he said, and tightened his arms around her. 'At last.'

16

~ *Lily* ~

When she wasn't at the Mack, Lily spent every spare hour painting self-portraits to perfect the style she was developing, and to make the time pass more bearably as she waited to hear the Royal Academy's verdict. Her heart lifted at the end of each day at the Mack when she saw Jack waiting for her on the steps. She'd decided to forget all about Sandy Munro and put aside the hope he'd given her, when the doorbell to the Garnethill flat jangled one afternoon after class. Still wearing an old-fashioned crinoline dress and a high velvet hat she'd put on for a self-portrait, Lily opened the door and Sandy Munro tipped his hat.

'How do you do, Miss Crawford? I hope you'll forgive me calling on you unannounced, but you didn't call on me so the mountain had to come to Mohammed, so to speak.'

Lily collected herself after a moment and stood back to let the art dealer in. 'Of course, please. Would you like some tea?'

'No, nothing for me,' he said, rubbing his hands together and making for the fire. It was a cold day, even for January. 'I don't have much time, but I'd like to see your work again – I recall you showing considerable promise for a young artist and wanted to make sure my memory wasn't playing tricks.'

Lily sent up a silent prayer that she had plenty of work to show him – six canvases were on the floor, propped up against the wall. She couldn't afford to frame them, but they were finished to her satisfaction, the oil paint dry.

Munro picked up a self-portrait that she'd been unsure of, experimenting with paler tones and using her thumb to blur the edges for a soft, dreamlike effect.

He held the painting at arm's length, and then approached her easel. 'Do you mind?' he said. Without waiting for her answer, he replaced the canvas she was working on with the one he was holding and stepped back to examine it, chin in his hand. Lily waited for his comments in silence, as she'd learned to do at the Mack.

Munro turned to her. 'This will do splendidly, this style. Do you think you could replicate it with another sitter?'

'Yes, of course, although I wasn't sure, I was trying something new.'

'New is good, as long as it casts the sitter in a favourable light, and this is simply beautiful, the way the light shines on your hair, the daring touch of red on the lips, the depth of feeling in the eyes. Splendid!' He clapped his hands together. 'So! Down to business. I have a commission for you – three in fact. The wealthy lady I was telling you about, the *jolie-laide*.'

'Ah yes, the torn scone.'

'The very one! I told her I'd discovered an artist, an up-and-coming talent, to paint her portrait. She was at first unsure when I told her this artist was a woman, but she has come around. And her husband is a jealous character, God knows why. He is delighted that his spouse isn't going to be closeted for hours with a lusty young man; and when I told him what the fee would be . . . You're not a name, so you can't command high prices, not yet anyway. But you'll get some steady work out of it – the lady in question couldn't wait to tell her friends and two of them want their portraits done too. She has two daughters, so if she's happy with your work there will no doubt be more commissions.'

Lily had been brought up to believe that talking about

money was vulgar, but she had materials to buy and her allowance barely stretched to cover the rent and coal bills. She took a steadying breath. 'How much will they pay?'

'Good, down to brass tacks straight away, we'll get on well, can't abide mealy-mouthed artists who pretend they're not interested in money. We all have to live.' He mentioned a sum that made Lily's eyes widen. She'd been trying to keep her cool, but it was more than she'd expected, and three times as much as Kit was being paid for her book illustration.

Munro held out his hand. 'Do we have a deal? As you get better known, I'll push for a bigger fee.'

Lily shook his hand. He turned back to her easel. 'Do you mind if I take this, in lieu of a commission – I'm usually fifteen per cent, but this would look pretty in my wife's sitting room.'

'Please, yes, take it.' As she opened the door for him, a thought occurred to Lily. 'How did you know where to find me?'

'Jack Petrie gave me your address. I'm on my way to meet him now – he's been pestering me to come and see you and I'll be glad to get him off my back.' Lily's hand went to her throat. Munro looked at her closely. 'You don't mind, do you? Jack said he's a friend of yours.'

'No, I don't mind at all. And yes, he is, a dear friend.'

17

~ *Lily and Jeanie* ~

Lily was late. She and Kit were supposed to have met Jack half an hour earlier at the opening of Nellie Grayson's exhibition. It was only around the corner from their studio flat but Lily had become absorbed in putting the finishing touches to her first portrait commission and lost track of time. She realised Kit was hurrying to keep up and slowed down. It was a Saturday and Sauchiehall Street was busy, the pavements crowded with shoppers enjoying the May sunshine. In their artistic dress, the two women drew the usual disapproving glares, as well as catcalls from a bunch of corner boys, cigarettes hanging from their lips. Lily tried to ignore them but moved away, frightened when she saw one of the lads break off from his gang as if to follow them. They stepped up their pace and the lout called out: 'Dinnae get your bloomers stuck in the crack of your arses. That's if you wear bloomers, mind.' His cronies guffawed and repeated his insults to each other.

Kit spun round. 'Och away and bile your heid, ya big jessie! Away hame to yer maw!' Astonished, the lad stared at her. His pals hooted with laughter and he turned red. One of the gang shouted out 'Go on yersel, hen!' and slapped him on the back. 'Come on, man, leave the lassies alone.' Their tormentor scowled at Kit and Lily, spat on the pavement and turned away, his hands in his pockets.

Lily tightened her grip on Kit's arm as they marched up the street and away from the stares of the people who had stopped to goggle at the street entertainment. Her breath was ragged when they stopped at the corner of a department store.

'Where did you learn to speak like that? Honestly, Kit, I thought he was going to go for us. You should be more careful.'

'That balloon? He couldn't have fought his way out of a wet paper bag.' She grinned and nudged Lily, who was looking at her, open-mouthed. 'Stop catching flies!' Kit laughed. 'Don't worry about me; I'm tougher than I look. I grew up with five brothers in a big house but on the edge of a rough part of Glasgow. We had running battles with the local children. Sometimes we even won.'

'Well, don't do it again, we might not be so lucky next time.'

Kit linked her arm into Lily's. 'We were surrounded by other people, he wouldn't have tried anything – it was all for show. Don't they have idiots like that in Kirkcudbright?'

Lily thought back to the bully boys at school, at how they'd teased her for talking 'posh' and made Jeanie's life a misery for being poor. It seemed you couldn't win: they'd find a reason to hound you for being different.

They walked on to the Corporation Gallery where they were to meet Jack. He was waiting for them and Lily smiled when she saw the familiar figure in its baggy tweed suit, his hands in his pockets and his hat tipped back. She could have picked him out from any crowd. When she'd hurried to find him at his studio after Sandy Munro's visit, he'd brushed off her thanks and insisted that he had only mentioned her name in passing, but Lily knew he'd gone out of his way to help her. She'd put her hand on his chest and kissed him on the cheek and smiled to see him blush. They'd grown closer in the months since the varnishing and when she'd won a silver medal from the Royal Academy for *Girl with a Rose*, he'd seemed as pleased as she was.

Jack had brought along Ned, who bowed deeply as Kit reached them a few steps behind Lily and out of breath.

'Where's the fire?' Ned said, lifting his hat. 'Or is there a sale of hideous frocks at the New Woman counter in Pettigrew & Stephens?'

Jack took Lily's arm. 'You both look beautiful. Ignore him, he's such a stuffed shirt with his stiff collars and frock coat.'

'Some of us have to work for a living,' Ned said, unperturbed. 'I couldn't turn up at the High Court wearing frayed tweeds and an artfully floppy cravat.' He flipped his friend's soft bowtie. 'I'd be taken straight to the prisoners' bench and clapped in irons.' He smoothed the velvet lapels on his coat, tailored to show off his slim figure. 'There's nothing wrong with a bit of Glasgow style – just look at that lot.' He pointed with his cane. 'I'm sure they'd agree with me. You scruffy artists could learn from them.'

The pavement ahead of them was taken up with a row of theatrical types, linked arm in arm. The women were heavily made up and wore elaborate hats and fur-trimmed dress coats that showed off tiny corseted waists, while the men wore top hats, gold watch fobs, white silk scarves and fur coats. Lily had seen performers like these before; Glasgow was full of theatres and music halls, and they loved to show off their finery by parading up and down Sauchiehall Street. Lily was slightly ahead of the others and was forced into the muddy road by the flamboyant characters, who were too busy laughing and talking at the tops of their voices to notice her.

'Excuse me! How rude!' she called after them crossly, emboldened by Kit standing up to the corner boy.

One of the women turned and said, 'Sorry, hen,' but stopped to stare. 'Lily? It's you, isn't it? I'd recognise that hair anywhere.'

85

Lily was about to tell her she was mistaken when the other woman lifted her veil to reveal a nut-brown face framed with dark curls.

'Jeanie! Is that you?'

'Aye, Lily, it's me, your old pal.' Jeanie grinned. 'Can you believe the state of me?' She spread her crimson silk skirts and curtseyed. Lily stared at her old friend for a moment, taking in the changes the years had brought: how she'd grown from a skinny little rabbit into a beautiful woman; the cocky walk; the raffish friends. But underneath the absurdly fashionable hat, it was unmistakably the girl she'd grown up with, and who had broken her heart by running away. Lily didn't know whether to hug her or shout at her. Jeanie broke the tension by holding out her arms, her voice catching as she said: 'Come here and give your old pal a kiss, you daft gowk.' The two women clung to each other and laughed between tears, and only drew apart when Lily's friends caught up with them. They stared open-mouthed at Jeanie and her entourage, who were making a great show of nonchalance, the men smoking and the women making tiny adjustments to their huge cartwheel hats.

Lily took Jeanie's hand in hers and turned, beaming to show her off. 'This is Jeanie. We grew up together in Kirkcudbright. And Jeanie, these are my friends, from the art school, Jack and Kit, and this is Ned, a friend of Jack's.'

'And definitely not an escapee from the art school,' Ned said with a grin.

Jeanie laughed. 'I can tell, you're more like one of us in your fancy duds.' She turned to Lily and clasped her hands together. 'Art school! Good for you – you always wanted to do that. And, as for me, I'm on stage now, a dancer just like I said I'd be, along with these fine folk, my professional colleagues in the entertainment business.' Jeanie shoved her thumb back at the other three, who smirked and preened.

Lily was trying to understand what she'd heard. So that's where Jeanie had gone, when she disappeared all those years ago. But why hadn't she said goodbye first? It still hurt, all this time later. There was an awkward silence. Ned was the first to break it. He bowed and lifted Jeanie's gloved hand to his mouth.

'Delighted, I'm sure.'

One of the theatrical men snorted behind his hand and Lily winced when she heard Ned's polite tones mimicked with a mincing 'deeelited aim shuer. Get this one, the Laird of Muddy Dykes!' Ned narrowed his eyes and was about to say something when Jack stepped forward and took Jeanie's hand.

'A dancer, you say? But you're perfect, just perfect!' Jack held onto her hand and pumped it vigorously.

Jeanie laughed. 'So I've been told! Can I have my hand back, before you have my arm off?' She shot a questioning look at Lily, who rolled her eyes.

'He means he wants to paint you. He's absolutely shameless when it comes to asking people to pose for him.'

Jack nodded without taking his eyes off Jeanie. 'She'd be perfect as a model.'

'She has a name, Jack, have some decorum,' Lily said with a laugh, which faded when she saw Jeanie's expression and the bigger of the two men tighten his fists.

'I'm not taking my clothes off for anybody,' she said, clearly affronted. 'Just because I'm on stage you think I'm a loose woman, is that it?'

Jack blushed and stuttered. 'Of course not, no, I'm sorry if I've offended you . . . I wouldn't dream of . . . I mean . . .' He took off his hat and ran his hand through his hair. 'What I mean is, I'd dearly like to come along and sketch you performing – all of you. You know, like Chagall and Degas and Toulouse-Lautrec, artists who did their best work in music halls and theatres.' At this the theatre folk looked slightly mollified. The big man's fists uncurled, and he grinned and nudged the other man, while the other woman giggled and said in an Irish brogue, 'Aye, why not? It might be good craic.'

Jeanie looked uncertainly at Lily. 'You always said you'd draw me dancing.' She put her head on one side. 'What do you say? I'll only say yes if you come too. It's the first night of a new variety show tonight at the Hippodrome. It's a bit of knockabout fun with a full bill – a play, dance routines, some comic turns. They've really pulled stops out for this one, spared no expense. What do you say, Lily? I'll leave comps for all of you at the box office.'

Jack tucked his arm into Lily's and drew her close. 'It looks like you have the final say.' She felt the heat of his body pressing into her and she glanced at Jeanie, who was watching them with raised eyebrows. Lily didn't mind; she was getting used to the idea of being a couple.

She turned to her old friend and smiled. 'It's a date, then. And afterwards I want you to tell me about everything that's happened since we last saw each other.'

Jeanie grimaced. 'Aye, well, it's a long tale. Come to the stage door afterwards and we'll have a chinwag. But I want to see you out in the audience tonight with your sketchbook, mind.' And with a flurry of skirts and a tapping of ebony walking sticks, the performers linked arms and sauntered away down the busy street, the men pausing to raise their top hats to pretty girls and the two women laughing and calling across them to each other.

Lily watched them go until Kit shook her arm. 'Hurry or we'll be late for the opening of Nellie's show.'

18

~ *Lily and Jeanie* ~

Lily shielded her eyes from the electrical lights' unnatural blaze, dazzled not only by them and the footlights but also by the line of dancers on stage. Jeanie broke ranks and took centre stage as the principal dancer. Lily's childhood friend was unrecognisable, transformed into a fairy creature, her dark curls caught up in a jewelled coronet and a rose tucked behind one ear. Her tiny waist was encased in a boned corset that pushed her breasts nearly out of the frilled bodice, and she wore a daring short dress made of fringes that exposed her legs from thigh to ankle. As the music swelled to a crescendo, she pirouetted like a spinning top and ended with the splits to wild applause.

Lily glanced at Jack and saw his eyes following Jeanie while his pencil flew across his sketch pad. Damn! She'd been so caught up in the performance she'd forgotten to draw the scene. Jeanie would be disappointed. Ned, sitting the other side of her, nudged her and leaned in, his whiskers tickling her neck.

'Jack seems smitten with your bendy little friend – although I don't know if it's the acrobatics or the fact that she's forgotten her skirt that impresses him more. You'd better watch he doesn't fall for the little gutter sparrow.' Lily elbowed him back, hard, and was rewarded with an *ooft!* Ned rubbed his side and looked aggrieved. 'I'm only saying this for your own good. Don't shoot the messenger.' He raised an eyebrow. 'You New Women should carry a warning label like they have at the zoo: *Don't come too close, wild animal.* Maybe you should have a word with Jeanie's boss, I'm sure he could do with a lady wrestler – now that would be an arresting sight I'd pay good money to see.'

He winked at her, and she could tell he was picturing her in tights and was furious to feel the heat rise into her face. Lily turned away, determined to ignore him and avoid any more of his sharp-tongued jibes. Ned was a mischief-maker, seldom passing up an opportunity to make a cutting remark and insert himself between her and Jack. But this attempt to make her jealous of Jeanie was pathetic. She ignored him and concentrated on Jeanie on stage as she curtsied and tripped about picking up the flowers that had been thrown, light as a sprite; she'd grown into a stunningly beautiful woman but retained a beguiling impishness.

The audience stood to applaud and call out Jeanie's name as she blew kisses to her adoring fans in between acts. There was no doubt she was the star, and Lily felt a swell of pride for her friend, remembering the dreams they had whispered to each other as young girls. Jeanie flitted about, natural and gracious as she presented her fellow dancers so the audience could applaud them too, but Lily knew her star turn would have been hard won and her journey from a tumbledown cottage on the outskirts of Kirkcudbright to here would have been a rocky one. She shifted in her seat; it had been a long night, the show too vulgar for her taste – an old-fashioned melodrama based on the life of Rob Roy, but with added dancing and singing and spectacular mechanical scenery. The last piece of theatre she'd seen was with Kit on the recommendation of a tutor – a difficult modern play called *The Blue Bird*, with exquisitely painted scenery and poetic language. It had been full of symbolism – a brother and sister's quest through the land of memory to the palace of night to find the blue bird of happiness – and they had stayed up far into the night to discuss its meaning. Lily wondered what Kit would make of this sensational drama enlivened by dancers in titillating costumes, but Kit had cried off after the exhibition, complaining of a headache.

Lily's thoughts were interrupted by cranking hydraulics as the stage rolled away to reveal a circular glass tank. Torrents of water gushed into the tank, filling it within minutes, and men appeared on horseback splashing through what she supposed was a raging waterfall, chased by soldiers shooting pistols. As the air filled with the tang of cordite and the holler of war cries, Ned settled back into his seat and clapped loudly.

'This is more like it!'

The dramatic action was followed by the grand finale played out against a fountain ingeniously coloured with lights, jets of water falling and rising in time with music played by the rather damp orchestra.

After the show, the three of them made their way to the stage door, where Lily asked a man smoking a cigarette if they could go in.

'What are your names and are youse expected?'

'Yes, we're here at the invitation of Jeanie Taylor, the principal dancer,' Lily said, put out by his officious manner.

He threw his smoked-down butt and ground it under his heel. 'Is that so? She'll be backstage scraping off the greasepaint and shaking the sequins out of her hair.' He stood aside to let them through the scuffed door. 'Follow the corridor all the way round and her dressing room is the third on the right, you cannae miss it.'

Jeanie greeted them in a small room crammed with flowers and people drinking champagne who all seemed to be talking at once. She grabbed Lily by the hand and introduced her and Ned and Jack to the crowd, firing off a bewildering litany of names and nicknames. She grinned at Lily's confusion.

'Aye, I know, you'll never mind anyone. It's too hot and stuffy in here.' She turned to the other dancers. 'Come on you lot, everyone, out! Lily and I'll see you at the Lauder once I've got this lot off and wriggled into my glad rags.'

When they were alone, Jeanie disappeared behind a screen where Lily could hear her splashing about with a basin. She started singing:

'I dream of Jeanie with the light brown hair . . .'

and Lily joined in:

'Borne, like a vapour, on the summer air;
I see her tripping where the bright streams play,
Happy as the daisies that dance on her way.'

Jeanie emerged from behind the screen, dressed and tidying her curls. 'Mind the boys at school used to sing that to me back in Kirkcudbright?'

'I do! You were a heartbreaker even then. I think that's why they tormented you – they fancied you.'

'Maybe, aye, especially that big ugly brute, he was always finding an excuse to walk by our cottage. I'd rather have stepped out with Ma's pig than with one those lads with the straw coming out of their ears.'

'What about now? Do you have someone?'

Jeanie turned around so Lily could fasten her dress. 'You mean like that handsome Jack the Lad of yours?'

'How did you guess?'

'I've seen how he looks at you with those big calf eyes. He's smitten with you, and I can tell you like him too, you go all pink when you look at him.'

Lily fastened the last hook and turned Jeanie round to face her. 'I was asking about you; don't change the subject.'

Jeanie leaned into the mirror and patted some rouge on her lips. 'I do have a fancy man, as it happens. You'll meet him tonight.'

~

The theatre people's table was the loudest in the restaurant and Lily wondered if the maître d' would urge them to be quiet, but he seemed unfazed, happy to send waiters scurrying with bottles of chilled champagne and platter after platter piled high with lamb cutlets, game pies and a whole halibut. Jeanie had insisted that Lily, Jack and Ned join them, and they took their places at a large circular table around which sat the comic, Mr Mirth – whom everyone deferred to – an actor Lily recognised as the lead in *Rob Roy*, several dancers and a well-dressed man in tails she didn't recognise, who seemed to be having a whispered argument with a sulky woman.

'Who is that dapper gentleman? Is that your young man?' Lily asked Jeanie.

Jeanie laughed through a mouthful of lamb. 'No, Viktor's not here yet. That's no gent, that's Tina the Toff.'

'A woman? But she's dressed as a man.'

Jeanie shrugged. 'That's her act, male impersonator. She's got all sorts of costumes – brickie, sweep – Champagne Charlie's the punters' favourite.'

'And who is that with her, the girl in tears?'

'That's Yolanda, her dresser, but they're more than that, if you know what I mean?'

Lily had heard about men falling in love with each other – who hadn't since the Oscar Wilde trial? – but she hadn't realised it could happen between two women. She nodded and started sawing at her lamb chop, not wanting to appear naive and say the wrong thing. Surreptitiously, she watched

93

as the drama and the voices across the table intensified. When she realised everyone was leaning in, rapt, she gave up the pretence and set down her cutlery. Tina stood up and shouted at the girl: 'You stole those earrings from me, you little bitch! Give them back. I won't have it, do you hear?'

The other woman pouted and covered her ears protectively. '*Nein, leibling,* these are a gift you gave me, for our anniversary, don't you remember?'

'Liar! Tramp! Whore! Do you think I don't know what you get up to when my back is turned, when I'm working my fingers to the bone on the stage, night after night? And now, to cap it all, you steal from me.' Tina lunged at Yolanda and tried to snatch the earrings from her lobes, but the other woman hung on grimly, screaming in German.

At that, the comic, who had drunk too much, roused himself and slurred: 'Now, now, Tina, settle down, there's a good fellow. Can't you see she's upset?'

'You stay out of it, Mirthless,' Tina snarled. 'The day you tell me what to do is the day you'll make me laugh, which is never.'

The comic lurched to his feet and took a swing at Tina, who dodged his blow and planted a right hook on his nose. Blood spurted over the table, staining the actor's white stock. The actor leapt up and began throwing punches at Mr Mirth while some of the others tried to hold both parties back. In the melee, Jack and Ned were knocked from their seats and soon joined in, arms flailing and fists swinging. Jeanie, her eyes shining, grabbed Lily's arm and pulled her away from the table.

'Come on, we'd better scram before the polis arrive.' She laughed at Jack and Ned, who were pushing and shoving and squaring up like the rest of them. 'Looks like your posh pals are having a rare tear. They seem to like a

94

good rammy just as much as the next Glesga keelie.' She led Lily, protesting, from the restaurant. 'Leave them, they'll be fine – but I'm not hanging around to get lifted.' When Lily looked back, food was flying across the restaurant and Yolanda was sitting astride the comic, her blonde hair hanging free from its pins, clawing at his face.

They pushed through the revolving doors and Lily took a gulp of air, glad to be out of the fug of the restaurant. A stiff breeze had blown away most of the smog, but the night was chilly for spring.

Jeanie took her arm and squeezed. 'I can't believe we're together again! We haven't had the chance for a proper blether yet; it's hard to get a word in with that lot. Can we go to your place? I don't think you'd like my digs – they're down at the Trongate and it's not a part of town a lady like you should be walking in at this time of night.'

'Please! I may have been the doctor's daughter once, but I'm not considered respectable any more. According to my father's last letter, after he found out I was living independently when a bill got sent to him by mistake, my name is mud among the good ladies of Kirkcudbright. They think I'm going straight to hell for living in the sinful city as a bohemian artist without a husband to keep me in line.'

'Who cares about those busybodies?' Jeanie said. 'Can you imagine what they'd say about me? The minister would have kittens if he knew what I was up to these days.' Her neck and shoulders bare in a low-cut dress, she shivered at the memory of the Church of Scotland minister who had made her mother grovel when she needed parish alms.

'You'll catch your death in that fashionable dress,' Lily said. 'Come on to my place in Garnethill, it's not far to walk. I can meet your beau another time.'

'Garnethill? Now, there's fancy.'

'It's a tiny tenement flat, not one of the big mansions.'

'Maybe one day, eh? When you're a famous artist.'

~

When they arrived at her close, Lily stopped to let a man bundled up in an overcoat run down the steps and past them, so close he nearly knocked her off their feet. She cried out and he whirled round.

'Why, Mr Geddes!' Lily was about to ask the tutor what he was doing, but he hurried down the hill and disappeared into a side lane. She remembered Kit was home, sick with a headache, and she took the stairs two at a time until she was at her front door, fumbling with the key. Lily burst in with Jeanie on her heels. The parlour was in darkness and at first she could hear nothing.

'Kit? Are you there?'

A small sound came from the other side of the room. Lily scrambled for the box of lucifers above the chimney piece and lit the gas mantle. The flickering light shone on Kit, lying on the divan, her hair and clothes in disarray.

Jeanie clutched at Lily's arm and whispered: 'That man we passed on the stairs, do you think— Is your pal in there alone?'

Lily's stomach turned over. She knelt at Kit's side. 'Are you all right? What has that brute done to you?'

Kit's eyes opened slowly, and she smiled. 'Only the most blissful things.'

Lily's concern turned to fury. 'For God's sake! I thought you'd been attacked!'

Kit sat up and put her arms around Lily's neck. 'Don't be cross with me.'

Lily shook her off. 'Are you drunk?'

'As a lord!' She stretched her arms above her head. 'I

don't think I've ever been happier. Henry and I are to be married – isn't it wonderful? We arranged to meet here, I hope you don't mind, only we wanted to be alone.'

'No, of course not.' Lily struggled to hide her dislike of Geddes, who she had watched trying his fascinating ways on many of the young women students. Inexplicably they, like Kit, seemed to idolise him, despite the mystical nonsense he spouted. But she didn't want Kit to think her a prig and she hugged her back. 'We must celebrate.' She gestured at Jeanie. 'We were about to have a nightcap. Shall we toast your news with the brandy we bought when I got my commission? Unless you and your fiancé have finished it off?'

'Henry brought champagne. Isn't he a darling?'

Jeanie spied an unopened bottle and began to twist off the wire around the cork while Lily fetched glasses from the press. Kit raised hers in a toast.

'To marriage!'

Lily clinked her glass and noticed that Jeanie, like her, didn't repeat the toast.

19

~ *Lily and Jeanie* ~

Lily understood Jeanie's reluctance to toast marriage when she met Viktor Ivanov. They were in Jeanie's dressing room, a few days later, where Lily had come to escape Kit babbling about her wedding plans and so she could let off steam about Geddes.

Jeanie puffed on a coloured cigarette. 'Sounds like a right arse, this gadgie your pal's marrying.'

'He's got a roving eye, and hands, if you know what I mean.'

'I know what you mean, all right, there's a few like that among the backstage johnnies.'

'Geddes isn't a bad man. It was wrong of me to think the worst of him that night in the flat. He's a puffed-up charlatan but I don't think he'd hurt anyone.'

'It was my fault, I put the idea into your head.' Jeanie faltered and Lily thought she was about to say something, but she stood up. 'Let's go and find Viktor, you'll like him, he's a real gentleman.'

Jeanie led her through a maze of corridors and onto the stage through the wings. Lily gasped at the size of the auditorium when seen from this side, at the galleries stretching up to the gods.

'It must take thousands of people,' she said.

'Aye, and I'm their wee darling,' Jeanie said with a dramatic sweep of her arm.

'Long may that continue, my little golden goose,' came a voice from the orchestra pit.

Jeanie crouched down at the front of the stage. 'Viktor, come up and meet my old pal.'

Lily was expecting him to be one of the young dancers or actors, but Viktor was an imposing older man who dwarfed Jeanie. With his greying hair swept back from his handsome, weathered face, and his expensive astrakhan coat and ebony cane, he had an air of authority and Lily could see the attraction. He leaned over her hand to kiss it in the French manner.

'Jeanie has told me about her artist friend, and that you'd like to attend rehearsals to draw the dancers. Come whenever you like.'

'How kind! I'm planning a series of paintings of dancers, backstage and rehearsing in the studio, and then on stage in full costume and make-up, under the lights. The contrast will be interesting, showing the hard work and strain that goes into training, and the final, glittering performance.'

Viktor nodded. 'You'd like to show our world in the round, so to speak.'

'Exactly. Fascinating to get a glimpse behind the scenes – and then the performances are so colourful and dramatic.'

'And they would be displayed in an art gallery – an exhibition?'

Lily faltered. 'Well, I don't have anything set up yet.'

'I'm a businessman, Miss Crawford, and recognise an opportunity to make money when I see it. An exhibition would bring people into the show – a better class of audience. I'll fund your exhibition. Do you have someone I can speak to? An agent?'

'Why, yes, how marvellous! The art dealer, Sandy Munro, I'll put him in touch with you.'

'And I'll buy any paintings you do of our star dancer.' He kissed Jeanie on the head, and she pushed him away playfully.

'You're a plaster.'

His tone was gentle as he looked into Jeanie's eyes. 'I would do anything for you, little bird.' He broke off abruptly and looked at his watch fob. 'Now, I have to meet the theatre manager, who is trying to cheat me once again out of my share of the box office takings.'

Viktor left and Lily turned to Jeanie. 'An exhibition! My first solo exhibition – I can't thank you enough.'

'Don't thank me, thank Viktor.' She took Lily's hands and they leaned back and spun each other around as they used to do as children. Jeanie, her eyes shining with glee and free of make-up and her curls tumbling wildly, still looked like the young girl Lily had known in Kirkcudbright.

Later, when they had found a quiet corner backstage and were sipping strong tea, Lily looked over her enamel mug at Jeanie.

'Earlier, I thought you were about to tell me something.'

Jeanie frowned. 'No, I don't think so.'

'Yes, when we were talking about Geddes, how we thought at first he'd attacked Kit.'

'It was nothing, I can't remember.' But her expression was troubled, and she couldn't meet Lily's eyes.

Lily put down her mug. 'I can tell it wasn't nothing. I know you. Something happened to you back in Kirkcudbright that made you run away.'

Jeanie pulled at a curl and chewed it. She was silent for a while. 'I haven't told anyone, only Tatiana knows. I don't want Viktor to find out, he'd kill him.'

'Who?'

'That dirty bastard, Calum Mackay.'

'Your stepfather? He always seemed so nice.'

'He was a two-faced snake, a lying shite and a toerag. And he wasn't my stepfather – he never married Ma, thank God.'

'Did he . . .?'

'He tried. Crept into my bed one night, but I was able for him and managed to get away. He wasn't expecting me to put up a fight.'

'He obviously didn't know you well.'

Jeanie managed a chuckle. 'Aye, right enough! I gave him a good boot in the balls for his trouble and ran like hell. Mind Tatiana?'

'One of the show people? The one who taught you to dance?'

Jeanie nodded. 'She took me in, offered me a berth and I ran away with them.'

'What happened to Mackay? Did your mother throw him out?'

Jeanie laughed. 'Aye, right! She wouldn't have believed me if I'd told her. She was besotted with that creep. I heard he left her in the end, stole her money and buggered off. Good riddance.'

Lily blinked. She couldn't imagine her mother, who had always fought her corner, taking someone else's side against her. Lily was heartbroken for her friend. She'd always known things were difficult at home, but she had never realised just how bad it had been for Jeanie.

Jeanie wiped her nose. 'I've a new life now, and I'll never be that hungry, dirty wee urchin again, thanks to Tatiana. She works here now as my dresser. I don't know what I'd do without her, she's more of a mother to me than Ma ever was.' Lily wanted to ask her more, but Jeanie smiled and tossed back her curls. 'So, tell me about Jack. Is it serious? Are you going to be the next one walking up the aisle?'

'I like him, it's true; more than that, if I'm honest. He's funny and kind and generous and thoughtful. I love being with him. But the thought of marriage . . . I don't know,

I've worked so hard to get here and I'd hate to give it all up to warm a man's slippers and wipe babies' bottoms.'

'I know exactly what you mean. That's why I'm with Viktor. I know people think it's because he's rich and powerful, and I can enjoy the high life with him, which I do – I've had enough of being poor and hungry – but I also know there's no chance he'll want to marry me. He's got a wife in Russia.' Lily blinked and Jeanie shook her head. 'It's all right, I'm no marriage wrecker. Anna left him ages ago. We're having a bit of fun, that's all. This way I can concentrate on my dancing without a husband wanting to tie me down.'

'And does Viktor think it's a bit of fun, too? He looked smitten to me.'

'Of course he does! He'll be on to the next pretty young thing once he's tired of me, you'll see.'

20

∼ *Lily* ∼

Kit was folding linen she'd been given for her bottom drawer when she stopped and looked around the sitting room of their studio flat, which was bathed in the early summer sun.

Lily looked up from the book she was reading. 'What is it?'

'This, all this; I'll miss it when I'm married. I'll miss you. I'll miss the Mack.'

Lily went to kneel beside her on the rug. 'We'll still see each other.'

Kit started crying. 'It won't be the same. Nothing will be the same.'

'It's not too late, you can change your mind.'

Kit shook her head. 'I love Henry, and I want to be a wife and a mother. I want children, I've always wanted children, and to have a big family like the one I grew up in.' She wiped her tears. 'I'm being daft, never mind me, it's wedding nerves.'

'I can't believe you're leaving the Mack.'

'Neither can I, but it's can't be helped. I'll be too busy running a household and hopefully looking after a baby.'

Lily clasped her hand. 'You're not getting married until the autumn. There's the whole summer ahead of us – why don't we have one last jaunt as carefree artists? Jack's been talking about Cockburnspath, the coastal village in the Borders. He says it's a haven for artists and has been badgering me to take a cottage. It would be all right if you came too, you could be my chaperone! What do you say?'

'One last summer of freedom?'

'Yes!'

'What would Henry say?'

'You're going away with me – what could he possibly object to? Besides, he's not your husband yet.'

Kit grinned and threw a hideous antimacassar an aunt had given her on the coal fire. 'You're on!'

~

Once art school had broken up for the summer, Lily spent a week at home with her parents in Kirkcudbright before travelling back to Glasgow to meet Jack and Ned under the clock at Central Station. Her father had been reluctant to let her go but her mother had pointed out there would be another woman there as a chaperone. She counselled Lily not to mention Jack.

'You know what your father is like, and what he thinks about artists. He'll imagine all sorts of things. I'm sure if you like this Jack, that he's a good man and will treasure you as I do.'

Now, as the train pulled away from the noxious smells arising from the breweries, tanneries and filthy waters of the Clyde and carried them south-east towards the light and clean air, Jack leaned forward in his seat.

'I can't wait to get to Cockburnspath. It's been an artists' colony since the days of the Glasgow Boys.'

Ned fumbled for his cigarette case. 'You're putting me off, dear boy. You sold this to me as a summer on the coast, not an outdoor art school. I hope to God there's a decent pub I can escape to while you're all swanning about annoying the local yokels by asking them to strike rustic poses with their cabbages and geese.'

Jack looked put out and Kit stifled a giggle. When Lily had told her that Ned would be coming with them, she'd been wary at first.

'He's a bit of a Smart Alec,' Kit had said.

'Ned's not so bad when you get used to him. He can be cutting but once he decides he likes you, he's a good friend.'

As if to prove them both right, Ned spent the train journey gently teasing Kit about her fanciful ideas, which ran in the opposite direction to his unflinching pragmatism. He led her into a trap by asking her politely about her beliefs in spirits and the occult before ruthlessly picking them apart with the forensic skills of a lawyer. But before she could take offence, he made her laugh by kindly enquiring whether a place had come up for her at Hawkhead Asylum yet, and whether Henry would be signing the commitment papers at the same time as the wedding certificate. Lily worried Ned was going too far with his relentless barbs, but Kit only laughed and batted him away with her small hands.

Even so, when the two men got up to stretch their legs, Lily leaned towards her. 'I'm afraid Ned doesn't know when to stop sometimes. Are you all right?'

'Don't worry about me. My brothers loved to torment me, and Ned's a pushover compared to them. The trick with people like him is never to mind what they say. He'll soon stop once he realises he can't get a rise out of me.'

Kit was right: Lily too had learned to laugh off the darts Ned aimed at her, and as a result she found him much easier company, although there was still a frisson of unease between them. Over the past few months she'd found it hard to be on her own with Jack, as Ned came everywhere with them. When they reached Cockburnspath he never left them alone, even when they painted *en plein air* down at Pease Bay and Kit stayed in the cottage, drawing hollyhocks in the garden or sewing under the shade of an apple tree. Every day, Ned would stroll down to the beach with Lily and Jack, his hands in his pockets while they struggled under their burden of umbrellas, easels and paint boxes. While they set up he'd stretch out among the dunes, hat over his eyes, and blow smoke rings, content to wait for them until they finished working. One afternoon when the sun was warm on their backs, Lily realised Ned had fallen asleep. She caught Jack's eye. Without a word, they moved to sit behind a sand dune where they were sheltered from the breeze that riffled the tops of the waves below. Jack cupped his hand behind her head and kissed her. His mouth was warm on hers. Lily moved closer and wrapped her arms around him. A while later she pushed him reluctantly away.

'Let's not get carried away.'

He groaned. 'I've tried to be patient, not to spook you, but I don't think I can bear to wait much longer. Why don't we get married?'

Lily went still. The sea stretched out towards the horizon in a blue haze and seagulls cried to their mates in the sky above them. She pulled at a tuft of sea grass. 'Don't joke about such things.'

'I couldn't be more serious,' he said and lifted her chin so she could meet his eyes. 'I want to marry you, Lily Crawford, and take you to live in France. We can have a studio together. There's a village I know where the light is like water and the colours so bright, they dazzle. The art we could make! What do you say?' She hesitated and he took her hand in his. 'Don't think; I can see you thinking. Say yes, say yes.'

106

A voice travelled over the top of the dune. 'Do say yes, Lily. I wish you'd hurry up and put him out of his misery, this is getting boring.' They looked round to see Ned, his hat at the back of his head and a piece of grass between his lips.

Lily smoothed her hair and looked for her own hat. 'I thought you were asleep.'

'It doesn't do to fall asleep in the sun, that's what the old man told me when he came back from India, anyway. No, I was awake and alert, plotting my next move in court, when what should I hear but a deliciously naughty scuffle followed by a sweetly romantic proposal. I must say, I was rather moved. You two should be on the stage at the Gaiety.'

'It's not gentlemanly to eavesdrop,' Jack said and threw his hat at Ned, who caught it deftly.

'I've never been accused of being a gentleman before. Take it back, there's a good man.'

Lily surreptitiously fanned her face while the two friends fell into their familiar back and forth. Before long they were swapping old school stories about people she didn't know, forgetting she was there, and once again she felt that Ned had won some kind of victory.

~

That night the four of them walked back to the beach with baskets filled with bread, cheese and a bottle of brandy. Lily watched Jack gather stones and build a fire as she sipped the alcohol to keep out the chilly air. They sat in a circle swapping stories with Ned taking centre stage, his anecdotes from the courts becoming more outrageous and hilarious as the brandy bottle emptied and the sky darkened, the stars emerging like diamonds scattered across a jeweller's velvet cloth. Jack laughed at his friend's scurrilous tales but kept glancing across the flames at Lily. She knew she would have to give him an answer. Her heart urged her to accept, but if she was serious about making it as an artist, she'd have to remain single. Lily lay back against the cold sand, her head swimming with the brandy, and watched the stars wheeling above her. Her blood sang in her veins and she was seized with reckless joy. She turned to look at Jack and found he was staring at her.

On the walk back to the cottage they lagged behind the other two and she whispered, 'Come to my room tonight.'

Later, she lay in bed, naked and shivering between the cold linen sheets, waiting. When Jack slipped into her room the moon was high and bathed them in mother-of-pearl. He stripped off and stood by the bed, his face in shadow.

'Are you sure?' he said.

'I'm sure about this, but I'm not sure about marriage. Can't we just enjoy what we have now?'

'I don't want to behave like a cad. You must know how I feel about you, how much I love you.'

'Jack, I love you too, and I want this.' She lifted the covers and he got in. His skin was warm and smooth over hard muscle. He kissed her, sliding his hands down her body until she arched against him. Much later, she cried out, her voice joining the cries of seabirds that swooped in circles over the darkening sea.

21

~ Lily and Jeanie ~

After Kit and Geddes were married, they moved into a mansion in the south side of the city. Lily was caught up with the new term and delayed her visit until winter had begun to set in. She took the train one rainy afternoon to the garden suburb where Kit's wealthy parents had bought the newly-weds one of the new houses. As she crunched up the gravel drive, she found herself thinking that Geddes had landed on his feet. Kit was sitting at the bay windows of her drawing room with her feet up, looking pale and being fussed over by a maid.

She waved the girl away and beckoned Lily over. 'I can't move with this wretched morning sickness. Even the smell of cooking turns my stomach.'

Lily sat down next to her and took off her gloves and removed her hat, which the maid took before scurrying away, clearly grateful to be away from Kit and her petulance. 'You poor thing! But tell me, how are you settling in as an old married woman?'

'It's a bit dull, to be honest. I thought I'd have heaps to do running a household but there's only the two of us and the maid takes care of the cleaning and cooking. I've been keeping myself busy making the baby's layette, but it can get lonely with Henry out all day teaching.' She leaned forward eagerly. 'How's everyone at the Mack?'

'Oh, you know, rushing about to get ready for the Christmas show.'

'Any gossip?'

Lily couldn't say she'd seen Geddes trying it on with a new student – the rumour was that he had followed her to her digs one night and begged to be let in.

'What about you and Jack? You were inseparable all summer at Cockburnspath; I was expecting an announcement when we got back. Well?' Kit grinned and seemed to regain some of her spirit.

At Cockburnspath, Jack had begged her to marry him, repeatedly, but Lily had remained resolute. He came to her room most nights, the risk of being discovered adding a thrill of fear to their encounters. Lily knew even the free-thinkers at the Mack would be shocked that she'd welcomed him into her bed, and she didn't want to tell Kit now. She changed the subject and asked about the baby, happy to let her friend talk.

On the short train ride back to Central Station, Lily realised Kit had a new life and that when the baby came, they would have less and less in common. The Garnethill flat without Kit's bustle and chatter felt empty, and since getting back to the city Lily preferred to work in one of the large shared studios at the Mack during the day. Jack was busy getting ready for an exhibition at the Art Club and every night she waited for his soft knock at the door. She was thankful there was no snooping landlady to disapprove of them, but lived in fear of a neighbour catching them out, even though Jack promised he was always careful not to be seen.

When she wasn't at the Mack, Lily would go and see Jeanie. She was free most days, resting from the previous night's performance, and when she was at rehearsals, Lily brought her sketchbook. She felt at ease with the actors and dancers and was working on a series of paintings for 'Nights at the Theatre', the solo exhibition Munro had booked after meeting Viktor. Lily spent hours sitting on a stool capturing unguarded moments behind the scenes: dancers sitting on the floor, bent over touching their toes; actors putting on their make-up; Viktor on stage beating out the rhythm with his stick while the dancers leapt and landed with gentle thumps. Lily noticed that the impresario paid particular attention to Jeanie and would adjust her position with a gentle touch of the hand, his face close to hers. She worried about Jeanie and her reputation, but the other dancers either didn't seem to notice or care if they did. Outside the theatre, she would have been shunned, but in this closed world where affairs were commonplace, Jeanie was the star turn, accepted and protected by her dance family.

On the days when there were no rehearsals, Lily and Jeanie liked to walk over to Kelvingrove Park together, wrapped up against the cold, or sit in the Willow Tearoom and talk about their childhood and their hopes and fears. Lily trusted her friend as she would a sister, and it was a relief to talk about Jack knowing she wouldn't be judged. One day, when it was too wet for the park and they had tired of the clatter of the tearoom, Jeanie suggested they go to the empty rehearsal studio so they could talk in peace while she stretched at the barre.

'Jack was badgering me for an answer to his proposal again last night,' Lily said, settling down at the covered piano. 'He's beginning to lose patience with me. I keep telling him that I'm not ready, but to be honest, I'm not sure if I'll ever be ready.'

'Do you love him?'

'Yes, more than anything, but . . .'

Jeanie was working through her feet and nodded without looking around from her task. 'I know what's stopping you. My ma became a drudge when she had all those bairns, and she thought the answer to her misery could be found

111

in bed with a man, any man, even a snake like Calum. Me, I never want to be tied down. I love my freedom and no man is going to take that away from me.'

'What about Viktor?'

'It's true, I'm right fond of the old bugger – he's a big softie, treats me like a queen, and we always have a good laugh together. But he doesn't own me. He knows that I can walk out any day and get a job with another company. Glasgow's hoaching with theatres and music halls.' Jeanie stretched her hands above her head. 'I'm a star now, a real star. Told you I would be.'

Lily laughed. 'Yes, you did.'

22

~ *Jeanie* ~

It was a cold December afternoon, but Jeanie had been hurrying and was warm enough to loosen the fur tippet around her neck as she walked along Argyle Street. She wasn't performing tonight and wanted to be alone to think about Viktor's proposal. Not a marriage proposal – she wasn't naive – but to join a new company, a touring company. Jeanie acted gallus but she'd never been out of Scotland. Viktor had told her the company was based in London and from there they'd travel to Paris, Rome, Vienna, Prague – all over Europe and beyond. Jeanie was both thrilled and terrified at the prospect and couldn't make up her mind.

'Grab this chance with both hands,' Tatiana had advised her. 'I gave up too soon and always regretted it. You're ready for this.'

Still Jeanie hesitated. She was the principal dancer here, the star who got top billing. In London she would be one of many and she didn't want to sink back into obscurity. Viktor had assured her that the principal in the new company was going to retire soon and that she would be first in line, but he couldn't make any promises, not yet.

Jeanie turned up Buchanan Street. She'd find Lily and talk Viktor's offer over with her; Lily was the person who knew her best in the world. The streets grew quieter as she reached Garnethill; she thought she heard footsteps behind her, and had the sensation of being followed. It was getting dark already even though it was only late afternoon. Jeanie hated the short winter days, which were worse in this city cooried into a valley with the damp creeping up from the Clyde. Once again, she sensed she was being followed, but when she looked round, she could only see a few people huddled against the cold, walking in the other direction. Jeanie shivered and drew her fur collar more tightly around her neck and sank her cold nose into the comforting softness. She strode on, her thoughts in a whirl. Perhaps Tatiana was right: she should take up Viktor's offer and see the world. She liked him and she liked what they did in bed together, but more than that, he knew how to put on a sure-fire hit. He also got the best out of his performers and could strike a hard bargain with theatre managers. Jeanie's career was in good hands and Viktor let her do what she wanted; he wasn't about to leave his wife and make her settle down and give up dancing – why kill the golden goose, as he often said.

As she reached the top of the hill, Jeanie's mind was nearly made up to take a chance with Viktor and go to London. But she still wanted to talk it over with Lily. She'd be thrilled for her, and Jack, too. Her friend had ended up with a kind, decent man. He was no pushover, though, and wasn't averse to laughing at Lily when she took herself too seriously. Jeanie hoped he'd be at the art school too; she couldn't wait to see their faces when she told them her news.

Jeanie had forgotten all about her earlier unease when suddenly a dark figure stepped out of an alley and dragged her into its dark mouth. The smell of gin was strong on the man's breath. She opened her mouth to scream for help, but her voice died in her throat when she saw who it was. Jeanie's insides turned to water. Calum gripped her by the shoulders and smiled.

'Well, hello wee Jeanie.' Her eyes widened as he moved his hands up to her neck, drawing her face close to his. 'What's wrong, hen? Won't you give your old Uncle Calum a kiss?' He mashed his mouth against hers and when he pulled away his breath was ragged. He grabbed her backside and slammed her into his groin. Jeanie struggled against him, bucking away from his grasp, but it only seemed to make him more excited. 'You always were a wildcat, now it's time you were tamed. There's some unfinished business between you and me.'

~

Calum buttoned his flies. He fished a cigarette butt out of his pocket and lit it, his features illuminated for a second by the flare of the match. Jeanie stared at him dully from the ground where she sat slumped against the wall. Her mouth was swollen and bruised, and she was bleeding from between her legs from where he'd thrust his way inside her, but she felt nothing, not even pain, only an over-whelming shame. Calum drew in tobacco smoke and leaned against the opposite wall companionably, as if settling in for a friendly chat.

'I can tell it wasn't your first time. You've turned out like your mother, a wee hoor.' He took a comb from his breast pocket and ran it through his blonde curls. 'Well, I'll be seeing you. I only live around the corner in Blythswood Square, got myself a nice wee set-up in one of the big town houses – Widow Fraser can't believe her luck, having a handsome bucko like me in her bed at her age.' He sauntered away whistling 'I Dream of Jeanie with the Light Brown Hair'. Jeanie leaned over and vomited, splattering the cobbles around her.

She lost track of time as she sat there, but when the

bells of St Aloysius' struck five, she realised it had only been an hour. She needed all her willpower to get herself to her feet, clinging to the wall as if she were on the deck of a ship in a storm. She staggered out into Rose Street and a couple stepped out of her path.

'It's terrible to see a young woman drunk and incapable like that,' the woman said. 'Something really should be done about the city's drink problem.'

Jeanie could have dealt with contempt and would have spat out an angry reply, but the note of pity in the woman's words undid her and she began to sob. The streets where she'd once felt invulnerable now seemed full of lurking shadows, every close mouth a yawning darkness hiding an attacker. The soot-blackened buildings loomed over her as if ready to swallow her up; she could taste the acrid yellow fog as it thickened. Footsteps clipped up the hill behind her – metal segs on the soles of a man's boots – and fear gripped her bowels. She pulled her coat close around her torn blouse, took to her heels and didn't stop running until she'd reached the familiar black doors of the Mack. She stopped before them. Her instinct had been to run to Lily, to find a friendly face. But now a wave of shame overwhelmed her, and she sank to the steps and put her head on her knees, defeated.

Jack found her, her hands blue, teeth chattering, the damp cold knifing through her bones. He bent over her and shook her shoulder.

'Miss? You can't sleep here, it's too cold.' She lifted her head and looked at him blankly before shrinking behind her hands.

'Don't hurt me any more.'

'Jeanie! It's me, Jack. What in God's name has happened to you?' When she didn't reply he lifted her gently into his arms. An overpowering need to sleep gripped her and she closed her eyes as he pushed his way through the doors and carried her to his studio.

~

The morning sun woke her and for a while she looked through the huge windows, wondering where she was. She raised herself on an elbow and saw Jack at his easel, brush in hand and lost in concentration. Her throat was dry and sore and when she tried to clear it, he turned around.

'You're awake!' He put down his palette, wiped his hands on a rag and came to sit on the cot beside her. He handed her a tin cup of water from an upturned crate and watched her drink. Jeanie handed the cup back to him with a trembling hand and closed her eyes. It hurt to swallow. That bastard must have had his hands around her neck. The events of the previous night came flooding back and she whimpered and pressed herself against the wall. As she did, her coat fell open and Jack gasped when he saw her torn blouse and the bruises on her throat and exposed breasts. Jeanie covered herself and looked away, paralysed with shame. His eyes hardened. 'Who did this to you?' She shook her head. If she didn't say the words then perhaps she could forget it had happened, but when Jack shifted up the cot to sit beside her, she began to tell him what had happened. He listened in silence until she'd finished.

'You promise you won't breathe a word to Lily. I couldn't stand for her to know. I don't want anyone to know. I don't want anyone to look at me differently. It's the only way I can go on. Please, Jack. Please.'

His expression was grim. When he spoke, his voice cracked. 'Are you sure that's what you want?'

Jeanie nodded and reached for his hand and crept closer to him, glad of the feel of his scratchy tweed jacket against her cheek and the strong, clean smell of him. She dozed for a while and then woke with a start, wondering what time it was. The students would be arriving for their morning classes soon. 'I've got to go, before anyone sees me like this.'

'I'll walk you back to your digs. Unless you want me to take you to Viktor?'

She shook her head and began to cry. 'No, I don't want him to know; I don't want anyone to know.'

Jack put his arm around her and rocked her like a child. 'It's all right, you're safe with me. And I won't breathe a word, I promise.'

23

~ *Jeanie* ~

Jeanie tried to put her ordeal behind her. She redoubled her training, pushing her body to its extremes as if to reclaim ownership of it. Night after night she leapt higher and higher and spun faster, taking risks that made the other dancers murmur with envy and the audience go wild. Under the spotlight she was powerful: a star, admired but untouchable. After the show she'd drink too much with the other performers, losing herself in hysterical laughter and strong wine until she could be sure of a dreamless sleep. She made excuses to not come to Viktor's hotel suite: she had women's troubles, she was tired from rehearsals, she had a migraine. He frowned every time she turned from him but accepted it. Jeanie imagined it wouldn't be long before he tired of her and looked for amusement elsewhere, but she couldn't worry about that now. She was trying her hardest to block out the memories of being raped and knew she'd be powerless to stop them flooding back if she climbed into Viktor's bed.

Jeanie was coping, just. But one night her landlady told her that a man had been round at her digs asking for her, a handsome man with blonde curls, *a real charmer.* The next morning, she couldn't get out of bed. Her limbs were heavy, and she felt sick every time she moved her head. She closed her eyes and went back to sleep filled with nightmares of Calum's hard eyes, his grip around her neck. In the delirium between sleep and waking she thought she heard a scrabbling at the latch of her window and found she couldn't move, only whimper until she surfaced into full consciousness.

Fear gripped her. Calum must have been following her; he knew where she lived; he'd be back. She cursed her carelessness and wondered desperately who she could go to for protection. It couldn't be Viktor – she didn't want him to think of her as spoiled goods, a tarnished star. Shame made her guts heave at the memory of that night. Only Jack knew her terrible secret. Jack, who had promised to keep it, even from Lily, would help her find a way out of this nightmare. Jeanie summoned the last of her strength and dragged herself to the window and called out to a gang of boys playing in the street who ran errands for ha'pennies. She wrapped a coin in a handkerchief and threw it down to the leader. He snatched it up and shoved it in his pocket and waited for her instructions.

'Do you know where the art school is, up in Garnethill?'

'Aye.'

'Ask for Jack Petrie. Tell him it's urgent, that Jeanie needs him. Bring him back here, and there'll be a shilling in it for you.'

The boy took to his heels and she sank to the floor and made herself as small as she could in the corner of the room. The dread that had assailed her began to recede, leaving her shivering and hollow.

Jack found her still curled up, her hands cushioning her cheek from the hard, wooden floor. He gently shook her awake and helped her to her feet and into a chair, tucking a blanket around her thin shoulders before sitting opposite her. He waited for her to speak. It was one of the things she admired about him: his stillness and patience. Unlike Ned, Jack never rushed people or talked over them but listened intently. It made him easy to talk to, and she knew why Lily was so fond of him. With a pang she longed to confide in her friend, but she knew it would be too hard to say the words; she had to look after herself now, she had to survive. A man like Calum, once he'd tasted power over a woman, would want to hurt again. It wouldn't be long before he came looking for her.

'You have to help me.' Jeanie blurted out her fears.

Jack pushed his hand through his hair while he thought. 'This man has to be stopped. We should go to the police. And you should see a doctor, you're pale and your forehead is burning up. He may have done some damage internally.'

Jeanie shuddered. 'I don't want another man pawing me.'

'What about a woman doctor? My friend Florence Anderson has just qualified. She's working in the Royal Infirmary. Will you let her see you?'

'Does Lily know her? I don't want Lily to know, or anyone else.'

'They know each other through me, but not well. Florence won't tell anyone. You'll be her patient and she has to treat anything she hears from you in absolute confidence.'

Jeanie closed her eyes and fought a wave of nausea. 'All right, ask her to come here. I don't think I can make it as far as the Royal.'

Jack put her to bed and the last thing she remembered before falling into welcome blackness was his kindly face leaning over her. Some time later she awoke when a cool hand was placed on her forehead. A woman in a neat, plain dress sat on the bed next to her, frowning as she took her pulse. There was no sign of Jack.

Florence smiled briskly and introduced herself. 'Jack tells me you're unwell, feverish and feeling sick. And that you were sexually assaulted, is that right?' Jeanie looked away and nodded. 'I'm going to examine you now.' Florence drew back the blanket, lifted Jeanie's nightie and felt her stomach before placing the end of the stethoscope on her belly.

'Put your heels together and let your knees fall away from each other. I'm going to give you an internal examination, is that all right?' Jeanie winced. 'Try to relax,' Florence said.

Afterwards, she went over to the washstand in the corner and washed her hands. 'When was your last monthly bleed?'

Jeanie blushed but knew she could talk freely to this grave young woman. 'I can't remember. A while ago, but I'm not regular.'

'You're undernourished, but that's not unusual for dancers. When did you last have relations with a man?'

Jeanie turned and faced the wall. 'That time, when I was attacked.'

'And that was when?'

'Couple of weeks ago, early December.'

'You're pregnant, from what I can tell, around four months, although with your slight build you could be further along.'

Jeanie went still. A baby. Viktor's baby. She'd never wanted a baby; it would be the end of her dancing career. There were ways she'd heard you could get rid of it, but her hands instinctively cradled her belly at the thought. A child. Her child. She'd held so many of her little brothers and sisters when they were born, remembered the pearls of their tiny nails, the pucker of their rosy lips, their faces turned up, seeking love, and she knew she couldn't do it.

Florence waited, her hands folded on her lap. Jeanie searched her expression for any sign of judgement but could find none. She was a kindly stranger who offered help with no expectation of friendship or gratitude, the sort of person Jeanie could trust. She thought of how Calum had hurt her and how she'd bled; she must have been pregnant when he raped her.

'Can a baby be hurt, if the man is rough?'

'What do you mean?'

Jeanie didn't want to relive that moment, but she had to know if the baby would be all right. 'The filthy animal who attacked me, he tore me, I was bleeding after and sore.'

'Your baby is fine, it's well protected inside you.' Florence frowned. 'Was this man known to you?'

'He was my ma's bidie-in. He'd tried it on before, when I was living at home. It's why I ran away to Glasgow, but now he's here too.'

'Did you report him to the police?'

Jeanie sat up in bed. Jack had suggested the same thing. She had been brought up to distrust the police. Maybe they were right. It was about time that Calum was punished once and for all – that he was put away so he couldn't hurt anyone else. But the thought of confronting him made her stomach clench like a fist.

'What if he goes for me again?'

'He'll be in custody, you'll be safe, and so will your child.' Florence placed one of her hands on Jeanie's. 'You're going to be a mother and you'll do anything to protect your child. And you'll wipe out this terrible deed by bringing another life into the world and by cherishing it.' Florence put her instruments away and closed her doctor's bag. 'Get plenty of rest and good, wholesome food. The sickness is natural at this stage and will improve if you eat a little and often. A little ginger in hot water may help. I'll come back next week to see how you're getting on.'

Once Florence had left, Jeanie turned on her side. Before she fell asleep, she knew what she was going to do: Calum would pay for what he'd done to her. She and her baby would be safe.

24

～ *Jeanie* ～

Jeanie dressed carefully to give herself courage. She knew the power of clothes: her costumes at the theatre transformed her into a star. The past few days of feeling sick had left her pale, with violet shadows under her eyes, so she dusted her face with a swan's down powder puff and rubbed rouge into her cheeks and lips. Crying jags had made her eyes practically disappear so she lined them with the kohl she wore on stage. Her favourite scarlet velvet dress, high heels for height, and a flamboyant hat trimmed with ostrich feathers made the desk sergeant stand up straight when she walked into the police station.

'How can I help you, madam?'

'I am here to report a crime. It's a delicate matter. Can we speak in private?' The sergeant listened respectfully and took notes while she talked.

'And you say you know this man? This is a very serious accusation – rape is a heinous crime. Do you have an address for him?'

'He lives at Blythswood Square, but I don't know the number. He let slip he lives with a widow, a Mrs Fraser.'

A constable – a giant of a Highlander – was dispatched to walk to the other end of town with her, and she waited as he knocked on a door to enquire about the whereabouts of Mrs Fraser. He led her to a door with shined brasses flanked with bay trees in pots. Jeanie stood nervously next to the constable as he rang the bell. A parlour maid came to the door and squealed when she saw the police officer.

'Is there a Calum Mackay living at this address?'

'Aye, sir.'

'Well be a good lass and fetch him.' The maid turned tail and half shut the door. They could hear a woman's voice.

'Who is it, Mary?'

'It's the polis, Mrs Fraser. Says he wants to speak to Mr Mackay.'

A few moments later an overweight middle-aged woman in black came to the door with Calum. He'd changed since the last time Jeanie had seen him: his hair was pomaded, and he wore a snow-white shirt under a well-tailored frock coat. He was clean-shaven and looked every inch the respectable gentleman.

Calum didn't even glance at Jeanie. 'How can I help you, officer?'

The widow broke in. 'This is most inconvenient, we were just about to go out.'

Calum smiled benignly at the police officer. 'Now, Helen, we must be good citizens and help the law. I think I know what this is about.' He turned to Jeanie. 'I see you've brought along an acquaintance of mine.'

'So, you admit you know this young woman, sir?'

'Oh yes. I know her family, the Taylors, in Kirkcudbright. She's a runaway, broke her mother's heart and then, like so many unfortunate girls these days, she fell on hard times. I'm sad to report that she has become a common prostitute. She accosted me in the street a few weeks ago, touting for business.' He shook his head sadly. 'Her poor mother.' The big Highlander turned to Jeanie, who found she was unable to speak up for herself. She was transfixed with horror.

'Well, miss, what have you got to say for yourself?'

'It's not true,' she managed. 'You raped me, you bastard.'

'Now then, no need for that kind of language, there's a

125

lady present,' the constable said. He stared meaningfully at her red dress with its low bodice and at her make-up and she realised she'd made a catastrophic mistake.

'But he attacked me, on December the tenth.'

'Sir? I must ask you what you were you doing that night.'

The woman stepped in front of Calum. 'My husband was with me all evening, tucked up in bed with a heavy cold and I was looking after him, wasn't I, Mary?'

The parlour maid, who had been hovering in the background looked terrified. 'Yes, ma'am, you're right. Mr Mackay had a real stinker, caught it myself later.'

'That'll do, Mary, off you go. Is there anything else, officer?'

'No, madam, sorry to trouble you.' The constable put away his notebook and turned to Jeanie, his expression hard. 'You'd better come with me.'

What followed was like a bad dream that Jeanie later struggled to remember clearly: the constable's hand on her arm as he half dragged, half walked her back to the police station where she was interviewed by the constable and a younger officer.

'I keep telling you, I'm a dancer.'

'Well, then, someone from the theatre will vouch for you.' The constable waited for her answer, his pen poised. Jeanie thought quickly: if Viktor came, he'd find out all about the attack and she didn't want that, not when she had to tell him about the baby now, on top of everything else. She needed to think about her future, about her baby's future. Anything that sullied her in his eyes could spell disaster. He would never look at her the same way again, never mind want to look after her and the child. Jack had promised to help her, perhaps she could put his name forward, but then a better thought occurred to her.

'I want my brief, Ned Raeside. He's an advocate.'

The constable grinned at the other officer. 'A street girl who can afford an advocate? You must be good at what you do. Right, we'll get him over here, but meanwhile you need to see the doctor.'

'What? Why?'

'It's the law. Under the Contagious Diseases Act, the police have the right to have any woman suspected of being a prostitute checked for venereal disease.'

'Will you hell!'

It was no good struggling. The police officer held her down while a tired young doctor swabbed her between the legs and pushed his fingers inside her.

'No visible lesions or discharge, but this woman is pregnant,' the doctor said.

'I could have told you that without you sticking your dirty fingers inside me, you filthy bastard!' Jeanie screamed and kicked the doctor in the face with her high heel.

A night on a hard bench in a freezing cold cell followed. Jeanie shivered so much her teeth chattered. When she dozed, her dreams were vivid and terrifying. Most of the night she spent wide awake, wondering what was going to happen to her. She'd heard of a place in Cowcaddens where women were locked up for being unwed mothers and forced into slave labour, their babies taken away and given to wealthy people with no family of their own. She fell asleep as the grey light was seeping through the barred window and woke to the sound of the guard unlocking the door. Ned came in, followed by Jack.

'Are you all right?' Jack sat down on the bench next to her.

'What are you doing here?' Jeanie said.

'Ned told me he'd been asked to represent you, so of course I came. What on earth is going on?'

127

Jeanie glanced at the guard and Ned waved him away. 'I need to talk to my client,' he said sternly.

Haltingly, she told Ned the whole story, from the night of the rape to the confrontation with Calum and her examination, while Jack stood with his back to them to give her privacy.

'So, you see, he's the one in the wrong, he's the criminal who should be banged up in the pokey, not me.'

'In theory, yes,' Ned said.

'What do you mean, "in theory"?'

'I believe you, of course, but rape is difficult to prove. No witnesses – it's a case of he said, she said, his word against yours. And unfortunately, his word holds more sway. A judge will be more inclined to believe him over a dancer.' Jeanie glared at him. 'I'm sorry, but I'm only stating the facts. Women in the theatre are assumed to have low morals by most judges. Also, the newspapers would have a field day and your name would become a dirty joke. You'd go through the ordeal of a trial and come out with nothing.'

'And Calum, he just gets away with it?'

Ned shrugged. 'From what you say, he's a smooth talker, a charmer. He must be convincing if he's managed to persuade some wealthy widow to marry him. I've met his type before, like a tick who attaches itself to a dog.' He paused. 'If it's any comfort, a man like that is bound to slip up sometime, and when he does, I'll make sure the full force of the law comes down on him. There's a detective I use from time to time, he'll keep an eye on Mackay.' He stood up and shot his cuffs. 'The most pressing matter is to get you out of jail. Assaulting the doctor wasn't clever, but Jack and I were at school with him and we've had a word. As a favour, he's agreed not to press charges.' He gestured to the open cell door. 'You're free to go.'

Jeanie stood up, her back stiff from the hard bench. 'Thank you, Ned, I owe you.'

'No, you have no cause to be grateful. I'm ashamed of our legal system, that it's so hard for women to prove they're not at fault when they're attacked.'

He stood aside to let her pass. After Jeanie and Ned had signed some papers, she was released without charges. Outside, Jeanie took a deep breath to get the smell of the prison cell out of her nostrils.

'What will you do now?' Jack said.

'Get as far away from Calum Mackay as I can,' she said.

25

~ *Lily* ~

Lily had been so busy the past few weeks she hadn't had time to see Jeanie, but assumed that she was just as busy with the pantomime the company were putting on at the King's Theatre. She was overseeing the hanging of 'Nights at the Theatre' when Jack walked into the gallery Munro had persuaded to show her paintings. Lily was too distracted to pay him much attention but when the technicians left she found him standing in front of a painting of Jeanie, her curls tumbling freely down her back as she danced in a sheer Arabian costume of scarlet and gold. She looked like a pillar of fire.

'This is quite extraordinary,' he said. 'The vivid colours, the movement.'

Lily tucked her arm in his. 'Thank you.'

They both looked at the painting in silence. After a while, Jack said, 'There's something I need to tell you.' He turned to face her. 'I'm going to France, to live.'

Lily blinked. 'What?'

'I'm suffocating here. I need the warmth and sunshine of France, to try my hand at the new Colourist movement. If I don't get away, I'll never make anything of myself. I've learned all I can at the Mack and I've only been hanging on here because of you.'

A gust of wind blew a sheet of rain against the gallery windows. Lily hugged herself. 'What about us?'

Jack held her shoulders, his face eager. 'That's just it – you could come with me. There's this village I know in

Provence: the light is ethereal and the air is full of the scent of wild herbs; the colour of the sky in summer almost blinding. You'd love it there.'

Lily moved away from him. 'This is the wrong time for me.' She gestured around the gallery.

Jack took a step towards her. 'But this is only one small exhibition – think of France: the food, the climate, the freedom we would have. We could live together openly instead of sneaking about.'

'But I'm beginning to make a name for myself here. I can barely keep up with my portrait commissions, and Munro is talking about taking this show to London. Why would I stop and give it all up to chase after you and your dreams? I can't leave now.'

Jack frowned. 'It's not just about me. It would be good for both of us, as artists, to live and paint free from constraints.'

Lily turned away from him. 'No, I won't go. I'm sorry.'

He spoke softly. 'Lily, please.' Jack put his arm on her shoulder, but she wouldn't turn round, unwilling to let him see her tears. She didn't want him to stay out of pity. After a while he dropped his hand. 'I'm sorry, but I have to go. If I don't go now, I never will. Goodbye, darling.'

The door jangled and Lily turned to look at Jack as he walked away. This time he didn't turn around.

26

～ *Jeanie* ～

Once again, Jeanie dressed carefully. This time she chose a green velvet dress; the red one had been given away. She was going to see Viktor.

He was in his office at the theatre, dealing with paperwork. He came out from behind his desk and held out his arms to her. 'Little bird!'

Jeanie held up her hand to stop him. 'Viktor, I have something to tell you.'

He dropped his arms. 'You're not leaving the company, are you? That mountebank Pickford's been after you for months.' Viktor seemed to grow in stature. 'How dare he try to poach my talent!' Jeanie was unperturbed, she knew it was all theatrics and that Viktor was a gentle giant.

'Cool your beans, it's nothing like that. Sit down so we can talk calmly.' They sat on the sofa he kept in his office. Jeanie turned to face him. 'I have two things to tell you. The first is that I'm going to take you up on your offer to join the new company in London. With one condition.'

He grinned. 'Name it.'

'That Tatiana comes with me as my dresser.'

'Done! What else?'

'I'm going to need some time off later this year, several months in fact.'

'But that's impossible! You'll have to learn new routines, there's a show to prepare for, a tour even.' He narrowed his eyes. 'Have you become a prima donna? Don't tell me I've created a monster.'

Jeanie shook her head. 'Viktor, shut up and listen. I'm expecting.'

'Expecting what?'

'A child, you idiot – your child.'

His mouth dropped open for a moment. 'But how can this be?'

'Surely I don't have to explain it to you?'

'No, I mean, I never took any precautions with you because Anna and I had tried for years. The doctor said she was fine, that it must be me.'

'You should have got a second opinion from a good Scottish doctor, because I'm four months gone according to mine.' She waited while he stared at her. 'Are you pleased or horrified? I can't tell from your glaikit expression.'

He took her face in his hands and kissed her. 'Little bird! You have made me the happiest man on earth.'

Jeanie took a breath – it felt like she'd been holding it since she walked in. She hadn't been sure how Viktor would take the news.

'I know I won't be able to dance for a while, but when I told Tatiana she said I could go back on stage three months after the birth. It's not usual, but if I work hard, I can be back in shape by then.'

He frowned. 'Let's have the baby first and see how you feel. But for now, get Tatiana to pack up your things. We're going to London.'

PART 3

~ Changing Times ~

1914–1919

27

∼ *Lily* ∼

As the weeks and then months passed into the spring of 1914, Lily tried not to think about Jack, but couldn't help longing for him. She smiled and chatted with her fellow students, but inside there was a blank she couldn't seem to fill with painting. The calm absorption it used to bring had vanished along with Jack. Thinking to distract herself with new skills and work for which she need not mine her emotions, she threw herself into other classes at the Mack: enamel jewellery, book illustration and binding, and embroidery and needlework. When the long hours in the studios were over, Lily returned to an empty flat. First Kit had left to get married, then Jack had left for France; the final blow was Jeanie moving to London.

'We'll write to each other, and you must come down to see me in London. Viktor's buying a place for us in Chelsea – get me!' Jeanie had said, unusually flushed and bright-eyed.

When Lily had asked if she was all right, not wanting to mention that her once wasplike waist had thickened – too many rich meals with Viktor, perhaps – Jeanie must have read her thoughts. 'I'm having a baby, you daftie! Can you imagine?' Lily looked worried, but Jeanie laughed. 'Don't worry, Tatiana's going to help me look after it, and Viktor says when we get to London, I must be Mrs Ivanov to everyone. They'll never know we're not married, and this way I get to keep my freedom without the scandal. I'll be back on the stage before you know it. Nothing has to change.'

Jeanie had left in a whirl of hugs and kisses. Afterwards the city felt like a lonely place. Where once Lily would have filled her spare time walking through the Botanic Gardens with Jack or sitting with Jeanie sketching and talking, now the hours dragged. The other students were friendly and interested in her work, but she wasn't inclined to confide in them the way she had with Jack and Jeanie. Ned popped in every now and then to take her out for tea, but inevitably they would end up talking about Jack, and she couldn't help questioning Ned about Jack's past. Ned seemed reluctant at first but soon supplied some worrying details: a girl Jack had jilted, an artist who had tried to end her life when he left her after an affair in Paris, and worst of all, the married tutor who had come close to leaving her husband for him.

'I'm afraid his charm hides a rather callous soul,' Ned said. 'Like most people endowed with extraordinary beauty, he can be rather careless of the feelings of lesser mortals.'

Lily wondered if he had already forgotten her, they had parted on such cool terms, both too angry and stubborn to give an inch. At night, when she felt at her most lonely and couldn't sleep, she'd sit by the window in her little sitting room and watch the sky lighten, feeling like the only person awake in the city. *I miss you, Jack. How could you leave me to face the world alone?* And she would allow herself the luxury of crying, unseen and alone.

As the trees began to unfurl their green buds, Lily felt strength and purpose returning with the longer, brighter days. One day a note arrived from Florence Anderson inviting her for tea. Florence was more Jack's friend than hers, but she'd grown to like and respect her.

'Enough of this wallowing in misery,' she told herself sternly. It was a fine spring day and she would stroll over to the West End and visit Florence. She walked through

Charing Cross and on to Great Western Road, and soon left the busy stream of carts and omnibuses behind when she reached Florence's tree-lined street opposite the Botanic Gardens. Lily's heart twisted as she turned her back on the gardens where she'd spent so much time with Jack.

At Florence's house, a maid opened the door and led her through to the drawing room where a fire burned in the grate despite the mild weather. These town houses, three storeys high with thick walls, remained cool throughout the warmer months. Florence looked up from the book she was reading and came to kiss Lily on the cheek.

'How lovely to see you! Come and meet my brother.' A tall, broad-shouldered man was standing by the window looking down at a table covered in maps. He came over to shake her hand. 'Hugh read medicine at Cambridge,' Florence said. 'But he gave up a promising medical career to bring God's Word to Glasgow's poor.'

'Thank you, Florence,' he said wryly. 'You make me sound so saintly and pious. I can see Miss Crawford desperately looking for an escape route.'

Lily laughed and shook her head. 'It would take more than a saint to scare me.' He smiled and, like Florence, it softened his austere features. His eyes were such a startling blue they did in fact give him an other-worldly air. Tall, broad and fair, he bore a resemblance to the Renaissance painting of the warrior archangel Michael, which Lily had studied in an art book.

'I'm afraid my sister doesn't approve of my urban mission. She's a practical soul and believes that the poor are better served with medicine and food in their bellies than they are with sermons, but man cannot live by bread alone.'

'Matthew's gospel,' Lily said automatically. Hugh looked surprised. 'Sunday school. Endless hours of boredom, even in the summer when I longed to be outside playing.'

'Ah yes, dusty church halls and parish ladies – Florence and I endured the same torture as children. It's one of the reasons I became a minister, to take religion out of the churches and into the streets. My mission is to bring the poor hope and a sense of God's love.'

Lily wondered what Ned would make of such fervour, but then Ned was a cynic and made fun of everyone. There was no doubting Hugh's sincerity and there was something compelling about his intensity and the way he was looking at her as if she were the most important person he'd ever met.

Florence left the room to organise tea and Hugh led her to a seat before the fire. 'My sister tells me you're an artist, a gifted one. That must be a hard road to travel. Forgive me for being so forward, but I detect a sadness about you. Will you tell me what's troubling you?'

Lily was taken aback by his directness at first but found herself telling him about Jack, how they had been pulled in different directions, and how lonely she was without him. Hugh listened gravely without interrupting. Lily stopped abruptly, embarrassed that she'd revealed too much to this stranger.

'I'm sorry, I'm boring you.'

His expression softened. 'You could never be boring. You're interesting to talk to; perhaps too interesting.' He smiled again and she wondered what he meant – was there a hint of flirtation there? Surely not! But he moved swiftly on before she could analyse his comment further. 'Forgive me for saying this, and I mean no offence by it, but artists in my experience tend towards the solipsistic. Perhaps, if you took up an activity to help those less fortunate, it would take you out of yourself.'

'Do you mean charity work?' Lily remembered the Kirkcudbright busybodies she'd escaped from and their endless coffee mornings and good works. She shuddered. 'I couldn't bear to be one of those women who fill their empty hours arranging sales of work and taking up collections.'

He leaned forward and once again she was transfixed. 'No, something far more challenging. If you could come with me into the backstreets of Glasgow and see the desperation of the poor, the drunkenness, the violence, the depravity, and the difference a woman of your talents could make . . .'

Lily shifted uncomfortably under his stare. 'You're mistaken. I don't have the faith and conviction to help you in your work.'

'Not everyone has to be a Martha to do God's work. "Consider the lilies of the field . . ."'

'". . . how they grow, they toil not; nor do they spin." Sermon on the Mount.'

He laughed. 'You see, the Scriptures stick even when you don't want them to. I could use your artistic skills at the mission I've set up in Cowcaddens. We have a ragged school for the street children, but I think they need more than their ABC, someone to show them that there's beauty in the world – an art teacher.'

'I'm not sure . . . I don't know what to say.'

'Think about it.'

Lily was relieved when Florence came back into the room with the maid bearing the tea tray.

~

Still, Hugh had left an impression on her. It didn't hurt that he was good-looking and that he seemed to embody the term Muscular Christianity. That night she tossed and turned in her bed and dreamed about the archangel

141

Michael, his foot upon the neck of one of Satan's rebellious army, his sword ready to deal a fatal blow. The warrior angel turned his head to look at her, and she saw it was Hugh. He lifted his sword as if to run her through and she woke in a cold sweat. It took a moment for her heart to slow and realise she was safe.

~ *Lily and Jeanie* ~

When Jeanie had her baby, Lily took the sleeper train to London to see her. The cherry blossom was in full bloom and scented the morning air as she walked through the pretty streets of Chelsea. Tatiana answered her ring at the mews cottage.

'I'm so happy you're here,' Tatiana said as Lily followed her upstairs. 'It was a difficult birth and she lost a lot of blood. She's been fretting and asking for you.'

'I came as soon as I got Viktor's telegram.'

Tatiana stopped at a closed door. 'Don't stay too long, she's still weak.'

Lily hovered in the doorway. The room was dark and there was a tang of iron in the stuffy air. Tatiana opened the shutters and pulled down the sash window.

Jeanie's pale face emerged from the tangle of covers on the bed. She covered her eyes. 'What are you playing at, Tatiana? Draw the curtains, I haven't slept a wink all night.' A mewling cry came from the cot beside her bed. 'Now look what you've done – the bairn's awake and I'll have to feed her again.'

Tatiana helped Jeanie sit up in bed and plumped her pillows. 'Look who's here.' Lily stepped into the room and Jeanie's face lit up.

'You came, I knew you'd come!'

Lily sat on the bed. When she kissed Jeanie's cheek, she noticed it was cold and clammy. 'How are you feeling?'

'Better now you're here.' Jeanie shifted in bed and winced

before beaming again. 'I've a baby, Lily, a wee girl, can you believe it?'

Lily laughed. 'I know, that's why I'm here, you silly thing.'

'Would you like to give her a cuddle?'

Lily wasn't used to handling babies and fumbled to pick her up, but Tatiana was by her side in a trice to help her. The child stared at Lily as if she could see into her soul. 'Aren't you a serious one? She's gorgeous.' She smiled at Jeanie. 'What's her name?'

'Stella.'

'Stella, Stella, you're a darling,' Lily crooned.

There were footsteps on the stairs and Viktor appeared, his arms full of parcels. He set them down and enveloped Lily and his daughter in a gentle hug. 'I see you've met our little star.' He bent down to kiss Jeanie. 'And here is our other star. You grow more beautiful every day.'

Jeanie pushed back her greasy hair and grimaced. 'Your eyesight must be going.'

Viktor stroked her cheek. 'Now your friend is here, do you feel like getting up and having a bath, maybe put on one of your pretty dresses and get some air? What do you say, little bird?'

Jeanie turned her face away. 'Aye, maybe I will, if you ever give us some peace. Away you go, you too Tatiana, and take Stella with you so we can have a right good blether.' She shook her head as they left. 'They're a couple of old hens, the way they fuss after me. You'd think I was made of glass.'

Jeanie leaned against the pillows and closed her eyes: there were blue shadows under them. Lily thought she had fallen asleep but when she tried to get up from the side of the bed, Jeanie reached for her hand. 'Oh, Lily, I'm so glad you're here.' She welled up and Lily squeezed her hand in alarm.

'Was it awful, the birth?'

'It was like being in a dark tunnel of pain. The baby wouldn't come out for ages. They thought I was going to die. I could hear Viktor shouting at the doctor and in the end they had to lock him out. I thought he was going to break the door down, the daft bugger.'

'You're all right now, though?'

'I'm no bad. Tatiana's been feeding me up – I never want to see another bowl of consommé or plate of fried liver again. The doc says I'm through the woods, but I can't get my head straight. I keep crying, for no reason, and you know that's not like me.'

'No, but you've just had a baby. Don't they say that's normal, to feel a little down in the dumps afterwards – the baby blues?'

'This is different. I'm not sad, I'm frightened – terrified that something will happen to Stella. I've never felt like this before, like I'd die for her.'

Lily smiled. 'You're a mother now – a fierce, protective, loving mother.'

'But what if I can't do it? What if I end up like Ma, letting her down? There are bad people out there, how am I supposed to protect her?'

'You won't, you'll be different from your mother. You're one in a million, Jeanie Taylor, and now you've got me crying.' They both wiped their eyes and laughed. 'Do you feel like getting up?' Lily said. 'I can run you a bath and sit with you while we catch up.'

When the bath was full of hot water and scented oil, Jeanie sank into it and sighed. Lily washed her hair, vigorously massaging her scalp.

Jeanie put her head back and closed her eyes. 'That feels grand. Viktor offered, but he'd be too gentle.'

'He adores you.'

'Aye, I know. He's a plaster.' But Jeanie's tone was warm. 'He's not a bad old thing.'

Lily had been struck by Viktor's tenderness. She'd only ever seen him before as the larger-than-life theatre impresario. Here in this mews cottage, away from the gilded theatres and plush hotel restaurants that were his natural habitat, his anxiety for Jeanie made him seem vulnerable and unsure of himself. He clearly doted on her and the baby. What must it be like to have someone so entirely devoted to your happiness? Lily thought with a pang about Jack.

As if reading her mind again, Jeanie said, 'What about Jack?'

Lily's hands stilled. 'What about him?'

'Are you still in the cream puff with him for scarpering to France?'

Lily was nettled. 'It's more serious than that. We had a fundamental disagreement.'

'Aye, well, whatever you call it, you've taken the hump.'

'Tilt your head back a bit more, I'm going to rinse off the suds.' Jeanie obliged and gave Lily a wink. 'I bet you still love him, you're just too pig-headed to admit it.'

Lily put down the jug and dabbled her fingers in the soapy water. 'You're right.'

'Of course I'm right! Have I not known you since we were knee-high to a grasshopper? Jack's a prince among men, you'd be daft to let him go.'

Lily was taken aback by Jeanie's fierceness. 'A prince! That's a bit strong!'

Jeanie turned and looked Lily in the eyes. 'Jack helped me through the worst time of my life.'

Lily frowned. 'What are you talking about?'

'He didn't tell you?'

'Tell me what?'

Jeanie nodded her head. 'Aye, I thought so. He promised he wouldn't, and he was as good as his word.'

'You've got me worried now. What happened?'

Lily sat in shocked silence as Jeanie told her about how Calum Mackay had raped her, and how Jack had picked her up from where she sat huddled and broken on the steps of the Mack, taken her in and comforted her, sent Florence to her when she was too sick and scared to leave her room. How he'd come with Ned to get her out of the police station. And how he'd kept all this to himself, because Jeanie had begged him to.

'But why didn't you tell me?'

'I didn't want anyone to know. I was ashamed. Viktor still doesn't know.'

'Oh, Jeanie—' Lily's voice broke.

'Don't start crying again, for God's sake! You'll set me off again and I've shed enough tears.'

Lily smiled and sniffed. 'The water will be getting cold and I don't want you to get a chill – Tatiana would have my guts for garters, as you'd say. Let's get you dried.' She held out a linen bath sheet for Jeanie and when she stood up, noticed how her ribcage showed. Lily wrapped the towel around her friend and held her until she wriggled free with a laugh.

'You're a bigger softie than Viktor,' Jeanie said. 'Don't worry about me, I'm strong and I've put it behind me. I wanted you to know what Jack did for me, so you'd realise what kind of man you were losing by being so thrawn.'

Lily looked down at her hands. 'He's in London.'

'What?'

'Jack, he's in London.'

'I thought he was in France.'

'He's been back for a while, talking to a gallery owner

147

about an exhibition. He wrote to me saying he'd like to come up and see me in Glasgow.'

'Where's he staying?'

'At the Chelsea Arts Club.'

'But that's only around the corner from here! Tell me you're going to see him.'

Lily rubbed Jeanie's back through the towel and kissed the top of her head. 'Never mind that now, let's get you dressed.'

29

~ *Lily* ~

They met in the garden behind the Chelsea Arts Club. Jack was wearing cream Oxford bags and his shirtsleeves were rolled back to show tanned arms. Lily thought they would be awkward together after their months apart, but it was just Jack, his familiar face smiling and open, delighted to see her.

They had the garden to themselves. Over China tea with slices of lemon they sat in the spring sunshine and slipped easily into talking about their work.

'I think I've cracked it,' he said. 'I'm working *en plein air* all the time, on landscapes. The colours are so vivid and the light so different, it's forced me to change my style. I used to try so hard to capture the gentle cerulean blue and soft greys and greens of Scotland, but now I'm reaching for burnt sienna, bright cadmiums – yellows and reds – and cobalt blues. It's like I can see properly, for the first time.' Three of his paintings were to be shown in a London gallery known for its daring. 'This is the break I've been waiting for all these years,' he said. Lily tried to be happy for him, but she couldn't help thinking that she hadn't had the same opportunities. Her thoughts must have betrayed her because he changed tack and asked about her exhibition in Glasgow.

'There were some decent reviews, and Munro has talked about taking "Nights at the Theatre" to London, but nothing has come of that so far.' She shrugged as if to show she didn't care. 'Meanwhile, I've been busy with commissions, and at the Mack, of course.'

'And how's Jeanie?'

'Weak after a difficult birth, but on the mend.'

'I'm glad to hear it, she's a fighter that one.'

Lily leaned forward. 'Jack, she told me what she went through, what you did for her, and how you kept her secret.'

He looked away, embarrassed. 'I'm sorry I couldn't tell you, she asked me not to.'

She took his hand. 'I've been wrong to push you away. I miss you. Can we start again?'

He raised her hand to his lips and smiled. 'You took the words out of my mouth. Here I was all set to beg you to take me back. I'm actually home for good. France is intolerable without you. I stuck it as long as I could out of idiotic pride and Petrie stubbornness, but I missed you too much.' He kissed her. Lily was light-headed with relief. After a while they pulled apart. 'Let's never be apart again.'

Lily laughed. 'No, never!'

Jack tucked a copper strand behind her ear. 'I've had plenty of time to think about us.' Lily tried to interrupt but he went on. 'No, it's all right, let me finish – I know how you feel about marriage and I've put aside my vanity and realised it's not personal, that you love me and I love you is all that matters, and convention can go hang. What I propose is that we are together in a union as strong and binding as any marriage, but live apart, with the freedom to work. How does that sound?'

'It sounds perfect: together, but apart.'

He stroked her face. 'You know I've taken a room here?'

'Yes, I do know that.'

'The staff are used to turning a blind eye to the scandalous behaviour of raffish artists – in fact, they're

150

disappointed if they don't get a handsome tip for looking the other way.'

'What are you suggesting?'

'Shall we begin our not-married life with a not-honeymoon?'

'I thought you'd never ask.'

30

~ *Lily* ~

Lily turned twenty-three at the end of her last term at art school, in June 1914. Since Jack had moved back to Glasgow, their arrangement had worked, allowing her the freedom to stay on at the Mack while they continued to see each other discreetly. Sometimes she caught him staring out of the window of her studio flat and wondered if he were thinking about France. He would always smile and shake his head if she asked him, but there was a new restlessness about him. Still, he was as good as his word and there was no more talk of moving to Provence.

The final weeks of term had been frantically busy as Lily prepared for the degree show, but now that summer had arrived, she too became restless. She'd hoped to teach at the art school but there were no openings, and Nellie Grayson advised her to try a high school in the meantime. Lily remembered Hugh Anderson's offer of work at his ragged school and began to give it serious consideration. With Jeanie away in London and Kit busy with her growing family, Lily had been spending more time with Florence and as a result had seen quite a bit of Hugh.

The brother and sister were drinking their mid-morning coffee together when she paid them a visit after she'd submitted her final piece to the degree show.

'Lily! How lovely to see you. Come and sit with us,' Florence said, leading her by the hand to the sofa. 'You'll take a cup of coffee?'

Lily had to suppress a smile as the siblings sat down at

either side of the fireplace like two bookends. They were both dressed in simple black and greys with white collars and cuffs, and had similar features, although Florence was almost plain while Hugh was strikingly handsome. Lily wondered how much his good looks had contributed to his following as an urban missionary. He had looked after Florence since the deaths of their parents while she was still at school, and Lily admired their kindness and selfless efforts to help people in need. Frankly, they were a relief after the giddiness and drama of her circle of friends. Jack was fond of Florence but neither he nor Ned were comfortable with Hugh.

'He's so saintly, it's sickening,' Ned had declared after she'd had them all round to her studio flat.

Lily had rolled her eyes. 'He just makes you feel wicked.'

'But I adore feeling wicked, I just find him rather tiresome. Florence is a sweetie but he's rather intense, don't you find?'

'I think Hugh's an interesting man, and he does a lot of good work.'

'Ah, good works, the curse of the lower orders.'

Lily had dismissed Ned's remarks as frivolous – he could only bear being around people who amused him, and she resolved to keep her two sets of friends separate.

Now she sank down on their sofa and accepted a cup of coffee.

Florence cast a professional eye over Lily. 'You look tired and you've lost weight. Have you been unwell?' The ticking of the mantel clock was the only sound to disturb the quiet of the drawing room as brother and sister waited for her to speak.

'I haven't been sleeping well. I'm rather at a loose end after the euphoria of finishing my degree course. I miss the Mack and I find I can't paint. I stand at my easel for hours, but everything turns out flat and muddy.'

153

Florence came to sit with her on the sofa and took her hand. 'Is there anything we can do?'

'Actually, there is. I was hoping that Hugh's offer to teach at his school for street children still stood.'

'It most certainly does, and I'm so pleased you're taking me up on it,' Hugh said. 'I'm sure the children will adore you.'

His eyes burned into her. Lily ducked her head and scratched off a dab of paint from one of her fingers. 'I don't know how much use I'll be as a teacher, but I'm willing to give it a try.'

~

Lily pushed up the sleeve garters she wore to keep the chalk dust from her cuffs and turned to her class. She smiled at the children's upturned faces.

'Once you have all drawn an oval, I want you to take your pencils and draw a cross over it like I have on the blackboard. The eyes and ears are on the arms of the cross and the centre of the nose on the upright bit.' She drew another line further down the oval. 'And the mouth goes here,' she said. 'Who'll be our model today? Tam, will you help me?'

A boy who looked about eight but who had told her he might be eleven or twelve came up to the front of the class, beaming with pride, and took a seat. Lily patted his shoulder. Tam, always eager to learn but full of spirit and mischief, had become one of her favourites at the ragged school. He had taught himself to read by picking up discarded envelopes in the street and taking them to a drayman who knew his letters. Hugh had filled in the other sorry details of the boy's life.

'His mother was imprisoned after she was found lying

dead drunk in the street, the infant Tam starving, naked and bawling his lungs out in the gutter next to her. The child was removed and put into the care of an aunt who gave him some kind of stability, but when Tam's mother was released from prison, she reclaimed her son after a screaming match. Tam stayed with his mother until the day he turned up at his aunt's door, naked. His mother had sold his clothes to buy drink. When his aunt died of tuberculosis last year, he was thrown on his mother's mercy once more, roaming the streets and scavenging for food until they brought him here.'

Hugh knew the sad circumstances of every one of the children who attended the school that he had started in a single room with filthy windows and a blocked-up fireplace. He and another evangelical missionary had scrubbed away the soot and pigeon droppings, polished the windows and got a fire going before going out in the streets to find the children, who they began to feed and teach. Now, thanks to donations, the school was in a new building called the Fellowship, which also had several meeting halls, a kitchen and a dispensary and clinic run by Florence when she wasn't at the Royal Infirmary. As well as the ragged school, the Fellowship held classes for mothers, teaching them practical skills such as sewing, cooking and how to clean a house. Lily could see that the evangelists who helped Hugh run the place were well-meaning, but she disagreed with the belief that it was a woman's Christian duty to run a clean home and provide a hot meal to keep her husband out of the pub. The Fellowship, in fairness, also held temperance meetings for men, and Bible classes where both sexes could learn to read and write. Still, Lily preferred to stay in the classroom and keep the children busy with paint and clay and papers and pencils.

155

Lily had been at the ragged school for a month now, and found that the work settled her so she could paint again. The contrast between her comfortable life and the children's desperate struggles just to survive galvanised her, and she began a series of street scenes. Growing up in the countryside, Lily had seen poverty at first hand, but the misery she saw in the city was more shocking. The slums were crammed with families of fourteen or more living in a single end: one room that served as kitchen, bedroom and sitting room. The lavatory was on the landing or outside and shared with other households in the close. Children played in the gutters or in the crumbling tenements' backcourts where rubbish was dumped in rat-infested middens.

'People do their best to be decent and raise a family, but life is hard,' Hugh had told her before she started teaching at the Fellowship. 'There's a whisky shop on every corner and drink helps them forget their sorrows. But when it takes hold, all the money goes on it and the children suffer, going hungry or being beaten by their drunken parents.'

It wasn't until Lily ventured into the slums with him for the first time that she really understood what Hugh meant. She saw barefoot children in filthy rags, their faces pinched and white under the dirt, malnutrition hollowing cheeks that should be plump and rosy. But she came to admire the people who had to survive in these slums for their wry humour and for the way they were always ready to help someone in need, no matter how little they had themselves. Here, there were no locks on the doors and neighbours ran in and out of each other's homes to borrow a twist of tea or a drop of sugar. Women hung out of windows to talk to each and monitor what was happening below on the crowded streets while their children played with whatever they could find in place of toys. The girls used ropes taken from the drying greens to skip, the ones 'cawing' the rope at either end usually with a baby sister or brother balanced on a hip, or they played hopscotch while the boys played leapfrog and built dens out of discarded bricks or go-carts out of broken bits of wood and old pram wheels. The little ones played shops with pebbles or 'chuckies' as tender, selling tin cans filled with weeds and any other rubbish they could find. Others floated paper boats down the streaming gutters or nursed dolls made from rags and old shoes. Often, Lily stopped to sketch, but after a while she would find herself surrounded by a swarm of children begging to see what she had drawn.

One day, after Tam had stopped coming to her class, she and Hugh went out to look for him in the backstreets of Cowcaddens.

As they climbed the filthy stairs to Tam's door Hugh said, 'His mother is a handful and won't take kindly to us being here.'

There was no answer when he knocked, and he pushed open the door. Inside, five or six women sat on the floor, pulling at pieces of muslin. Yellowing newspapers covered the broken windows and a single candle guttering in the corner was the only light in the room. Lily saw that there wasn't a stick of furniture and guessed it must have been pawned. One of the women looked up and scowled at them.

'What are youse after?'

'Hello, Aggie,' Hugh said. 'This is Miss Crawford, Tam's teacher. We were wondering why he hasn't been at school.'

'Aye, well, there's a reason for that.' Aggie turned to the hole-in-the-wall bed and shrieked, 'Tam! Get in here.' The little boy appeared from the dark recess, his hair tousled from sleep. When he saw Lily he ran towards her and clung to her. She saw that he was wearing nothing but a woman's skirt tied around his skinny chest and under his arms with a piece of string.

'His breeks fell to bits and he couldn't go out in the street like that. I couldn't afford another pair,' his mother said. She sighed and reached for a bottle by her side and tipped it into her mouth. Lily nearly made a comment about having enough money for liquor, but Hugh shook his head at her.

'Well,' he said. 'If you don't mind, Aggie, I'll take this fine young man to get him some clothes. And there's a spare room at the Fellowship, perhaps he could stay for a while?'

The woman's eyes narrowed. 'I need him to help me earn. His wee fingers are good at working the muslin.'

'I could see about getting him an apprenticeship, and of course, I have something to help tide you over.' Hugh bent down and dropped some coins in her lap. She counted them and a crafty look lit up her face.

'Aye, all right, you can take him. But mind he remembers his mammy on payday.'

'I'll make sure of it. What do you say, Tam? Would you like to come with Miss Crawford and me?'

The little boy nodded mutely and held out his hand to Lily. She took it in hers and they hurried down the stairwell before his mother could change her mind.

Only a few weeks later, Lily was in class admiring one of Tam's drawings. There was no doubting he had an eye. She couldn't quite believe the transformation that had taken place since he'd been away from his mother. In the clinic, Florence had bathed him and treated him for lice and scabies, and he was now recovering his health thanks to regular meals. Hugh had found him an apprenticeship with a draughtsman, who had taken him to live with his own family once he realised what a hard worker and a quick learner Tam was, and he continued to attend the ragged school. The boy had talent and was thriving.

Lily smiled at Tam as she handed him back his drawing. She knew she shouldn't have favourites, but her heart lifted when he smiled shyly and whispered, 'Thanks, miss.'

31

∼ *Jeanie* ∼

Jeanie pushed the pram along Knightsbridge, hoping the movement would soothe baby Stella to sleep. She wanted time to think. Until now she'd been content with motherhood, too busy with the endless demands to think about anything else, and too exhausted to contemplate dancing. Then yesterday Viktor had taken her to see a renowned Russian prima ballerina who had moved to London. The walls of her drawing room in Golders Green had been covered in paintings of the dancer in various roles created for her, the tables in silver-framed photographs of the dancer with various royals and heads of state. Jeanie found her airy name-dropping deeply boring and irritating but Viktor had been captivated.

'Diaghilev was an absolute tyrant, but a genius, too, you know? And Nijinsky, so beautiful, but not my type, too pretty. Besides, I always thought he and Sergei might be lovers.'

Jeanie sat in the corner with Stella on her lap, feeling invisible while the great ballerina talked about the Ballets Russes, how she loathed Stravinsky's music, and on and on, while Viktor hung on her every word and leapt to pour her more tea from the samovar. The prima ballerina had insisted they go out to the garden to feed her pet swans, but one had hissed at Jeanie and pecked at her foot with its serrated beak, drawing blood. Jeanie had had enough and, scooping up Stella, had insisted they go home.

Now she seethed with frustration as she marched down

the King's Road. That awful woman had played the grande dame, and after a few cursory questions about Jeanie's dancing career, she'd found out that she had been a mere 'hoofer' and ignored her the rest of the time. Instead, she'd aimed the full wattage of her considerable charm on Viktor, who was helpless with adoration. Jeanie was used to being the star and hadn't realised until now that giving up the stage meant losing that privilege. Hanging up her dance shoes had been a colossal mistake. As she walked through the busy streets, she noticed that men no longer turned their heads to stare at her with desire. She stopped to look in the window of Woolland Brothers. Her reflection showed a dumpy little woman who was still carrying her pregnancy weight dressed in loose clothes in drab shades of brown and grey. Jeanie thought she really did look like a little bird now – a drab sparrow.

'Bugger that!' she said out loud, startling a woman standing next to her. Jeanie straightened her back and pushed the pram into the department store. Emerging an hour later, she smoothed the emerald-green skirts of her new silk dress and glanced at her reflection again, pleased with the effect of the new lip rouge and face powder she'd bought. The shop girls had made a fuss over Stella and kept her amused, but as they left the shop, the baby began to keen with hunger. Jeanie's nipples pinched with milk and she quickened her pace. When she reached home and the baby had been fed and put down for her nap, Tatiana eyed Jeanie's new dress.

'It suits you. And it's good to see you with some colour in your cheeks.'

Jeanie picked up a slice of cake and was about to take a bite but put it down again. She looked up at the older woman.

'I'm going back on the stage. Will you help me get back in shape?'

Tatiana took the cake away and put an apple in front of Jeanie. 'I thought you'd never ask.'

32

∽ *Lily* ∽

The days lengthened into summer and began to take on a rhythm. Lily had recently taken a studio in Bath Street where she worked on portrait commissions as well as turning her hand to fancy inlaid boxes, mirrors with frames of beaten pewter and copper, and delicate, flower-shaped jewellery that bloomed with the semi-precious stones she'd come to love: purple amethysts, honey-coloured amber, luminous moonstone and the fiery glitter of opals. The wealthy merchants' wives couldn't get enough of these decorative objects, and Lily was beginning to make more than a decent living. In her spare time she worked on the paintings that were closest to her heart, working from the sketches she'd made at the Fellowship and on the streets of Cowcaddens. When Lily had three paintings she thought were ready to be seen, she sent a note to Sandy Munro and was gratified to receive a note back the same day: he would have great pleasure in coming to see her work.

She'd asked Jack to her studio for moral support, and while they waited for Munro to arrive Lily paced up and down the studio, pausing every now and then to put one canvas in a more prominent position, only to change it again.

'For goodness sake, you'll wear out the rug!' Jack led her to a chaise longue she'd draped with a silk Paisley shawl. 'Sit down and try to look composed; you don't want to look too eager. Sandy's a businessman, after all, and he'll smell the desperation coming off you.'

'But I'm not selling a necklace or a snuffbox, these are my paintings. I can't be calm and dispassionate about it. This isn't business, it's art.'

'I know, and they are utterly astonishing, like nothing I've ever seen before. I'm proud of you, Lil.' He took her hand and she leaned her head on his shoulder. But she couldn't stop her insides churning and leapt up at the sound of the doorbell.

'Keep your cool,' Jack said. 'Remember, Munro needs us just as much as we need him.'

Lily took a couple of deep breaths before opening the door. The art dealer bustled into the room, sweeping his hat off and bowing over her hand in the French style.

'My dear Miss Crawford, I was thrilled to get your note.' He bowed briefly in Jack's direction. 'Mr Petrie, you must allow me to come and see your work.' He turned back to Lily. 'But I'm here to see your paintings, my dear. Your portraits have been going down a storm. Those haughty faces, the bold eyes and the impertinently tilted heads! Charming! Quite charming! And so original! The full-length portraits are particularly popular – they're calling you the new Whistler, or at least that's what I've told them to call you.' He laughed and clapped his gloved hands together. 'Don't keep me in suspense a moment longer. Show me what you've been working on.'

Lily led him to a wall where the light was good and where she'd stacked her Cowcaddens paintings. Munro looked at them one at a time. After ten minutes she could bear it no longer.

'Well? What do you think?'

He straightened up from where he had been crouching in front of a portrait of Tam in his cast-off skirt, his eyes enormous in a face stamped with hunger. Lily had diluted the paint for the background with turpentine, so it looked as streaked and stained as the walls in his miserable home. Despite the obvious poverty, Tam shone like an angel, his expression suffused with joy and hope. It was the painting of which Lily was most proud.

Munro held the canvas at arm's length. 'Remarkable, quite remarkable, almost a masculine style, I'd venture. Bold, too. I see you're not afraid to experiment. You've become a serious artist, my dear, congratulations.'

Lily beamed. 'So, you will take them? I've planned a whole series. I thought perhaps another solo exhibition?'

The art dealer replaced the canvas and dusted off his gloves. 'Oh no, I'm afraid I can't take these.'

Lily's mouth went dry. 'What do you mean? You said they were remarkable.'

'Ah, yes, they are indeed. But the subject matter is far too grim. The poverty, the deprivation, the ugliness you lay bare – my clients don't want to see that, let alone hang it on their drawing-room walls. As an artist, you must paint what you must paint, of course, but if you want to sell your work then you must make art that people like – and they don't like to be reminded that poverty, neglect and cruelty sit at their doorstep like stray dogs begging for a crust.'

Lily's cheeks grew hot as the blood rose in them and she could feel her temper taking over, like a wave of scorching heat. She would not be beaten on this: she knew it was the best work she had ever done.

'What about the Glasgow Boys with their paintings of poor farm workers and their children?'

'Quite different, my dear – they were bucolic scenes and the rosy-cheeked little peasant girls and boys chasing geese and cutting cabbages are in faraway glens and villages, not swarming through the streets of Glasgow, picking pockets. No, these poor souls you have painted are too close to home and too realistic. Personally, I think they're sublime, but I have to be businesslike.' He put his hat back on. 'My advice to you is to stick to portraits of society women. Or why not do some more delightful theatre scenes? Those pretty ballerinas sold like hotcakes – far more suitable as subjects for a lady artist.'

After he'd left, Lily put her head in her hands and tried not to cry. Jack put his arm around her.

'Don't give up. You heard what he said – they're sublime. He just can't sell them.' She gave a sob and his arm tightened. 'Hey, don't be downhearted. Think of what you've achieved so far and carry on.'

Lily nodded but wasn't consoled. It was all right for Jack, he had another exhibition coming up in London – and Munro had never balked at his experiments. As a woman artist, she was expected to play it safe. She bit her lip. Lily had never played it safe and wasn't about to start now.

33

～ *Jeanie* ～

Jeanie's back ran with sweat and her ligaments strained as she stretched along the barre.

'Further.' Tatiana instructed.

Jeanie slid her leg away from her and felt the burning ache. 'I can't go any further, I'll pull something.'

'All right, have a rest. But then we start again. You've a long way to go.'

Jeanie sank onto the floor and took off her shoes. One was filled with blood. Tatiana inspected her mangled, swollen toes. 'I'll get you some iced water to soak your feet in, otherwise you'll never get your shoes back on.'

When Tatiana had left, Jeanie rested her head on her knees. Looking down, she could see her belly bulge. Her stomach rumbled and she thought longingly of the scones lathered in cream and jam she usually ate at this time of day, but she knew she shouldn't have anything other than water, not if she wanted to return to the stage. The wardrobe mistress had tutted at her measurements and told her briskly to lose ten pounds. Eating less was easy, though, compared to regaining her strength and suppleness. Every muscle in her body ached. Tatiana said it was because she'd lost strength in her stomach and back muscles and she'd have to work doubly hard to get back into shape.

Jeanie leaned against the mirrored wall and closed her eyes. She was tired but this was different from the fatigue she felt looking after Stella all day; every twinge and ache meant she was growing fitter and more agile. The studio door opened, and she opened her eyes, expecting to see Tatiana. It was Viktor with Stella in his arms. His expression was thunderous.

'I found our daughter in the dancers' dressing room, being fed chocolate.'

'So? She was being looked after.'

'She should be with her mother.'

Jeanie's tiredness was pushed aside by a surge of fury. 'Gie's peace, man, she's fine. Stella loves being at the theatre, don't you my wee darling?'

The baby gurgled and reached out chubby arms to Jeanie, who pushed herself painfully to her feet and took her. She glared over Stella's head at Viktor. 'I'm going back on stage, and that's that.'

He looked downcast. 'I thought you liked staying at home and being a mother.'

She put her hand on his. 'You know I need to get back out there.'

'Aren't Stella and I enough for you?'

'I'm a dancer as well as her mother. You don't want me to be unhappy, do you?'

'But you have a home of your own, a family of your own – that would make most women happy.'

'My home is the theatre, whether it's in London or Paris or Rome. I'm too restless to stay in one place – and so are you. And just think of the childhood Stella will have, the people she'll meet and the places she'll see.' Jeanie waited, but his expression was still troubled. 'Viktor, please.'

He sighed. 'I thought I was building a nest for my little bird, but it was a cage.'

Jeanie rolled her eyes. 'You Russians! Always so dramatic.' She waited. 'So, yes?'

'Yes.' He kissed her and then abruptly he was all business.

'I've bought the rights for a new variety show. It has the perfect role for you.'

'The principal role?'

'Of course.'

Jeanie smiled. 'You can tell me about it tonight, in bed.' She handed the baby back to Viktor. 'Now, off you go and take the bairn with you. I'll never fit into my costume if I stand around blethering to you all day.'

34

~ *Lily* ~

Lily turned up the gas mantle. She stoked the fire and sparks burst up the chimney. In the next room, the bath was running, and she looked forward to a soak after a long day in the studio. She stretched her back and looked around the little parlour she'd decorated with William Morris wallpaper, and sighed with contentment. Her new flat in Garnethill was evidence that she was an independent woman who could buy her own property. It only had three rooms counting the indoor bathroom. She'd paid for the flat with money saved from her commissions and from a trust fund she'd come into, and from September she would have a regular salary.

Fra Newbery had offered her a job teaching at the Mack starting in the autumn term, and meanwhile she was still busy at the Fellowship. The rest of the time she worked in her Bath Street studio, and most evenings she met up with Jack or wrote to Jeanie, who had sent her the playbill for the new variety show she was starring in on the Strand. *Come and see us and bring dear Jack and that rogue Ned,* Jeanie had written. But although Lily missed her friend terribly, she didn't see how she'd find the time. Her quirky portraits were still in demand with wealthy patrons. Her life was busy and full. Only the outbreak of war with Germany had cast a shadow over the summer, but everyone said it would be over soon.

The war in Europe seemed far away this evening. As she stood at the window of her flat and watched swallows arcing through the silvery dusk, she remembered another late summer evening on the beach at Cockburnspath, with Jack, his hat tilted to keep the late sun out of his eyes, laughing at something Ned had said. As if conjured by her thoughts, the doorbell rang, and she was gratified to see Ned standing on her doorstep.

'I was just thinking about you,' she said and ushered him into the parlour.

He surprised her by kissing her cheek three times in the Parisian way and handing her a box tied up prettily in a bow. 'How gratifying! In return, here are some *bonbons*, sweets for a sweetie.'

'How very French! What's all this for?'

'Well, that is a tale I need to tell.'

'How mysterious! Let me turn off my bath and we can have a nice long gossip. Tea?'

'Tea would be most fortifying. And I'm afraid you're going to need it when you hear my news.' When they were settled with cups of tea, she urged him to tell all. 'You'll never guess what Jack and I have done,' he said.

Lily frowned. 'I haven't seen him for a couple of days, which is also mysterious. What have you two been up to?'

Ned put down his cup. 'Well, that's the exciting news. Jack and I have signed up. You're looking at an officer of the Highland Light Infantry. We're doing basic training first and then it's off to La Belle France.'

Lily stood up and wrung her hands. 'But you can't, you must not!'

'But we can, dear heart, we must, and we have. It will be a lark, a great adventure. And I die to wear the kilt and a Glengarry – only imagine how dashing I will look.'

Lily began to pace around the small room. 'This isn't a game, Ned. You could get yourselves killed.'

'Nonsense, we'll be home before you know it, boring

everyone rigid with our war stories.' Ned stood up to go and held out his arms. Lily buried her nose in his neck, smelling the expensive pomade and citrus cologne he favoured. 'When do you leave?'

'Tomorrow, first thing.' Lily clung to him more tightly and began to cry. Ned detached her and laughed. 'Steady on, you'll have me bubbling next. Don't worry, dear heart, we'll be back in no time, having sent the Germans home to listen to interminable Wagner operas and eat their ghastly *schnitzels* and *wursts*.'

When he was gone, she looked out a photograph that had been taken at her solo exhibition to give to Jack. Across the back of it she wrote:

Be careful, my darling Jack. I love you always, Lily.

That night, Lily clung to Jack as if she were drowning. 'I don't want you to go.'

'I can't stand by like a coward and let other men do the fighting. Now, dry your tears, we haven't much time left.'

35

~ *Lily* ~

Although Jack wrote to her often from basic training, Lily missed him terribly. As autumn passed into winter and the war showed no sign of coming to an end, she fell into a routine of teaching at the Mack and at the Fellowship, and painting in her studio, but the world seemed to be holding its breath. Lily longed for Jack to be home on leave, but when he arrived looking strange in his uniform, they only had a few days together before he was off again. Meanwhile she kept his letters in a silver casket studded with amethysts that Kit had made for her. His letters were full of anecdotes about Ned teasing the other men.

I have to watch his back, as he will insist on goading the toughest chaps in the company. You know Ned, he doesn't know when to stop and I've had to pull him out of many a scrape.

It seemed the celebrations to bring in 1915 had barely passed before Jack reached France in February. The tone of his letters changed. After the initial excitement of reaching the front, he'd bedded down in trenches with his regiment in miserable weather.

We are drenched from morning till night. Our kilts may keep us warm, but they provide a perfect home for lice, which hide between the pleats, and in the mornings they're also stiff with ice. The shelling is

ear-splitting but I've learned to sleep through it
standing like a horse.

In the margin, he'd sketched a picture of a kilted soldier, his Glengarry pulled over his eyes, propped up asleep against his rifle.

As spring led into summer, there seemed no end to the fighting. Lily took to attending Hugh's outdoor sermons in the slums, standing shoulder to shoulder in the street with whey-faced women and their children to listen to him talk about hope and the end of these dark times. Hugh had started working alongside Florence at the Royal Infirmary, tending the wounded men returning from the war.

'A lot of them have terrible facial injuries, their features destroyed by shrapnel,' he told her. 'We've taken down all the mirrors in the wards after some of the men fainted at the sight of their reflections. Some of them don't want to go home to their families, they're so ashamed.'

When Florence volunteered for the Red Cross in France, Lily felt her world was falling away bit by bit. As the months dragged by, her days teaching at the Mack and at the ragged school kept her darkest fears at bay, but the news she was dreading came just a year after she had said goodbye to Jack. In late October, her doorbell rang, and it was Ned on the doorstep. His face was drawn and there were dark shadows under his eyes. She ran to embrace him and felt a shudder go down his back. He wouldn't look at her or answer her questions until she had led him to a chair by the fire and handed him a cup of hot, sweet tea, and then he could only repeat her name, as if he couldn't quite believe she was there. His hands trembled violently when he tried to drink, the cup rattling in its saucer. Lily took it gently from him and poured him a brandy and helped him drink it. When some colour had come into his cheeks, he sighed and closed his eyes and fell asleep sitting upright, wrapped in his greatcoat, his long, sooty eyelashes like those of a child, his dark hair damp with fevered sweat.

Lily fetched a blanket and laid it gently over him and drew the curtains as the sun set over the city rooftops, lighting up the red sandstone with an eerie golden light under the darkening sky, as if it were the end of the world. She moved a chair to sit by him and settled down to wait. Dread gnawed at her insides as she watched over her friend as he slept. After a while Ned woke with a cry. He looked around the room, stricken, until he saw Lily and reached for her hand.

'Dear heart, I can't tell you what a tonic it is to see you.'

'And you, dearest Ned.' She rubbed his cold hand in hers. 'I don't want to rush you, but what news do you have of Jack? I haven't had a letter from him in weeks.'

Ned closed his eyes and shook his head. 'I'm afraid I have terrible news.' His voice broke and he put his face in his hands and wept openly, like a child. Lily hugged herself and rocked, the hollow place inside her filling with something worse – a searing pain that gnawed and tore at her like a wild beast.

'Jack?' she managed to whisper.

Ned reached into his pocket and handed her a letter, the envelope smeared with mud and rusted blood. It was addressed to her, in Jack's hand.

'He gave me this to give to you. Just before we went over the top at Loos, he went out to no man's land to scout out the enemy's position and draw a map of the landmarks. The shelling started while he was out there, and he didn't make it back.' Ned looked anguished. He hid his face in his hands and sobbed. 'Oh, Jackie-boy!'

Lily opened the letter with clumsy fingers. As she read, she realised it was a farewell.

Darling Lily,

*Forgive me for the tired epithet but you are my
dearest, darling, and I love you so much it pains me.
I write this on the eve of battle and I've an awful
feeling that I won't come out of this one. I know Ned
always said I'm a lucky beggar, but I fear my luck
has run out. I've become terribly superstitious out here
– we all have. You see, your photograph was my
lucky charm, but it must have fallen out into the
sump. So, that's it, I know I'm for it. I'm dog-tired
and I won't be sorry to leave this dreadful place and
this hideous war. The only thing I regret is from before
the war – that seems like a lifetime ago! – stupidly
going to France without you. I thought we had all the
time in the world, that you would eventually agree to
marry me – so stubborn, my darling! – and we would
have children, lots of them, all as beautiful and spir-
ited as you.*

*Know that I've always loved you, and if there's
another life after this, I'll wait for you. I hope you'll
go on to have a happy and wonderful life, filled with
love and a family, and, above all, that you continue
to paint. Don't waste the precious gift you have, and
don't waste your life grieving for me. I'll say goodbye
now, darling, and goodnight.*

All my love,

Jack

Lily folded the letter carefully and put it in her skirt
pocket. She crossed over to the window and opened the
curtains. The moon was full and bright, the sky studded
with stars. *Jack*, she thought, *my own Jack*. Why had she
not agreed to marry him and start a family? She would at
least have had Jack's child, but now she had nothing of his,

only memories. She was twenty-four but felt as if her youth was over. She leaned her forehead against the cold glass and the tears came. Ned put his arms around her waist, and she turned and leaned into his greatcoat and they clung to each other and wept for their loss.

36

～ Lily and Jeanie ～

Jeanie took the stairs two at a time and rang Lily's doorbell. After a while she hammered on the door and shouted through the letterbox. When the door opened, she was shocked by Lily's appearance. Her face was haggard, and her nightgown was stained. She peered out from her tangled hair and blinked.

'Jeanie? Is that you?'

Jeanie put down her overnight bag and held out her arms. 'Oh, Lily, I'm so sorry. I came as soon as I heard.'

Lily leaned heavily into her and began to cry. 'I've lost him.'

'I know, darlin', I know, I'm here now. Let's get you inside.' The flat was stuffy and in darkness, the windows shuttered and curtains drawn. Jeanie led her to the sofa and opened the windows, letting in a blast of cold air that made Lily shiver. Jeanie found a blanket to cover her, and as they sat together she looked around the room. There were dirty clothes and books strewn everywhere and shattered pictures scattered the floor. It looked as if Lily had ripped apart the flat in her grief.

Jeanie smoothed Lily's ragged hair away from her face. 'When did you last have something to eat?' Lily shrugged and closed her eyes. Jeanie wished Tatiana were here – she'd know what to do. She thought back to how she'd comforted her mother when one of her men had left her. 'I'll make us a nice cup of tea. Would you like that?' Lily nodded and Jeanie eased herself away from her and went into the little scullery. She got the range going and found the kettle in the sink under a pile of encrusted dishes. While the water boiled she washed up and threw away opened tins and mouldy food. When the tea was ready, she took it into the parlour only to find Lily asleep, a frown like a knife cut between her eyes. Jeanie poured herself a cup of tea and sipped it while she watched over her sleeping friend.

~

It was dark when Lily awoke to the smell of beef consommé and toast. She pushed off the blanket and saw someone had tidied and swept the parlour, which glowed with lamplight. There was a fire in the grate, and she rubbed her hands in its heat. She found she was ravenous for the first time in weeks, since she'd heard about Jack. Her shoulders sank under the weight of her grief and she put a trembling hand to her cheeks to wipe away the tears. A clinking sound made her look up from the flames. Jeanie stood before her carrying a supper tray, and Lily felt the pain in her chest ease.

Jeanie stayed for a month, sleeping in the same bed as Lily, holding her tightly when she wept, coaxing her to eat, and helping her bathe and dress. Lily didn't want to talk about Jack at first, but when she was ready, Jeanie listened as she poured out her anger.

'He shouldn't have gone to war. It was foolishness, stupid manly pride. I told him not to go, but he wouldn't listen to me, thought he knew best, putting his King and Country before us.'

After the anger came bouts of sobbing and wailing, Lily keening like a hurt animal as Jeanie held her and murmured into her hair. When there were no more tears, Lily sat curled up in an armchair, staring into the fire, and began to talk about Jack, finding comfort in reminiscing about their time together. When Lily was ready to receive visitors, Jeanie replied to the condolence letters. Florence, back on leave, and Hugh were the first to arrive. Jeanie went into the scullery with Florence to have a quiet word with her about Lily's state of mind. When she came back into the parlour, Hugh was sitting close to Lily talking quietly to her. Jeanie cleared her throat and he turned to smile at her.

'Bless you,' he said as he took the cup of tea she held out to him. 'I was telling Lily that we're praying for her and that she's sorely missed at the Fellowship. It might be time for her to come back to teach.'

'I don't know if your prayers will do any good,' Jeanie said. 'But going back to work might help take her mind off things. What do you think, Florence? You're the doctor.'

Hugh smiled but his eyes were cold. 'I'm also a doctor.'

'Aye, but no a proper one like your sister.' She patted Florence's hand and was rewarded with a warm look.

'I think it might be beneficial,' Florence said.

Hugh leaned forward to say something when Lily sat up straight. 'There's no need for you all to discuss me as if I'm not here. I'll make up my mind when I want to go back, if that's all the same to you.'

'Excuse us for breathing,' Jeanie said, but she was pleased that Lily had regained some of her old spirit. And when the visitors had left, she helped her get her teaching materials together.

'I'll start back at the Mack tomorrow, go and see Fra, and then I'll go back to the Fellowship next week.'

Jeanie turned away and collected the teacups so Lily wouldn't see the worry in her eyes. She cleared her throat. 'That sounds grand. I'll take these into the scullery and then I'll pack. There's an early train I can take tomorrow.'

Lily put her hand on her arm. 'Thank you, Jeanie, I don't know what I'd have done without you.'

Jeanie took in the colour in Lily's cheeks, the way her copper hair shone and her clear eyes. 'No need to thank me – you'd have done the same for me.'

37

∼ *Lily* ∼

For the next three years Lily threw herself into teaching and painting, but the thought of Jack was never far from her. After a year or so, the pain had blunted and she found comfort in talking to him when she was on her own, telling him news from the Mack and pausing, brush in hand, while she asked his opinion. She received the occasional letter from Ned, who had gone back to the front, but they were short, chatty missives that never mentioned Jack. In his last letter, he'd pleaded with her not to knit him any socks. *Can you imagine how hideous they would be – embroidered with skinny hags holding roses. Fiendishly uncomfortable. Frankly, I'd rather have trench foot.* Ned's letters made her smile and long to see him again, and she wondered when he would be demobbed and heading home; she missed his friendship. Lily would have been lonely if it hadn't been for Hugh. They'd grown closer as she spent companionable evenings at his home or helping him at the Fellowship. When the war ended, he gave up his post at the hospital and returned full time to his urban mission and Lily saw even more of him. She found an odd solace in how different he was to Jack, but hadn't noticed how much she had come to rely on him until the day Sandy Munro turned up at her flat looking for her.

'My dear, do you still have your paintings of those sweet little slum children?'

'Of course, I've added to them over the years. But I thought you said they were no good.'

He put a gloved hand to his heart, as if stricken. 'I never said such a thing! I told you they weren't the most commercial work you'd ever done, but tastes have changed because of the war. The critics are mad for all this dark stuff coming in from Europe, and your grimy urchins in their depressing rags will go down a treat.'

Lily fetched the paintings for Munro to look at and found herself once again waiting for his verdict.

'Such gloom and doom,' he said with relish. 'There's a gallery in London that will lap this up.' He named a gallery that made Lily's heart skip. It was the same gallery Jack had exhibited with, known for showing experimental art. 'What do you say?' Munro said. 'Can I have them all? They'd be perfect for a solo show. Usual commission, of course.'

When Munro left Lily was so elated and surprised, she forgot for an appalling moment that Jack was dead. Her first thought was to rush to his studio and tell him the news. She was halfway down the stairs when she remembered. Lily sank down onto a step and wept as her heart broke all over again.

After a while she dried her eyes. She couldn't face going back to the empty flat and decided to distract herself by visiting Hugh. The thought of him filled her with comfort and she hurried down to Sauchiehall Street to catch a tram to the West End. When Hugh opened the door in his shirtsleeves, he looked so solid and ordinary that she had to fight the urge to embrace him. It would be good to feel a man's reassuring arms around her, to feel a starched cotton shirt against her cheek. Instead she smiled and he stood aside to let her in.

'An unexpected pleasure!' he said.

'I'm sorry if this is inconvenient.'

'Not at all, I'm always glad to see you.'

183

Hugh led her to a seat in front of the fire. Despite her gloves, her hands were blue from the cold that had set in with the dreary advent of November. She hated this month, when the city looked its drabbest and the rain came in sideways on gusts of freezing wind. Hugh didn't ask her why she was there but waited in silence for her to speak. It was one of his strengths: he could listen to people's burdens but did not demand they lay them down. In the quiet, Lily began to feel calmer.

'I forgot Jack was dead today.' She glanced up at him. 'How could I forget?'

He inclined his head. 'It's normal. You've suffered a great loss, but in time the pain will ease.'

Lily put her head in her hands. 'But I don't want it to go – I don't want to lose him all over again.'

Hugh knelt before her and she drew back, surprised. 'Lily, I know you're grieving, but you must go on with your life. You need a home of your own, children to look after, a husband.'

Lily went still. She was fond of Hugh and admired him, and he was an attractive man. But she didn't love him, at least not the way she'd loved Jack.

He seemed to guess her thoughts. 'I know you'll always miss Jack, but I'd like to comfort you, to heal you with love. Lily, will you marry me?'

She held her breath. 'Why?'

He laughed. 'Because, you goose, I've loved you from the day I first met you. I've hidden my feelings until now, but with everything changing and the war over, this could be a new beginning for both of us.' He held her hand. 'Lily, if you'll be my wife, I promise to protect and cherish you as you deserve.'

He waited.

Lily thought of how bereft and lonely she'd been since

Jack died. She'd once been so sure that art was enough for her, that she didn't need a family of her own, but now the years stretched before her, an endless bleak landscape of solitary dinners in her little flat as she grew older. Jack was still so vivid in her memory, but did she have to live with this sadness for the rest of her life? Hugh was a good, decent, strong man who loved her. Still she hesitated. *Jack, my Jack, help me. I don't know what to do.*

She looked down at Hugh's hand covering hers. 'I can't give you an answer, not yet.'

38

∾ Lily and Jeanie ∾

Lily's London exhibition was a success, the opening night
packed and the critics who had seen the preview unreserved-
ly enthusiastic, as Munro had predicted. He'd taken the
precaution of printing brochures with her name as L. M.
Crawford to avoid any prejudice against Lily as a woman
artist. After a late supper with Munro and the gallery owner,
Lily caught a cab back to Chelsea with Jeanie.

'I'm sorry Viktor couldn't come, he's been a bit under
the weather recently,' Jeanie said.

Lily yawned and settled into the back seat of the cab.
'That's all right.' She yawned again. 'I'm so tired. I've been
so nervous about this exhibition and looking forward to it,
then it seemed to be over in a flash.'

'It's the same for me with the opening of a new show
– all those nerves before and then the performance is over
before you know it.' She squeezed Lily's hand. 'It was a
great night, I'm so proud of you. Jack would have been
proud too.'

Lily looked out of the window and her ghostly reflection
stared back at her. She felt a pang of guilt as she realised
she hadn't thought about Jack for a while. The last few
weeks had been hectic crating up her work for London,
overseeing the exhibition notes and endless meetings with
Munro. She hadn't even had time to think about Hugh's
proposal, although she planned to talk to Jeanie about it.
Now, with the opening night behind her, she really should
make up her mind and stop dithering.

'You know, Jeanie, it's been three years now since Jack died, and with the war over, perhaps it's time for big changes.'

Jeanie leaned her head on Lily's shoulder and yawned. 'That's exactly what I was saying to Viktor, that we've got to make changes, take the company on tour, get new material to bring in the punters.'

'You're going on tour?'

'Yes, for a year. We're nearly there with rehearsals and we've a few dates booked already.'

'But you'll come back to London in between dates?'

'No, it's not worth it.' She nudged Lily. 'But I'll send you postcards – you know I'm not a great letter writer.'

'I know! I'll miss you. Even though we don't see each other very often, it's a comfort knowing you're only a train journey away.' They were both silent for a while. 'I've something I've been meaning to talk to you about.'

Jeanie yawned again. 'What?'

'You remember Hugh Anderson?'

'Oh, aye, the Holy Willy. What about him?'

'He's asked me to marry him.'

Jeanie sat bolt upright. 'In the name of the Wee Man! You never told me you were winching with him.'

'That's the thing: we've been friends until now. With Jack gone, and you in London, he's become a bit of a rock. I'm very fond of him, and he's a good man.'

'That doesn't sound very romantic. Not like you and Jack.'

Lily sighed. 'I'll never meet anyone I love as much as I loved Jack. But does that mean I'm never to have a family of my own, a husband? I'm so lonely, Jeanie, and I'm tired of being sad, of grieving for Jack who is never going to come back, no matter how many tears I cry over him.'

Jeanie tucked her arm into Lily's. 'I want you to be happy – do whatever you think best, and I'll stand by you.'

Lily smiled through her tears. 'Like in the playground back in Kirkcudbright.'

'Aye, mind those wee bastards? We saw them off together, and I'll always be there for you if you're ever in any trouble.'

'And I for you.'

39

~ Jeanie ~

The next few weeks passed in a whirl as Viktor organised the tour, sending telegrams to theatre managers in Europe and negotiating terms, auditioning performers to replace the ones who wanted to stay put in London. The small house in Chelsea was thick with cigar smoke and full of a stream of writers, directors and choreographers. Viktor would stay up long after they'd gone, poring over librettos and scripts, a balloon of brandy in his hand. Jeanie woke early one morning to see he hadn't come to bed at all and crossly pulled on a dressing gown. Downstairs, he was slumped over his desk by the open window. The room was chilly with wintry air.

'For goodness sake, Viktor, you'll catch your death of cold like that, come to bed.' She shook him by the shoulder but couldn't rouse him. Panic fluttered in Jeanie's chest as she pushed him upright against the back of the chair. His eyes were closed and his face white and cold. 'No, no, don't you dare!' she shouted at him, seized with terror. She loosened his collar and listened frantically at his chest, but all she could hear was the hammering of her own heart. What else? Her mind was frozen. His pulse – she could try to feel for that. She put two fingers against his wrist but could feel nothing. 'Please God, please don't let him die,' she muttered. She ran to Tatiana's room and pulled back the bed covers. 'It's Viktor!' she choked. The two women ran to the drawing room.

Tatiana leaned close to Viktor. 'He's still breathing,' she said.

'Thank God!'

'Help me get him onto the sofa.' With one of his arms around each of their necks they dragged him, gasping at the dead weight. Tatiana was calm as she covered Viktor with a blanket. 'Stay here and keep him warm while I fetch the doctor.'

When the doctor arrived, after what seemed an age, Jeanie sat in the hall with Tatiana, waiting. She wrung her hands and wept. 'This is my punishment. I never said I loved him, all these years and I've never told him that. I didn't even know that I did – I thought I couldn't love anyone, and that it suited me to stay with him, for my career and for Stella. But I do love him, I do, and now it's too late, he'll never know.'

Tatiana held her close and stroked her hair. 'He knows, this Russian with a big heart. You had a tough start in life, so did I, so did Viktor. Like me, he grew up on black bread and cabbage soup. He knows what it is to have to fight to get what you want, but he also knows that underneath that hard shell you have a tender heart.'

The doctor came out after what seemed like an age. 'He's had a heart attack, but he's comfortable now.'

'Can I see him now?' Jeanie said.

'Yes, but don't stay long.'

'We're going on tour next month – the company, to France.'

'Out of the question! I'll arrange for a nurse to come and stay with him around the clock. He needs bed rest and complete quiet – no more cigars, no alcohol, no more rich meals, and above all, no work pressure. I've been warning him for years that this would happen.'

In the drawing room, Viktor was propped up with

cushions on the sofa and his colour was better. He held out his arms and Jeanie sank into them. 'I was so frightened,' she sobbed. 'I thought you were dead, Viktor.' She sat up and wiped her face. 'I thought you were dead, and I've never told you I love you.'

'There was no need to tell me. Loving you is like loving a wild creature – it's a privilege when a fox, say, dares to let you near it and takes food from your hand, and a marvel when it comes back, a miracle when it puts its head on your knee.'

'So, I'm a fox now, not a bird? I wish you'd make up your mind.'

His laughter turned to a wheezing cough and Jeanie sat up in alarm. He waved his hand at her and after a few moments was able to speak again. 'That fool of a doctor says I can't go on tour, and I suppose I must listen to him, but there's nothing to stop you and the rest of the company. The director is perfectly capable of operating without me, and Madame Lebret will keep you all on your toes.'

Jeanie handed him a glass of water and helped him to drink. She put the glass down and looked at him sternly. 'I'm staying right here, with you.' And to her surprise, Jeanie meant it. She would give anything to keep him alive – nothing else mattered.

Viktor cleared his throat and spoke with his old authority. 'I'm still the boss of this company, and I insist you go. This is the right time for you – you don't want to miss it and let someone else take the spotlight. Stella can stay here with me, and Tatiana will look after both of us.'

Jeanie considered. 'But . . .'

'I don't want any argument. I insist.'

She sighed. There was no moving Viktor when he was set on a course of action. 'Very well, have it your way, you

191

stubborn old bear.' She smoothed his hair back from his forehead. 'Poor Tatiana! She'll have some job trying to feed you chicken soup and keeping you away from your cigars and brandy.'

40

~ *Lily* ~

Lily stood on Hugh's doorstep, nervously twisting her gloves. She'd planned on giving him an answer as soon as she got back from London, but Florence had told her he was away on a retreat on Islay. Now he was back, and Lily found herself eager to see him. She knew Florence was working at the hospital and Hugh would be on his own, and at this late hour the servants would be in bed. When Hugh opened the door, they stood looking at each other for a while. He held out his hand and she took it and he led her inside. She sat on an armchair by the fire and he knelt before her, rubbing her hands to warm them. They still hadn't said a word to each other. Lily didn't know if it was his proximity and her nerves, but she sensed a quickening in the air between them. On an impulse, she leaned down and kissed him on the lips. Warmth coursed through her and for the first time in years she felt a man's hands in her hair, his mouth on hers. He drew away but she pulled him back to her.

'It's all right.'

He nodded and pulled her to the floor to lie beside him. Lily reached for his shirt buttons and tugged his shirt from his shoulders and tasted the smoothness of his skin, kissed the beating pulse at the base of his throat and felt his hands lift her skirt. His body was heavy on hers and his fingers clumsy with nerves and excitement, but she didn't care. When he pushed inside her and gasped, she emptied her mind of all the pain and grief she'd carried for years and bucked against him, letting go of the despair she'd clung to for so long. *I don't care. I don't care. It doesn't matter. Nothing matters any more. He is dead and never coming back and I must live.*

When it was over, Hugh fetched glasses and a bottle of whisky, and Lily winced as the alcohol burned her chafed lips. Their lovemaking had been fierce and desperate, nothing like the tenderness and wonder she had had with Jack, but strangely and darkly satisfying all the same. Hugh sat down on the floor beside her and topped up her glass.

'I thought drink was the devil's poison, that's what you call it when you ask people to take the pledge,' she said, meaning to break the tension with some teasing. The firelight played on his face so she could not read his expression.

He raised his glass and winked at her. 'It's for medicinal purposes.'

'Ned's wildly disapproving of you because he thought you were teetotal.'

'Ah, Ned – he obviously carries a torch for you and doesn't approve of any man who gets near you.'

'I don't know, he's a wild card. I can never make him out. Are you jealous?'

He set down his glass and kissed her gently. 'Only if he comes galloping back from wherever he is to claim you.'

She laughed. 'I can't imagine Ned galloping anywhere – sauntering is more his style.' The whisky reached her empty stomach and sang in her blood. She nudged Hugh's foot with her own. 'What would the Fellowship say if they could see us now? Their adored preacher lying in sin with a bohemian artist.'

He pulled her towards him, and she laid her cheek on his smooth chest. 'Well, I'll just have to make an honest woman out of you. I take it you've made up your mind, and that's why you're here.'

194

Lily looked up at Hugh and felt at ease for the first time in years, as if she had sailed into a safe harbour after a storm at sea. 'Yes, I have.'

'And?'

'I thought it was obvious. Yes, I'll marry you, Hugh Anderson.'

He kissed her forehead. 'Good, I was getting worried about your loose morals, Miss Crawford.' She pushed his chest and he laughed and took her in his arms again.

41

~ *Lily* ~

Now that the decision to marry Hugh was made, Lily concentrated on painting and teaching. They took a trip to Kirkcudbright so Hugh could meet her parents and ask her father's permission. Donald Crawford was delighted at the prospect of his only daughter marrying not only a man of means and property but a doctor and clergyman to boot.

'I told you he'd like you,' Lily told Hugh after he'd come out of her father's study and they were alone in the drawing room. 'You're making a respectable woman out of his wayward daughter. The family's honour has been restored.'

'Didn't he like Jack?'

Lily tried to ignore the stab of pain she still felt at the mention of his name. 'Papa never met him – I didn't think there was any point. He'd never have approved.'

'And your mother?'

Lily smiled at the memory. 'She came to see me often in Glasgow and she adored Jack – he was always so charming. She said he was like a big puppy.'

'I'm not at all sure she's so enamoured by me,' Hugh said. 'I'm not really the puppy type.'

Lily laughed. 'No, you're more like one of those wolf dogs: what are they called? The ones they used in the war.'

'A German Shepherd?' He held her face and kissed her. 'You're right, I'm more of a guard dog, but perhaps that's what you need, someone to protect and guide you.'

Lily frowned and was about to reply when her mother

called her. 'I promised Mama I'd go and see her after you'd had your chat,' she said to Hugh.

Upstairs in her bedroom, Lily let her mother brush out her hair in front of the dressing-table mirror. 'Such rich colours – copper and gold, not silver like mine.'

Lily caught her mother's hand and kissed it. 'You're still beautiful, Mama.'

Her mother put down the brush and sat on Lily's bed. 'Life goes so quickly. You think it's going to last forever when you're young, and then one day you wake up and you're nearly fifty.'

Lily turned around and faced her. 'I know you're worried about this marriage, but I know what I'm doing.'

Her mother sighed. 'Are you sure? This Hugh is so different from dear Jack.'

'I know, Mama, but I can't live the rest of my life mourning him. Hugh looks after me; he's a good man.'

'Oh well, your father and him get on well.'

'Yes, did you hear them both talking about the Reformation at dinner?'

Her mother rolled her eyes. 'Your father's hobby horse – agony! At least I didn't have to listen and could think about my next project – botanic art has caught my fancy. Come and see what I've been working on.' Lily followed her mother into the sewing room she used as a studio, relieved not to be talking about Hugh any more.

～

When they arrived back in Glasgow, they went straight to Hugh's house to tell Florence, who, in a rare show of emotion, clasped Lily in her arms.

'What lovely, lovely news! I've always wanted a sister! I couldn't be more pleased.' She broke away from Lily but held onto her arms. 'He's not always the easiest person to live with, so if he gives you any trouble, let me know and I'll sort him out.'

Lily laughed. 'I think I can handle him.'

Florence smiled and turned to Hugh, her arm around Lily. 'I hope you realise how lucky you are, brother dear.'

Later, when Florence had gone to bed, Hugh filled their brandy glasses and took Lily over to a circular table in the bay window of the drawing room.

'I've something to show you,' he said and unfurled a map, weighting it down at each corner. Lily's curiosity was piqued.

'The Fellowship is running smoothly now, and I feel it's time for me to move on to another mission.'

Lily traced the ragged coastline and the archipelago of islands. The names were redolent of fragrant teas, of spices, of blue and white porcelain: Formosa, Soochow, Nanking, Shanghai.

'China? But it's so far away – the other side of the world. I thought we were getting married soon.'

'We will. And I want you to come with me.' Lily blinked, lost for words, and Hugh rushed on. 'I've been sent my orders from the China Inland Mission and now I just have to book our passage to Shanghai.' He reached for her hand. 'I want to do this. It would be the culmination of my life's work. There are millions of souls to be saved, and what better time to go than now, with so many of Europe's thinkers turning against God after the war.' He looked intently at Lily. 'And I would like nothing better than for you to be at my side, as my wife.'

She looked again at the map: the painters she admired had all been to the Far East and come back raving about the sights they'd seen – the doll-like women in kimonos, the exotic street scenes. And she had several of the woodblock prints in delicate inks they'd brought back hanging on the wall of her Garnethill flat.

Her breath quickened as a new life beckoned; there would be strange new sights and colours to paint.

Lily spoke before she could change her mind. 'I'll come with you.' Hugh beamed and took her in his arms, and she looked over his shoulder and out of the window. *It will be a new beginning. I'll be far away from this city with its reminders of Jack on every corner. Hugh is a good man who makes the world a better place.* So she reasoned as the rain began to fall outside.

42

~ *Jeanie* ~

The dance company had completed the first leg of its tour of France and Jeanie was elated. Paris had been a glorious dream, and their show had been a sell-out night after night. After a heady week the company was on the move, taking the railway down through France, filling up whole carriages with their laughter and music and rowdy talk. Now they'd reached Provence, and had stopped to rest in a village inn. It was hotter than Jeanie was used to, and she found it hard to sleep. Jeanie had turned in early to be ready for the next day's performance – they had stopped at this little village to break the journey from Paris to Nice – but she was restless. In the distance she could hear fireworks, shouts of laughter and strains of music coming from the square. The landlord had told them it was the village's summer fête and the celebrations would go on far into the night. She slipped out of bed, pulled on a skirt and blouse and crept out of her lodgings. A walk to the centre of the village would help her sleep, and besides, she could never resist any kind of festivity.

In the square, men and women in traditional costume were dancing to a band playing folk tunes and the tables outside the estaminet were busy. Jeanie thought a glass of wine would help her sleep and was looking in vain for a free table when she spotted a man sitting on his own watching the dancers, his hat tilted back on his head in a way that seemed familiar. She approached his table. He had his back to her.

'*Excusez-moi, monsieur.*'

When he turned around it took her a while to understand what she was seeing. It was Jack. His handsome face was ruined, the skin on one side a relief map of burns. They stared at each other. Jeanie reached for the table to support her weight. Jack reached for a cane and struggled to his feet to pull out a chair for her, and she sat down heavily.

'I never thought I'd see you again,' Jeanie said.

'It must be a shock. I suppose you thought I was dead.'

'That's what I heard.'

'That bloody war. That's where I got this.' He touched his cheek. 'And this.' He massaged his thigh and winced. 'But I survived. Everyone back home thinks I'm as dead as a doornail.' He barked a laugh. Jack hadn't just changed physically, he was bitter, a war casualty in more ways than one.

Jeanie didn't know what to say. Lily had been so desolate, thinking her Jack was dead, and here he was, alive and almost well. She knew she should be angry but all she felt was an overwhelming sadness, and pity for him.

'Don't you want to go home?' she said at last.

He grimaced. 'What, back to bonny Scotland? No fear, the country's a busted flush, full of pious hypocrites, ministers and priests setting the population at each other's throats, the whole place strangled by respectability.' He knocked back his drink and signalled to the waiter, who brought them a fresh bottle of white wine.

Jeanie sipped at her drink and watched Jack from over the edge of her glass. He seemed agitated, fidgeting and jiggling his good leg. To distract him, she began to tell him about the show. When she thought he was relaxed enough, she gently asked him what had happened.

He winced and looked away. After a while he spoke, his voice distant as if he were seeing the events unfold in his mind's eye. 'We were at the front. Days and nights of miserable cold and mud, the lice driving the men mad if they hadn't already been sent round the twist by the constant boom of the big guns. One night, I couldn't stand it any more, the claustrophobia of the trench, the waiting, the boredom. I went out to do a recce with my sketchbook, took the place of one of my men. Wasn't an act of bravery, just had to get out and away for a bit.'

Jack paused and lit a cigarette with a trembling hand. Jeanie saw the skin here was red and lumpy too. He inhaled and coughed. 'I did what I needed to do and was about to head back when the guns went quiet and the smoke cleared for a moment. It was eerily quiet. I heard this unearthly groaning. Spooked the hell out of me. Turns out, it was some poor bugger caught on barbed wire. I managed to untangle him and get him down into a foxhole, but he was done for, shot in the chest and neck.' He took a deep breath as if to control the emotion that had crept into his voice. 'Had to cut away the chap's jacket and shirt. All the while he was shivering and calling for his mother. A Frenchman. Told me his name was Alain, kept saying how cold he was, so I took off my jacket and wrapped it around him. Then this awful gurgling started, down in his throat. Said he couldn't breathe, kept clawing at his neck.' Jack sucked on his cigarette and Jeanie waited while he composed himself.

'After he died, I held him in my arms for a while. And I thought, bugger this, I've had enough. I took off his dog tags and put them on, and then I shot him in the face. I didn't really have a plan, I just wanted to get out of there and get away, as far away as possible. I wasn't thinking straight – there was nowhere to run to, trenches on both sides. I stood up like an idiot, in the middle of bloody no man's land. The guns started up again, and a grenade landed in the foxhole. I was trying to scramble out when it went off.'

Jeanie pressed her fingers against her mouth, but Jack didn't seem to notice. His eyes looked out over the square as if he were back on that bloody field. 'Next thing I know, I'm waking up in a French hospital. My leg was riddled with shrapnel and my face was covered in bandages. Couldn't remember my own name, and they kept calling me Alain. The name rang a bell, so I just nodded. It was only later, when I didn't need so much morphine, that I realised what had happened – the real Alain was wearing my jacket and tags. By that time, I didn't care. The war was over for me – I'd be no use on the front line with a gammy leg – and one field hospital was much the same as another. I got into a funk. Wouldn't speak. Wouldn't eat. Couldn't. It was like being in a black tunnel, no way out. Wanted to die. I was ashamed, I suppose, because I'd tried to run, hadn't cared about leaving my men behind. And there I was, useless, safe in a ward, while they were in hell. But truth is, I was scared.'

Jeanie put her hand on his arm. 'Of course you were scared, who wouldn't be?'

He wouldn't meet her eyes and moved his arm away. 'In the end, the French doctors put me into an asylum for soldiers like me; a loony bin, really.' He gave a shaky, high-pitched laugh that chilled Jeanie to the bone. 'Shell shock they call it, but I knew what I was – what I am – a coward, hiding from the war. And that's where I stayed for the rest of the war while my friends were slaughtered.'

Jeanie bit back tears. She knew the last thing he wanted was her pity.

'But people back home, don't you want to let them know you are safe and well? What about Lily?'

He pushed his hand through his hair and looked

desperate. 'There's nothing left for me back home.' They sat without talking with the sounds of merriment all around them. 'And you,' Jack said after a while. 'Are you all right now, after what happened to you? I can't imagine you'd be keen to go back to Scotland either.'

Jeanie closed her eyes. She didn't want to remember that night in the dark alley; Calum whispering obscenities in her ear. But she no longer cringed with shame at the memory; she had Stella and Viktor, and she was principal dancer on an international tour. She shrugged and forced a smile. 'I've put all that behind me.'

Still, she couldn't stop a memory of Calum's face leering into her own, the whisky stink of his breath and his wet mouth on hers. She willed herself to think of something else: Stella laughing in the bath as a baby, her round stomach poking out of the water like a little island; Stella in her ballet tutu under Madame Lebret's strict tuition, Viktor looking on proudly; Viktor in his astrakhan coat, his hair streaked with silver; the rapturous applause and the glorious, blinding spotlight as she curtseyed again and again. Jeanie's heartbeat slowed and she turned her attention back to Jack.

'Lily would want to know you're alive.'

He covered his face with his hands. 'I can't tell her, not ever. I'm ashamed. I couldn't go back as a cripple, not knowing whether she'd taken me back out of love or out of pity. And I couldn't bear her pity. I couldn't bear any of their pity. Besides, the army would consider me a deserter, and they'd be right. I'd be shot for my trouble and Lily would have to go through it all again, and she's suffered enough.' He cleared his throat and wiped his eyes. 'No, it's better this way, with everyone thinking I'm dead. After all, it's true, the old Jack who thought he had the world at his feet is dead. And good riddance to the smug bastard.'

Jeanie looked around her, at the old men in berets and the widows in their black dresses, at the children running around the square. 'And this is enough for you?'

Jack raised the glass he had refilled to his lips and drank it down before answering. 'It's cheap to live here. I do odd jobs. People leave me alone. I still paint a little, although my hands shake too much to do anything good. It's a half-life, but it's enough for half a man, don't you think?'

Jeanie rose to go, determined not to cry. She embraced him. 'Look after yourself, Jack.'

He smiled and once again he looked like his old self. 'Wee Jeanie.' She turned to go, and he caught her by the wrist. 'One last thing.'

'Anything.'

'Promise me you won't tell Lily.'

She hesitated.

'Jeanie, please.'

She nodded. But Lily had to know – she had talked about marrying Hugh, and surely she wouldn't if she knew Jack were still alive. Jeanie knew there was someone she could tell, without breaking her promise. Ned would know what to do.

43

~ *Lily* ~

Lily and Hugh were married in September. Florence was their bridesmaid and she adjusted Lily's veil outside the kirk before Lily went in.

Florence said, 'I'm so happy for you both: my two favourite people.'

Lily embraced her. 'Don't worry, I'll be a good wife to your brother. But how I wish you were coming to China with us! I'm going to miss you terribly.'

'No tears, or else your eyes will be like little red rubies and Hugh will think you're having second thoughts.'

It was a simple ceremony with only close family and friends attending. Lily's mother wept as Lily walked down the aisle with her father. Her face had creased with concern as she helped Lily into her wedding dress. 'Are you sure about this, darling?'

Lily, who had been trying to ignore a feeling of dread, dismissing it as nerves about leaving the country, found herself intensely irritated. 'We've talked about this. Stop fussing, I'm a grown woman.' Her mother bit her lip and Lily instantly regretted her harshness. She kissed her on the cheek and spoke gently. 'I'm quite sure, Mama, please be happy for me.'

Now Lily scanned the pews and saw the loving faces of her friends: Kit, craning to see her, pregnant again and looking rather drawn next to Henry, who was carrying a toddler and trying to control two boys fidgeting beside him in their velvet bloomers and lace collars. Behind them sat

Fra and Jessie Newbery. But the friend she'd longed to see most at her wedding wasn't among the guests: Jeanie. Viktor had written to say she was on tour in Europe and couldn't return in time. He'd added that she was going down a storm and the company had extended the tour.

At the wedding breakfast, Lily went looking for Kit, who looked cross and uncomfortable. '*Oof!*' she said as she sat down. 'I get bigger with every baby.'

'Congratulations! You'll soon have four beautiful children.' Lily looked over at Henry, who was surrounded by his offspring, the boys vying to clamber on his knee while he held the toddler out of harm's way. 'He seems to have taken to fatherhood well.'

Kit grimaced. 'He's devoted to our children, but I'm afraid rather neglectful of me. I seem to have lost my allure since becoming a mother.' She lowered her voice. 'I've had no end of trouble with him.'

Lily tried to look surprised. 'Young students? Are they still bowled over by him?'

'Students, neighbours, friends, servants – I've lost count of the maids whose tears I've had to dry before packing them off with some money and a good reference.'

'I'm so sorry.'

Kit looked at Hugh, who was listening to some elderly aunts. 'It'll be different for you. He's solid, not like my gadfly Henry. Better a good, reliable man than a faithless charmer. To think I gave up being an artist for him.'

Fra Newbery came bustling over and kissed her on both cheeks. 'Congratulations, my dear, I hope you'll be very happy. And remember to keep painting. Marriage needn't stop you. It didn't stop my Jessie.'

Kit had moved away to sort out her brood, and Lily glanced in her direction. 'But Kit gave up.'

'It needn't be the same for you. Kit is unhappy in her

207

marriage, and they struggle for money, I hear – Henry has run through her trust fund already.' He took her hand. 'You, my dear, are altogether tougher than our sweet Kit.'

'I'm not entirely sure I like the sound of that but thank you. It's just as well I'm moving away as the art school won't be the same without you. I hear you're moving to Dorset. You'll be sorely missed.'

'As you will be, my dear, you're a fine teacher.'

Nellie Grayson was the hardest to say goodbye to – for this was also a farewell party for Lily and Hugh.

'You will write to me in Shanghai, won't you?' Lily said, succumbing to tears at last.

'I'll keep you up to date with the art school gossip. How can I replace you? The students will be short-changed.'

~

As she prepared to go, Lily looked around the assembled company and felt a pang. As well as Jeanie, there was one other person she dearly wished could have been there. 'I couldn't get hold of Ned,' she said to Kit. 'He's still being demobbed somewhere; the MoD wouldn't tell me where his regiment was.'

'Perhaps it's better that he's not here,' Kit said. 'He's always been rather keen on you, the way he used to try to come between you and Jack.' Kit's face fell when she realised what she'd said. 'I'm sorry, Lily, you won't want to be reminded, not today of all days.'

Lily shook back her tears and smiled. 'It's all right. I'll never forget Jack – I don't want to. But I must get on with my life, it's what he would have wanted for me.'

The high emotions had wrung Lily out, and once most of the guests had gone, she was relieved when Hugh noticed she was tired and suggested he find her a cab to go back to her flat and finish packing.

'I'll look after the stragglers and come around in a couple of hours to pick you up and take you home,' he said. 'I imagine you'll want some time on your own to say goodbye to your old place.'

She stood on tiptoe to kiss him. 'You're the most thoughtful man. I'm very lucky.'

When she arrived at her flat, she took off her wedding dress with its tight corset and pulled on her comfortable handmade dress. Lily heard someone at the door and when she opened it, she saw Ned standing there, grinning. Lily threw her arms around him; she was glad to feel the soft wool of a civilian coat rather than an army greatcoat against her cheek.

'Ned! Darling Ned! How well you look.'

He grimaced. 'Don't squeeze too tight, there's a dear. Caught some shrapnel in the last act.'

Lily's hand flew to her mouth. 'Are you all right?'

'As rain! Florence patched me up. You should have seen her out there with a whole team of medics and nurses running about doing her bidding double time. She'd have made a wonderful general, better than the fools we had at any rate.' He smiled. 'Enough talk of the war! I never want to think of it again. I'm home now, back in sunny Glasgow.' He glanced out of the window at the leaden sky and she laughed.

'It's good to have you back.'

'Yes, we have lots of catching up to do. And there's something I have to tell you.' It was then that he looked around the room and noticed the half-filled trunks and cases. He turned to look at her quizzically.

'Heavens!' Lily said. 'I should have told you straight away, but I forgot in the excitement.'

'Gratified to have had that effect, I'm sure. Well go on, then, spill the beans! Are you moving to a bigger place now that you're beating off the commissions with a stick? Don't tell me you're finally leaving Bohemia for the respectable West End? My snooty neighbours will be lining up to be painted by the talented Miss Crawford.'

Lily moved a hatbox off an armchair. 'You'd better take a seat for this.' She waited until he'd sat down. 'I'm not going west but east – all the way to China.'

He stared at her. 'Very funny.'

'I'm serious, Ned. I married Hugh this morning and we sail from Glasgow as soon as he's bought our passage. He's secured a position as a physician with a hospital in Shanghai to pay the bills, but he's really going to do missionary work.'

Ned sprang to his feet and glared at her. She'd never seen him angry before and shrank back.

'You fool, you utter fool.'

'Ned!'

He grabbed her by the shoulders. 'Don't go, you're throwing away your life on someone you don't really love, not like Jack.' She recoiled at the second mention of his name that day, but Ned didn't seem to notice. 'And what the hell are you going to China for? What about your work? What about me?'

'I am going to China with a good man, to help him with his work.'

'His work? Ranting at people who don't care about his precious God, shoving his religion down the throats of the poor and gullible, just as he does here.'

'That's unfair, and you know it. Hugh's mission has done wonders for the poor in Glasgow.'

A sneer turned Ned's beautiful face ugly. 'His pretty words don't put food in their bellies or protect them from injury at work or keep them out of the clink when they can't pay their debts to the moneylenders. I never thought you'd fall for the sainted Hugh, but he must be good in bed, good enough to make you forget Jack anyway.'

Lily pulled away her hands and pressed them together to stop herself slapping him. She turned away so he couldn't see how much he'd hurt her. Lily had forgotten how cruel Ned could be. With her back to him she told him to leave. She could hear him breathing heavily, as if he'd run a race. After a while she felt his hand on her shoulder.

'Lily, please, let's not part like this.'

She shrugged off his hand. 'Get out, and don't come back.'

When she heard the door close behind him, Lily sank onto the sofa and wept.

It was only days later, as she stood on the deck of the boat bound for China and watched Glasgow fading into the distance, that she wondered what Ned had wanted to tell her.

44

~ *Jeanie* ~

When Jeanie arrived back in London from France at the
end of the summer, she didn't notice anything was amiss
at first. Stella at six was a ball of energy; she couldn't wait
to show her mother what she was learning at dance school
and plied her with questions about the tour.

'Why can't I come with you?' Stella said as she tapped
across the flagstone kitchen floor, ending in a flourish.

Jeanie could never resist her daughter's dimpled smile.
She was an enchanting child, a mixture of Viktor's dark
Russian and Jeanie's wild gypsy looks, with eyes and hair
so dark they were nearly black.

'Let me talk to your father about it.' Jeanie had every
intention of taking Stella with her when the company left
for Vienna. She missed her daughter and she missed Viktor,
but when she broached the subject, Viktor was evasive.

'It's early days,' he said. 'You go on ahead without us.
We can catch up with you.'

He seemed slower since his heart attack and had aged.
His hair was almost completely white now and he shuffled
a little when he walked bent over, like a much older man.
He complained if there was a draught and let Tatiana fuss
over him. They no longer went out in the evenings to meet
friends or go to the theatre; instead, he sat by the fire with
a blanket over his knees while Tatiana read from Tolstoy.
Jeanie stuck it out the first night, fidgeting in the stuffy
heat, unable to even follow the story, which was in Russian.
That night, lying in bed next to a snoring Viktor, she

passionately wished herself back on the road. She missed the freedom she'd had on tour, not having to think about pleasing anyone but herself. After that night, she went out with some of the dancers to catch a show and stayed out late at Daltons, the new nightclub in Leicester Square.

One morning, Jeanie came down late and stood at the dining-room door, struck by the sight of Viktor and Tatiana having breakfast together. They weren't doing anything wrong – he was reading out snippets from the newspaper while she buttered his toast – but there was something so intimate and fond in the way they looked at each other that Jeanie felt like an intruder. She cleared her throat and tried to sound casual.

'I think, perhaps, I will go ahead on tour without you.'

Viktor didn't take his eyes off the paper. 'That's a good idea.'

'And I'll take Stella with me. She's old enough now.'

He nodded. 'As you wish.'

If he'd put up a fight to keep them with him, she would have stayed, but Jeanie knew that she was in the way of the quiet domesticity he had come to enjoy with Tatiana. She was nearer his age, they spoke the same language and shared the same culture, and, unlike Jeanie, she was un-demanding. Jeanie knew that she was temperamental and volatile – traits that had once enchanted Viktor but now tired him, as did Stella's exuberance. Tatiana smiled at her from across the table and Jeanie couldn't find it in her heart to hate her, but she couldn't bear to be in this house a moment longer.

Her coffee tasted bitter and she put down the cup. 'I've a few days before the tour starts again. I'd like to go to Scotland first and catch up with some old friends.'

'You should do that – shame you missed Lily's wedding.'

It had been a blow to come home only to find out that

Lily had married Hugh. Jeanie had been astonished at the speed of the marriage, and then shocked to find another letter waiting for her from Lily telling her she was off to China, of all places. Ned had obviously not been able to tell Lily about Jack. She would go and see him in Glasgow and see if there was anything he could do.

PART 4

~ *New Ventures* ~

1919–1925

45

~ *Lily* ~

~ *Shanghai, 1919* ~

When they steamed into Shanghai on a damp, grey morning, five weeks after leaving Glasgow on the SS *Teiresias*, Lily was astonished to see the waterfront lined with magnificent buildings in the Beaux Arts style. She searched in vain for the willow-pattern pagodas of her imagination. They had already passed cotton mills and a power station belching smoke when they entered the Huangpu River at Wuson, leaving behind flat farmland scored with canals and creeks. Now, along Pudong on the opposite bank, she could see an ugly jumble of shipping wharves, paper mills, a cigarette factory, engineering works and a behemoth of an oil installation, all swathed in noxious clouds of vapour that smelt and tasted acrid. The only indication they were not sailing up the Clyde was the cluster of small houseboats that clung to the embankment wall of Shanghai, their inhabitants squatting over cooking pots or hanging out laundry, and the sampans and junks bobbing alongside the modern steamers.

Daniel O'Leary, a Roman Catholic priest they had befriended during the voyage, came up to stand between Lily and Hugh at the railing.

'That's the Bund,' he said as they passed a curve of magnificent buildings to port. 'It's mostly banks and trading houses, with a few grand hotels for the wealthy European traders, the *tai-pans*.' He pointed at a Renaissance-style structure. 'That's the McBain Building, home to the Stock

Exchange, and next to it is the new Shanghai Club, smartest place in Shanghai.'

'I'd love to dine there – it would make a change from the captain's table night after night,' Lily said.

'Men only, I'm afraid,' Daniel said. 'It's famous for its Long Bar and swanky billiard room.' He nudged Hugh. 'We should leave off our dog collars one night and pretend we're a couple of *tai-pans* talking shop over a dram of your fine Scotch whisky, or even better, a drop of far superior Irish whiskey.'

Hugh nodded absently. He would, Lily knew, be contemplating the task ahead and the burden of saving as many of the millions of souls that populated this strange land as he could. The long sea voyage had been a respite for Hugh. Daniel's jovial company had helped; he had a wealth of stories about his Shanghailander parishioners.

'There's one old biddy who spends so long in the confessional telling me about her fabricated sins that my backside is aching by the time I give her a decade or two of the rosary to get her out of my hair,' he told them as he sipped his customary brandy and ginger ale. 'Once I fell asleep and woke to hear her saying: "just as long as he pulls my nightie down when it's over, I can put up with it, but do I have to do my duty every night, Father? Even the Almighty got a day off.'"

Hugh had thrown his head back and laughed. 'I suspect, Daniel, that she has developed a fondness for you and is trying to inflame your desires by detailing her sins of the flesh.'

'In the name of the Wee Man! Do you think so? What a thought!'

'It's a danger we men of the cloth are all too aware of – the worshipful looks from lonely women,' Hugh said.

Lily suppressed a smile at the thought of the pious women at the Fellowship, their hearts under their plain dresses bursting with secret passion for Hugh.

'Ah,' the priest had said, 'but you have such a charming and lovely wife, I'm sure you have no trouble resisting any temptations of the flesh thrown your way.'

Hugh smiled fondly at Lily. 'I am indeed a fortunate man.'

Daniel had beamed at Lily. 'Hugh tells me that you're an artist, and a talented one at that. You will find China has many fascinating subjects to set your imagination alight.'

The priest was knowledgeable about art and they had many happy conversations as the steamship ploughed its course through the Suez Canal into the Arabian Sea and out past the Bay of Bengal. By the time they reached the South China Sea, Lily and Daniel were firm friends.

Now, as the steamship was nudged into the public dock by a flotilla of small boats, Lily found she was loath to be parted from this jolly man who had become a welcome third wheel in their new marriage. She tuned back into Daniel, who was still giving them a guided tour of the Bund, pointing out the Hongkong and Shanghai Bank and the Customs House with its tall clock tower.

'You'll feel quite at home when you hear its chimes, they're copied from Big Ben,' Father O'Leary said. 'At the far end of the Bund you'll find the Public Gardens, which are strictly reserved for foreigners. Even the *amahs* who take the European children to the gardens are not allowed to sit on the benches around the bandstand.'

As the gangway was being put into place, Father O'Leary told Lily a little about the city that would become her new home. 'You'll want to go to Nanking Road, the smart shopping street of the International Settlement – that's the area of Shanghai founded by the British and Americans. There's a new department store that all the ladies go mad for, built only this year, the Wing On. Further along, after the Jing'an Temple, it becomes Bubbling Well Road.'

'What a pretty name!' Lily said.

'A pretty name for a pretty place; it has wide streets lined with trees – lovely for a stroll. It's where all the wealthiest westerners live and play; there are theatres, grand hotels and, of course, the Shanghai racecourse, a boon to an Irishman like me with a love of the horses.'

This last comment seemed to rouse Hugh from his reverie. 'I'm afraid I haven't any time for that sort of thing, but Lily might enjoy all the new sights and experiences.'

Lily seized her chance. 'Perhaps you could show me around Shanghai, Daniel. It sounds like I'm going to need a friend with my husband tied up with his work at the hospital. I should hate to lose touch after all these weeks spent in your company.'

'Don't worry; you won't get rid of me that easily. You can always find me at St Ignatius, the cathedral in Frenchtown. That's what foreigners – or Shanghailanders, as you must learn to speak of them – call the French Concession.' He smiled at her. 'I should also like to stay in touch, and I'd be delighted to show you around, if that's all right with your man, of course.'

Hugh was watching the crew unloading the passengers' luggage and spoke distractedly. 'Of course, Lily can do as she pleases.'

They walked unsteadily down the gangway into a sea of movement and noise. The cacophony came from everywhere: the hordes of flashy American cars that choked the road, honking like angry geese; the shuddering blare of ships' horns that ripped apart the air, and the bloodcurdling shrieks from steamers' whistles; the clatter of rickshaws and the squeak of wheelbarrows; the incomprehensible cries of street hawkers and coolies. Beneath these piercing sounds was a polyglot hubbub of a million conversations between the Chinese, Europeans and Russians crowding the quay.

Lily waited while Hugh went to find their luggage. Although she was used to the bustle of Glasgow, the sheer number of people here overwhelmed her. Shanghai was a larger, busier and more impressive sight than any city she had seen before.

'Dreadful place, isn't it? But I do love it,' Daniel said as he caught up with her, clutching a battered portmanteau he was trying to keep away from an over-eager coolie. 'There's a saying the Chinese have: Shanghai is like the Emperor's ugly daughter; she never has to worry about finding suitors.' He gave up his struggle and let go of his luggage. 'There, you can have it, you devil. I suppose you want to be paid too, to carry it four feet to my rickshaw?' Lily saw him empty his pockets into the Chinaman's hand.

She leaned over and kissed the priest on his pink shaven cheek. 'You're an old softie, Daniel.'

'Less of the old! I was considered quite the catch in Tipperary. You should have heard all the lassies weeping and wailing when my mother sent me to the seminary.' He grew serious suddenly. 'Lily, I hate to leave you here in this city: it's a wonderful but terrible place. I know you have your husband, but you will spend a lot of time alone. The life of a clergyman's wife can be a lonely one. If you ever need anything, anything at all, just send word to me at the cathedral.'

'I will, Daniel, but we Scotswomen are remarkably resilient. I will get in touch but only to beg you to visit us – I'll need your company. You're right, Hugh is going to be busy here between the hospital and the China Inland Mission.'

'Well, my advice is build a life for yourself. And come and see me, often.' He mopped his face with a handkerchief and blew his nose, a ruse, she could see, to hide his tears. 'Now where's that blasted coolie? If he's stolen my bag,

221

he'll get a fright when he opens it and finds nothing but rosary beads, holy water and my even holier underwear.'

He bustled away to the waiting rickshaw and Lily turned to search for her husband. Surrounded by a press of people, she felt desperately alone and was about to start panicking when she saw Hugh, a full head taller than most of the Europeans and towering over the Chinese. Relieved, she waved at him and he made his way through the crowd towards her. Everything was strange and deeply foreign; Glasgow seemed so far away. Lily wondered what Jeanie was doing and felt a pang of regret.

46

∼ *Jeanie* ∼

Jeanie got off the train at Central Station and went straight to Ned's office in West Nile Street. He looked thinner and more lined, but otherwise as elegant as ever. He seemed pleased to see her and insisted on taking her out for lunch.

'We have a lot to talk about, but not on an empty stomach – there's nothing a rare steak and a fine claret can't make better,' he said, pulling on his coat.

At the restaurant, once the maître d' had stopped fussing over Ned and they were finally alone, Jeanie found she had no appetite. She pushed aside her plate and drank some wine.

'What happened, Ned? I was relying on you to tell Lily about Jack. I couldn't, he made me promise not to, but I didn't think you'd be so squeamish.'

'Your telegram didn't get to me for weeks. I was being demobbed and moved around a lot, a tedious business. By the time I got back to Glasgow it was too late and she'd married that ghastly man.'

'What possessed her? She couldn't have picked a more different man from Jack.'

'Lonely, I suppose, and weary. Misery can be so exhausting, don't you find?'

'Still, to marry someone because you're lonely doesn't seem right.'

Ned raised his eyebrows. 'But it's all right to be a mistress out of convenience.'

Jeanie glared at him. 'How dare you!'

He smirked. 'Don't mind me, old girl, I'm the last person to judge, but you and Viktor aren't exactly love's young dream. At least I can understand what you get out of it, but what on earth can Lily be thinking of, trekking off to the other side of the world and leaving everything and everyone behind.

Jeanie thought of the house in Chelsea, the drawing room with Russian ornaments and keepsakes cluttering every surface; of the chintzy cushions lovingly bashed into shape every day by Tatiana, house proud the way Jeanie had never been. 'Maybe she just needed to get away.'

'Damned selfish of her! What about me?' He looked like a sulky schoolboy for a moment and Jeanie smothered a laugh.

When they finally laid down their napkins, Jeanie could barely move. After starving herself to get her figure back, she wasn't used to eating so much and waved away the dessert trolley.

Ned leaned towards her across the table and became serious and businesslike. 'I do have some news you'll be interested in, so your journey isn't a complete waste of time.'

'Oh yes? Have you found a way to get Lily out of this marriage?'

'Sadly, no, there's nothing I can do there, and don't think for a moment that I'm going to tell her about Jack now.'

'No, that would be cruel. But, can't you go out to France and persuade Jack to come home?'

'There's the small matter of his desertion. He'd be arrested as soon as he set foot in Britain.'

'Surely you can do something? He can't have been in his right mind. Isn't that a defence?'

Ned shook his head. 'The government has come down hard on deserters and he wouldn't stand a chance. At best,

I could get him committed, but that's no life. No, he's better off where he is, living freely under an assumed name.' He signalled the waiter. 'Brandy?' he said to Jeanie, who shook her head. He ordered coffees before turning his attention back to her. 'Now, to prove that I'm not completely useless, I've tracked down our old friend Calum Mackay.'

Jeanie clutched her hands together under the table. After all these years the name still had the power to make her come out in a cold sweat. 'Is that bastard still in Glasgow?'

'Yes, but safely banged up in Barlinnie Prison, and for a long, long time. I told you the law would catch up with him.'

Jeanie steadied her breathing. 'What did he do?'

'After bleeding poor gullible Widow Fraser dry, he ran off with her niece. They'd been carrying on under her nose for quite some time. He would have got away with it if the niece hadn't been fourteen. Her father's high up in the Corporation and made sure he went down for it. Sadly, they didn't catch Mackay until he'd abandoned her and pawned her jewellery, but it did mean he was given a longer sentence.'

Jeanie sat back in her chair and blew a curl away from her eyes. 'You know, I think I will have a brandy. No, I'll tell you what, let's have champagne.'

Ned grinned at her. 'That's my girl!'

The lead weight that had been pressing on Jeanie's chest since she'd stepped off the train lifted. Calum had got what was coming to him at last. It was a pity she hadn't been in court to see the weasel's smug face fall. Her feet twitched; she wanted to dance through the streets, shouting and singing, and she longed above all else to tell Lily what had happened. Jeanie sighed. Glasgow wasn't the same without her old friend. She wondered if she would ever see Lily again, and what she was doing right now.

225

47

∼ *Lily* ∼

Lily's head was down the toilet. She retched and brought up clear bile. Hugh hovered in the doorway to their hotel suite.

'Shall I ask for some ginger ale?'

'It must have been something I ate. But it feels more like seasickness. Oh God, here I go again.' Lily bent over the toilet bowl again.

Hugh helped her to bed and she slid between the sheets. The waves of nausea receded, but Lily still felt miserable. Their first week in Shanghai had been a disappointment: she'd been desperate to explore the city but had felt so unwell that she'd been confined to the hotel room.

Hugh placed his cool hand on her forehead. 'You don't have a temperature. I may be wrong, but could you be pregnant?'

Lily's eyes snapped open and she made a quick calculation. She hadn't had a monthly bleed since before her wedding, more than two months ago. She'd been so caught up with the wedding and the move to China that she hadn't noticed. She looked up at Hugh's concerned face and nodded. His expression softened and he kissed her forehead.

'You'd never think you were a doctor's daughter and married to a doctor.'

Lily instantly forgot all about her nausea. Suddenly she was ravenously hungry. She turned to Hugh. 'Let's go down to dinner.'

'Are you sure?'

'Quite sure.'

'Your colour looks better. Perhaps it would do you good, make a change from this room.'

Lily had a bath, carefully soaping her tender breasts. She put on her best dress and the moonstone drop earrings Hugh had given her as a wedding present. He came up behind her and put his arms around her.

'You smell divine and look luscious, like a ripe peach. I want to take a bite out of you.' His teeth nipped her earlobe and she laughed and shrugged him off. He lifted Lily's hair and kissed the nape of her neck, sending delighted shivers down her spine. 'Pregnancy suits you. I've never seen you looking so well. Plump as a partridge.'

She slapped the hands that were sliding down the front of her dress. 'How ungallant you are! Are you saying I've put on weight?'

'Only a little.'

'Well, I'm glad it wasn't the nine-course dinners on board ship.' Lily placed her hands on her flat stomach and wondered at the life growing inside her. A baby! Hugh put his hand over hers and she sighed with happiness. She was carrying the child she had never had with Jack. Lily pushed her fingers through Hugh's blonde thatch of hair, and he leaned down to kiss her.

When they drew apart, there were tears in his eyes. 'I've always wanted a child; it's a miracle.'

Lily laughed. 'Perhaps not such a miracle given how much time we spend in bed.' Ever since their first time, their lovemaking had grown wilder, and sometimes she'd find bruises and scratches on her body afterwards. It was so different from the tenderness of Jack's lovemaking, but then Hugh was so different – driven and zealous, and filled with stormy emotions, where Jack had been playful and charming. Lily shook off the wave of sadness that had crept up on her and tried to recapture the joy she'd felt a few moments earlier: she was going to be a mother!

She checked her hair in the mirror and turned to Hugh. 'Let's go to dinner. I'm so hungry I could eat a scabby horse.'

'What a disgusting expression,' Hugh said mildly. 'I must try it on O'Leary when I see him next.'

48

∼ *Jeanie* ∼

The train journey back to London gave Jeanie plenty of time to think about her future. The tour of France had opened her eyes to the world, and she was eager to see more of it. And without Viktor around, she'd had more authority in the company, the choreographer and director asking for her opinion more and more. The thought of going back to the little house in Chelsea, which had been such a sanctuary when Stella was a baby, now made her shrink into her seat. She loved Viktor, but he was frailer now, and she knew he had welcomed the chance to stay at home rather than go on the road. Really, she shouldn't leave him again; he was so unwell. And he'd done so much for her, lifting her out of poverty and giving her the chance to shine as a professional dancer. Without him, she'd still be scrubbing floors. Even so, as the train grew nearer to London, Jeanie felt as if she was being swallowed up.

She arrived home to find Viktor dozing by the fire. He woke and smiled sleepily when she bent to kiss him on the forehead.

'How was Glasgow?'

'Cold, wet.'

'You'll be glad to be back home, then.'

Jeanie tried to muster a smile. Viktor patted the arm of his chair. 'Come and sit beside me, little bird.' He took her hand. 'I've been thinking, while you were away, that this is not much of a life for you. But you'll be back on tour soon.'

She slid onto his lap. 'I've been thinking, too, that I

should stay here with you, look after you, make sure you're not sneaking the odd cheeky cigar.'

Viktor was silent for a while. He pushed her gently off his lap and she sat opposite him. 'I don't want you here as a nursemaid, looking after me. I want you to be free – I've always wanted that for you. What would make me happy, is for you to be free. I want you to leave me.'

'What?'

Viktor smiled at her. 'I'm glad I can still surprise you.' He pointed at his desk. 'There's a banker's draught giving you enough money to set up on your own, and to look after Stella and pay for her schooling. My will is there, too, leaving this house and the rest of my estate to you. Otherwise, Anna will get the lot, and she already has more money than she knows what to do with.'

Jeanie wrung her hands. 'Why are you saying this? Don't you love me any more?' A thought stopped her. 'Viktor, have you got worse? What did the doc say?'

He put up his hand to calm her. 'I'm as well as can be expected for someone who has had a heart attack and who has led a good life. No, I'm thinking about your future – yours and Stella's. And I don't want you stuck here, resenting me. Jeanie, my little Jeanie, take this as a gift of love, from me to you.' Viktor leaned his head back against the chair and closed his eyes. 'I'm not going to argue any more. I'm too tired.'

Jeanie sat and watched him sleep. After a while she stood up and pulled the tartan rug up over his chest. Upstairs she found Tatiana packing for her. Jeanie stood at the door. When Tatiana looked up, she said, 'You knew what Viktor was going to say to me.'

'Yes, he told me. And I think he's right.'

Jeanie walked into the room and sat on the bed. 'But I owe him so much. I can't leave him now, when he's so weak.'

230

'That's exactly why he wants to let you go. He's a proud man and doesn't want you to see him like this.'

Jeanie picked up a silk shawl and ran it through her fingers. Viktor had bought it for her. 'Will you stay with him, to look after him?'

Tatiana turned from the wardrobe. 'No.'

'He's happier with you than with me. Besides, my cooking's mocket.'

'No, Jeanie, I'm not anyone's consolation prize. I'm coming with you and Stella.'

'Aye, but—'

'You thought because we're both Russian and I made Viktor borscht and read Tolstoy to him that he was beginning to prefer me? I could tell from your face when you came back from France what you were thinking. I've known you a long time, Jeanie.'

'I wasn't jealous, you know.'

'I know. But I'm not your easy way out. Viktor has given you the chance to leave with your love for each other intact – take it.'

Jeanie looked at her hands. 'Who's going to look after him if the two of us scarper?'

'There are plenty of women needing work. I've already found one to live in as his nurse.'

'You've got everything planned out. I can see the pair of you've been thick as thieves while I've been away.'

Tatiana sat down next to Jeanie and put her arm around her. 'Don't sulk. This has been a long time coming. Viktor knows that if he tries to keep you in a cage, you'll grow to hate him one day.' She stood up. 'Enough chit-chat! We have work to do. You'd better go and talk to Stella while I pack.'

231

49

～ *Lily* ～

Lily and Hugh had been in Shanghai for two months. Hugh had taken up his post at the hospital, and he spent his spare time on so-called Missionary Row, a road dotted with Protestant churches that ran behind the British consulate on the Bund. Left to her own devices most of the time, Lily began to explore the streets around the hotel now that her morning sickness had lifted. She went with Hugh once to the Union Church to meet the other men and their wives, but could tell by their frozen expressions that she didn't quite fit the bill for a missionary's wife. The others took an immediate dislike to her, which Lily reciprocated, and for a moment she longed to be back in Glasgow, at the Mack, surrounded by colourful eccentrics.

Hugh didn't seem to notice the frisson of antipathy in the air and talked about his plans all the way back to the Palace Hotel. He burned to go into China's wild interior, taking the Word of God to remote villages just as he had taken it to the poor in the slums of Glasgow. What's more, he wanted to dress in native costume like the great missionary Hudson Taylor. In their hotel room, Hugh showed Lily the simple blue trousers and padded tunic a tailor had run up for him that morning and rushed to try them on.

When he stood in front of her, she bit her lip and tried not to laugh. 'If you think it would help, I suppose you could wear that.'

'But?'

'But I see from my daily walks along the Bund and down Nanking Road that the Chinese are small in stature and you're so tall and broad. Many of the Shanghainese men wear suits and the women are strikingly glamorous – they wouldn't be out of place on Bond Street, let alone Sauchiehall Street. The only people I see dressed like that,' she gestured to Hugh in his blue cotton trousers and tunic, 'are rickshaw men and coolies.'

Hugh frowned at his reflection. 'Of course you're right, damn it. I look ridiculous. I worry, though, that when I go into the interior, where many people will never have seen a foreigner before, that I will stand out.'

'Darling, you're going to stand out no matter what you wear.'

Hugh changed back into his black suit jacket and trousers, although she saw he folded his Chinese clothes and put them in a sailor's duffel bag he had bought for his trip. Lily was beginning to find out that Hugh could be stubborn and wasn't used to people disagreeing with him.

But Lily was also used to getting her own way and made excuses not to go with him again to Missionary Row. Instead, she spent her evenings sitting in the hotel's rooftop garden, where she could hear the strains from the band that played in the Public Gardens, and her days wandering the streets of the International Settlement and the neighbouring French Concession, while Hugh was with his fellow missionaries or at the hospital. She soon discovered she preferred Frenchtown, redolent with the scents of baking bread and roasting coffee beans.

Lily's heart, heavy after years of mourning for Jack, lightened as she strolled in the cool of tree-lined Avenue Joffre, peering through arched and gated entrances to the *lilongs* or alleys. These bustling lanes were like tiny villages, home to several three-storey houses where families lived virtually on top of each other. Some were quite beautiful; a melange of Chinese and Western styles had produced the Shikumen houses – brick terraced buildings with elaborately carved doorways unique to Shanghai. Lily was fascinated by these glimpses into everyday Chinese life just off the grand shopping boulevards, which struck her as surprisingly like the wide tree-lined streets of European cities; she could have been in Holland Park. It was here that she drank tiny cups of strong coffee in smart cafés and nibbled at French pastries while admiring the elegant women strolling past dressed in the latest Paris fashions.

Lily soon realised the home-made, embroidered aesthetic-style dresses she'd worn in Glasgow marked her out as an oddball in chic Shanghai, while her more conventional clothes seemed dowdy and unfashionable and, as her waist thickened, were becoming too tight. She decided to go shopping on Nanking Road and spent a few happy days visiting Hall & Holtz and Weeks & Co. as well as the two new Chinese department stores, the Sincere and the Wing On, where the fashionable Chinese women shopped. The assistants seemed to be mostly aristocratic but impoverished Russian women, émigrés from the revolution that had stripped them of their privilege and their nationality. Despite their mournful expressions, these women had remarkable taste and fitted Lily in the new simple, sleek style. She adored the casual elegance and was relieved to see she would not have to return to wearing a punishing corset as the clothes were loose and cunningly draped to flatter the figure.

On the last day of her fittings, she collected her parcels and made her way back to the Palace Hotel. It was night-time but the Nanking Road was brightly lit with neon signs and fluttered with red and gold banners in Chinese script. The pavements were thronged with pedestrians and the road was a bright river of cars, carriages, rickshaws, wheel-barrows and bicycles. Winter in Shanghai was chilly and damp enough to make her bones ache, so she was glad of her final purchase: a warm coat trimmed with Siberian fox fur. She wore it on the rickshaw drive home, her nose buried in the soft fur, surrounded by packages beautifully wrapped in coloured paper and tied with silk ribbons.

Hugh came back to the hotel that evening after a double shift at the hospital where, she later found out, he'd attended a breech birth that had ended badly. Both mother and twins had died. When he came in, exhausted and white-faced, he still had dried blood under his fingernails and his eyes were sunk deep and hollow. Lily, elated and invigorated by her day, didn't notice the state he was in when he walked in to find her surrounded by tissue paper, with dresses, coats, hats, jackets and shoes spilling from boxes. She had been admiring herself in the floor-length mirror, wearing one of her new purchases – a bottle-green, velvet coatdress trimmed with sable and tied loosely at the waist – and spun round to show it off.

'What do you think?'

Hugh folded his arms, his face carved in granite. 'I think it is a waste of money that could have been spent on our cause.'

At first Lily didn't detect the danger in his quiet tone and thought to tease him out of his mood. She laughed lightly as she leaned into the mirror and smoothed an eyebrow. 'Don't be such an ogre, darling. I'm an artist, I love clothes, and these ones are so gorgeous and modern. Besides, it's not mission money but my own.' She glanced at his reflection and saw his expression darken, realising too late how angry he was.

His voice was strangled with fury. 'Perhaps you forget we are husband and wife now, and that it is I who control the household budget. First thing tomorrow, you will return every single one of these fripperies. People are starving in this country and you're spending our money on clothes when you have a wardrobe full of them.'

Lily turned to face him, her own anger mounting. 'Don't be ridiculous, I can't and I won't return them. They've been tailored to fit me and I need suitable clothes. Or do you expect me to go out naked? I'm not sure those po-faced sticks at your precious mission would approve.'

Hugh strode across the room and yanked open the hotel door. Before she could speak again, he had slammed it behind him.

Hours later he returned. She didn't look up from the book she was pretending to read in bed.

He sat next to her and stroked her hair. 'Forgive me, my darling. I was a brute. I should be more careful of your condition.' His hand slipped to her belly, but she lifted it off.

'I've never allowed anyone to talk to me like that, and I won't start now. I may be your wife, but I'm not your chattel. You frightened me – I've never seen you like that before.'

He passed his hand over his face. 'I don't know what came over me. This place has pushed me off balance. I'm expected to be always at the hospital where I feel I'm wasting my time treating rich, spoiled Shanghailanders rather than tending to the poor and needy who really need my help, both as a medic and a priest. Then today, well . . .' He told her about the young woman who had come pregnant with twins. 'She called on God, but it was no use. It was up to me to save them, but I couldn't. I failed.'

Lily placed a protective hand on her belly, and he placed his hand on hers. This time she didn't throw it off. 'You're just tired. You've been doing too much since you came

236

here. Perhaps you're coming down with something? Daniel said the miasma from the river causes all sorts of fevers we're unfamiliar with back home.'

'No, it's not that, I'm not sick. I feel I'm losing my way.' He rubbed his eyes. 'What good am I doing in the hospital? I hate being a doctor, and all around me there's so much misery and squalor and corruption. I thought the Glasgow slums were bad but it's worse here, to see such obscene wealth and decadence while people starve to death in the streets.' He clenched his fists. 'The city is riddled with brothels, dance halls and opium dens. I feel I'm drowning in sin and powerless to do anything about it.'

Lily listened wordlessly: her husband's Sodom and Gomorrah vision of the city didn't tally with the one she was beginning to know.

Hugh reached for Lily's hand. 'It will be better when I'm in the interior, away from this filth, breathing the country air and mixing with simple men and women. I promise this bout of temper will not happen again.'

That night, Hugh was unusually tender, careful not to hurt her in bed, and Lily was reassured. She had been shocked by his temper. Perhaps she was partly to blame – she had got carried away and spent too much. But she wasn't used to answering to anyone about her spending.

Lily turned to a cooler side of the pillow. They'd had their first fight as a married couple. It was normal. In his sleep, Hugh turned his back on her, and she put her arm around him and listened to the slow, steady beat of his heart.

50

~ *Jeanie* ~

The theatre doors swung shut behind her and Jeanie held her head high and walked off down the Strand. This was the fifth company she'd been to see, and each and every one of the impresarios had showered her with compliments before giving her the same answer with varying excuses: *Sorry, I'd love to have you on board but funds are tight . . . I've just taken on a principal . . .* She had left Viktor's company, feeling it wasn't right to take his money and stay on as his principal dancer now they were no longer together. Turning her back on the tour had been a wrench, but she had her principles, not to mention her pride. Jeanie had assumed she could walk into any company in London, but she was finding it harder than she'd imagined. Now she straightened her shoulders and walked on to the next theatre. There was one last manager to see.

Rinaldi came out of from behind his desk to greet her. '*Cara mia!* You grow more beautiful every time I see you.' He kissed her on both cheeks and ushered her into a chair and leaned against his desk, beaming at her. 'How can I help you?' He wagged his finger playfully. 'I hope you're not here to poach one of my dancers.'

Jeanie laughed and looked up at him through her lashes; a little flirting wouldn't hurt. 'You know I've always admired the way you run your company – the marvellous shows you put on and how you treat your dancers like family.'

He stretched out his arms. 'It's true, I'm Papa Rinaldi

– everyone's father, from the youngest lighting apprentice to the leading lady.'

'And that's exactly what I want – to be your leading lady.'

Rinaldi's expression shut down abruptly and he moved back behind his desk. 'I'm afraid that's impossible.'

Jeanie, exasperated, dropped her coy act and glared at him. 'Why? Why is it impossible? I know for certain that you lost your principal dancer and that you haven't started auditions yet. I thought, with my reputation and star appeal, you'd bite my hand off.'

Rinaldi sighed and moved a pen and ink set fractionally to one side. 'I could tell you a pack of polite lies, but I respect you too much. The truth is everyone is too afraid of Viktor to take you on. Word is out that you split up.'

Jeanie went still. Outside the office window, a tram rumbled past. 'But Viktor wanted this separation, I'm here with his blessing. We're still pals and there are no bad feelings between us.'

Rinaldi shrugged. 'That's what he says, but you know how emotional the Russians can be, they're as passionate and volatile as we Italians. Ivanov is a powerful man and he has the financiers in his pocket. All he has to do is have a quiet word and they'd withdraw their backing. I can't risk it, I've too many people depending on me for a living.'

Jeanie could feel herself beginning to panic. Was she washed-up already? She stood to leave, and Rinaldi got up to open the door for her.

'My advice to you is to start teaching – a nice little dance school for the *bambini*, eh?'

He looked down at her with such benign concern that Jeanie could have slapped him. Instead she summoned her best, most dazzling stage smile. 'Don't worry about me, Carlo, I'll be fine.' She held back her tears until she was inside a cab, where nobody could see her cry.

51

∼ *Lily* ∼

After their fight, Hugh was on his best behaviour, attendant to Lily's every need and the cravings that sent him running to the street vendors to bring back *xiaolongbao*, the fried pork dumplings with their hidden explosion of hot salty broth. Lily began to find his solicitude for her and the baby she was carrying suffocating: he wanted her to stay in the hotel and insisted on going with her on her walks.

'It's not safe for you to go out alone. This city is a sewer. Some of the things I've come across would make you faint with horror and disgust,' he said.

Lily, whose eyes had been opened by visits to the Cowcaddens slums and the salty company of her theatre and dance friends, doubted she would be either horrified or disgusted, but she kept her counsel and tried to put up with Hugh's attentiveness. There was a new feverish brightness in his eyes, and she was wary of starting another fight while his nerves were still overwrought. All the same, she missed her solitary walks and her fingers itched for pencil and paper to draw the scenes that were so new and strange to her. When they were out together, Hugh kept up a swift pace, talking at her all the while. He seemed not to see the men hunched over mah-jong, the barber plying his trade outside a doorway, the hot water shops with their bright copper kettles and pans. Hurrying after him and casting wistful looks over her shoulder at the homely bustle she glimpsed in the narrow alleyways, Lily vowed she would be back with her sketchbook as soon as she could get away.

Deprived of the freedom to absorb the city through drawing and bored by the afternoon naps Hugh insisted on for the health of their baby, Lily grew more bored and frustrated. Her great adventure in China was proving to be a weary prison sentence. One day, while Hugh was at the Inland Mission's headquarters, Lily stared out of the hotel window at the junks going down the river. As she watched the movement of the water, her mind stole back to that first summer in Cockburnspath with Jack: how carefree she had been, how she would lie in his arms for hours afterwards as they talked until dawn and he left her, replete and sleepy, for his own room. Lily felt a flutter and put a hand on her growing belly.

'It will be better when you're here, not long now,' she whispered to the baby inside her. But when she counted off the months of her pregnancy – five – she felt impatient for the birth.

Lily's enforced idleness came to an end shortly afterwards, when Hugh announced he would be leaving on his first trip into the interior and would be away for three months. She slipped into their bathroom and stifled a scream of joy with a towel. When she emerged, she calmly helped him pack his duffel bag.

'The Mission ladies will look after you while I'm away,' he said. 'The Smythson sisters have identified a house they think will be suitable for us, so you should call in on them to thank them.' He handed her a piece of paper. 'Here's the address for the place they've found us.' Lily shuddered at the thought of the two spinster sisters whose mouths had puckered when they met her, reminding her of an expression Jeanie had often used for someone whose face looked like they'd been 'sooking lemons'. Now she only smiled and agreed she would call on them the following day and make arrangements to move into the house.

241

Instead, the next morning, minutes after she had waved Hugh off, she raced back to the room to collect her drawing materials, her heart soaring and her mind clear of the fog that had been clouding it for so long. Energy crackled through her veins, propelling her across the busy road through the honking taxis, the cars and the rickshaws, to the waterfront. Here dock workers shouted to each other while struggling under heavy burdens and Chinese women worked on their houseboats, cooking and stringing washing along the ropes. Lily unfolded her canvas stool and didn't move from it for hours, her hand racing over the paper.

Finally, she stretched her back and looked out over the wide curving river. The fog had lifted, and the day was a bright new penny despite the January cold. Relishing the familiar weariness in her back and arms, she tucked her drawing bag under her arm and made her way to the backstreets of Frenchtown, inhaling the sharp tang of spices and sweet smell of fried food. Suddenly hungry, she followed her nose down a lane and came across a Chinese family sitting outside their door eating a meal, elbows on the table and bowls held to their chins to scoop the rice into their mouths without dropping a grain. The father, a middle-aged man with a kindly expression, waved his chopsticks at her.

'Welcome, madam! Are you hungry? Come and join us!' He spoke with a peculiar accent that Lily was sure held traces of Scottish. The man turned to speak to his wife. She went back into their house and came out with a steaming bowl, which she handed to Lily with a bow and a friendly smile. Lily shook her head, unwilling to take food from the mouths of the children, but the woman frowned and tugged at her sleeve. She beckoned Lily over to the table and sat down next to three red-cheeked boys, who were doing a poor job at stifling their giggles. Lily tried in her rudimentary Mandarin to say a halting thanks, which only resulted in the children laughing so much that the smallest boy, his cheeks bulging with food, fell off his stool. The father barked a warning and turned to Lily.

'Forgive my son, he has forgotten his manners,' he said.

Lily waved away his apology. 'You speak perfect English.'

He bowed slightly. 'Thank you! I worked for many years for a Scottish family, the Buchanans, before they moved back to Aberdeen. I was their Number One Boy, and I also helped Mr Buchanan, a tea merchant. I helped him do business with the Chinese. He was a canny man.'

Lily smiled at the familiar word. 'But I'm Scottish too, although not from Aberdeen.' She held out her hand and he took it, to more snorts of laughter from the children. 'I'm Lily Crawford— I mean Lily Anderson.'

'Huan Liu, at your service.'

As they ate – the food was delicious, and she tried not to eat too greedily – Lily told Huan Liu she was an artist. After she had finished her bowl, she amused the children by making quick-fire sketches of them. They looked at her with shining eyes and spoke all at once and so quickly she couldn't understand them.

'I'm sorry,' she said to Huan Liu. 'I've been learning Mandarin but it's terribly difficult for me. What are they saying?'

He chuckled. 'The reason you can't understand any of their silly babblings is that we speak Shanghainese, a variant of Mandarin but different enough to make it hard for Europeans to understand. My own mother tongue is Cantonese. I came up from Kowloon in the south to find work and married a girl from Shanghai.' He smiled at his wife, who ducked her head shyly. 'Who has blessed me with three fine sons.' He nodded at his children, his eyes full of warmth. 'My boys are asking if you would draw more pictures of them, but they have chores to do.' He spoke sharply and they scuttled into the darkness of the house. His wife bowed to Lily and followed them, pausing at the doorway to issue a volley of sharp instructions to the gigglers inside.

Huan Liu proved to be fascinating company, telling Lily about the tea trade and life in Shanghai. When she told him she was about to move into a house, he asked if she would be looking for staff.

'I would be honoured if you would take me on as Number One Boy,' he said with another small bow.

'I think that's a splendid idea,' Lily said, and made a careful note of the *lilong* as she said goodbye.

It was dusk when she got back to the Palace Hotel to find an invitation to tea from a Nancy Thornton.

A friend of mine, whose husband works with yours at the hospital, told me you're new to Shanghai – nothing escapes our gossipy little community! I'd be so pleased if you'd come to tea tomorrow. I enclose a badly drawn map and directions so you don't get lost.

The address was near St Ignatius. Lily could visit Daniel afterwards. She had made one new friend that day and felt sure she was about to make another. At last, she began to feel less strange in Shanghai.

~

Nancy Thornton was a thin American with a bright eye and an amused expression. Her hair was in a Marcel Wave and she wore the dropped waist and elegant silhouette Lily so admired.

'What brought you to Shanghai?' Lily said. Nancy took

a cigarette out of a silver case and tapped it expertly to pack the tobacco before lighting the end. She raised an eyebrow and offered the case to Lily, who shook her head. The American inhaled and blew smoke out through her nose. She was like a terribly chic cowboy, Lily thought.

'My dear!' Nancy drawled in an accurate imitation of an English upper-class accent. 'One never asks why someone has come to Shanghai. It's assumed everyone has something to hide.'

Lily was intrigued. 'And do you?'

'What?'

'Have something to hide?'

Nancy laughed and reverted to her own accent. 'You're awfully direct for an English gal.'

'Scottish. We don't mince our words where I come from.'

'Quite right too! I shall never get used to the mealy-mouthed politeness of the Shanghailanders, a vicious tribe of philistines who would eat you alive as soon as look at you.' Lily laughed as she pictured the Mission ladies with bibs around their necks clutching silver cutlery, ready to tuck into their latest victim. Nancy flashed a wide smile. 'In answer to your question, sadly, I have nothing to hide. I'm not nearly interesting enough.' She lowered her voice. 'But I can tell you who does.'

Lily blinked. She was wary of gossip, but she couldn't resist this charming woman. After a pause she murmured: 'Do tell!'

'First, you must be introduced to the main characters in our little Shanghai drama. My delicious morsels of scandals will taste all the better once you know who's who in our giddy social circle. And there will be plenty of opportunities, as your husband is away and our babies are not yet here.' She laid a hand on her nearly flat stomach. 'It's a perfect time for you to dive into the social round.'

Lily was instantly drawn to Nancy, a journalist with a string of published novels that were doing well both in North America and Britain. She had come to Shanghai when her husband Joe, also a journalist, was offered a senior position at the *North China Daily News*.

'I've always been a sucker for adventure, so here we landed a couple of years ago. Joe's paid twice what he would get in the States; I can mooch off him while I wait for glorious motherhood.' Nancy was eager to help Lily – a kindness, she began to realise, that was common among expatriates, who knew what it was like to land in a foreign country where you know nobody. The American woman offered to take her shopping.

Inwardly wincing at the unhappy memory that threw up, Lily said: 'I've already been on a shopping spree, I'm afraid, and spent my clothing allowance.'

'Let me at least introduce you to my tailor. You'll need your clothes adjusting as the baby grows, as well as after the little bundle of joy arrives. I'll ask him to call on you at the Palace Hotel, if you like?'

'That would be kind, thank you.' Lily paused. 'But my most pressing need is a new home. Some ladies at the Mission have found a place for us, but I'd be glad of your advice.' Lily handed her the slip of paper with the address, and Nancy frowned.

'This is in the International Settlement on quite a busy street.'

'It's near Mission Row and the hospital where my husband works.'

'But I thought you liked Frenchtown.'

'I do. I adore it. I'd much rather stay here. It's so peaceful and I love the streets lined with plane trees.'

Nancy crumpled the piece of paper and smiled at her. 'You have a good eye, not unexpected in an artist. I know of a house only a block or two away from here that's just been freed up. The family moved out last week and I know it's still empty. It's a peach. Shall we go and see it tomorrow? Joe can take us as he speaks the lingo fluently and haggles like a Shanghainese, otherwise the landlord will charge you triple the price, if not more. My Joe will make sure you get a fair deal.'

'Would you? I'd be so grateful for your help. Only . . .' Nancy waited while Lily wondered what Hugh would say when he found out she'd ignored the advice of the Misses Smythson. No matter, she'd think of something. She smiled at Nancy. 'All right, you're on, thank you.'

Lily's spirits were still high when she arrived later at St Ignatius and asked for Father O'Leary. He came hurrying down the aisle in his black cassock.

'Now aren't you a sight for sore eyes!' He glanced at her belly. 'And congratulations!' He ushered her into a side door. 'Come away in here where I've a drop of whiskey to chase away the cold. I can't wait for spring; you'll like the city when the blossom is out and the air is sweeter.' Over a warming glass, Lily told him about her early explorations of the city. 'I'm glad to see you're getting to know the city and beginning to make friends,' the priest said. 'But tell me, how is Hugh? Is he settling in as well as you?'

Lily hesitated. Recovering, she tried to smile, but failed.

'What is it, my dear?' He took her hand. 'I can't imagine it's easy being married to a man of the cloth.'

'I'm worried about Hugh. He's been different since coming to Shanghai. Everything is more difficult than he imagined, and he's appalled by the poverty and the way the rich don't seem to care about the poor. He's also frustrated about having to spend so much time at the hospital when he'd rather be out in the countryside saving souls.

He's gone off on a mission now, to the interior, and I hope that sorts him out.'

Daniel looked into his whiskey tumbler, and Lily waited for him to speak. 'Hugh is a good man, but it's not easy having a vocation.' He looked at her. 'Would you like me to talk to him?'

Lily was relieved. 'I know he would love to see you – it would be good for him to talk to another priest. Perhaps you could visit us when he's back? He so enjoys your company and you seem to bring out his lighter side. It might help him put everything in perspective.'

'He's taken on a formidable task with this inland mission. The Chinese aren't too keen on us Christian missionaries, and after a few years out here I'm inclined to think they may be right.'

'Why don't you come for dinner when he's back? I may have found a house and we should be settled in by then.'

'I'd like that very much.'

52

~ *Jeanie* ~

Tatiana had found them somewhere to live. It wasn't much to look at – a dingy basement flat in Ladbroke Grove – but it was within walking distance of Holland Park.

'This area's full of posh families and they're the ones who like to send their little darlings to dance school,' Tatiana said as Jeanie took in the cobwebs and cloudy windows. 'Don't look at the dirt, that can be fixed. There's space for a dance studio, a small one, but big enough for us to teach in.'

Jeanie despised housework and had always left it to the maid in Chelsea, but once she'd rolled up her sleeves and started scrubbing the filthy floorboards and polishing the windows, she found herself humming as the flat began to smell fresh and clean. They whitewashed the walls them-selves and Tatiana found a firm to install the mirrors, a barre and a sprung wooden floor. It took up most of the money Viktor had given her and all her savings. For the first time in years, Jeanie was worried about money.

'Thank goodness Viktor is still paying Stella's school fees, otherwise we'd be really stuck,' she said to Tatiana as they looked around the finished dance studio.

Jeanie used the last of her money to place newspaper advertisements and there followed a nerve-wracking few days of waiting. On the fourth day the doorbell rang and standing there was a harried mother with a little girl of five.

'If you could take her off my hands once or twice a week, that would be a blessing,' the mother said.

The little girl looked mutinous. 'Don't want to.'

Jeanie crouched down so she was level with the girl. 'Do you know, I started dancing when I was your age, and I loved it. Would you like to see some of my costumes? They are very, very sparkly.' The girl nodded mutely and let Jeanie take her by the hand and lead her in. Over her head, Jeanie mouthed *I'll take it from here* to the child's mother, who slipped out of the door with a grateful backward glance.

It was a start, and soon word got around Holland Park that Jeanie Taylor's Dance Academy was *an absolute find* and the fees started rolling in. Having practically brought up her own brothers and sisters as well as Stella, Jeanie knew how to keep children entertained and, unlike most of her charges' mothers, didn't mind joining in the fun and games she devised. Tatiana took the older girls and was stricter about teaching them positioning. She disapproved of Jeanie larking about with silk scarves and balls, but had to admit she got results.

'It's no use trying to teach little ones about *pliés* and *port de bras*, they have to think they're playing,' Jeanie said. She found she liked teaching, but there were some days, when her head was pounding, that she longed to be back on stage, or back with Madam Lebret in the rehearsal studio.

~

Jeanie had been running the dance school for five months when the doorbell rang one evening. It had been a tiring day and she was trying to muster the energy to sweep the studio and put the lights out when the doorbell rang. She shouted for Tatiana, but remembered she'd gone to pick up Stella from school.

'Bugger, drat and bloody hell,' she said as she struggled to unbolt the door.

'That's a nice way to greet an old friend.'

250

'Ned!'

'In the flesh, dear girl.' Ned took off his coat to reveal a blue tweed suit with red piping. 'I'm gasping for a soothing glass of bubbly after the Tube – ghastly way to travel, like moles scrabbling about in tunnels.'

Jeanie took his coat and led him to the parlour. 'There's only the sherry that I keep for the dance pupils' mothers.'

Ned picked up the sherry bottle and looked at the label before setting it down with a slight shudder. 'It's true, then, you've fallen on hard times. Viktor wasn't exactly forthcoming at first when I popped in to see you in Chelsea, but he eased up a bit once we'd had a couple of snifters and told me you'd set up an extremely successful dance school for all the little Holland Park brats.'

'How is he? Stella goes to see him every weekend, but it's been easier for both of us for me to stay away.'

'He's aged since I last saw him, but still good company. We had a few drinks and talked business. Which is why, my dear, I've come to you.' He took out his cigarette case. 'I must say, I never thought I'd see you reduced to teaching dance classes to little rich girls.'

Jeanie was stung. 'I have a daughter to support.'

Ned lit his cigarette. 'Then you might like the business proposal I have for you. I ran it past Viktor first, and he thinks you can do it.'

She leaned forward, intrigued. 'Spit it out, Raeside.'

He let out a stream of smoke and grinned at her impatience. 'There's this chap I know in Glasgow, rich as Croesus. His family made their fortune from sugar and he's just come into his inheritance. He fancies getting into show business – thinks it's glamorous.'

'Aye, right!'

'I know, the fool! But the thing is, he's looking to back a dance troupe – along the lines of the Folies Bergère.'

251

'Tits and arse.'

'And legs, don't forget the legs. The chaps all go mad for that, apparently. I told him I knew just the woman to start up a really fabulous troupe, all sequins and feathers and spectacular numbers to knock the socks off the Glasgow punters and make them think they are in Montmartre. What do you say?'

Jeanie stared at him. 'Are you serious? Me? My own company?'

'I certainly am. Who better?'

Jeanie took a deep breath; her own company! She pulled Ned to his feet and kissed him. 'You're some man, Ned Raeside. I used to think you were a bit of a prick, but you're all right.'

Ned laughed. 'You've a mouth like a sewer, my dear. I take it that's a yes?'

'It's a yes, yes, yes!'

He raised an eyebrow. 'Now that's something I never thought I'd hear from you.'

53

~ *Lily* ~

Nancy was taking Lily to see the house she thought would be perfect for her. They turned into an unprepossessing lane off a leafy street, Nancy's husband Joe loping ahead. He was a tall, rangy man with a casual manner. When Lily had turned up, he'd suggested they walk to see the property.

'Unless you'd like to get a rickshaw? Nancy here is as strong as a horse, but perhaps you're more delicate?' He nodded discreetly at Lily's bump.

'Not at all, I love walking and I never get tired when I'm in Frenchtown, there's so much to see.'

After a short walk, they stopped in front of a pair of iron gates and Joe talked to a Chinese man at the gatehouse who then let them into a sandy courtyard. The outside of the house was painted a warm yellow and, despite being hidden behind a lane, a large garden planted with plum and cherry trees stretched away to the side and round to the back. Lily pictured the blossom in the spring. A plane tree stood in front of the house, which had three floors and a low extension to the side – the garage, kitchens and servants' quarters.

The landlord arrived to let them in, and Lily's heart lifted as she stepped indoors. The inside walls were also painted yellow and the windows looked out on a courtyard filled with pots of honeysuckle and jasmine and the garden with its fruit trees. At that moment, the clouds that had lowered over Shanghai all morning parted and sunlight flooded the house.

She turned to Joe and Nancy. 'It's perfect. Will you ask him what he wants for it, please?'

There followed a barrage of Shanghainese. The lengthy bartering ended with both men bowing to each other. Joe told Lily the rent Mr Lee was asking in taels – the shoe-shaped silver currency used by the Chinese for rent and salaries – and helpfully translated it into Mexican dollars and cents, which were used for everyday purchases. Lily still struggled to convert the sum into pounds, shilling and pence, and was grateful when Nancy whispered how much the rent was in sterling. It was a third of what she had been quoted for the house the Misses Smythson had found. Lily clutched her hands together and nodded at the two men, who broke into smiles and bowed to each other and her. Before she left, she had signed the lease.

As they left, Nancy said, 'We need to get you some staff. You'll need a reliable Number One Boy and he'll hire a Number Two Boy as cook, and an *amah* to look after the baby.'

'Don't worry, I have someone in mind already.' She kissed Nancy on impulse. 'You're a lifesaver, thank you so much for all your help, but I need to run.'

Lily flagged down a rickshaw to take her to Avenue Joffre; she could remember the way to Huan Liu's *lilong* from there.

~

Later that day, back at the hotel, Lily dashed off a note to the Misses Smythson, explaining she had already found a house and thanking them for their trouble. She packed in a fever of excitement while the hotel organised for a porter to retrieve her trunks from storage and take them to her new home.

Huan Liu had sprung into action when she'd turned up at his door, rushing off to order furniture from a store aimed at foreigners and their strange notions of comfort. He also assured her he would find a reliable Number Two Boy that very day. By the time Lily arrived at the Yellow House, as she had decided to call her new home, a carved cherry wood bed had been installed and made with linen sheets and a silk eiderdown, stoves burned in every room, and Wang Yong, the Number Two houseboy and cook, was presiding over a spitting wok and steaming kettles of water on the kitchen stove. Huan Liu explained that there was no oven as roasting and baking were not the Chinese custom. He led her into the sitting room where two coolies were setting down a red enamelled cabinet inlaid with ivory and delicately painted with flying cranes in gold leaf.

Lily clasped her hands in delight. 'Huan Liu, you've worked a miracle in a few short hours. I don't know how to thank you.'

He bowed to her. 'It is my pleasure, Mrs Anderson.' He ducked his eyes and smiled shyly. 'I'm glad to be your Number One Boy. And my wife and children are also happy, as we've been able to move out of my mother-in-law's house and into comfortable quarters here. I'm a lucky man.'

'It is I who am lucky, to have found you, Huan Liu.'

He smiled. 'Perhaps I could also sometimes help your esteemed husband in his dealings with my countrymen? It would be an honour to serve a clergyman and a doctor.'

Lily realised she hadn't thought to ask what Huan Liu's salary might be. She had never run a household before, only looked after her own small flat in Garnethill. He named a sum and she made a quick calculation. The money she would save on rent would more than cover his salary and the furnishings for her new home. Hugh had already allocated a budget for household staff, so she could see no reason why he wouldn't welcome this arrangement. She wanted to tell Hugh there and then but knew he would not return until May, when spring would be well under way and the blossom out in the garden. Lily calculated she would be seven months pregnant by then and getting larger and clumsier, so there was no time to waste turning the Yellow House into a home.

~

Huan Liu proved himself indispensable time and again. He took Lily to buy porcelain from shops tucked away in back alleys, haggling down the exorbitant prices she would have otherwise been charged and steering her away from the cheap imitations sold in the larger shops to ignorant foreigners. Lily discovered it wasn't always the most ornately decorated pieces that were most prized but the plain bowls from the Song dynasty that she would have dismissed as simple peasant pottery. Only the way the light shone through the milky glaze betrayed its true value. Huan Liu also showed her how to buy jade ornaments and silk hangings, and soon the Yellow House shone like an amber pendant.

As the house took shape over the next few months and she grew accustomed to her surroundings, Lily burned to discover more about Shanghai and reach beyond the borders of the Concessions. It was Huan Liu who made this possible, taking her on rickshaw rides and pointing out pagodas and parks, and the streets where the rich Chinese lived behind guarded walls in grand European-style garden villas with Tudor beams and enormous, manicured lawns.

During this time, Lily also found herself taken up by Nancy and her husband. They were about to be first-time parents too, although Nancy insisted on banning baby talk. With the American couple's help, Lily widened her circle of friends, encouraged by Nancy to attend the balls and national celebrations that made up the social round in Shanghai, so that, even with Hugh away, Lily was never lonely. Nancy was often without her husband, who worked long hours at the newspaper, and she often popped round to share gossip about the people Lily was beginning to get to know. Nancy and Joe were only too happy to take her along to the functions they were invited to, where Joe would slip off to talk to contacts in Shanghai business and politics – what he called 'keeping my ear to the ground' and Nancy called 'sticking his nose in where it don't belong'.

But after a few weeks the novelty of Lily's new social life began to wear off. She began to feel like a pampered colonial wife, spending her days on empty pleasure when she knew that Shanghai, like Glasgow, was home to the poor and helpless. She had been too distracted by the social whirl and tired by her pregnancy to turn the street sketches she'd been making of Shanghai into paintings. And she began to miss the weight teaching at the Fellowship had given her life. Recurring thoughts of her studio in Bath Street, of friends like Nellie Grayson and her pupils at the Mack, made her more homesick. Astute Nancy picked up on Lily's restlessness, and after some probing discovered she'd taught street children.

'Why, I know just the fella who'll be glad of your help. Tony Forsyth is one of the richest men in Shanghai, but he's also one of the kindest. He runs St Joseph's, a school for abandoned Eurasian children – some of the *tai-pans* become a little too entranced with the exotic ladies of the Orient, and the resulting children are rejected by both sides.' She whipped out her address book. 'What do you say? Shall I introduce you to Tony?'

Before she knew it, Lily found herself teaching a host of bright and chatty children who lived and were taught in a large garden villa run by nuns. She soon slipped back into the role she had left at the Fellowship, teaching the rudiments of art to her eager charges. These Eurasian children were fed and clothed better than the slum children she'd taught in Glasgow, but they had the same desperate need for affection and, like them, blossomed when a benign adult paid them attention. Having a purpose helped Lily settle in more than anything else. Letters from home, from Kit and Nellie and her parents, arrived in a bundle along with parcels and copies of the *Glasgow Herald*, bringing news from Scotland and making her feel not quite so far away.

~

Life in China took another unexpected and pleasant turn for Lily. Not long before Hugh was due to return from the interior, Huan Liu took her on a half-hour taxi ride to Jessfield Ferry on Soochow Creek and pointed out a handsome houseboat. He called out to the skipper, a Chinese man in a Homburg felt hat, who helped them aboard before retiring to the stern, where he sat smoking a pipe and fanning himself.

Huan Liu told Lily the mast could be lowered when the boat passed under bridges and showed her how the foredeck led down to two big cabins. There was a galley kitchen and beyond that the stern, where the crew's quarters were covered by a wooden awning. The boat could be manoeuvred with the *yuloh*, a large stern oar that needed three crewmen, and steered with the help of long bamboo poles.

'It's going cheap,' Huan Liu said. 'The owner has died, and his widow is going back to France and wants a quick sale. If you'll allow me to negotiate with her *notaire*, I can get you a good price.'

Lily peered into the cosy cabin with its chairs and bunks. From here she could sketch scenes as they rolled past the changing landscape. It would be a chance to see the real, old China of her imagination, far from westernised Shanghai. Still, she had spent so much money already on the house.

She looked regretfully out over the creek at the wisps of mist playing on the surface of the water. 'I've no idea about boats and neither does Hugh. We'd end up in the river!'

Huan Liu explained that the *laodah*, the Chinese skipper, lived on board to prevent theft and would do all the sailing. 'When you want to take a trip on the inland canals and waterways, the *laodah* will find five coolies to crew, only fifty cents a day each, and you can bring Number Two Boy to cook.' He cast his eyes down and she knew a request was coming and suppressed a smile. 'I could come too, to oversee. My father was a fisherman and I was sailing since before I could walk. It's the best and safest way to travel and a good way to get out of the dirt and noise of Shanghai. Mrs Anderson, you'll see many wonderful sights to inspire you as an artist.'

Lily thought of the last of the money she had kept from her commissions and was tempted, but remembered how furious Hugh had been with her over the clothes purchase. She could justify the house rental and staff as they were within the agreed budget, but this houseboat was an indulgence, a real luxury. Still, she had the funds, and with Huan Liu overseeing the household expenditure and making sure they were not paying inflated prices for food and fuel, they were spending a great deal less than Hugh had budgeted. She shaded her eyes and looked to the horizon, where the soft blue of the creek merged with the sky. Huan Liu was right, the waterways were a safer way to travel than the trains, which were often attacked by bandits known to kidnap foreigners and demand a ransom for their safe return. Lily made up her mind.

'All right, see if you can beat the *notaire* down to a fair price. And of course, if you are to be our boatman as well as our right-hand man' – she could not bring herself to call this gentle and educated man Number One Boy – 'you must allow me to raise your salary.'

He bowed. 'That would be most kind, thank you, Mrs Anderson.' Within an hour she was the owner of a houseboat.

'What will you call her?' Huan Liu asked her as they stood side by side on the quay and admired the boat.

Lily hugged herself in delight. 'The *Jeanie*, after a dear friend who taught me about the importance of adventure.'

54

~ *Lily* ~

When Hugh returned from his missionary trip to the interior he was too ill to take in the new house. Weak with fever,
he was only grateful that Lily had made a comfortable
home. Always lean, he was now gaunt and for the first time
seemed frail. Lily was worried and sent Huan Liu to the
hospital to fetch one of Hugh's colleagues.

'He needs to rest,' the doctor told Lily later. 'Little else
can be done for him, other than letting it run its course,
I'm afraid. It could be any number of tropical fevers. I've
done all I can for him. Now it's up to God.'

Terrified she would lose him, she tended her husband
night and day, coaxing his appetite with clear broths and
bathing his burning skin with cold cloths when he was in
the grip of sweats, covering him with blankets and her own
body warmth as he shivered pitifully in the aftermath.
Through the long nights sitting by his side, watching his
eyelids flicker as if with the luminosity of his fever-dreams,
Lily thought about all the good this man had done in the
world: the street urchins he had saved from disease, death
and worse; the inebriate children he had scooped up from
the whisky bonds where they were paid in spirits to clean
out the stills and often fell dead drunk into the Clyde; the
factory girls he had taught how to read at night school; the
violent, drunken men who had changed their ways after
hearing him preach. She knew that Psalm 23 was one of
his favourites:

Yea, though I walk through the
valley of the shadow of death, I will fear no evil;
for thou art with me . . .

It was true: Hugh's faith made him fearless. He could walk the darkest backstreets, filled with cut-throats and desperate men, without a thought for his own safety and return unscathed. And here he was in Shanghai after having travelled into a countryside full of bandits and warlords, where foreigners were feared and killed without mercy, desperately ill but still alive. Surely God would not abandon him now?

Whether it was down to her assiduous nursing, divine intervention or mere good luck, Lily didn't know, but Hugh began to show signs of recovery. By the time the cherry and plum trees were in full bloom, he had grown strong enough to sit out in the garden and take gentle walks. Lily tried to talk to him about his trip, but he only shook his head.

'I cannot speak about it yet.' He clutched his head and his voice broke. 'I'm not sure if I can go on. I'm horribly afraid that my life's work has been for nothing.'

Alarmed, Lily put her arm around him. She had never heard him speak like this. 'Come now, it's the illness that is making you wretched,' she said. 'When our child comes, you'll feel different.' She placed his hand on her stomach so he could feel the baby kick. 'There, you see, he's saying hello to his papa.'

Hugh managed to smile. 'How can you be sure it's a boy?'

'The *amah* Huan Liu found read my fortune.'

Hugh sighed. 'You're such a little heathen. You know I'm too weak to object. It's most unsporting of you to take advantage.'

She laughed, heartened to hear his dry humour return. 'There is one other thing I must confess to while I have you at my mercy,' she said.

'Well, let's have it. No wonder the Misses Smythson of this world disapprove of you.'

She frowned. 'I didn't think you'd noticed that I was *persona non grata* at the Mission, but I care not a jot for the prejudices of the sainted Misses Smythson.' Lily pulled him to his feet. 'Come with me. This is a surprise you must see to understand. I'll get the driver to take us there. It involves a trip over a few days, so I've packed our things.'

'How mysterious you are, and how unpredictable! Remind me why I thought it was a good idea to marry a woman with an artistic temperament.'

Lily shrugged. 'There were plenty of pious and well-behaved women you could have had in my place. For instance, you could have married one of the Misses Smythson: I caught them looking at you with more than frank adoration.'

He made a face. 'No, thank you, I'll stick to my artistic hoyden and her impulsive ways. You make life interesting. The Misses Smythson, on the other hand, do not.'

～

They set off in their car with Huan Liu, Wang Yong and their luggage. When they reached the jetty, Hugh stood for a while looking at the *Jeanie*. Lily held her breath.

He turned to her. 'Is she ours?'

'Every inch.' Lily held onto his arm. 'Do you like her? It'll be a wonderful way for you to recover, out of the city air and this humid heat, which I'm told will only get worse as summer progresses. I know you prefer open spaces and even I, who love the bustle of city life, find Shanghai too much at times.'

He walked up the gangway to where Huan Liu was waiting. Knowing Hugh was still weak, he discreetly helped him aboard and settled him on a cushioned seat on the flat prow while the *laodoh* and his five coolies carried the baggage on board. A pelican flew overhead, and Hugh watched its course. Huan Liu pointed out the boat train further down the creek and they watched the coolies push off from the bank with their long bamboo poles to guide the boat, tow ropes at the ready to hitch a ride with the steam launch, along with other houseboats. The boat train let out a shriek and chugged down the creek and away from Shanghai. The *Jeanie* cut effortlessly through Soochow Creek at a gentle pace. A fresh breeze riffled the water and Hugh took off his hat. Lily knew from the brightness of his eyes that he was taken by the boat.

He grinned at her. 'As soon as the baby is born, we'll make a little sailor of him.'

When he made his way towards the prow where Huan Liu was checking the tow rope, Lily jumped to her feet to help, but Hugh waved her away. She saw that he was already steadier and stronger, as if the river was replenishing his strength. Delicious smells arose from the galley as Wang Yong prepared a four-course meal in his miraculously inventive way. They would sleep on board tonight while the *Jeanie* cut through the river and canals, and in the morning they would reach the medieval walled city of Soochow with its pagodas and camel-back bridges. They would breathe clean air and see mountains for the first time since they left Scotland, and Hugh would become whole again. Lily smiled to herself: she had been right to follow her instincts, right about the Yellow House and right about the *Jeanie*. And she'd been right to marry Hugh, no matter what Ned or her mother had said.

55

~ *Jeanie* ~

Ned was showing Jeanie around a three-storey town house in Glasgow's West End.

'The seller has gone bankrupt and is desperate to sell, so it's a bargain,' he said, mentioning an asking price that made Jeanie wince.

'That's more money than I could earn in a lifetime,' she said.

'Richardson is going to put down the deposit and he'll guarantee your mortgage.' Jeanie hadn't expected to like Harry Richardson, her financial backer, expecting a spoiled rich boy who wanted to play the impresario. But he had turned out to be a serious young man who listened while she laid out her plans for a dance company. He had acquiesced to all her demands, and only had one of his own, that a box be reserved for him on the opening night of each show. They'd shaken hands and Jeanie had stepped out of Ned's office the owner of the Taylor Girls.

Jeanie still couldn't quite believe it, but here she was inspecting premises only a day later.

'This place is going to be a gold mine,' Ned said. 'The public rooms will make excellent rehearsal studios and you can put a dance school in the basement.'

She looked at him sharply. 'I thought you disapproved of my dance school, you were so sniffy about it when you came to London.'

'That's before I went over the accounts with Tatiana

– dance classes will give you a steady stream of income to shore up the dance company.'

Jeanie stood at the window overlooking the private gardens, where women were pushing prams and minding toddlers. There would be plenty of mothers looking for dance classes. But she wanted this school to be different, to become a centre of excellence that turned out professional dancers, and with scholarships for talented children from poor backgrounds, so they could have the chance that she had had all those years ago. Jeanie turned to Ned. 'I'll take it, but I want to bring in Tatiana as the head of the dance school.'

'Good idea to get people in you know and trust. May I suggest a costume designer?'

Jeanie raised her eyebrows. 'Who were you thinking of?'

'Kit Mackenzie.'

'Lily's pal from art school? The one that married that dobber?'

He laughed. 'Well put – Henry Geddes is indeed a complete and utter dobber. But his wife is an absolute darling and talented with it. She's a talented embroiderer and designed the costumes for the art school's masked balls.'

'Won't her numpty of a husband object to her earning her own money?'

'He's had to leave town. Kit's parents paid for a one-way ticket to America to get rid of him. There was a scandal at the art school – an irate father whose daughter tried to kill herself because of him – and they sent him packing. As did Kit, I'm delighted to say. She's a redoubtable little thing, stronger than she looks, one of those types who are easy-going until provoked, and then you'd better run for cover.'

Jeanie grinned. 'She's not the only one.'

266

'Don't I know it! You should see some of the terrors who turn up in court – they're ten times tougher than the men. Anyway, Kit is on her own now with four children, and looking for work she can fit in around them.'

'Aye, well, I know what that's like. Tell her to come and see me and we can go over some ideas for costumes.'

Ned jumped into a cab to go back to his office, but Jeanie wanted to walk back to the hotel to give herself time to think. Everything had happened so fast and so many people would be depending on her to make this work. What if she failed? She strolled through Dowanhill and found herself outside a house she recognised. A maid was scrubbing the front steps, her hair in tangles and her face red with effort. Jeanie remembered scrubbing those same steps; it seemed a lifetime ago.

She called to the girl: 'You're working hard there.'

The maid stopped and sat back on her heels. 'Aye, but it's a fine day.'

Jeanie smiled. 'It is that.'

56

~ Lily ~

When the cherries hung in ripe clusters in the Yellow House's garden and the Shanghai air was still and hot and thick with humidity, Lily gave birth to a baby girl. Rosie had copper hair, creamy skin and a rosebud of a mouth, and she waved her plump little arms in fury when she mewled for milk; Lily was enchanted. She was content to sit propped up in bed under the mosquito net feeding her baby while Li Na, the tiny but astonishingly strong *amah*, fussed around her with cold drinks and nourishing bowls of glass noodles in broth.

Hugh was a devoted father, swooping down on the child and cradling her to his chest when he was home from the hospital. But he seemed to spend all his affection on the child and Lily noticed he had become distant with her since the birth. Nancy told her that some men did this, and that it would pass as he became used to her as a mother and not just his wife, but it pained her that he wouldn't touch her in bed at night. When she finally got up the nerve to speak about his reluctance to make love, Hugh insisted it was too soon, that he was afraid he would hurt her. Lily, feeling fat and milky, worried that he no longer found her attractive; her breasts were swollen and hard, traced with blue veins, and her nipples coarser and larger from breast-feeding, her belly slack as a deflated balloon.

Hugh still refused to talk about his trip to the interior and since Rosie's arrival, had put aside his mission work. A cholera epidemic had broken out in the city and he was away for long hours working across the five Settlement hospitals run by the Shanghai Municipal Council. He still suffered bouts of fever – the doctor thought malaria likeliest – and Lily was worried about him, but he refused to rest while there was so much to do. Lily would often wake in the middle of the night to find his side of the bed empty, only to find him in his study, head in his hands staring at nothing, an open Bible on the desk. Or he would be standing in the garden in the darkness looking up at the stars, as if searching for answers. He cut a lonely figure among the night-blooming flowers, eerily luminous in the moonlight, the air perfumed with their scent. Lily knew she couldn't reach him at times like these and would slip back to bed unseen. In the mornings he would be gone, a rumpled newspaper and an empty teacup the only signs he'd been there at all.

In those early days of motherhood, with Nancy and Joe gone to the lake city of Hangchow to cool off while they waited for their baby to arrive, Lily was often at home alone for days on end. She relied more than ever on Huan Liu, who would stop his work to go through the books she had bought on Chinese art, explaining the legends and customs behind the images of dragons and the elaborate costumes. While Rosie slept, Lily liked to sit on her balcony and watch him play with his children in the courtyard, sketching the boys as they ran shrieking pursued by their father. Huan Liu was proving to be a good and loyal friend, as she had always known he would be. But there was still an unspoken restraint between them, as mistress and servant, and she could never quite let her hair down with him. She missed Ned and his waspish humour, and Jeanie's salty asides, and her outrageous theatre friends. Lily thought wistfully of the Mack, of Fra and of Nellie Grayson and her students. She wondered if Kit had felt like this when she became a mother, as if she had lost herself. Lily wished now that she had gone to see her more and been a better friend; she'd had no idea motherhood could be so tiring and frightening. Every time she picked up Rosie she was overcome with a fierce desire to protect and care for her, but when Li Na took the baby away, she was torn between not wanting to let Rosie out of her sight and guilty relief that she could sleep undisturbed and walk about with empty arms.

In these quiet times, alone in her room and trying desperately to rest before the baby woke, she missed Jeanie, who knew her best. She longed for female company and to talk about familiar subjects, but there were so few foreign women in the Concessions. Confined and constrained and confused by motherhood, and without Nancy to gee her up, Lily was lonely.

Since coming to Shanghai, she'd avoided being drawn into the tight social circle of female missionaries led by the formidable Misses Smythson, but one day a small flock of them descended on the Yellow House bearing gifts of baby cardigans and all-in-ones they had knitted. Lily fingered the scratchy wool that would be far too hot for Rosie and thanked them.

'I'd put one on her now if I were you. Poor little mite, babies are prone to catch chest colds in this damp climate, you know.' This from a Miss Sullivan, who glanced disapprovingly at Rosie's delicate muslin frock embroidered with silk lotus flowers, a gift from Huan Liu's wife. A heavy-set woman wearing a dented hat sniffed when she saw the baby in Lily's arms instead of swaddled in a cot.

'You don't want to handle her too much. Too many foreign children turn into spoiled brats in Shanghai, coddled and fussed over by the *amahs*.' A stern look at Li Na, who smiled and bowed. The woman sniffed again and lowered her voice to a quiet roar. 'Another thing, dear, you don't want to get too familiar with the servants else they won't respect you. She calls you Missy, the respectful name they give their foreign mistresses, don't she?'

Lily caught Li Na's eye and managed to stifle a giggle. 'No, of course not, she calls me by my first name.'

The woman looked so appalled she was lost for words. Lily took the opportunity to call for a soothing pot of tea, making sure it was strong, Indian and heavily sugared rather than the pale, straw-coloured China tea she had grown to like. She thought the ordeal was nearly over and was irritated when the Smythson sisters arrived just as the other women were leaving. The elderly sisters begged to see the baby and Lily didn't have the heart to say no. They peered at Rosie in Lily's arms, and she braced herself for more unsolicited advice. Instead, one of them put out a finger and beamed when Rosie grasped it in her fat little fist.

'Oh look, Maud,' she breathed.

Her sister stroked the baby's red curls with a papery hand. 'Like silk.'

'Yes, like silk.'

Lily looked from one gentle face to the other and realised she had been mistaken about the Smythsons, or Iris and Maud as they asked her to call them.

'You must let us take the dear little thing for a walk in her perambulator when you want a spell.'

'We'd be pleased to. Really. Such a poppet.'

'Yes, such a poppet.'

Lily remembered she had neglected to thank them in person for their efforts to find her a house, only dashing off a note. She'd been unfair, assuming they were busybodies when really, they had been only trying to help her find her feet. She was ashamed of her unkindness now.

'Would you like to hold her?' She held Rosie out to Iris,

271

who blushed with pleasure and opened her arms to receive the infant. The baby cooed and looked unseeingly into the older woman's face as if searching for clues to this mysterious world where she'd so recently arrived.

After that, the sisters were regular visitors to the Yellow House and Lily always made an effort to fuss around them with tea and cakes and ask them brightly for their news. But she found it hard to concentrate on their chatter about the latest sale of work to raise money for hymnbooks or how they were asking people to cross-stitch kneelers. The sisters talked without pause, finishing each other's sentences so seamlessly there was no chance for Lily to interject any of her own thoughts, and at the end of their visits she would feel wrung out. They were kind and clearly adored Rosie, and had endless patience with her, even when she was fussing, but what Lily longed for more than anything was to talk to a woman of her own age, someone she could confide in. She found her thoughts returning to Jeanie more often, longing for the closeness they had shared.

57

~ *Jeanie* ~

The move to Glasgow had not gone as smoothly as Jeanie had planned. Tatiana had helped with the practicalities of winding up the dance school in London, but Stella had been distraught about leaving London. At eight she already knew her mind and wasn't afraid of speaking out.

'What about Daddy? I'll never see him,' she'd wailed at her mother while she was packing the contents of her wardrobe.

'You'll see him on school holidays, we'll visit.'

'It won't be the same! Scotland's so far away. And, what about school?'

'There are schools in Glasgow, you know, it's not the Wild West.'

'But my friends won't be there.' Stella had thrown herself on her bed and sobbed into the silk eiderdown.

Jeanie had relented. She'd sat down next to her and stroked the little girl's dark curls that, like hers, refused to be tamed no matter how many times they were brushed. 'You'll make new friends. It'll be an adventure, you'll see.'

But Stella wouldn't be consoled. All the way up on the train, she'd been sullen, staring pale-faced out of the window as they travelled north, leaving England behind. Jeanie, who had been only too glad to leave her home in Kirkcudbright, found it hard to understand her distress. Tatiana had taken her to task several times in the run-up to leaving London.

'You were leaving a horrible situation and breaking free

– and you were older. Stella has only ever known happiness in London, and she adores her father. She's a daddy's girl.'

'I wouldn't know what that's like either, not having a father,' Jeanie said. She could hear the bitterness in her voice but carried on. 'Viktor's spoiled her rotten and I have to be strict with her, so she doesn't turn into a brat, like the stuck-up little madams she calls her friends.'

Mother and daughter had both worked themselves up into a furious temper by the time they got on the train. Shaking her head at their stony expressions, Tatiana had said, 'You're as bad as each other – two peas in a pod.'

Now that they'd moved into their new home, Jeanie hoped that Stella would settle once she started at a private all-girls' school in the West End. But she came back from her first day in tears.

'I hate my new school. They all laugh at the way I speak. I hate those girls, and I hate you!' she screamed at Jeanie before slamming the door to her bedroom and turning the key. Jeanie knocked at her door, pleading to be let in, until she lost her temper.

'You can stay in there and stew. A big girl like you, having a tantrum. I'm ashamed of you. You're spoiled – I never had anything you have. You're an ungrateful wee besom.'

It was Tatiana who managed to coax Stella out of her room and down to dinner that night, and who shook her head as Jeanie was about to make a fuss about Stella's sulky face and to comment about being careful in case the wind changed. Jeanie sighed and tried to concentrate on the auditions she'd held that day for her new company.

The stormy atmosphere in the West Princes Street town house eased when Kit arrived, brimming with cheerfulness. She took one look at Stella and pressed her to her breast in an enormous hug.

'What a wee beauty! Jeanie, you're so lucky to have a daughter. I've nothing but big lummocks of sons.' She put her arm through Stella's and confided, 'You and I are going to have such fun together! I hear you're a wonderful dancer. Would you like me to design a costume for you?'

'Oh, yes please, I'd love that, thank you,' Stella said in her politest, most charming voice.

Kit clapped her hands. 'Marvellous! We'll get started straight after I talk to your mother. If you toddle off and draw up some preliminary sketches of your ideas, I'll come and find you.'

Stella beamed at her and skipped away. Jeanie was relieved to see her daughter's mood lift but also peeved that she should be so pleasant with someone else.

'What a darling little girl!' Kit said, looking after her fondly.

'Aye, well, that's a matter of opinion,' Jeanie said after the door had closed behind Stella. She turned to Kit. 'Right, you, let's get to work.'

58

~ *Lily* ~

It was early summer in Shanghai, the heat still bearable. One day, while Rosie was sleeping in her cot under her mosquito net, eyelashes casting shadows on her porcelain-doll cheeks, Lily heard the doorbell. Huan Liu was out on one of his mysterious errands, and Wang Yong was shopping at the market, while Li Na was in the garden picking fruit, so Lily dragged herself off the couch and opened the door herself. Standing in front of her was Hugh's sister, looking neat and composed and carrying her doctor's bag. A large Gladstone bag sat at her feet. Lily felt her knees buckling and Florence let fall her bag and held her up.

'Are you all right? You've gone quite pale. I'd hoped this would be a pleasant surprise but I'm afraid it's more of a shock.'

Lily recovered and threw her arms around her sister-in-law. 'Florence! How wonderful to see you! Why didn't you write and tell us you were coming? Hugh will be so delighted, as of course am I. Oh, Florence!'

Florence smiled but took her hand firmly. 'Now, no tears, even if they are of joy. I hope they are?' Lily nodded, unable to speak. 'Take me into your delightful Chinese home and give me some tea, won't you? I'm parched and somewhat shaken after that rickshaw ride.'

Over jasmine tea, which Florence pronounced to be 'water knocked stupid', she told Lily why she had come to Shanghai.

'When I got your letter telling me you were pregnant, I was of course overjoyed. However, I realised that with the post so slow, by the time I wrote to you and told you I was coming to see you all, I could have sailed here myself. So, that's what I did. I shut up the house in the West End, gave notice at the Royal Infirmary, and took the steamer to Shanghai. And here I am.' She squeezed Lily's hands between hers. 'How I've missed you both. And now I have a little nephew, or niece perhaps? What is he or she called?'

Lily picked up her teacup to hide her smile. How like cool and pragmatic Florence to sit calmly drinking tea rather than rush in to see the new baby. 'Rosie, we called her Rosie.'

Florence frowned. 'Our mother was Eleanor and I'm named after our grandmother. Is that a family name on your side?'

'No, but you'll understand when you see her.' She led Florence into the nursery where they found Li Na bathing the baby. Florence nodded at the *amah* as if she were one of her staff nurses and cast an approving eye over her bathing technique. She bent down to inspect the child and Rosie squirmed in Li Na's hands.

'I can see why you called her Rosie. It's perfect and so is she. May I hold her?' She deftly lifted the baby out of the water and wrapped her in a towel with swift, assured moves, a legacy of her time attending births in the East End of Glasgow. Rosie stared up at her aunt with big blue eyes. 'My, she has quite a fierce look about her. Good! A girl needs a strong will in this world, don't you, my wee darling. Look at that colouring – she could only be a Scottish lass. What a gorgeous girl! Yes, you are! Yes, you are!'

Lily was amused to see Florence cooing just like any

277

other fond aunt. It reminded her of how the childless Smythson sisters had melted into puddles of affection on seeing the baby. For the first time, Lily thought about the sacrifices Florence had made in order to become a doctor. Her sister-in-law had been deprived of the chance of having a family of her own, a fate that had so nearly been her own. Lily's thoughts turned to Jack. What would he make of her now, a mother and running a house? She remembered what he'd said in his last letter to her, that she shouldn't waste her talent. Lily hadn't thought about her artwork for weeks: since she had given birth she had been wrapped in a fog of motherly love. Perhaps, now that Florence was here to help her, it was time to dig out her sketchbook and get back to work.

With Rosie back in Li Na's care, the two women settled down in the garden for a long talk. At last, after months of bearing them on her own, Lily was able to confide her worries about Hugh.

'He's overwhelmed at the hospital with the epidemic. I know he would prefer to be doing mission work, but he seems to have lost his way after a disastrous trip to the interior. It must have been bad, as he still won't talk about it.' She smiled at Florence. 'I'm so glad you're here: we both missed you so.' Lily clasped her hands together and noticed the way the sunlight played on her white muslin skirt. 'I've been feeling rather lonely lately. It sounds silly as I've been so busy with the baby and I'm never really alone with a houseful of servants, and there are visitors, from the Mission, who look in.' Lily realised her words were coming out in a rush and she took a breath. 'I know I sound ungrateful. Rosie is a blessing, an easy baby, and I have an *amah*, but still, it's hard.' Florence laid her hand on her shoulder and Lily began to cry.

Florence said, 'It is hard. You could have a squadron of

nannies to help but you're still the mother, your baby needs you. The broken nights alone are exhausting. I've no illusions what it's like to look after an infant round the clock, day in, day out. There's many a new mother who's not been able to cope. Don't be so hard on yourself – you've had to cope with this in a foreign country without family to help you. But you've got me now.'

Lily took Florence's hands. 'It's wonderful that you're here.' She cleared her throat. 'Would you help Hugh, too? He works day and night, growing more haggard and exhausted. I know he'd welcome your help at the hospital. It would comfort him to have you by his side. I hope your visit will be a long one. Might I persuade you to make it permanent? We've plenty of room and your niece already adores her clever auntie.'

'My niece is too small to recognise me let alone gauge my intelligence, but it's kind of you to say so, and I would love to watch her grow into a bundle of strong-willed trouble.' Florence kissed Lily on the cheek. 'I was hoping you'd ask me to stay on, and I can do as much good in the hospital here as in Glasgow – perhaps more.' She frowned. 'Now, about Hugh. I'm concerned firstly about his physical health. We can address the state of his mind once he's stronger. He shouldn't be working at full tilt after being so ill.'

'He won't rest, and he won't listen to me.'

'No, he can be a stubborn old stick. I'll talk to him, but I suspect he's punishing himself for his failed mission. I'll talk to him and try to get to the bottom of what happened on this trip.'

Florence was as good as her word. When Hugh returned from his hospital rounds that evening, he found her waiting for him. Lily could see the immediate effect on his spirits, and dinner was a lively affair as they eagerly

279

drank in the news from home. After the meal had been cleared, Florence shot Lily a look. She took her cue and rose from the table.

'If you'll excuse me, I'll settle Rosie and go to bed. I'm sure you both have a lot of catching up to do.'

59

～ *Lily* ～

The next morning, after Hugh had left for work, Florence knocked on Lily's bedroom door.

She yawned and stretched and the baby, who had fallen asleep in her arms after a feed, made a tiny protest. 'You're up early and dressed already. I'm afraid I've got into the habit of staying in my nightgown; I've grown decadent in the Orient, as you can see.' Lily touched her breakfast tray, beautifully laid by Wang Yong, who had toasted sliver-thin slices of bread and cut a pawpaw into a decorative shape where it lay on a porcelain plate with plums from the garden. Florence sat on the edge of her bed and devoured a slice of toast with one bite.

'Aren't you spoiled!' she said. 'We did sit up late but I'm not in the least tired. I can get by on a few hours' sleep and besides, I did nothing but rest on the boat over.' While Lily sat back against the pillows and drank her morning tea, Florence patted the baby back to sleep and relayed her talk with Hugh. 'You were right: his morale is low. He told me all about the trip to the interior. He feels humiliated, an utter failure. In all those months he spent travelling from one village to another, he made not one convert. He was chased out of more than one place, pelted with stones and mud. The Gospels he handed out were burned for fuel. He found the poverty horrifying.'

'Surely, his work in the Glasgow slums must have prepared him?' Lily said.

'He says there's no comparison. There are regular

famines that kill the children, old people and the weak. Droughts or floods often destroy crops and the people starve. Trees are stripped of leaves, grass is made into thin soup and children suck pebbles and clumps of mud to get nourishment. In the hunger times, mothers smother their babies or leave them out in the open to die, especially if they are girls. Hugh said he—' Florence cleared her throat and cupped a protective hand around Rosie's head. 'He saw a dog snarling and snuffling at a bundle on the ground. When he drew near, he saw it was a baby's arm.'

Lily covered her ears. 'Stop, Florence, please.' She looked out of the window into the garden and took several deep breaths. 'They must be savages.'

Florence shrugged. 'The peasants are no different to us. Starvation leads people to do terrible things. A girl baby is no good to a starving family who must find a dowry for her unless they sell her as a slave. A son can work the fields and it's his duty to look after his parents in their old age.'

Lily shook her head. 'It's no wonder they didn't listen to Hugh – starving people can't eat sermons.' She took Florence's hand. 'How we've missed you! You keep Hugh's feet on the ground.'

'My brother realises any further trips to the interior will be futile. He feels he has come to the other side of the world on a fool's errand and he's deeply ashamed – and angry.'

Lily plucked at the embroidered bed cover. 'He was better off in Glasgow, then?' The thought of leaving Shanghai just as she was settling in filled her with dread.

'There's no need for that, but I told him he should go back to what he's good at – urban missionary work. In Glasgow, the curse as we know is drink, with poor people blotting out their misery with cheap gin and whisky; here it's opium. Hugh tells me that the police are cracking down, but they're fighting a losing battle when even their own Chinese policemen smoke on their breaks.'

Lily sat up straighter in bed. 'What did he say?'

'He was fired with enthusiasm, couldn't understand why he hadn't thought of it himself. He's going to see the China Inland Mission people later today, and I've promised to take up some of the slack at the hospital so he can follow his vocation.'

Lily was impressed. In a few hours, Florence had got to the root of Hugh's unhappiness and found a solution. Later that day, when he came back from work, the transformation was immediately apparent. He laid out his plan before Florence and Lily, full of his old fire.

'I've heard Shanghai called the Paris of the East, but really it's a cesspool drawing every conman and adventurer from every corner of the world looking to make his fortune,' he said. 'Opium is everywhere, a scourge we British brought to China, destroying souls so we would have something to trade for their silk and tea.' He turned and looked out of the French windows into the garden, where the last of the plums hung heavy and ripe. 'Out of sheer greed, we flooded China with opium, creating a monstrous hunger that spawns the most heinous crimes.'

Lily thought of the villas in Shanghai with their tennis courts and sleek cars in the drive, the British *tai-pans* in their imposing trading houses, of the race meets and the armies of servants: inconceivable wealth built on a rotten foundation. Her eyes widened when Hugh named a family with castles and estates in Scotland who had started off as opium importers before diverting their wealth into more respectable trade channels. These were topics that were never discussed at the parties and functions she attended, but clearly everyone must be aware of them, from the wives

283

in their furs and jewels to the wealthy traders playing billiards in the Shanghai Club.

Hugh was in full flow now, almost oblivious of their presence. 'The worst degradations are found in the brothels, where women are sold like cattle, many of them Americans or Europeans recruited by unscrupulous madams, or Russian emigrés who flooded Shanghai after the revolution.'

Lily heard the zeal in her husband's voice and began to have doubts. How could one man hope to make a difference? She suspected he was setting himself up for another impossible task that could only end in failure.

'Hugh, I don't want you to put yourself in danger. You have a family now and we need you.'

He waved his hand. 'I'll be fine, I never had any problems in Glasgow, and I won't here.' He unfolded a map of the city with certain streets marked in red. 'I don't deny it's an enormous task – there are nearly a thousand licensed madams running brothels in the International Settlement alone – but with faith and determination I'm sure it's possible to stem this tide of misery, or at least try.'

Lily was sceptical. She remembered the streetwalkers she'd seen in Glasgow standing in tight groups, loudly propositioning men; how they'd snicker at Hugh and the other Fellowship missionaries. She imagined the sing-song girls in Shanghai would be just as resistant to 'do-gooders' as their Glasgow sisters. Lily began to regret asking Florence to speak to Hugh. What had she set in motion? The brother and sister pored over the map, making suggestions and jotting down notes, as if Shanghai were a puzzle that only needed their clever minds and hard work to solve. She heard the baby cry in the next room and stood up. Lily only wanted to make a small difference where she could, at St Joseph's teaching the Eurasian orphans.

While Florence and Hugh were busy with their plans,

she slipped out of the room and went in search of Li Na and Rosie. They were in the nursery. Lily took the child and kissed the top of her head, breathing in her sweet baby smell. Rosie was all she cared about; let others try to save the fallen women of Shanghai.

60

~ *Lily* ~

Florence brought an air of calm to the Yellow House. Lily was no longer lonely and began to venture out into the streets of Shanghai once more with her sketchbook. When she had first arrived in the city, she'd been a 'griffin', a newcomer trying to get to grips with the city; now she was eager to show her sister-in-law around her favourite spots in Frenchtown and on the Bund. They even managed to drag Hugh away from his mission work long enough to go on weekend trips on the *Jeanie*, meandering through waterways and going ashore to explore the ancient delta city of Soochow, strolling through the quieter lanes that ran alongside canals to buy fruit and sweets from handcarts. They wandered through the Humble Administrator's Garden with its peculiar pitted rocks, quaint teahouse and lotus ponds. Lily loved the poetic names of the pavilions – Faraway Looking and Sound of the Rain were her favourites. They joined the crowds to admire the temples and pagodas, and squeezed through the crush of bodies along Lindun Lu, peeking into the narrow alleys where jade cutters, silk merchants and ceramicists plied their trades and pedlars hawked tongue scrapers, joss sticks and ivory combs.

On these trips Hugh was at his most relaxed, as if the water soothed him. In the mornings they sat on deck, watching the cormorant fishermen in their wide straw hats, plying their trade on narrow skiffs. Instead of fishing poles, they tied string around the birds' necks, and the cormorants dived for fish to add to teeming baskets. In the evenings, the sun stained the sky rose gold and the red lanterns on the shore lit up as darkness fell. Lily was at peace, with Rosie warm and sleepy in her lap, listening to the water lapping the side of the *Jeanie* and the low murmur of voices from the crew.

As summer wore on and turned Shanghai into a steam bath, the crowded streets and noxious air became unbearable. Huan Liu arranged a trip to Hangchow, the mountains and lake making it a popular summer bolthole for Shanghailanders. The two women couldn't persuade Hugh to leave the sweltering city, but Florence took leave from the hospital, where she had quickly made herself indispensable.

'I must take a break else I shall be no use to man nor beast,' she said to Lily.

The two women, Rosie and the servants went by train, renting a garden villa on the shore of West Lake and in the lee of Phoenix Mountain. They took boat trips, played tennis and went for long walks along the edge of the lake where giant water lilies grew and men flew kites with their children, the wind tugging at the delicate paper shapes. Lily's brush captured the layers of grey and blue that stretched out over the water and faded into the mountain range in the distance. The lake was fringed with weeping willows that cast a cool shade, and she was reminded once more of Jeanie and the willow tree that used to be their secret hideaway as children.

When they returned to Shanghai, Florence still had some days of leave left and they took turns pushing the child in her perambulator through the wide tree-lined streets of Frenchtown and the Public Gardens. Nancy Thornton had had her baby and began to join them on their walks with her son, Beauregard. The American woman seemed unchanged by motherhood and deemed any mention of feeding times, naps and winding 'too tedious for words'. She was still a mine of gossip, despite her recent confinement, and welcomed Florence as a new audience, ignoring her obvious dislike of idle talk. The three women were walking through Gus Park in Frenchtown with the babies one day when Florence bumped into an Irish nurse from the hospital. Nancy and Lily went ahead while they talked shop.

'Do you see that fine gentleman with a paunch?' Nancy whispered to Lily. 'The one with the whiskers who keeps looking at his fob watch?' Lily nodded. 'He's a leading light at the American consulate. This is where he meets the wife of one of his underlings. They've been carrying on under her husband's nose for several years. *Le tout* Shanghai knows about the affair, everyone, that is, except the patsy he married. Now watch this.'

After a few minutes a much younger woman approached the portly man, who jumped back in a show of surprise. He glanced around several times before doffing his cap to her and walking off with her. As they walked away Lily stifled a giggle.

'What a dreadful ham!'

'I know, he'd be booed off the stage on Broadway,' Nancy said. 'Now, pay attention: this is the best part.' And with that, the diplomat shot out an arm and pulled his young companion into a flowering bush. 'I really think we should move on before that bush starts trembling, it's too killing!'

'What's so funny?' Florence asked when she caught up with them. But Lily couldn't speak for laughing.

When Florence went back to work, Lily found herself immersed once more in the social whirl of Shanghai. Nancy had no intentions of letting motherhood slow her down, and Lily saw a lot more of her as both their husbands were working long hours. Joe had been promoted to night editor, so he was at the office from ten o'clock until the small hours, and he'd sometimes stay even later, rolling up his sleeves to help the Chinese printing staff get the paper out. He'd also take off on trips to the interior with his portable typewriter in an attempt to bring back news of what he called 'the real China' for his mostly British and American readers, who were more interested in the goings-on of the London and New York stock exchanges and their own society events.

'I don't know why he bothers since nobody gives two hoots about the skirmishes between warlords up country,' Nancy drawled. 'All they're interested in is the next paper chase.'

Nancy and Beauregard were soon a regular presence in the Yellow House and Lily didn't even notice when Florence began to spend longer and longer at the hospital. It was only later that Lily realised that her sister-in-law had discreetly withdrawn once she was no longer lonely.

~

The next three years were a period of calm and happiness as Rosie grew into a delightful toddler with winning ways and a sunny outlook. Lily widened her circle of friends, encouraged by Nancy to attend the balls and national celebrations that made up the social round in Shanghai. Hugh worked at the hospital during the day and most evenings on urban missionary work, so Lily had plenty of time to fill. She enjoyed the drama and glamour of the balls, but more for the aesthetics and the women's fashionable cocktail dresses than the chatting and drinking. The parties with their incessant stream of gossip and frothy conversation tired her out after a couple of hours, and she was always glad to get home and drink a cup of green tea alone in her garden at the Yellow House, relishing the solitude that allowed her to think and dream of her next painting. She was planning a series of street scenes that would show the contrasts of the city: the European traders in their sedan chairs, their wives in muslin dresses sitting pretty in rickshaws pulled by half-naked, sweating coolies; but also people haggling over the catch at the morning market, the old men sitting in doorways in the back alleys drinking tea from tiny cups. Lily liked to get up early, when it was still cool and fresh, and wander the streets, sketchbook in hand. She would return at breakfast and eat with Florence, Hugh and Rosie, content with her small family and the steady rhythm of her life.

Father O'Leary was also a regular visitor to the Yellow House. 'You've made this place a home, Lily,' he said one morning, dandling a plump Rosie on his lap after Hugh and Florence had left for the day. 'I can see that Shanghai suits you. But, tell me, how is Hugh after his illness? He seems recovered. Not working too hard, I hope?'

'Of course he's working too hard, he wouldn't be Hugh otherwise. He spends all day at the hospital then goes out into the streets at night on his mission.'

'And how's that going?'

'I've absolutely no idea. He doesn't like to talk about it and, quite frankly, I'd rather not hear about it.'

The priest frowned. 'Is that wise? I'm no expert when it comes to marriage, clearly, but shouldn't a husband and wife share more? Forgive me for being forward, but it seems you have separate lives.'

Lily rankled. 'Well, we don't live in each other's pockets, if that's what you mean. I used to accompany Hugh on his missionary work in Glasgow, but I have Rosie to think of now. Do you expect me to go into brothels with him?'

'Of course not, and I can see I've offended you. I'm sorry, I should have kept my big mouth shut. I'm turning into an interfering old woman. I could give the Misses Smythson a run for their money.'

Lily was mollified. 'I see their fame has reached St Ignatius. Actually, they're perfectly lovely old dears and Rosie adores them, don't you darling?' Her daughter was too busy playing with the priest's rosary beads to look up. 'I've grown fond of the Misses Smythson, of Maud and Iris, or is it Iris and Maud? I can never tell which is which.'

As a foreign woman, life in Shanghai was easy for Lily. Her nights were her own since Rosie had begun sleeping in the nursery with Li Na in a trestle cot at the end of her bed, and Huan Liu and Wang Yong ran the household like clockwork, with delicious meals on the table and laundry appearing neatly pressed and folded before she had risen from her bed. She had acres of time and, determined not to turn into a bored colonial wife who had little to occupy herself with other than balls and race meets, started drawing and painting in earnest. She sketched candid portraits of Beauregard and Rosie as they played together in the shade of the plum and cherry trees or in the bathtub where they gurgled and hit at the water with fat fists. One day, Lily walked into the sitting room to find Nancy leafing through her sketchbook. She held up a drawing of Beauregard on his hands looking backwards through his legs while Rosie squatted beside him, head tilted as if they were having a conversation.

'Why, these are simply enchanting!'

Lily laughed, embarrassed, and made to take the sketchbook, but Nancy whisked it out of range.

'Please, Nancy, give me that back. Nobody is supposed to see these, they're just doodles, really.'

'Doodles that people would pay cold, hard cash for

– Shanghailanders would love nothing better than portraits of their precious darlings.'

'But these aren't my real work. I used to do portraits back home, but I prefer to work on street scenes, I find them more authentic.'

Nancy tutted and handed her the sketchbook, and Lily shoved it into a cupboard. 'Authentic? Oh, brother! You Brits are so coy about money, but trust me, you could earn a small fortune in commissions. Don't tell me you couldn't do with some extra cash.'

Lily had to admit that money had been tighter since Hugh had cut his hours at the hospital and started spending more time on his missionary work. The China Inland Mission paid buttons and her own savings had dwindled alarmingly as she quietly subsidised the household budget. This past year she had spent a lot on tailored gowns suitable for balls and race meets and regattas and had not thought it wise to discuss the expenditure with Hugh. Meanwhile, Huan Liu had told her the berthing fees for the *Jeanie* were due, as well as some repairs. She had had no idea the upkeep for a boat would cost so much. She'd overheard a wag at the yacht club describe owning a boat as 'standing under a shower and tearing up ten-shilling notes'. Lily made up her mind: she would start doing portraits again. Besides, none of her peers in the art world would see them. And she could still paint her street scenes.

She smiled at her friend. 'All right, if you think it would work.'

Nancy clapped her hands. 'I'll be your agent, ducks.'

She lost no time putting the word around that Lily was a talented and famous artist who was open to offers. Soon prominent Shanghailanders were queuing up to have their and their offspring's portraits painted, delighted by Lily's ability to bring out a person's character with the tilt of a head or the thrust of a chin. Lily found herself enjoying the work. There was an unexpected bonus when Tony Forsyth, who was one of the board members of the Hongkong and Shanghai Bank, said he'd like nothing better than to put on an exhibition of her Shanghai street scenes.

'These are quite remarkable,' he said one day, on a visit to the Yellow House, where he admired the watercolours she'd framed and hung on her sitting-room walls. 'You've captured the ordinary people of Shanghai.' Tony turned and smiled at her. 'My mother was Eurasian, you know. These scenes remind me of the times she took me to the old Chinese part of the city to eat dumplings and noodles in the street and spend time with her family.'

Nancy was delighted. 'I'm taking all the credit for your success, of course,' she said in the room Lily now used as a studio while the toddlers played happily in the garden watched over by their *amahs*. 'And an exhibition, no less! Tony will be as good as his word. He's worth a mint and once he starts buying, the rest will follow. This bunch of yokels won't know what's hit them when they find out there's a real artist in their midst. Did you know we had a mobile library for a while? There was so little demand for the books it had to close. Philistines to a man and woman.' Nancy squinted at a portrait of a chinless wonder and scion of a shipping family whom Lily had persuaded to pose in tartan trews and a Glengarry bonnet. 'I don't know how you've done it, but you've made Mackenzie-Robertson look almost human.'

Lily was uncertain. 'It's perhaps not my best work. I didn't want to flatter him, but you know, that chin.'

'I know! You could eat your breakfast off it. Don't mind me. Take the money and run, I say. Just draw the line when

293

they start asking you to paint their pets.' Lily bit her lip and Nancy dropped her jaw in mock astonishment. 'Don't tell me, you brazen hussy, have you no shame?'

'Lady Mackenzie-Robertson begged me for a portrait of her Pomeranian, Poubelle. I couldn't say no, much as I wanted to. However, it died last week.'

'A narrow escape, then, for our acclaimed lady artist, winner of several medals?'

'Unfortunately, no: she's having Poubelle stuffed so the portrait can go ahead.'

'Jeez, painting a dead pooch. You have sunk to a new low. But say, isn't *poubelle* French for garbage can?'

Lily laughed. 'Yes, it is. Lady M-R heard her Parisian maid say it and thought it such a sophisticated name. I didn't have the heart to tell her what it meant.'

Nancy put the portrait back against the wall with a shudder. 'I guess you have to get your kicks where you can find them with these people, otherwise you'd go as nuts as they are.'

~

Hugh became so immersed in his mission that he negotiated for Florence to take over his position full time at the hospital. The brother and sister were now rarely home for meals and Lily was often out in the evening with Nancy, and sometimes Joe, if he could get away from the paper. Caught up in her work and new friendships, Lily pushed the nagging doubt planted by Daniel O'Leary about how she and Hugh were living parallel lives to the back of her mind and concentrated on her exhibition. It was to be called 'Old Hundred Names' – the name the Chinese called themselves after the hundred most common surnames.

Tony Forsyth clapped his hands when she'd told him.

'Yes, yes! *Laobaixing* we say, "Old Hundred Names". It's perfect!'

Besides her art and working at St Joseph's, Shanghai kept Lily entertained and distracted from the growing distance between her and her husband. There were endless race meets, balls, cocktail parties and nightclubs with American bands playing the latest jazz. She never tired of the bustle – eight people walking abreast on the pavements; roads rammed with Oldsmobiles, rickshaws, electric trams and people pushing wheelbarrows or wobbling past on bicycles.

As her fame as an artist grew, Lily became a popular guest at dinner parties thrown by wealthy Shanghailanders, where she struggled through course after course of rich food shipped in from Fortnum & Mason and Crosse & Blackwell. There were boat trips and regattas and the annual cross-country paper chase with riders in pink jackets on shaggy Mongolian ponies. Immersed in the hectic, ceaseless social rounds of the Concessions, she inhabited a strange life filled with Europeans, Americans and the rich Chinese with their Westernised ways. She was barely aware of the old walled Chinese City, where half of the three million population of Shanghai lived set apart from the foreigners, or of the industrial districts of Chapei and Yangtzepoo with their cotton mills, silk filatures, chemical and engineering works, power plants, shipyards and arsenals. These districts and Nantao, a jumble of streets along the old quarter, were deemed too dangerous for foreign women to visit. The only Chinese Lily knew were her household staff and the sons and daughters of wealthy compradors, bankers and industrialists. These Charlies, Philips and Wendys, with surnames like Pei, Jung, Kuo and Soong, lived in Frenchtown in mock Tudor villas with swimming pools and tennis courts and limousines; the young men wore fedoras, leather brogues and impeccably tailored suits, the women the latest Paris fashions, their black hair bobbed and marcelled, their faces artfully made up with kohl, pale powder and crimson lipstick. Lily saw them at tea dances at the Astor or the Majestic, at the Shanghai Race Club or at Sincere's and Wing On, chattering like brightly plumed birds. They seemed a breed apart from the ordinary Chinese who filled the factories and cleaned, cooked and ferried around the foreigners. Sometimes, when Joe Thornton talked about his work, Lily would be aware of this other side of Shanghai. It was a tale of two cities, one poor, one rich – as was Glasgow.

'There's trouble coming,' Joe said one evening, his rangy limbs relaxed in an easy chair at the Thorntons' apartment, a tumbler of bourbon in one hand and a cigarette in the other. 'There were more arrests last night after the rallies.'

'What was it all about?' Lily asked.

'The Chinese Communist Party is gathering strength and one of its leaders, Mao Tse-tung, is a real firebrand, stirring up the students. Mark my words, we're living in a bubble, but things are changing. Shanghai is a powder keg – the government has no power and isn't doing enough for the ordinary Chinese, and the country is in a state of anarchy with gangsters running the city through opium, gambling and kidnapping rackets. Meanwhile the country-side is controlled by warlords and their armies of looting bandits.'

Nancy raised her eyebrows at Lily, but she was interested and urged Joe to carry on. He was happy to oblige and recrossed his legs, settling in for a lecture. Nancy sighed and picked up the latest copy of *Harper's Bazaar*.

'You see,' Joe said, lighting a cigarette from the butt of the last one. 'China is rapidly industrialising, but most of the population are peasants and most of the country is agricultural, so the wealth isn't trickling down to the masses. In the cities, factory conditions are appalling – think the worst excesses of the last century in Britain – and there has been a wave of strikes and labour unrest recently.

'So, you have the Communists stirring that lot up. Meanwhile, their deadly rivals, the Kuomintang, the banned Nationalist Party, have been biding their time and word is they're gathering an army together from their base in the south and are getting ready to strike. There's even talk of their leader, Sun Yat-sen, forming an alliance with the Reds to start a revolution and overthrow the government.'

Lily listened carefully but her knowledge of China's recent history was sketchy. She knew about the different dynasties by their art and porcelain, coached by Huan Liu, but nobody in her circle talked about the Boxer Rebellion or the Opium Wars; they were too shameful and too recent to sully a dinner party conversation. Lily had never seen signs of unrest in her untroubled Shanghai life and thought Joe might be exaggerating the danger for effect. As a journalist, he had a flair for drama.

'Surely any such trouble will be far away and won't affect us,' she said. 'In Shanghai, we're still run by our home countries and protected by extraterritoriality laws. The Chinese central government in Peking knows to leave the foreign concessions alone.'

Joe shook his head. 'That's what you'll hear the *tai-pans* say – they can't imagine their empire falling apart. But we Americans know that revolution can and does happen and that the colonisers are always overthrown in the end.'

Nancy lowered her magazine and made a face at her friend. Lily smiled at her wifely exasperation. Joe was like Hugh in many ways: he thought he had the power to change the world by shining a light on exploitation and injustice. But Lily had no stomach for crusades; she was only concerned with the here and now and how she could capture it in bold oils or elusive watercolours: the shadow thrown on a face; the myriad tones of green, blue and purple in a landscape; the molten gold spreading over a hill at sundown; the gossamer down on her infant daughter's cheek.

Even so, Joe's talk of revolution disturbed her, his gloomy warnings bringing back troubled memories of the war and of Jack she'd tried to bury. Back at the Yellow House, Lily went to a trunk in her bedroom and brought out an old sketchbook. Inside, a bundle of old letters in Jack's hand was tucked between studies of Jeanie for the 'Nights at the Theatre' series. Lily put aside the letters, unable to bear reading them, but she turned the pages of the sketchbook to see Jeanie dusting her ballet shoes in chalk, Jeanie in conversation with Ivanov, his arm carelessly draped around her shoulders. The last page was a charcoal sketch of Jeanie on stage, her arms arched above her head as if reaching for the stars. Lily put the book back in the trunk and closed the lid, overwhelmed by sadness.

61

~ *Jeanie* ~

Jeanie was in her office, poring over costume designs with Kit while her backer, Harry Richardson, sat in the armchair by the window, reading out newspaper reviews of the previous night's show. The Taylor Girls had seen their success grow in the last four years, but Jeanie knew that the buzz of publicity around the new show had drawn the critics and the punters as never before.

'The *Evening Citizen* says we're *spectacular*,' Harry said. 'The *Glasgow Herald, Daily Express* and *Daily Record* all loved the show – "*Ooh la la!* Like an evening in Paris" – but the *Scotsman*'s a bit sniffy – "too much flesh on display for our readers' refined sensibilities". That critic's always been a po-faced bastard, begging your pardon, Kit.' Harry had taken a shine to Kit and gazed adoringly at her over the top of the newspaper.

'He's done us a favour – we'll have to beat the punters away with a stick,' Jeanie said. She fanned out a sheaf of papers and beckoned Harry over. 'What do you think of Kit's designs for the new act?'

Harry pointed to a drawing of a jockey in colourful silks, tight white breeches and riding boots. 'I like this one for the leading man, very dashing. Quite fancy it myself.'

'That's for a race scene,' Jeanie said. 'The girls will be in fancy frilled dresses, hats and parasols. He'll leap off the horse after winning the gee-gees, and they'll clamour round him, whipping off their long skirts for the song and dance routine.'

'Did you say horse? Isn't that awfully expensive?'

'We can't have a jockey without his horse. Don't worry, I've found an ex-police horse that costs buttons and won't be spooked by the crowd, who are, by the way, going to lap this up.'

'In that case, I love it! And Kit, may I say, you're a genius.'

Kit smiled and shuffled through the papers on the desk. 'Here's what I've designed for Jeanie.' She picked up a colourful drawing in brilliant greens and blues, trimmed in gold. A magnificent peacock's tail rose behind the figure of a dancer in her tight bodice. The tiny skirt that showed off her legs was made from feathers.

Harry whistled. 'Now, that's what you call a show-stopper! This is going to be our most extravagant show yet.'

~

The company might have grown from strength to strength over the last four years, but Jeanie was the first to admit it had been a slog. They'd started small in provincial theatres but gradually scored theatres in Glasgow, Edinburgh, Aberdeen and Dundee, and the likes of Liverpool and Manchester, although they hadn't been given any bookings in London. Harry had stuck with them in the slow climb but he'd been prudent with his investment, unwilling to spend too much until the Taylor Girls had become established and the offers from the big theatres started coming in. Jeanie was thirty-three now and knew she only had a few more years as a dancer left; already her joints ached, and she was more prone to injury. But Stella at twelve was now a gifted ballerina, and one day she'd take her place in the spotlight, outshining her mother. Jeanie had pushed her hard since she was a little girl, knowing how impossible it was to make up practice missed in the early years. Her heart swelled with pride when she saw Stella dance, but she found it difficult to show it.

'You're too hard on her, she's only a child and needs time to play,' Tatiana said a few days after their meeting with Harry when Stella had stormed out of the studio in tears after a particularly fraught rehearsal with Jeanie. 'You make her too anxious – she should enjoy her practice.'

Jeanie sighed. 'She's got some notion of herself – thinks her shite doesn't smell, and I can tell she thinks I'm as common as muck.' She sat down heavily next to Tatiana. 'We never used to fight like this when you were teaching me. What am I doing wrong? The other girls in my classes listen to what I say and respect me. She's always correcting the way I speak, the cheeky wee bitch. I would never have given you backchat.'

'That's because you're not my daughter. Didn't you fight with your mother?'

Jeanie thought back to how she'd treated Ma, how she'd despised her for being so weak with men and been ashamed of her washerwoman's red and callused hands, of her reputation as a slut and a slattern, and how she'd secretly longed for an elegant, softly spoken mother like Lily's. 'Aye, we did, I gave her a hard time. Now it's coming back to bite me.'

Tatiana placed her hand on Jeanie's arm. 'Be patient. She's growing into a young woman. It's a difficult time but it'll pass.'

'I hope to God you're right. She's a right pain in the arse.'

They tidied and swept the studio and Jeanie began to feel contrite. She handed Tatiana the broom. 'I'd better go and see how Stella is. Wish me luck.'

She knocked on Stella's door. There was no answer and she tried the handle, expecting to find it locked. The door swung open to reveal an empty room; the wardrobe doors hung open and the chest of drawers looked as if it'd been ransacked. There was a note on her pillow:

Gone to London to see Daddy. I'm not coming back.

PART 5

~ *Old Friends* ~

1925–1928

62

~ *Lily* ~

Shanghai, 1925

It was Lily's fifth Shanghai summer, but she'd not got used to the suffocating heat. The city, built on mudflats and the banks of the roiling brown waters of the Huangpu, was a sauna, the air a miasma of pollution from the steamboats choking the harbour. Drinking water had to be boiled and treated with alum to kill parasites, and epidemics of cholera, typhoid, malaria and bilharzia were frequent. Lily, sapped of energy and unable to work, retreated to Moganshan, a hill station, with Rosie. The little girl, now a pretty doll of a five-year-old, was doted on by the servants and her parents. Hugh was busier than ever with his missionary work, but Lily had finally managed to persuade him he needed to rest in the cool, clean air of the hill station, where they could swim, play tennis and take long walks in the bamboo forests.

'Besides, Rosie is beginning to forget what her father looks like,' she had said to him, shamelessly using his love for the little girl. Rosie had grinned as if on cue, clambered onto Hugh's lap and thrown her arms around his neck.

'Please come, Papa, please. I love you so.' Hugh had smiled over her ringlets at Lily.

'How can I resist? Very well, then, I shall come with you.'

But Florence, working day and night in the overflowing hospital wards, would not be persuaded to accompany them and proved immune even to Rosie's pleading. They reluctantly left her in sweltering Shanghai.

~

Lily and Hugh were sitting in the shade of a fir tree drinking tea while Rosie pretended to build a fire with pine cones when the British consul came toiling up the hillside. He was red-faced in a linen suit and sweating under his tight collar when he stopped a few yards from them and raised a weary hand in greeting. Hugh leapt to his feet and offered the man a chair.

'Sir Alec! I had no idea you were here. Please, come into the shade and rest.' Lily poured him a cup of tea and they waited while the consul caught his breath. He mopped his brow and sat twisting his handkerchief between his hands, unable to meet their eyes. At last he looked up.

'I'm afraid I've come here on a grim errand. There's no easy way to say this, you must be brave.' He stood up and put his hand on Hugh's shoulder. 'It's your sister, Florence. I'm terribly sorry, but she's gone.'

Hugh's head dropped into his hands. Lily couldn't move. Not calm, cool, capable Florence; it was impossible.

She turned to the consul. 'You must be mistaken, surely? We only left her four days ago and she was in the peak of health. Tired with the long shifts, but fine.'

'I'm sorry, but there's no room for error. Miss Anderson fell ill with a fever. The other doctors and the nurses did everything they could, but it was hopeless. They think she may have been ill for some days and was medicating herself to keep going during the crisis.' He seemed to remember he was still wearing his hat and took it off. 'She was a marvellous woman, selfless to the end.' He got up, his knees creaking as if the humidity of Shanghai had made them rusty. 'I'll leave you now. Don't hesitate and so forth.' He walked off down the hill, his back rigid with embarrassment. Hugh stared at the ground. Rosie got up from her play and ran to her father holding a small blue flower.

'Look, Papa, for you.' She tucked it behind his ear and put her arms around his neck. Hugh held her and began to sob as if his heart were breaking. It was only then that Lily realised it was true: Florence was dead. She would never again see her gentle face, gravely listening or wryly amused; she would never again hear her low, steady voice.

They left for the city that day. That night, back at the Yellow House, Hugh shut himself in his study and locked the door. Lily stood outside, frightened. He began to howl, like an animal in pain. She could hear objects being thrown, the shatter of glass and porcelain, the thump of tables and chairs being overturned.

It was just before dawn that he came for her. Lily woke to find herself pinned to the bed, Hugh holding her wrists above her head with one hand and pulling up her nightdress with the other.

'Stop, you're hurting me!'

He clamped his hand over her mouth and thrust inside her. Lily wasn't ready and it felt as if he was burning a path. He grunted and drove into her with more force. Lily cried out, muffled by his hand. She couldn't breathe and bit his hand hard, tasting blood.

'You bitch!' Hugh rolled off her and sat up, sucking his hand while she scrambled off the bed, knocking over the bedside table, and curled herself into a ball on the floor in the corner of the room. He came towards her. In the half-light, Hugh's face was a mask of hatred. Lily tried to shrink away from him but there was nowhere to go. He raised his hand and with an open palm slapped her so hard, her head knocked against the wall. She was too stunned to cry out.

307

The slap seemed to resound around the bedroom. Hugh spoke into the silence.

'It's you who should be dead, not her. Florence was a saint, not a painted whore like you. Why are you alive and not her?' He took a step nearer but a noise at the door made him turn around and gave Lily a chance to get to her feet and run across the room. She pulled open the door and found Huan Liu standing there.

'Madam, is everything all right? I heard a crash.' She felt Hugh behind her. He placed his hand on her shoulder.

'I stumbled over the bedside table going for a glass of water. You can go back to bed.' Hugh's tone was affable as he moved past Lily. 'Bring some tea to my study, there's a good fellow. Now that I'm up, I might as well get on with some work.'

Huan Liu bowed his head. Hugh closed the study door and he looked searchingly at Lily. 'Are you sure you're all right?' Lily shook her head miserably and placed a hand on the side of her face that was already swelling. 'Oh, Mrs Anderson, you don't deserve this.' He clenched his fist. 'If only I could . . .'

'Don't do anything, Huan Liu, you'll get into trouble, and it'll be worse for me. Hugh's not himself, I'll call the doctor when it's light.'

'Lock your door. I'll put something in his tea to calm him down.'

~

The doctor came and prescribed a sedative and rest. Lily didn't mention what had happened, but she could see him looking at the bruise on her face. In the days that followed Lily instructed Li Na to keep Rosie occupied and out of the house as much as possible and Wang Yong to leave trays of food outside the study, where Huan Liu had set up a camp bed for Hugh. Lily locked her door at night and stared into the darkness, unable to sleep, wondering how she had got to this place in her life, afraid of her own husband, the two of them mired in grief and mutual hatred.

Lily moved through the days like an automaton for Rosie's sake, but one morning she knew she had to do something to either help Hugh or leave him. She wrote a note to Father O'Leary asking him to come and see them. Desperate to confide in someone, she also wrote to Jeanie about what had happened, pouring out her fears about Hugh. Lily asked Huan Liu to post the letter and call for a rickshaw to take her to the Misses Smythson. When she arrived at their house, Maud and Iris had heard the news. They put their birdlike arms around her.

'You poor thing.'

'Yes, poor thing. There, there; there, there.' They patted her gently on the back and Lily began to cry for the first time since she'd heard about Florence. After the sisters had given her a cup of strong, sweet tea – *for the shock, my dear, nothing like a cup of tea* – they settled down with pencils and notebooks and began drawing up lists.

'So much to be done under these sad circumstances, just when you're not feeling up to it.' Maud turned to Iris. 'We know, don't we, dear.'

'Poor Mama.'

'Yes, poor Mama.' Iris patted Lily on the knee. 'Don't worry, we'll see to everything. But there will be papers for you to sign, a casket to choose, people to notify – oh, it's endless. The only good thing is that at this time of year, because of the heat, everything is done most expeditiously. We'll help you with the bureaucracy.'

Lily didn't know how she would have got through the next few days without their help. The sisters took her to the hospital and sat with her while Florence's colleagues gathered around and explained how she'd died; they went with her to the consulate and to the municipal council to fill in forms and sign the paperwork, and to the funeral parlour where she set about the grim task of choosing a casket. Lily was grateful for their help as Hugh still refused to come out of his study and remained silent as she relayed the arrangements she'd made through the locked door. She was afraid he wouldn't attend the funeral service – Florence would have been saddened not to have her brother there. It was only when Father O'Leary arrived, all bustle and bear hugs for her and a doll for Rosie, that a shaft of light seemed to pierce the thick mantle of grief and anger that had settled over the Yellow House. He rapped at Hugh's door.

'You must let me in this minute, sir.' Lily had never heard the priest sound so commanding and she realised that there was steel under his affable demeanour. The door opened and the priest slipped into the room. An hour later he emerged alone. 'He's coming to the funeral,' he said.

'Thank goodness. How is he?'

Daniel shook his head. 'In despair. He thinks God has abandoned him. His faith has been shaken. I won't lie to you; I'm worried about him. As you know, your husband is a man of extreme passions.'

Lily couldn't bring herself to tell this kind man that her husband had raised his hands to her. 'He can't lose his faith; it would kill him. He was like this before, when he came back from the interior, after his mission failed.'

Daniel looked thoughtful. 'Some men are prone to these episodes of darkness; it's a kind of eclipse of the soul. What brought him out of it last time?'

'His sister.'

'Oh, dear.'

Lily tried to think what Florence would have done. 'She got him back to work. They drew up a plan for a new mission. She said a man like Hugh needed a purpose, to feel he was making a difference.'

'Then, that is what we shall encourage him to do – go back to work. What was the mission?'

'An urban mission, working with the Moral Welfare League in the brothels.'

Father O'Leary made a face. 'I always feel sorry for the fallen women. Have they not enough on their plate without missionaries trying to save their souls?'

Lily laughed for the first time since Florence's death. 'I don't know how much headway they are making, but Hugh has been away a lot.'

'I can't imagine he's got very far with the Voluptuous Vampires from Vladivostok. Those Russian women are quite something. They should have stayed and fought the Bolsheviks. Lenin and the rest of those lads wouldn't have stood a chance. Last time I ventured into Avenue Edouard VII at night, one of the dance hostesses jumped out of a doorway and grabbed hold of me with a grip of steel and went, "My prince, please you buy little Sonya one small bottle vine."' Lily laughed again. The priest put on a passable Russian accent and she'd heard the Russian women were notorious for their fondness of the imitation champagne they called 'vine'. He shook his head. 'And wouldn't you know, I was wearing my cassock and dog collar, if you please! Little minx!

'I know that Grace Flaherty, too, the American madam with a bawdy-house on Kiangse Road. Quite an enterprising businesswoman, she is, dresses her girls in saucy costumes – spangled harem trousers for the dance of the seven veils and so forth. Sails out to San Francisco regularly to get new recruits and sends out cards to her regulars to

311

announce the new arrivals. She even sent one to me after I'd been to see her to give the last rites to some poor girl. Aye, she's a devout Catholic, when it suits her.'

Lily was amused. 'For a priest, you seem to know an awful lot about the seedy side of Shanghai, and you don't seem that disapproving.'

'These venal sins are of little importance in the grand scheme of things. Sure, didn't Christ himself consort with prostitutes: *cast the first stone ye who are without sin,* and all that? I tell you, there are worse people knocking about Shanghai than Gracie Flaherty and her Paramount Peaches.' He stood up. 'But if Hugh thinks he can change their ways, who am I to disagree? And if that's what it takes to remember that God loves him, then I'll do my best to encourage him back to work.'

63

~ *Jeanie* ~

Jeanie read Lily's letter again. Lily needed her: poor Florence was dead, and her friend's marriage was in trouble. Jeanie put the letter in her desk drawer next to the others, and went to see Harry. The company was now more popular than ever, with London theatres eager to welcome the Taylor Girls and the audiences that flocked to see them. It meant Jeanie could see her daughter, who was back at her old school and living with Viktor. When Stella had run away, Tatiana had counselled her not to be heavy-handed and drag her back to Glasgow.

'Let her work it out for herself. She'll come back to you of her own accord.'

But two years went by and Stella was showing no signs of leaving Chelsea for Glasgow. When Lily's letter arrived, Jeanie had an idea that would bring her daughter back to her and help her friend. After seeing Harry, she called a meeting with Tatiana and Kit, both of whom now had shares in the company.

'I want to put together a new show, more modern, with new dance steps, extravagant sets and costumes. Harry's signed off on the budget.' She showed them the figures and Tatiana clapped her hands together.

'There's more,' Jeanie said. 'There's going to be a new dancer.'

'Who?' Kit said.

'Stella. I was watching her dance last time we were in London. She's ready.'

Tatiana nodded. 'At fourteen she's young, but she's always been talented, like her mother.'

'And there's something else.' They looked at her expectantly. 'We're going on tour.'

'The West End?' Tatiana said.

Jeanie tried to hide her smile; she'd been waiting to break the good news. 'A little bit further afield than that. How does Paris sound?'

Kit gasped. 'Paris! I've never been to Paris.'

'And Rome, Vienna, Berlin.'

Tatiana grabbed Kit's hands 'The places I can show you! You will love them all.'

Kit laughed. 'I can make the trip to Paris, but you forget I have four children who need their mama.'

Tatiana waved her hands. 'Then we'd better make sure you make the most of Paris.'

Jeanie leaned against her desk and crossed her arms. 'There's more.'

The two other women stopped and stared at her. 'More?' Tatiana said.

'Harry's going to get us deals with theatres in Moscow and St Petersburg. Then we go to Shanghai.'

There was a moment's silence, then Kit and Tatiana said in unison: 'Lily's in Shanghai.'

Jeanie allowed a grin to spread across her face. 'I know.'

64

~ *Lily* ~

By the time winter arrived, the Yellow House had settled into a dreariness that had become normal. Nancy still came to visit but Lily was still in mourning and had stepped off the Shanghai social carousel. Hugh, persuaded back to work by Daniel O'Leary, was now out day and night, pursuing his mission with a grim fervour that began to worry Lily. When he was home, he locked himself in his study where he still slept on a camp bed, but at least he didn't come near her at night and she began to sleep more easily behind her locked bedroom door.

Hugh had grown gaunt, reminding Lily of when he returned from the interior. But he seemed different this time: his red-rimmed eyes were sunk into deep hollows and if he had to stay at home for any length of time, he became restless, shivering and pacing with nervous jerks. He'd often stay out overnight and when he returned his clothes were pungent with an odd, sweet odour, like burned flowers. From being a devoted father to Rosie, he seemed to have lost interest in the little girl. When Lily could persuade him to stay in for dinner, he'd barely touch his food and kept glancing at the door as if seeking escape from Rosie's prattling and his wife's desperate attempts at conversation. Released from the table, he'd peck Lily on the cheek and pat Rosie distractedly on the head before bolting out of the house.

At first Lily tried to make allowances for her husband and put his odd behaviour down to grief. Daniel counselled her to give him time and space to recover his spirits, but the longer it went on, the angrier she felt for her daughter, who couldn't understand why her darling papa had changed into this surly stranger. When she tried to broach the subject, Hugh just stared at her silently until she stopped talking, his eyes as cold and expressionless as a shark's.

Lily stayed at home mostly, trying to read, and unable to work. The 'Old Hundred Names' exhibition was on hold out of respect for the mourning period, and Lily shrank into herself. The shadows in the corners of her carefully decorated rooms seemed to want to swallow her up and the house, which had always been her sanctuary from the bustle of the city, now seemed more like a prison with its high gates. At the end of the summer, Rosie started attending a British girls' school, and Lily missed her cheery babble and was always glad when her daughter burst through the door, full of news from the classroom and the small dramas of her circle of little friends. One windy December day, when Lily was trying to cheer the house up with some Christmas decorations, Huan Liu brought her a note. She read it and her hand flew to her mouth.

'Bad news, madam?'

Lily read the few lines again. 'Quite the contrary, it's wonderful news. My oldest friend is in Shanghai – Jeanie's here, right now.'

Huan Liu smiled. 'I'm glad. An old friend is what you need to help you through this dark time. Is she moving to Shanghai with her husband?'

Lily read the note again. 'No, she's on tour, in a show – she's a dancer.' Lily clasped the note to her chest. 'Oh, Huan Liu, I can't tell you how happy this makes me!'

There was a noise at the front door and Rosie ran into the sitting room and started talking before Li Na could help her out of her coat.

'Mama, Mama! You'll never guess! Juliet and I are best friends.'

'That's wonderful, darling. And you'll never guess – my best friend has come to Shanghai. She's a dancer and she's going to appear in a show.'

Rosie's eyes grew round. 'Can we go and see it? Please, Mama?' She turned to the *amah* and took her hand. 'And Li Na too. She can come too, can't you, Li Na?'

The *amah* smiled down at the little girl's upturned face. 'After chow time.' Li Na left the room to talk to Wang Yong about dinner.

Lily pulled Rosie towards her and stroked the little girl's curls. Her daughter had grown so pale and there were dark smudges under her eyes. A night at the theatre would do them both good and chase away the gloom that lay over the house like a grey army blanket. Lily could hardly believe she would see Jeanie again. She hugged her daughter until she squealed in protest.

'Of course we must go to the show and take Li Na too.' Rosie shrieked with delight and Lily laughed. Her thoughts turned to the last time she'd watched Jeanie perform on stage, a lifetime ago and halfway across the world. She tipped Rosie off her lap and went to the lacquer armoire. From its depths she called out 'Ah, here it is!', brandishing an old sketchbook in triumph and beaming at Rosie. 'Would you like to see some drawings of my friend dancing?'

Rosie clambered back into her lap and helped her turn the pages. 'She looks like a princess.'

'Jeanie can leap and pirouette like a spinning top. If you promise to eat all your vegetables at dinner, we'll all go together to see her perform. Now, go and wash your hands while Li Na sees to your tea.'

~

317

Later that evening, Lily hurried to get ready. They'd need to buy tickets but when she checked her purse it was empty apart from a few coins; she hadn't been to the bank for a while. She remembered Hugh kept cash in his roll-top desk. He usually locked his study but when she tried the door handle it opened easily and she stepped into the darkened room.

Feeling unaccountably guilty, she opened the central drawer of his desk and found the battered shortbread tin where he kept cash for emergencies. She took out some notes, stuffed them into her skirt pocket and was about to put the tin back when she noticed the corner of a photograph peeking out of a buff folder. Lily wondered if Hugh had been looking at family pictures and longed to see Florence's face once more. She sat down at the desk and pulled the folder towards her. The first photograph was of a young Chinese woman seated on a wooden carved throne. Her hair was piled into the elaborate style decorated with combs and bells traditionally worn by Mandarin women of another era, her face a mask of make-up, the skin ghostly white, eyebrows thick charcoal lines, mouth a dark rosebud. She was naked from the waist up, dressed only in silk pantaloons, her slippered feet just skimming the floor. This porcelain doll stared boldly at the photographer, the fingers of one hand resting provocatively on a nipple. On the back Hugh had written one word: *Coral.*

Hands trembling, Lily shuffled through the rest of the photographs. The same girl photographed from behind, naked apart from her shoes and hair ornaments. In other pictures she was dressed in various daring costumes, partially revealing her thighs and buttocks, the hint of a breast. Nudity didn't faze Lily – she had seen many life models – but she was shocked by these photographs of this young woman offering herself up to the camera without a hint of coquetry, as if she were going about her daily household duties, her expression serene, eyes staring boldly into the lens. These were disturbing pictures and they must have something to do with Hugh's mission work, she decided, but he shouldn't have brought them into the house. What if Rosie were to find them? Lily slid them back in the buff envelope and put it back where she'd found it. She didn't know what to think, but dark suspicions were already nosing their way into her mind.

65

∼ *Lily and Jeanie* ∼

Jeanie was putting on her stage make-up when Harry
Richardson came up to her. He was always jittery when
they arrived at a new place and he paced up and down in
front of her.

'Ticket sales are going well but we haven't sold out. Why
haven't we sold out? How often does a show like this come
to Shanghai? What else is there to do in this godforsaken
corner of the world? We should have stayed in Russia: they
appreciate our talents there. Peking was a disaster.'

Jeanie sighed. They'd been a success in Peking, selling
out every night except for one when it poured with rain.
It was far from a disaster. She stretched her hamstrings
and yawned. The overnight train from Peking had been the
latest in a series of sleeper rides across the Steppes and
down through Manchuria. The clanking as the train drew
into a station always jolted her awake, and she found the
crowds in China disconcerting. She'd be glad to get back
to Europe. Harry was still fretting so she walked over to
the curtain that hid backstage and flipped open a corner
to scan the crowd.

'It looks like a nearly full house to me. Stop worrying,
will you? You're supposed to keep us calm, not the other
way around.'

'You're right – Shanghai will fall in love with you, just
like all of Moscow and all of St Petersburg, all Paris, all
Vienna . . .'

'Aye, I get the picture. Now will you beat it, I have to

warm up.' She smiled fondly and closed the door on his hopeful face. Jeanie knew that she only had to say the word and he'd jump into her bed. Harry was wealthy and generous with it, and not bad looking to boot, but she knew he had also been making a play for Kit. Besides, Jeanie didn't want to go down that road again. She was proud of having built this company up by herself and how far she'd come from being Viktor's protégée.

There was a knock at the door and Jeanie sighed. 'Harry, I told you, I need to get ready.'

Stella put her head around the door. 'Mummy, it's only me.'

Jeanie's heart lifted. 'Come in, hen.' Stella came and sat next to her. She'd been such an affectionate little girl, never happier than when she was on Jeanie's lap, her arms around her neck, but she hadn't hugged her mother for years. Jeanie smiled at their reflections in the mirror. She had to content herself that her daughter was at least with her. It hadn't been as easy to persuade her to come on tour with her. Viktor had stepped into the middle of the inevitable shouting match.

'This is a chance any other dancer your age would jump at, if you don't go on tour, you'll regret it all your life,' he'd said, uncharacteristically firm. 'You have real talent. Trust me, I know what I'm talking about.' He'd smiled at Jeanie and for a moment she was back on Kelvinbridge as a young girl. Viktor had held out his hand and Jeanie walked into his arms filled with sadness for what they'd had.

Now Stella laid her head on Jeanie's shoulder and smiled back at her in the mirror. 'Two peas in a pod, just like Tatiana says.'

Jeanie cherished the moment of closeness. Stella was like an aloof cat who occasionally sits close to its owner as a show of affection. Jeanie put her arm around her and, rather than freezing, Stella relaxed into the embrace.

Jeanie spoke through her tears. 'You're the best thing that ever happened to me.'

'I thought I got in the way of your dancing career.'

Jeanie held on more tightly. 'Becoming a mother made me a better person and a better dancer. You gave me courage to fight for you and to fight for myself.'

Stella shook herself free and the moment was over. 'I've got to get changed for the first act. Tatiana will be waiting for me.'

Alone in her dressing room, Jeanie dabbed her eyes and fixed her stage make-up. She had her daughter back and tonight she would see Lily again. Her stomach fluttered, and for once it was nothing to do with first-night nerves.

~

'Excuse me, I'm sorry, I do beg your pardon . . .' Lily was flustered as she squeezed along the row to find their seats past people in evening dress who tutted in annoyance as they reluctantly stood up to let her pass. Their driver had been held up by the rush-hour traffic and Rosie had started to whine and fidget inside the stuffy car. Now they were here, the little girl was excited by the grand theatre. Lily and Li Na each held a small hand to make sure she didn't lose her footing. When they were finally seated, Lily tried to concentrate on the orchestra as it played various popular tunes, but she was impatient to see Jeanie. Beside her, Rosie fidgeted, and Li Na gazed up at the chandeliers. It was warm in the stalls and Lily shrugged off her coat and looked out her programme. At the top of the bill was Jeanie's name *appearing with the fabulous Taylor Girls*. Lily had been so proud of Jeanie when she'd written to tell her about forming her own company. And now she'd be seeing her soon. Time seemed to slow, and Lily barely took in the opening number danced by the chorus line. Rosie clapped her hands, entranced. Finally, finally, the spotlight lit up a lone figure and Jeanie leapt on stage, a vision in feathers and spangles, and Lily was transported back to another theatre in another time and place.

At the end of the show, to thunderous applause, the company of dancers held hands and approached the footlights to give their *reverence*, with Jeanie taking centre stage. Her curtsey was graceful, but she was unable to suppress a wide grin that Lily would recognise anywhere. Lily stood, her heart beating like a military tattoo, and clapped until her hands ached, blinking away tears as Jeanie gathered roses thrown from the audience. When the applause finally died down, Lily asked Li Na to take Rosie home, and made her way to the stage door. If ever she needed a friend, it was now.

In her dressing room, Jeanie was in her dressing gown taking her make-up off with cold cream when she heard a knock at the door. She called out 'Come in!' and turned as it swung open. There, standing in front of her, was Lily. Jeanie leapt up into a tight embrace, sending her chair sprawling. The two friends clung to each other, laughing and weeping. It was some time before they could find the words they needed to say and they stared at each other, searching each other's faces for familiar expressions and the changes wrought by time. It was Lily who broke the impasse.

'Jeanie, I can't tell you how happy I am to see you. Oh, I've missed you!'

'And I've missed you. What did you think of the show?'

Lily laughed. 'Always the performer!'

'Sorry, I know, I can't help myself. But did you like it?'

'Loved it! As did my daughter.'

323

'I can't wait to meet little Rosie. Your last letter said she was four or five?'

'Five. And Stella, she must be fourteen now.' When Lily had seen her on stage in the chorus line, she'd caught her breath; she'd looked exactly like Jeanie at the same age.

'Aye, and a talented wee dancer, just like her mammy! I'm so proud of her. You'll meet her later.'

'I picked her out straight away. She's a beauty!'

'She is, aye, and doesn't she know it, the little madam. She can twist Viktor round her little finger.'

'How is Viktor?'

'Frailer, but same old Viktor. We've stayed friends.'

'I'll never forget how he put on my first solo show back in Glasgow. Did he help you set up this company?'

Jeanie grinned. 'Naw, I'm my own woman these days. I own the Taylor Girls, thanks to Ned.'

Lily's face fell. 'How is Ned? I'm afraid we fell out before I left.'

'He mentioned that, but you know our Ned, bounces back every time. He's just as big a pain in the arse as ever, but I owe him everything – he found me a backer and helped me set up the business in Glasgow, and it was his idea to rope in Kit as costume designer.'

'She sent me some sketches with her last letter – I couldn't believe it when I saw all those ostrich feathers and risqué costumes. What happened to all the damsels in distress and knights in shining armour she used to swoon over at the Mack?'

Jeanie laughed. 'She's moved on, right enough. In more ways than one. Her shite of a husband's no longer on the scene, and recently she's become quite pally with Harry Richardson.'

Lily's eyes widened. 'Your backer? No! She didn't mention that, the sly dog.'

Jeanie crowed with laughter. 'Butter wouldn't melt!' She dabbed at her eyes so the kohl wouldn't run. 'But that's enough from me. I've been hogging the limelight, and I only do that on stage as a rule.' Jeanie caught Lily's hand. 'How are you? I set up this tour so I could come and see for myself. If that husband of yours is still knocking you about, I swear I'll . . .'

Lily winced. 'Things are bad, really bad. They have been for a while.'

Jeanie listened quietly while Lily told her how Florence's death had devastated Hugh, how he'd changed. When she started to talk about the night Hugh had first attacked her, she couldn't go on.

Jeanie put her arms around her. 'I was heart-sore about Florence when I read your letter. She was a good person. She helped me after I was attacked, and it was her who told me I was expecting a child.'

Lily wiped her eyes. 'She never breathed a word at the time.'

'I know, she was good at keeping secrets, like Jack.'

'I wish they hadn't, I would have been at your side in a trice.'

'I wouldn't have let you in. I didn't want anyone to see me after the rape. I was raging, raging at the whole world.'

Lily took her hand. 'I'd have hammered down your door and made you take my help.'

'It was nobody's fault, what happened to me, except for that bastard Mackay, but he's where he can't hurt anyone else, banged up in the Bar L for ruining a lassie not much older than Stella.' Jeanie shook herself. 'You say Hugh's taken it bad about his sister – I'm not surprised, they were so close, but it's no excuse for what he did to you.' She peered into Lily's eyes. 'Is there something else you're not telling me about Hugh?' Lily glanced at her hands and

Jeanie grimaced. 'I was afraid he wouldn't make you happy. I'm sorry, but of all your friends I never really warmed to him. Maybe I didn't get to know him properly, but he's so different from Jack. Even so, I never thought he'd treat you like this.' She hesitated and then blurted out: 'Do you still love him, after all he's done to you?'

Lily was caught off guard. She dug her nails into her palm. 'He's my husband and the father of my child.' But she couldn't meet Jeanie's eyes and her friend wasn't fooled.

'There's something else, isn't there?' She squeezed Lily's hands. 'You can tell me, we've known each other since we were bairns.'

The last remnants of Lily's reserve fell away and she found herself telling Jeanie about her marriage, trying to find clues to the way it had spiralled into a nightmare.

'When I married him, he was a kind and decent man, but he's changed so much since we lost Florence, and if I'm honest, it started before that, not long after we first moved to Shanghai. There were these black moods, and a temper, a kind of rage of frustration. I don't think he's been happy here, but he won't give up his mission.' Lily clasped her hands, unsure whether to go on. Jeanie sat beside her and put her arm around her. They leaned their heads together and the warmth of her friend's embrace gave Lily courage. 'Then there's how he is in bed.' She told Jeanie about the nights that Hugh had held her down by her shoulders, leaving bruises, about the way his face distorted with disgust when he climaxed, and how he pounded away at her as if he were exacting punishment, not pleasure. 'It's not like Jack was – tender and loving – he's rough and sometimes he's hurt me.'

Jeanie clenched her jaw. 'Bastard.'

'Since that night, when he attacked me, he hasn't come near me in bed. I don't know what's worse – he's so cold and distant. And then, today, I found something in his desk . . .'

Haltingly, she told Jeanie about the photographs, pictures she now realised he might have taken himself.

Jeanie frowned. 'There's plenty of men have dirty pictures of girls. It's a shame you had to see them, but I don't know why you'd think they're anything other than a bit of pleasure when he's on his own.'

'I know, I'm not naive. But he's been going to brothels in Shanghai, to save the prostitutes, it's his new mission.'

'Aye, I bet.'

Jeanie's cynicism gave voice to Lily's own suspicions. 'But there's more. I'm pretty sure, now that I think about it, that Hugh took the pictures, and there are so many of them, it's like he's obsessed with her. Her name – Coral – he's written it on the back of the photographs. And there's this odd scribble on the envelope, something about the greatest mission.'

Jeanie wrinkled her nose. 'Maybe he wrote it when he was half cut. Does he take a drink?'

'Only now and then, but he's been acting strangely recently. He looks terrible, all drawn and haunted. I saw plenty of drunkards while I was working in the slums, but he doesn't slur his words or stumble about or smell of drink.'

'What do you think this great mission could be?'

'He's trying to shut down the brothels.'

Jeanie lifted an eyebrow. There was an uncomfortable pause and Lily bit her lip. 'Look, you're not daft,' Jeanie said. 'There's nothing worse than having suspicions and not being sure of your ground. You'll have to confront him. A row may be just what you need to clear the air. But first, you need to be sure of your facts and find out once and for all what he's up to.'

'And how am I supposed to do that?'

'You're going to have to follow him.'

66

~ *Lily* ~

Lily tossed and turned all night, thinking about Jeanie's suggestion. At first she'd dismissed it as underhand; Hugh had never looked at another woman while they'd been together, and he was, at heart, a good man, wasn't he? The two women spent the next day together until it was time for Jeanie to get ready for the show. Lily tried to enjoy her friend's company, showing her around Frenchtown and the Bund, but Jeanie wouldn't let it go. When they stopped for coffee and pastries in Lily's favourite café, Jeanie said, 'You know what you have to do, right?'

When she got home, Lily waited until Hugh went out and then crept back into his study and eased open the desk drawer, the light from the lamp casting huge shadows on the walls. The buff folder was still there. She picked it up but hesitated, the thought of what lay inside turning her stomach. There was a sound at the front door, and she dropped the folder as if scalded and slipped back into the drawing room just in time. Hugh came in and walked past where she sat in the dark on his way to the bathroom, and Lily ran into their bedroom and slid under the covers, feigning sleep until she heard him shut the door to his study. As she lay there, she made up her mind: she couldn't live like this, tormented by doubts. There might be a reasonable explanation as to why he had taken such an interest in this Coral. There was only one way to find out. Tomorrow night, she would follow him.

~

Jeanie was busy with a matinee performance so Lily had all day to worry about what might go wrong. In the evening, after Hugh had left the house, she waited a moment before pulling on her coat and hurrying after him. Ahead, she could just make out his dark shape as he walked out of the gate and into the lane. Lily followed him, careful not to waken the nightwatchman, who was dozing, chin on his chest, at the door of the gatehouse.

It was a Friday night and the wide tree-lined boulevards were still brightly lit and busy with merrymakers strolling along on their way home from dinners and theatre shows or heading to nightclubs. The air was damp, a sharp wind blowing in off the Huangpu, bringing with it the river's unholy smells. Lily followed Hugh down Avenue Joffre. He ducked down a side street and she had to quicken her pace to keep up with him as he weaved in and out of a bewildering maze of narrow alleys. Washing was strung between windows and the air was pungent with the sweet and spicy smells of the street sellers' roasted pork and duck. In only a few paces they had left the comfort of European Shanghai and plunged into ancient China. Lily quickened her pace, aware that she stood out. She was used to walking these streets when she was out sketching, but what seemed picturesque by day took on a more sinister air at night. Hugh stopped at a door with a red lantern hanging over it. Lily hung back in the shadows and watched him go inside. She sidled up to the door and just had time to read the sign in English – 'The House of Heavenly Pleasures' – when she felt a tap on her shoulder, and spun round to see a grinning Chinese man.

'You beautiful. You come with me.' He smiled and lunged in for a kiss. Without thinking, Lily pushed him hard in the chest, and he reeled back against a wall. She turned on her heel and fled back through the alleys without noticing where she was going. Panic set in as she plunged into unknown streets and had to retrace her footsteps when she found herself in a dead-end. At last, she turned a corner and, sobbing with relief, saw the bright lights and plane trees of Avenue Joffre. Her heart didn't stop hammering until she was safely home, her back against the locked front door. Lily peeled off her clothes and ran a bath. In the warm water she soaped herself and thought about what to do next. She had risked going out by herself at night but had found out nothing. Hugh was at the hospital during the day – he had resumed his duties there since Florence's death. She could go back in daylight and see if she could find out more about this Coral. She sank further into the water and felt a pang of uncertainty. Her husband was a doctor who saved lives and a man of God. What was she doing?

67

∽ *Lily and Jeanie* ∽

It was nearing the end of Jeanie's run in Shanghai. Lily invited her and Harry to dinner at the Yellow House, along with Father O'Leary, Nancy and Joe. Hugh had disapproved of her theatre friends in Glasgow, and Lily thought the priest would keep him company and make him behave in a civil manner to their guests. Still, she was worried: Hugh had been so morose and bad-tempered. But dinner was an unexpected success. Wang Yong had pulled out all the stops and plate after fragrant plate was served to gasps of pleasure, while Huan Liu kept the wine and champagne flowing, and soon the dining room was redolent with good-will and laughter. Lily realised how much she'd missed convivial gatherings, her colour high with excitement. Nancy and Jeanie hit it off immediately, while Joe and Hugh talked gravely about the growing unrest in Shanghai. Daniel was on top form, cracking jokes with Harry, who was expanding into the role of impresario. After the cheese course was cleared away the men were left to their port and cigars and Lily, Nancy and Jeanie went out into the garden where they wrapped themselves in blankets Huan Liu brought out along with a pot of green tea. It had been raining but the clouds had cleared, and the night sky was bright with stars.

Nancy stretched out in her chair. 'I'm stuffed – what a meal! Remind me to steal your cook.'

Lily laughed. 'Not a chance! I don't know what I'd do without Wang Yong, or Huan Liu and Li Na.'

Jeanie snorted. 'You'd manage like most of the women in the world who can't afford servants to run about after them and their bairns.'

'What about Tatiana? You couldn't dance let alone run your company without her help with Stella,' Lily said.

'Right enough, I'll get down off my high horse.'

Nancy yawned and rubbed her round belly. 'This baby is making me sleepy and we should get back to Beauregard. I'd better round up Joe before he bores the other guys to death.' She kissed Lily and waved goodbye to Jeanie. 'So long, don't forget to look us up next time you're in Shanghai.'

When they were alone, Lily spoke quietly to Jeanie. 'I followed Hugh the other night.'

Jeanie sat up in her chair. 'What did you find out?'

'Not much, he went to a brothel, but that could have been mission work. I'm thinking of going back during the day, but I feel rotten about it.'

'Why?'

'Because Hugh doesn't deserve it. And I'm frightened about what I'll find out.'

'It's better to know, it's always better to know.'

Lily looked up at the stars. 'You're right, secrets are poison.'

Jeanie was quiet for a while. 'There's something I haven't told you, because I made a promise to someone. But I think you have to know the truth now.'

After she'd told Lily what she'd kept from her all these years, Jeanie fell silent. Lily's chest felt tight as the words whirled round and round: Jack was alive; her Jack was alive. For all this time, he'd been living alone and in pain while she too had been living a half life. She saw with sudden clarity what she'd been doing: teaching at the Fellowship, her marriage to Hugh, the social whirl of Shanghai, St

Joseph's. It had all been to distract her from her grief and keep her putting one foot in front of the other. A giant charade, none of it real, except for her work, and Rosie. Her child was real. Lily felt a tug at her heart as she realised that without the loss of Jack and without her marriage to Hugh, she would not have her daughter.

She dug her nails into the palms of her hands. 'Why didn't you tell me before?'

Jeanie's voice was gentle. 'I couldn't, Jack made me promise, but I wrote to Ned, thought he would know what to do. He didn't get the letter until he was back in Glasgow, and by that time it was too late.'

Lily's stomach turned over. 'That's what he wanted to tell me, and why he was so angry when he found out I'd married Hugh.' She let the tears fall unchecked. 'And now it's too late.'

'At least you know, and it'll help you decide what to do next.'

Lily rubbed her face. 'I know exactly what I'm going to do. I'm going back to that place and I'm going to find out the truth. No more secrets.'

Jeanie leaned over and took her hand. 'In that case, I'm coming with you.'

68

~ Lily and Jeanie ~

The next day, Lily and Jeanie stood in front of the door with the red lantern and rang the bell. A young Chinese woman opened the door and waved her hand from side to side to bar their entry.

'You go! No ladies! No good for you!'

Lily tried to smile at the woman's fierce closed face. 'Coral. We are here to see Coral.'

'No, you go now!'

Jeanie opened her purse and handed the woman a silver dollar. She grunted and tucked it into her pocket, and let them in. They stepped over the high wooden threshold into the lobby of a Shikumen-style house. Lily had never been inside one before and looked around, her curiosity getting the better of her nerves. An interior window from the study opened out on the lobby, and through it she could see a desk and a phone on the wall, reminding her of shipping offices in Glasgow. The woman shut the street door behind them and tottered ahead on tiny, bound feet. The practice had been outlawed in 1912, but Lily had heard it still went on in secret and women with three-inch 'golden lotuses' were prized. They were led into a small sitting room space and the woman gestured that they should sit on the European-style chairs placed around a low table laid with a tea tray, a box of cigarettes and an ashtray.

'You wait. You need talk Missy Alice.'

The maid disappeared into the next room. The wall between the two rooms didn't meet the ceiling so Lily and

Jeanie could hear an exchange in pidgin English. A white woman with dyed red hair and a face thick with make-up came out and glared at them. She was wearing an emerald-green dress cut too low and trimmed with too many flounces for her age. The madam stood in front of them, arms crossed. Lily rose and extended a hand, but the woman ignored it. Lily swallowed. She plucked a name from the air. 'I'm Jane Smith and this is my sister, Helen.'

'And I'm the Queen of Sheba. Jane Smith! What eyewash!' The woman had an American accent. 'You want to see Coral? We don't usually get requests from women, but she'll do as she's told.'

Lily could feel the heat in her face. 'No, it's nothing like that, I just want to talk to her. You see my husband . . .' Alice's eyebrows shot up and Lily realised it would be simpler and more effective to come clean. 'My husband's a missionary, Hugh Anderson, and he's been here, to work, but I'm worried about him, he's not been himself lately. I found some photographs of Coral and I thought perhaps . . .' She suddenly felt hot in her cloak and shrugged it off her shoulders. 'I don't really know why I'm here, but I'm at my wit's end.'

Alice laughed. 'You mean you think he's taken more than a Godly interest in her? He wouldn't be the first man of the cloth to give into temptation – my sing-song girls are the best in Shanghai. I know your husband. Tall guy, long, gloomy face, never cracks a smile?'

'That's him, face like a wet weekend,' Jeanie said.

Alice turned to her and her painted mouth twisted in a cynical smile. 'I knew you weren't sisters. You couldn't sound or look more different.' She eyed Jeanie's red velvet dress with its low neckline and tight corset. 'I could use a girl like you, a little firecracker.'

Jeanie's brow darkened. 'Forget it, missus, I'm not for

335

sale.' She opened her purse and laid some notes on the low table. Alice's eyes bulged. 'Let's get down to business,' Jeanie said. 'We just want to know what's going on between her man and your Coral. Is he a customer?' She reached for her purse again and added some more notes.

The madam took them and counted. 'Yeah, he's one of my best customers, always asks for Coral. He pays top dollar for special services, if you know what I mean.'

Lily closed her eyes. This couldn't be happening. Jeanie ploughed on. 'What kind of special services?'

'He likes the rough stuff. I've had to get the doc in a couple of times, but no broken bones.' From upstairs came the strains from a gramophone. 'And he's fond of the opium pipe. Never touch the stuff myself and don't let my girls use it, but I know the signs when someone's hooked.'

Lily thought of Hugh's gauntness, his twitchiness and lack of appetite. She could almost understand that he was trying to blot out his grief, but hurting this girl so badly she needed a doctor – it was abhorrent. Perhaps his visits here really were part of his mission, but then she thought of the fierceness of his lovemaking, right from the start of their marriage, and how he'd hit her, which she'd put down to his grief over Florence. She'd been too forgiving, perhaps. Lily's head hurt.

'He told me that coming here was part of his mission, to try and put a stop to prostitution,' she said, hoping that this woman would reassure her.

Alice cackled. 'That's a good one! I'm sure he does call on God when he's here, but not to pray, if you know what I mean? No, dear, he comes here for the same reason as all my customers. I have the most expensive bawdy-house in Shanghai and we only service Westerners, so he must have plenty of money to burn. He comes here every night, without fail, and asks for Coral. But you can't see her, it's

336

against house rules. 'Sides, she doesn't speak a word of English.' She folded her arms and glared at them. 'Now, if there's nothing else, get going.' Lily and Jeanie got up. At the door Alice pulled Lily's arm so she had to face her. 'There's no need to look so shocked, young lady. If you'd looked after your man better, given him what he needs in bed instead of making his life a misery, he wouldn't have needed to come here.'

Lily shook her arm free. 'Is that what he tells you?'

Alice shrugged. 'It's what they all say. He's no different.'

69

∼ *Lily and Jeanie* ∼

'A cup of strong tea, well sugared, with milk – it's good when you're upset,' Jeanie said when they were back in the Yellow House. Lily tried to take the cup and saucer, but her hands were shaking too much and the tea spilled. 'You need something stronger,' Jeanie said and went to the drinks cabinet to pour them both a brandy.

The alcohol warmed Lily and she stopped trembling enough to take several more sips. Her thoughts crashed around her mind like half-seen monsters in the mist. After they had returned home from the brothel, she had rifled through Hugh's desk and found a notebook with *Saving Eve: A New Method* on the cover. She hadn't wanted to believe what she'd read. Now, unbidden, passages in Hugh's hand swam behind her closed eyelids.

Only the seed of a Godly man can wash away the sin of a fallen woman like Coral. In the beginning, I tried prayer and reading from the Scriptures, but nothing worked. I realised that women like Coral are like animals and lack souls. She's possessed by a great evil and tempts me with her sly looks and whorish tricks. I take her to purify her with the emissions. And afterwards, I beat the demon out of her.

Lily put down her glass and picked up the notebook again. Every inch of every page was filled with Hugh's writing; usually small and neat, it had grown large and spidery, the pages blotted with ink and the words smeared, as if he had scrawled them in haste. Jeanie gently took the notebook from her.

Lily looked into the empty grate and shivered. 'He's gone mad. My husband is insane.'

Jeanie spoke firmly. 'You mustn't fall to bits now, you need to be strong. I don't like what I'm reading here – I think you're in danger.' She opened the notebook and pointed to the last lines.

My wife, too, is possessed. I knew she'd sinned before we married, but I believed I had saved her by encouraging her to do good works and by the sanctity of matrimony. But since coming to Shanghai, where temptations of the flesh are everywhere, she has reverted to her true nature. I have concluded that she is beyond redemption, and that it's my God-given duty to exorcise Satan's demons from her, just as I do to Coral, in order to save her soul.

Jeanie shook her head. 'He sounds jealous and suspicious, and dangerous. What does he mean that you sinned before becoming his wife?'

'He knew I'd been with Jack, that we were lovers. I didn't hide it from him when he asked.'

Jeanie shook her head. 'That wasn't very bright. Your arty friends and my theatre chums turn a blind eye to that sort of thing, but to Hugh you'd committed a terrible sin. Never mind he's up to the shenanigans with a prostitute himself.'

'But he seemed so tolerant and modern in his thinking when I first met him,' Lily said. 'He'd spent so much time in the slums of Glasgow and seen such deprivation, I assumed he'd be less judgemental, show some Christian forgiveness.'

'Ha! The do-gooders are the worst of all: sanctimonious pricks who like to tell everyone else how to live their lives. It's one rule for them and another for the rest of us poor mugs.'

Perhaps Jeanie was right. Hugh drank at home but insisted on abstinence from those he ministered to in the slums. Lily had heard that men would jump out of windows and flee to the backcourts when they heard he was on the way, in order to avoid taking the Pledge.

She also realised that Hugh had tried to clip her wings by taking her to China, away from the friends he disapproved of and from her independent life. Since meeting Nancy, she'd found a new social circle and had started working again, following her own whims and going where she pleased. She'd taken Hugh's lack of comment as tacit approval, but all the while he'd been silently judging her. Lily put her head in her hands. She couldn't square the Hugh she'd first met in Glasgow, the good, kind man who wanted to help people, with the troubled person who had written these terrible things. Florence's death must have tipped him over the edge and opium brought on these terrible delusions.

'Poor Hugh,' Lily said. 'He must be in such pain.'

'Poor Hugh, is it? Get a hold of yourself, Lily! He's a bully and the only way to deal with bullies is either to stand up to them or get right away from them, like I did with Calum. There's no use making excuses for him – I've seen that expression you're wearing many a time on my Ma's face.' Her voice was harsh with fury. 'Don't feel sorry for him, he's a rabid dog that needs putting down before he tears you to pieces.'

Lily was shocked. 'I don't think he'd hurt me again. He hasn't been near me since then – that was a one-off. I just think he needs help.'

'Did you not hear what that madam told us? Lily, she had to get the doctor in to treat the hoor he beat half to death.' Jeanie got up to sit next to Lily and put her arm around her. 'Listen to me, I know about men like Hugh, Ma was shacked up with plenty of them and she'd never hear a word against them, even when they blacked her eyes or broke her ribs. They'd cry and say they were sorry, but it only stopped when she finally kicked them out, or they'd moved on to someone else.' Jeanie rested her head on Lily's. 'My Ma was blinded by love, but you're not. I know you don't love Hugh, and that your heart still belongs to Jack.' Her voice became more urgent. 'You can still be happy. Go and find Jack. We only have one life. Take your daughter and run, run like the wind and don't look back.'

Lily went still. In the maelstrom she'd nearly forgotten that Jack was still alive. But she was married, and Hugh was the father of her child. She shook her head. 'I can't leave my husband, at least not without confronting him and trying to talk some sense back into him, if not for my sake, for Rosie's.'

'Are you going mad yourself? Aye, you can leave him, and you should. Think of what he wants to do to you – it sounds like he wants to punish you, with this talk of exorcism.' Lily winced, unwilling to remember those dreadful words he'd written. But Jeanie was remorseless. 'He's not only mad, he's wicked.'

'I don't know what to do, I can't think clearly. Hugh's obviously not well, he hasn't been since his sister died. I can't abandon him when he needs my help. I owe it to him, to our marriage, to at least talk to him about all this.'

Jeanie smoothed Lily's hair away from her damp forehead. 'I have to leave Shanghai tomorrow, but I don't like to think of you on your tod in this house with that man. I don't trust him.'

Lily looked around the room, cold without the fire lit, the corners of this house she had once loved so much now dark with waiting shadows. Instead of a haven, it had become oppressive since Florence's death, and the atmosphere wouldn't help Hugh. Perhaps he needed a break from it all, a trip on the boat, where the water would soothe him and the clean air restore him. Lily made up her mind: she would get him away from Shanghai and that awful brothel, and out on the water, where he had always been calmest. Li Na could look after Rosie so they could talk freely and have time alone together to work through this. How she wished Florence were still here! She would have known how to help her brother.

70

~ *Lily* ~

Jeanie left Shanghai on the steamer in a whirl of hugs and kisses, leaving Lily flat and empty. Her resolve to confront Hugh would have wavered had it not been for Huan Liu, whose solid presence made her feel safe. She told him that Mr Anderson was not well and that a boat trip to Soochow would lift his spirits.

'I'll make the arrangements and get the boat ready. It will do you good as well, madam.' He looked at Lily with concern. Since the night Hugh had struck her, he'd always found an excuse not to leave her alone with him.

When Hugh came in from the hospital that night, he was dog-tired and went straight to his camp bed unusually early. Lily felt his forehead.

'You're not hot, but you're overdoing it. What do you say to a trip upriver?' She spoke lightly but held her breath, expecting an argument. Instead he turned over, preparing to go to sleep. 'Yes, whatever you want,' he mumbled. 'I'm so tired, so tired.'

They left early the next morning. Hugh was quiet in the car on the way to the jetty but seemed to brighten once they were on board the *Jeanie*. Lily stood on deck, shivering in her thick coat. The water was black and oily and the mist so thick she could only make out vague outlines of other boats. She could hear the crew and Huan Liu talking quietly in the prow, and the dip of the oars as they pulled away. As they moved into more open waters and the mist cleared, Lily kept an eye on Hugh. He was looking out at the widening horizon and turned to smile at her. He seemed more relaxed already, and Lily congratulated herself on taking him on this trip.

They spent the day quietly, Hugh reading and Lily sketching, and after dinner, when the crew had retired to their quarters, she put her hand on her husband's arm to get his attention.

'I need to talk to you.' He looked down at her hand and then at her. Was that fear in his eyes? They had never talked about the night he'd hit her; he'd carried on the next day as if nothing had happened.

'What about?' he said.

Now that they were at this point, Lily didn't know where to start. She decided it was best to be direct and took a deep breath. 'I know you've been going to a brothel.'

'Yes, of course, it's my work.'

She met his eyes and ploughed on. 'I went there, to the House of Heavenly Pleasures, and talked to the madam. Hugh, I know about Coral, and what you do with her, and how you hurt her.'

The look he flashed at her was bewilderment hardening into anger. 'You've been spying on me, following me.'

'I'm not proud of myself, but I was worried about you. I also found photographs you took of her, and your note-book.'

A look of horror crept over his face and he sat down and buried his head in his hands. Lily went over to him and put her arm around him.

'I know you're troubled and that you have this idea in your head that you are somehow saving this woman, but it's not true, is it, Hugh? You're trying to blot out the pain of Florence's death with drugs and sex. I don't like it, what wife would? But I understand. You're not well, and you need help.'

344

He shook her off and glared at her. 'How dare you judge me!'

'But I wasn't, that's the point I was trying—'

He had stood up and was looming over her, roaring: 'Shut your filthy mouth! I don't have to listen to a cheap whore like you.'

Lily's pity evaporated, replaced by a molten anger that welled up inside her, shoving aside her resolve to be sympathetic.

'You'd know all about cheap whores, and you clearly prefer spending time with them in a sordid brothel than being at home with your wife and daughter. You're the worst kind of hypocrite – playing the man of God when you're really rotten to the core.' She turned her back on him and tried to calm down. 'I want you to do the decent thing and let me out of this marriage. I'm leaving you and taking Rosie with me.'

Hugh grabbed her and spun her around, nearly pulling her arm from its socket, his face contorted with fury. 'You will not take my daughter and turn her into a whore like you.'

Lily wrenched her arm out of his grasp and rubbed her shoulder, trying not to cry. 'I'm leaving you and there's nothing you can do about it. I should never have married you in the first place. I never loved you, not really. You took advantage of me when I was grieving, the way you scoop up desperate people to follow you. But I'm not desperate any more. I've found out that Jack's alive – Jeanie told me where he is – and I'm going to him. He's the one I love, who I've always loved, not you.'

She stared at Hugh, whose eyes had gone blank, the pupils huge in the dark, his face murderous. It was as if she was really seeing her husband for the first time and she knew with dreadful certainty that she had been naive and that Jeanie had been right: he was dangerous. She stepped back but tripped over a small table, falling backwards to the floor. Her eyes widened with panic in the gloom of the cabin; she tried to rise but one stride took him to her side in the confined space. He gripped her by the shoulders and pulled her towards him. Up close, his breath was sour and his eyes manic. *He looks like the devil.* The thought crossed her mind just as he shook her hard. Her neck whipped back, and her teeth jarred. Hugh raised his arm and she shrunk back, but she couldn't get away. When the blow came the shock was as bad as the black pain that made her cry out.

'It's bad enough that you go snooping through my desk like a scullery maid, but now you have the gall to want to leave me for another man and take my daughter with you. I'd rather you died than let him have you.' He struck her a second time, with more force, and Lily thought she would pass out. She struggled to get free, but his grip was too strong. Terrified, she heard herself beg for mercy. But just as he lifted his hand again, a wave from a passing vessel made the boat lurch and Hugh lost his footing and let her go. Lily grabbed her chance and ran for the steps. She scrambled up them and onto the deck, her breath ragged in her throat.

'Huan Liu! Help! Help me!' she cried. She heard a noise behind her and spun round to face Hugh.

'I should have known you were a no-good slut when you gave yourself to me that first time, as easily as a whore opening her legs in a Glasgow back lane. And now you think you can go back to that wastrel Petrie, a man who didn't have the decency to marry you.'

The mention of Jack's name gave Lily courage. 'Jack's ten times the man you are,' she said. 'You make me sick. You're an animal; worse than an animal. I'm leaving you and I'll make sure you never see Rosie again.'

346

Hugh screamed and lunged for her just as the boat tilted on another wave. She ducked under his arm but another blow hit the back of her head with such force she could feel her scalp split. She put her hand to her head and her fingers came away slick with blood.

Hugh was over by the edge of the deck, panting, his eyes wild. 'How many other men have there been, here in Shanghai, while you've been whoring about with that American bitch? You're not fit to be a mother. I won't let you have our daughter. The courts will give her to me. The law's on my side. You'll never see her again.'

He crouched as if he were about to leap at her again and Lily fled to the other deck. She looked over the side into the roiling waters. They were too far from shore now for her to swim, but she put a foot on the railing anyway, desperate to escape. She knew he would kill her. Time slowed as if in a nightmare as he walked towards her, his face contorted. Lily froze. She thought she knew her husband, but she'd been sleepwalking through her marriage. Shanghai had been a dream: the perfumed, broad, tree-lined streets, the glittering parties, and the haven of the Yellow House, all was a distraction from the rotten core of this life. And now she was about to die, and her daughter would be left without a mother. Hugh bore down on her and Lily closed her eyes and prayed as she'd never prayed before. There was a rush of air next to her, a sickening thwack and a splash. When she opened her eyes, expecting to see Hugh towering over her, she saw Huan Liu standing there, an oar in his hand. She whipped round to see a dark shape slowly rolling in the wake of the boat: Hugh.

She shouted at Huan Liu: 'We must turn the boat around! We must help him!'

'He was going to kill you! I couldn't let him do that!'

Huan Liu's voice shook. He dropped the oar and sank to the deck, his face in his hands.

Lily leaned over the side. She could only just make out a dark shape. 'We can't leave him to drown!' Her fear and anger forgotten, she grabbed the lifebelt and threw it into the water, but Hugh's body only bobbed further away in the wake. Lily turned to Huan Liu and shook him by the shoulders.

'Tell the crew to turn the boat around. Hurry!'

Huan Liu seemed to wake from a daydream. He hurried to the prow where she could hear him talking urgently to the *laodah*. The boat circled round but there was no sign of Hugh, the crew shining hurricane lamps into the river. Hours later, Huan Liu gave a shout and climbed down the steps so he was only inches from the water. One of the crew handed him the boat hook. Lily could make out Hugh, floating face down. Huan Liu managed to hook his jacket after a few tries, and the coolies hauled him on deck. When they turned him onto his back, Lily knew it was too late. His blue eyes stared into the night sky as if seeing beyond the stars to unknown realms.

Lily turned to Huan Liu. He had a wife and three sons, and his life would be over if the authorities knew what had happened here, no matter that he'd saved her from death. He was a Chinaman who had killed a white man. He'd hang.

'There's been a terrible accident, Huan Liu,' she said. 'You did what you could to save Mr Anderson after he slipped and fell overboard. He must have hit his head on the side of the boat.'

Huan Liu looked down at Hugh and back at her. He nodded. 'Yes, a terrible accident.'

348

71

~ *Lily* ~

The British consul arrived quickly at Jessfield Ferry, where the *Jeanie* was back in her berth, and dealt with the Shanghai Municipal Police. If Sir Alec had any suspicions about Hugh's death, he kept them to himself, both at the time and during the coroner's inquiry. The *North China Daily News* reported the coroner's verdict of accidental death without alluding to the feverish gossip Shanghai-landers were busy swapping at parties. The official version was that Hugh Anderson, a respected doctor and missionary, had lost his life during a regrettable boating accident. He'd simply lost his footing and fallen overboard.

But the rumours fell fast and thick. The most popular doing the rounds was that a grieving Hugh had taken his own life following his sister's death; another, which no doubt passed from Miss Alice to other clients at the House of Heavenly Pleasures, that Hugh had fallen overboard in a drugged stupor. All Lily knew was that Huan Liu was safe. The crew had been asleep at the other end of the boat, so she was the only witness.

In the weeks following Hugh's death she slept fitfully, troubled by a recurring nightmare in which her husband rose from the waters to drag her down to the depths with him. Lily would wake, panting, her skin covered in a film of cooling sweat. Too frightened to go back to sleep, she'd stand at the window and watch the sky lighten until the Yellow House came alive with the clatter of pots and the smell of cooking.

She would have liked to sit in her room with the door closed all day, but Rosie's chatter and the demands of motherhood saved her from sinking into despair, and made it impossible to wallow in the guilt that consumed her – and, worst of all, the anger she hid like a suppurating wound. She tried to remember the goodness and selflessness that had drawn her to Hugh in earlier days, but his face contorted with violence haunted her, even during the funeral service. While the head of Mission spoke of his good deeds and piety, she had been gripped by the fear that at any moment she would be unable to stop herself from standing up and denouncing Hugh as a hypocrite, an abuser of women and a violent sexual predator. She couldn't understand how she could have been so mistaken in his character and fretted over the past, looking for clues that hinted at the blackness that had risen within him. Lily remembered that her mother had wept at their wedding, and Jeanie and Ned hadn't hidden their dislike of him. Still, nobody could have known his faith would be twisted into a kind of madness.

Winter marched on, bringing a noxious fog from the Huangpu that settled over the city, turning it a ghostly grey. The mist settled over the Yellow House and got into Lily's bones: she couldn't get warm, no matter how close she drew to the fire. She was watching the flames sputter and turn from blue to yellow when Father O'Leary bustled in, taking off his coat and shaking it.

'My feet are like blocks of ice! Do you think we could have some tea, or something stronger?' He looked hopefully at the drinks' cabinet. Lily nodded and he fetched them glasses of brandy. They sat in silence while she avoided his eyes. After a while, he leaned towards her and took one of her hands. Lily began to sob. He murmured 'my dear child', patting her hand while she cried noisily, gulping for breath, releasing tears that she had kept dammed inside her since Hugh's death. When she quieted, the priest handed her his handkerchief and waited while she composed herself.

'Hugh is with his Heavenly Father now. You must take comfort in that.'

Lily screwed the handkerchief into a ball and shook her head. 'That's just it, he can't be.'

'I know you doubt your faith, but this isn't the only life and Hugh is in the arms of Jesus. I've heard the talk about suicide. Sir Alec asked me about Hugh, and I had to tell him he'd been troubled and depressed since the death of his sister. I'm sorry that I didn't come over earlier, I was out of town. Maybe if I had, that night would have turned out differently.'

Lily picked up her glass and took a sip. The brandy's heat warmed her. 'It's not your fault.' She took another sip for courage. 'If it's anyone's it's mine.'

'There's always guilt when there's a death, particularly if your marriage was going through a bad patch. Hugh could be stern and unbending, a true Calvinist, but he was a good man and that's how you must remember him.'

Lily swallowed the rest of the brandy. Its fiery trail seemed to illuminate her body and give her back some of the boldness she'd lost.

'That's just it, he wasn't a good man, not at the end anyway.'

Her fierceness made the priest sit back. 'You can talk to me, call it a confession.' Lily hesitated. 'I'm a priest, whatever you say will go no further than this room.'

'But I'm not Roman Catholic.'

He shrugged. 'Do you think God cares about that?'

Haltingly, Lily told him about her discovery of the photographs of Coral, about her suspicions and how she followed Hugh and found out he was seeing a prostitute and taking

351

opium. When she came to the part about the notebook, she couldn't carry on. Instead, she fetched it from Hugh's desk and let Daniel read it.

After a while, he closed the book and rubbed the deep lines between his eyebrows. He went to the fire and placed the notebook on the dying embers. They watched the pages catch and curl into ash.

Lily poured them more brandy and told him of how she had confronted Hugh with the truth and offered to get him help, and how he had attacked her before plunging overboard.

'I thought he was going to kill me. He came at me and Huan Liu stepped in to stop him, and Hugh fell into the water. We tried to save him.'

Daniel nodded. 'I thought there was something odd about the whole thing.'

'If I'd told the coroner the truth, it would have been the end for Huan Liu, when really I owe him my life. I couldn't do that to him. What good would it have done? The truth would have ruined several lives. I'd have had to testify and the whole sordid, awful story would have come out and any good Hugh did in his life would have been wiped out. Rosie would have grown up dogged by scandal. She loved her papa and, despite how he had changed towards me, Hugh loved his daughter. I couldn't do it, not to any of us.'

Daniel sighed. 'You did what you had to do.'

Lily wrung her hands. 'It was my fault Hugh died. If only I'd realised sooner how he'd changed, I could have helped him. I couldn't see what was going on under my nose – shouldn't a wife know what's going on in her husband's head?' She stood up and began to pace. 'I wish I could wake from this nightmare, but Hugh won't let me.' She wrung her hands. 'Daniel, he haunts me, every night he comes to me.'

Daniel held her fretful hands between his. 'You've done nothing wrong. Hugh's mind was already fragile. He couldn't cope with failing as a missionary, and Florence's death was the final blow. Try to forgive him, but don't torture yourself. You did what you had to do to survive.'

Lily pressed her fingers to her temples. 'I can forgive Hugh, but I can't forgive myself.'

'Then, let God forgive you.' He laid his hand just above her head and said: '*Deinde, ego te absolvo a peccatis tuis in nomine Patris, et Filii, et Spiritus Sancti.* Thereupon, I absolve you from your sins in the name of the Father, and of the Son, and of the Holy Spirit. Amen.' He made the sign of the cross. Lily felt a movement in the air, like the beating of wings. When she opened her eyes, Daniel said, 'It's time you went home. You and Rosie need to get away from Shanghai, start your lives again.'

Lily gazed into the fire. There was no trace of Hugh's notebook. 'You're right. I'll go back to Scotland. And then there's someone else I must see, another broken man. I couldn't save Hugh but perhaps there's still a chance for him.'

72

~ *Lily* ~

Leaving Shanghai took longer than Lily had expected, and the cherry trees were in blossom by the time she locked up the Yellow House for the last time. Nancy and Joe came down to the dock to say their goodbyes.

'What am I supposed to do in this cultural desert without you?' Nancy wailed.

'How could you possibly abandon my poor wife,' Joe said. 'With only the racing season, the paper chase and an endless round of charity balls to amuse her, how will she cope?'

Nancy shot her husband a furious look. 'I'm sure I'll be quite inconsolable.' She hugged Lily. 'You will write, won't you? From the gloamings and misty glens of Scotland? And send me some lucky heather?'

Lily laughed. 'I shall send you a whole box of heather if you'll only write back and tell me all the Shanghai gossip.'

'Now that you're leaving, the gossips will have only poor little me to talk about. I'll have to make sure I keep them entertained.'

Huan Liu and Li Na were waiting by the gangway. Li Na held Rosie tight and whispered into her ear. She smiled through her tears and gave the little girl a cloth doll she'd made. 'You be good girl,' she managed to say before running into the crowd. Rosie clutched the doll and her face crumpled.

'I want Li Na!' she said and sobbed as Lily picked her up and cradled her.

Lily distracted her with the doll and soon she was sitting on a trunk, prattling as she played with it. Lily turned to Huan Liu.

'Thank you, Huan Liu, thank you for everything. I don't know what I'll do without you.'

He bowed. 'I'll always remember your kindness, Lily.' She smiled at the use of her first name and put her hand in his.

'I'll never forget you,' she said.

'Nor I you.'

Lily looked around at the sweep of the Bund and remembered the day she'd arrived. It had all seemed so strange then, but now she was sorry to leave Shanghai. She'd miss the tree-lined streets of the French Concession, the sweet smell of Osmanthus blossom that perfumed the air in October, the friends she'd made in this strange and wondrous city. Huan Liu picked up Rosie with one arm and shouted some instructions for a coolie to stow away their luggage.

'Remember what Li Na told you and be a good girl for your mother,' he said, and kissed her on the cheek. She wriggled and he let her down. Huan Liu bowed and Lily ducked her head before hurrying up the gangplank, her last look at the Bund blurred by tears.

Rosie howled for Li Na on the boat home, but as the weeks fell away she began to forget her *amah* and became absorbed with the games on deck, making friends with the other children on board. The crew and passengers all made a fuss of the bright-eyed fatherless child and soon took to calling her Goldilocks for her rose gold hair and pink cheeks.

Lily was relieved that Rosie was too young to properly grasp the idea of death and now no longer asked for her father every day. She seemed comforted by the idea that he was in heaven and talked to him every night when she

355

said her prayers. Rosie's earnest whisperings to God to look after Papa made Lily's throat ache but she was careful not to cry in front of the child.

By the time they docked in Glasgow, Hugh was only a quick *God bless Papa* among the litany of names that included Li Na, Mama and the pet tortoise she'd been allowed to bring with her – all more solid and real to her than the father she was forgetting.

Lily's parents met them off the boat. Her mother's hair was nearly all silver now and her father seemed smaller than she remembered, his bluster nearly all gone. Her mother was enchanted with Rosie and bent down to give her a hug.

'What a wee poppet!' She smiled up at Lily, her eyes full of tears. 'She looks just like you when you were that age.'

Lily's father patted Rosie on the head and reached into his pocket. 'I've a present for you. Do you like presents?' She nodded and he held out a hinged wooden box. 'Open it, lassie.' But his tone was warm, and Lily saw how much he'd softened over the years. Rosie overcame her shyness and lifted a lid. A tiny ballerina twirled to music, and she clapped her hands.

'Look, Mama! Like your friend!'

Lily's parents had found them a house to rent in Kirkcudbright, painted duck-egg blue among a row of other houses in pastel colours. After a few days, Lily was satisfied her daughter was back to her usual inquisitive, happy self; her memories of Shanghai were already fading, supplanted by the novelty of doting grandparents, a new house, new school and a host of curious new friends.

Lily went to see her old tutor and spent a peaceful afternoon in his Japanese garden while they talked shop. She rented a studio cottage from a woman who had taught at the Mack before her time and now ran an artists' colony in the lane behind her house. Lily was reminded of how small-townsfolk loved to gossip when she heard scandalised accounts of the colony's 'goings-on'. Her housekeeper was only too eager to bring her up to date.

'They're shameless,' Mrs Annan said, furiously polishing the brasses. 'Can you believe they go swimming in the burn at the bottom of the garden without a stitch of clothing?'

Lily suppressed a smile. 'We're having such a warm summer, perhaps they're just hot?' The housekeeper only sniffed louder and rubbed harder at the brasses.

No matter how hard she tried or how long she spent in the studio, Lily didn't seem to be able to work and her brushes stayed clean. She went for long walks along the beach and through green valleys, striding through fields of sheep, crossing streams and climbing stiles and up the smooth, rounded hills, all bathed in that peculiar golden light she had missed so much. Her lungs filled with clean, sweet air and her eyes were glad of the wide, high sky and the cool Scottish air.

The nightmarish last days with Hugh gradually faded, but thoughts of Jack would not give her peace and she knew she had to find him so they could finally be together. Jeanie had warned her that he had changed, but who hadn't? None of them were the wide-eyed children they'd been. Lily was thirty-four now, a mother and a widow. She knew she had changed and matured, that life had battered her, but her love for Jack was a light inside her, and although she'd hidden it for years, it remained undimmed.

Still she put off going to France.

One day, she came downstairs to find Ned standing in the hall. She stood still, the breath knocked out of her.

'There you are! Talk about the Scarlet Pimpernel!' He looked a little unsure of himself and Lily wondered briefly if he had changed too before running down the last few steps and throwing her arms around him. He rocked back on his heels and laughed. 'Steady on!'

She sank her head into the comforting softness of his coat. 'Is this cashmere?'

'Of course! I'm afraid I'm a worldly man who loves the finer things in life.'

Lily raised her head and smiled at him. 'But that's what I love about you, you're shamelessly materialistic.' She felt his arms tighten around her. 'Oh, I've missed you!' she said. 'I'm sorry we fell out, but I know why now. Jeanie told me about Jack.'

He pushed her away and gave her a hard stare. 'I couldn't tell you. It was too late.'

'I wish you had.'

'So do I.'

They were quiet for a moment before he pushed back a strand of hair that had escaped from Lily's pins. She'd been helping Mrs Annan clear out the grates and realised she looked a state.

'You should have warned me you were coming,' Lily said, wiping at the soot smudges on her face.

'What? And have you fly the coop again with no forwarding address? It was hard enough tracking you down this time. I wouldn't have known you were back if Jeanie hadn't told me. She's back from her tour now.'

'I'm sorry, I should have been in touch, but I've had a difficult time of it recently.'

His expressions softened. 'I heard you'd been widowed. I'm sorry. That's why I'm here, to offer my services. I can help you sort out your husband's estate.'

'Thank you, that would be kind.' But Lily didn't want to talk about Hugh, not with Ned. She held out her hands. 'It's good to see you, you haven't changed a bit.'

'Haven't I? I suppose I've always looked this old and worn-out.' He smoothed back his hair in a familiar way that gave her a pang. He did look just the same, and the touches of silver and lines around his eyes seemed to soften his features.

Lily took his hands. 'Come and have some tea. I want to talk to you about Jack.'

~

Ned was silent, staring at the rug between his feet. Lily couldn't read his expression.

'Are you sure you want to find him in France?' he said.

'Yes. I couldn't be more sure. Jeanie said she'd come with me, once her tour was over.'

Ned cleared his throat. 'I wrote to him, you know, and he wrote back.'

Lily's hand flew to her mouth. 'What did he say?'

'He asked me not to come, that he didn't want to see anyone. But I can't stop you going. I know how much you two loved each other. It used to cause me agonies of jealousy.' His eyes shifted, embarrassed, before he straightened up and looked her in the eye. 'I've loved Jack as long as I've known him, which is all my life. But I knew, when I saw you two together in Cockburnspath, that I had to step aside, that he could never be mine.'

Lily blinked. It explained why Ned had treated her with such hostility at first; why he'd planted seeds of doubt in her mind about Jack and his intentions.

'That's why you kept warning me that I shouldn't trust Jack, that he wasn't serious about me.'

He shrugged. 'They say all is fair in love and war. I knew the game was up by the way Jack talked about you – his face would light up like a Christmas tree, the sentimental

359

old thing. That day, at your flat in Garnethill, I came around to tell you that Jack was alive. I couldn't bear to think of him alone in France, without you, no matter how much he insisted he wanted to be left alone. But then . . .'

'I told you I'd got married to Hugh and that I was leaving for China.'

Ned nodded unhappily. 'There was no point torturing you with the truth.'

Lily stared out of the window at the clouds being chased across the sky. If she'd known, would she have stayed despite the marriage? She'd never know now; it was a lifetime ago.

Ned stood and pulled her up with him. 'Come on then, get your things packed.'

'What do you mean?'

'Well, we can't sit here fretting and moaning about missing the old boy. It's time you fetched him home. I'll keep you company on the train to Glasgow. I haven't seen Jeanie for nearly a year. I've grown quite fond of the annoying little besom over the years.' Lily turned to pack, but Ned laid a gentle hand on her arm. 'You know, Jack may have changed, moved on.'

She barely heard him. 'Of course, we've all changed, how could we not have? But, underneath, we're still the same people surely, with the same hearts? Stop looking so gloomy and come and help me pick out my prettiest dress.' She touched her face. 'Have I aged dreadfully?'

Ned's frown softened. 'Lily Crawford, you're still one of the most beautiful women I know, and one of the vainest. At least Shanghai has taught you how to dress stylishly.' He shuddered. 'Those ghastly home-made frocks you used to wear . . .'

73

~ Lily ~

~ Brantes, south-eastern France ~

The journey to Provence seemed to take longer than the one from Shanghai. As they journeyed south, Lily began to wonder if she'd been too impulsive: like her, Jack would have built another life. Perhaps he wouldn't want to see her – she had changed so much and was no longer the young, idealistic artist he had known. Jeanie had told her he'd been wounded, terribly scarred, yet Lily was scarred too, although she carried her scars inside. But she had to see Jack; if she didn't, she would regret it for the rest of her life, and she lived with too many regrets already. Lily pushed away her doubts and grew impatient to see Jack again – her own Jack who she had loved more than anyone. The train seemed to slow to a crawl for the last few miles and Lily would have gone mad with impatience had it not been for Jeanie, who entertained her with stories about her tour. *After Kit turned him down, sensible lass, Harry tried to go after a Russian countess in Moscow – what a stooshie that was. The husband was furious and challenged him to a duel, so we all had to leg it on the midnight train. What a roaster!* Finally even Jeanie grew quiet as a taxi took them to the village of Brantes, perched high above the Toulourenc valley.

Lily could see why Jack had chosen to settle in this village with its stone houses that seemed to huddle around the seventeenth-century chateau like children hiding in their mother's skirts. The air was perfumed with wild thyme and lavender and the narrow, labyrinthine streets were bathed in sunshine. The driver dropped them off at the village square and a café owner gave them directions.

Jeanie put her arms around Lily. 'You go on ahead, I'll wait here at the café. I'm here if you need me.'

Lily began to climb a set of uneven, winding stairs lined with pots of geraniums, their petals blood-red against the honey-coloured stone. She stopped to catch her breath and looked out over the valley below. A green blanket stretched towards the blue-grey smudge of Mont Ventoux. Now that she was here, within minutes of seeing Jack again, Lily didn't want to go on. Her feet seemed to be made of lead and her skin was cold, despite the warmth of the sun. She forced herself to take a deep breath, held it, and let it out slowly. *It will be all right. Everything will be all right.* Her heartbeat slowed and she climbed the last few steps and made her way to Jack's address.

The street door was half open and led into a courtyard. Lily heard voices and paused on the doorstep and peered in. A little boy was playing with a wooden truck. His golden hair shone in the sunlight and his eyes were as blue as the sky above them. A voice called out 'Pascal!' but the child, caught up in his solitary game, stayed where he was. A young woman with dark hair came out, carrying a basket of washing. She spoke to the boy in a stream of French too rapid for Lily to follow. She must be the housekeeper; it was typically kind of Jack to let her bring her child to work. The boy ran to her and she put the basket down to lift him in her arms and kiss him. Lily could see that she was pregnant – quite far gone by the looks of it. She took a step forward to push open the door when a man emerged from the house, limping heavily. It was Jack. Lily was about to cry out his name when he put his arms around the woman and murmured into her neck. The boy reached for him, crowing with pleasure, and the three of them made a tight knot of love. Lily's legs weakened and she shrank back into the shadows, knocking over a pot of flowers. Jack turned his head and she could see the scars that marred his face. He called out: '*Qui est là?*' She moved further back and stilled her breathing until he turned away and led his family into their home and shut the door behind them. Lily stumbled towards the steps and sat down on a wall below which was the valley. It would be so easy to lean back and fall, to stop everything. She thought of Rosie in her room at home, twirling to her music box. Lily buried her head in her arms and let the tears fall.

By the time she got back to the café, she was oddly calm. She had sat on the wall for a while, her mind a blank, the wind in her hair. As the sun warmed her, she lifted her face to the sky. After the first shock, she realised seeing Jack had not been what she'd expected: he wasn't the Jack of her memories, bathed in a golden halo of nostalgia and young love. This flesh and blood man had a wife and child, with another on the way. She summoned her strength and accepted the truth: Jack was no longer the bitter and cynical broken man Jeanie had met. He seemed content. And Lily would not take that hard-won peace away from him.

At the café, she sat down next to Jeanie and put out her hand across the table. Jeanie raised it to her lips.

'Och, Lily, I'm heart sorry.'

She frowned. 'You knew he had someone?'

'I guessed when you came down so quickly on your own. I suppose a man like Jack, with such a gentle heart, needs love. At least you know now. Did you speak to him?'

Lily shook her head. 'They have a child and are expecting

another. What good would it have done? If I asked him to come back to me, it would be like stealing another woman's life.'

Jeanie nodded. 'Let's go home.'

74

~ *Lily* ~

~ *Kirkcudbright, 1927* ~

Lily was looking through a sketchbook in her bedroom. The window was wide open to let in the air that smelt of the first coal fires of autumn, so she heard Rosie calling up to her from the garden where she was playing in a pile of raked leaves. Lily closed the book, crossed the room and leaned out. 'What is it, darling?'

'There's a lady here who wants to see you.'

Lily leaned out further but couldn't see who it was. Whoever it was must be standing close to the door. Sighing with irritation, she closed the window and went downstairs one slow step at a time. She had started painting again in earnest and hadn't been in touch with anyone since she'd come back from France. The housekeeper had been given strict instructions to turn away any visitors, but it was her day off. Lily had needed time to let the memories of her marriage settle like a wrecked galleon sinking to the seabed; time to get used to the idea that she was on her own, and to say goodbye to Jack all over again.

She opened the door to see Nellie Grayson. She was a little thicker around the waist and fuller in the face, otherwise her old tutor looked much the same. Once again, she was aware her hair was a bird's nest and no doubt she had charcoal smudges on her face. Lily tried to smooth her hair, then realised her fingers were stained cobalt blue with oil paint that had refused to budge despite several scrub-bings with rags soaked in turpentine.

'Nellie! You should have said you were coming!'

'I wanted to surprise you.' Nellie stepped inside and took off her hat and shook out her hair, fashionably bobbed now. 'You look well. China has rounded you out and made a woman of you.'

'You mean I look older and fatter. I'm a mess!' Lily laughed.

'Nonsense! It's been what, eight years? You look exactly as you should: an artist at work, single-minded, with no distractions.' Nellie looked around her and spotted Lily's paintings – the street scenes she'd brought back from China and that had never had the chance to be exhibited. 'These are interesting.'

'I nearly had a solo exhibition with them in Shanghai, a millionaire art enthusiast was going to put it on, but then, well, life got in the way.'

'They're extraordinary. You should show them to Sandy Munro.'

'Is he still on the go?'

'Very much so, there's no keeping Sandy down. I'm sure he'd find buyers for you.'

~

Over tea, Nellie said: 'I must confess I have an ulterior motive in coming here. The Mack needs you. Our head of painting is leaving, and I can think of nobody better than you to replace him.'

Outside, the curlews were piping their eerie cries. 'I'm at peace here, finally,' Lily said. 'Don't they say you should never go back to a place you once loved?'

Nellie put down her cup. 'Listen to me, Lily Crawford.

You're a born teacher and you could help another generation of women become artists, give them the chance that you had. Otherwise it'll be a boys' game again, and we'll all be forgotten.'

Lily smiled. 'You're a hard woman to say no to, Nellie.'

Nellie leaned forward in her chair. 'Shall I tell the director you'll take the job?'

Lily thought of the Mack, of the tall windows letting in the light, the calm studios, the quiet concentration of students at their easels, of living once again in that great city with its galleries and seats of learning, the red and honey sandstone buildings leaning protectively over wide streets full of raucous, gallus people. She realised how much she had missed it all.

Lily filled Nellie's teacup. 'Shall we talk terms?'

~

A few days later, Rosie came bursting through the door, her cheeks flushed and her eyes bright. 'Mama! Mama!'

'Slow down, darling, what is it?'

'The dancer lady's at the gate. The pretty one from the ballet in Shanghai. She gave me this.' Rosie waved a porcelain doll in a flouncy dress and bonnet. 'And she said she's going to teach me how to go around and round on one leg like the ballerina in my music box. It's called a pirouette, you know.'

Lily smiled and took her little girl's hand. 'That's Jeanie.'

'Your friend.'

'Yes, my friend.'

Epilogue

Two girls sit under a willow tree, heads bent over a daisy chain, one an older child, the other younger. The late summer sun burnishes their hair: conker brown and fiery copper. The artist dips her brush into ochre, yellow and magenta and mixes the paint on the canvas, working quickly to catch the light. Gold is already pooling over the farthest green hills and the shepherd in the field below is gathering his flock, his dog a black and white streak against the green.

'For God's sake, tuck your skirt into your bloomers when you do that!' Ned removes the grass stem from his mouth and sits up to watch Jeanie walking on her hands. Lily puts down her brush.

'At least she's wearing them. It wasn't always the case.'

Ned pushes his hat back down over his eyes. 'Don't tell me, I have a sensitive nature and shan't sleep tonight.'

Lily laughs and bends again to her canvas to capture Stella and Rosie's rapt expressions. The sun begins to sink beneath the Galloway hills and a deep peace and contentment fills Lily as she watches the girls weave their dreams into a garland of flowers.

Spanning the period of dramatic change from 1909 to 1929, *Daisy Chain* was inspired by the eventful lives of the artists known as the Glasgow Girls. Charles Rennie Mackintosh's wife Margaret Macdonald was one of these pioneering women artists and designers who carved out a place in the male-dominated art world to create the distinctive Glasgow Style. These women – students or teachers at Glasgow School of Art – were recognised in their day but fell into neglect until they were rediscovered in the first retrospective exhibition of their work in 2000, when they were named Glasgow Girls as a counterpoint to the earlier Glasgow Boys.

The turn of the century was a time of opening opportunities for women. Most of the Glasgow Girls studied under the innovative Francis Newbery, who led the way in education reform and provided equal opportunities for women. In his time as director, 50 per cent of the students at Glasgow School of Art were female.

One Glasgow Girl in particular inspired this novel: Eleanor Allen Moore, who emigrated to Shanghai in the roaring 1920s when the 'Paris of the East' was a glamorous, wicked boom town. Her adventurous life was the model for my heroine, who, like the real artist, attended Glasgow School of Art and moved to Shanghai with her husband, a doctor, and their daughter. Despite the many social changes taking place during this turbulent period, Shanghai and Glasgow had much in common as industrial boom cities that thrived on the shocking disparity between the privileged wealthy few and the desperately poor masses.

To research the novel, I was granted a Society of Authors grant to travel in Eleanor's footsteps, tracing her 6,000-mile journey from Scotland to China and exploring the historic parts of Shanghai to get a feel for her life. Walking the same streets of Shanghai as Eleanor, and experiencing the same sights, smells and sounds, gave me a unique insight into the rich, colourful life of this intrepid woman.

~ *Acknowledgements* ~

My heartfelt thanks to the Society of Authors, who gave me a travel grant to Shanghai to research *Daisy Chain*. I'm also indebted to John D. Van Fleet of the Royal Asiatic Society of Shanghai and Patrick Cranley of Historic Shanghai for their insights into the city during the 1920s. And a big thank you to the kind Shanghailanders who befriended me in a strange city – Grace, Vikki and Jamie, and Will. I don't know what I would have done without you.

My thanks also to Lisa Highton and the superlative editorial team at Two Roads who helped shaped this book into a much, much better one, and, as ever, to my agent, Jenny Brown, who has such faith in me. I hope I justify it.

Thanks to Jeremy Raison for his expert notes on an early draft, and to my writer friends, Phil, George, Siobhan, Carmen, and Jackie for their encouragement.

And, finally, thanks for everything to my husband, Michael, and son, Adam.

∾ *About the Author* ∾

Maggie Ritchie's novel, *Looking for Evelyn*, was shortlisted for the Wilbur Smith Adventure Writing Prize for Best Published Novel of 2018. Her debut novel, *Paris Kiss* (2015), won the Curtis Brown Prize, was runner up for the Sceptre Prize and was longlisted for the Mslexia First Novel Competition. She travelled to Shanghai on a Society of Authors' grant to research *Daisy Chain*, her third novel. Maggie graduated with Distinction from the University of Glasgow's MLitt in Creative Writing. A journalist, she lives in Scotland with her husband and son.